CONQUER THE NIGHT

"I have gone insane, and at the moment, I don't care. I could devour you whole and never suffer a moment's regret."

Without replying, she pressed herself against him and kissed his lips. He made a hissing sound as if she had burned him but did not push her away.

Instead, his voice erupted in a groan of pure passion and he held her tightly, his arms a welcome vise. And then the kiss was no longer hers, but something of his own invention. His mouth claimed hers, possessed hers, at once both giving and taking. She gasped, startled.

He pulled back immediately and she could see his struggle to turn away from her.

"Sandro," she said, "don't stop. Please."

"My God," he said, "do you think I'm made of iron?" His hand trembled as he loosed the string that laced up the back of her blouse. "I couldn't stop now if I tried."

"Real and true and unforgettable."
Booklist

By Susan Wiggs

LORD OF THE NIGHT

SUSAN WIGGS

LORD of the NIGHT

AVON

An Imprint of HarperCollins*Publishers*

**This book is dedicated to my grandmother,
Marie Banfield,
with all my love.**

AVON BOOKS
An Imprint of HarperCollins*Publishers*
10 East 53rd Street
New York, New York 10022-5299

Copyright © 1993 by Susan Wiggs
Excerpts from *Memoirs of a Scandalous Red Dress* copyright © 2009 by Elizabeth Boyle; *Lord of the Night* copyright © 1993 by Susan Wiggs; *Don't Tempt Me* copyright © 2009 by Loretta Chekani; *Destined for an Early Grave* copyright © 2009 by Jeanine Frost
ISBN 978-0-06-108052-4
www.avonromance.com

First Avon Books paperback printing: May 2009
First HarperTorch paperback printing: October 1993

Avon Trademark Reg. U.S. Pat. Off. and in Other Countries, Marca Registrada, Hecho en U.S.A.
HarperCollins® is a registered trademark of HarperCollins Publishers.

Printed in the U.S.A.

10 9 8 7 6 5 4 3 2

Acknowledgments

As always, I gratefully acknowledge the critical skills of my fellow writers—Joyce Bell, Alice Borchardt, Arnette Lamb, and Barbara Dawson Smith, and my editor, Carolyn Marino.

My research of Venice in the sixteenth century drew from hundreds of sources, but I would like to cite particularly the scholarship of Lynne Lawner in her book, *The Lives of Courtesans*, and Giorgina Masson's *Courtesans of the Italian Renaissance*.

The book could not have been written without the services of Pat Jones and Suzanne Rickles of the Houston Public Library, and the Friends of Fondren Library, Rice University.

Special thanks to Ed Pape for the Italian words.

To be able to say how much you love is to love but little.
Petrach, *To Laura,* canzone 16

1

The Republic of Venice
February 1531

Sandro Cavalli's day took a turn for the worse when he walked into the airy, sunlit studio and encountered a naked woman. Though it was beneath his character to gawk at unsuspecting nude females, he hesitated in the shadow of a marble arch and forgot his pressing business with the artist, Titian.

Thirty-nine years of gentlemanly propriety demanded that Sandro make his presence known, then avert his awed stare while she covered herself in the gauzy material on the couch beneath her.

But Sandro Cavalli found himself, for the first time in his life, utterly at the mercy of his glands.

She was oblivious to his presence, her dreamy-eyed stare directed out the window, which framed a view of the bulb-shaped cupolas, fluted chimneys, and red tiled rooftops of Venice. Her hand glided along the cushions, the movement artlessly sensual.

Filled with guilty pleasure, Sandro absorbed her

beauty like a connoisseur inhaling the scent of fine perfume. From the skylight, shafts of rare winter sunlight streamed over her. She had one leg outstretched and the other drawn up, her wrist resting on one knee and her fingers relaxed like the drooping petals of a lily. Her more interesting parts were draped in some filmy stuff that made her nudity all the more glaring.

Nearly as startling as her state of dishabille was the color of her hair. In an age that set golden tresses as the standard of feminine beauty, this woman's hair was ink black, glossy as onyx, a tangle of silken midnight cascading down her back. A stray lock drifted over the curve of her shoulder and curled around one exposed breast.

Sandro's gaze lingered there, on the pale flesh shaped by a lusty man's dream, the tip soft and rosy with the color of the first blush of ripeness on a plum; then his glance moved to an endless leg topped by a smooth, creamy buttock, to the shadows concealing the feminine mystery at the apex of her thighs.

She was a flesh-and-blood fantasy, a goddess sprung from the mists of time to bestow her charmed presence on mortals.

Sandro began sweating profusely. It was not like him, captain general of the Night Lords of Venice, to be lusting after a strange woman. He had, for an instant, no notion of why he had come to Titian's house. Her presence, her mysterious allure, made him remember that he had been young once, that he had been a dreamer.

Unbidden remembrances made a bothersome clutter in Sandro Cavalli's well-ordered mind. Annoyed at himself, he banished a host of unbidden fantasies and cleared his throat. "Where is the maestro?"

The woman turned her face from the window. Neither startled nor embarrassed, she settled a look of polite curiosity on him. Her blue-violet eyes were larger than life, her face young and fresh and vulnerable. "He's gone to get a dove," she said, rising from the red couch.

Tall. She was tall and stunning, her luxurious curves a tease to his manly needs. Furious at his reaction, Sandro scowled as she took a blue silk robe from a hook and draped it around herself, tying it loosely at the waist. She tilted her head to one side, studying his expression of confused impatience. "You don't look like a man who's ever bought a dove."

"Why would I—" Sandro wondered why her question inspired a feeling of inadequacy. "No, I haven't."

"He wanted one for the portrait," she explained, gesturing with a fluid, dancelike motion at the easel.

Curious, Sandro took off his black velvet biretta. He shrugged out of his crimson-lined black cloak, flung it over a chair, and went to study the painting. To his eyes, the composition needed nothing but a hint of modesty.

Titian's skill as a colorist was dramatically evident here. The play of light and dark added a glowing scintillation to the reclining woman. Ripe as a rain swollen bud, she was displayed on a cloud of fabric; her chamber was a loggia opened to the sky from which a cascade of gold coins showered her.

"Danae," Sandro said past the thickness in his throat.

"Yes. The virgin princess being offered to the gods. Do you like it?"

"Were I a god, yes." Sandro could not take his eyes off the painting. His first impression was one of lustfulness, but as he examined her face, he saw that the rapt gaze was absorbed in an idea far loftier than bodily pleasure. The woman in the painting had two natures, the open-eyed innocence of a maiden, and the earthy wisdom of a courtesan.

"Do you wonder what she's thinking?" The girl spoke from close behind him, her voice a soft breath below his ear.

Sandro stiffened. He pretended to examine the puffs of clouds in the background. In reality he was examining the voluptuous mounds of the model's breasts. "I'm afraid I'm not well-versed in art." He turned to face her. Close. She was standing much too close. He could see the winter light refracted in her violet blue eyes, the sweet curve of her lower lip, the wispy tendrils of hair at her temple.

"Oh. Will you stay, then, er . . ." She bit her lip in precisely the spot Sandro wanted to bite it.

Catching himself, he cleared his throat. "Cavalli," he said. "Sandro Cavalli."

She moved even closer to him, her eyes wide with fascination. "You're the Lord of the Night!"

"Yes," he said, knowing the title defined his entire existence. "And you are? . . ."

"Laura Bandello."

Petrarch's Laura, he thought. Yes, she could move a man to poetry. Some other man, he reminded himself. Not Sandro Cavalli. The only verse he knew was the rhyme of the criminal and the meter of desperate souls.

Her gaze clung to him as if he'd grown a halo. "The Lord of the Night," she repeated. "I've heard so many wonderful things about you. You saved a boatload of women from the Turks." She counted off his achievements on her fingers. "You defended the saltworks of Ravenna from the French. You stopped the German lansquenets from closing the foundling hospital."

Her admiring expression and breathy tone discomfited him. He cleared his throat again. "Yes, well, I've not yet mastered the art of walking on water."

Her laughter rang like the chiming of glass bells. In that instant, she seemed unreal to him. Surrounded by a nimbus of light streaming through the pointed arch of the window, she seemed as ethereal as the mist off the lagoon, a creature of air and mirth.

Strange, thought Sandro, shaking his head, and he did not know whether he meant Laura Bandello or his response to her.

"The maestro should be back before long," she said. "Will you have a glass of wine while you wait?"

Sandro thought of the mutilated corpse he had found at dawn. He had no time to idle away with a too-beautiful and too-young artist's model. He heard himself saying, "Some wine, perhaps."

With a graceful movement that made him understand why Titian wanted to paint her, she seemed to float to a tall cupboard, carefully moving aside pots of pigment and soiled rags. When she bent to contemplate a row of jugs in wicker holders, her backside undulated beneath the thin silk robe. Sandro reminded himself that he was a Christian, a defender of feminine virtue. His body assured him that he was a healthy, red-blooded man.

"What would you like?" she asked over her shoulder.

You, he thought. He gritted his teeth; for a moment he had forgotten the art of speech.

"Here's a lovely marsala," she remarked. "The best vintage in fourscore years. Or perhaps this raisin wine. A merchant from Smyrna gave it to the maestro as a gift."

"It doesn't matter," said Sandro. "All wines taste the same to me."

She pulled herself swiftly upright. Her breasts stood out against the silk of her robe. "You don't know painting, and you don't know wine. I thought all patricians were connoisseurs of wine, literature, and the arts and sciences."

"Not this patrician," Sandro said wryly.

"My lord, what man of our age can afford to be ignorant of such staples as wine? Let's try the raisin wine," she suggested, filling two Murano glass goblets. "The maestro declares it's too sweet." She handed him a cup and took a sip from her own. She closed her eyes and parted her moist, shining lips. She looked like Danae in a state of anticipated rapture, awaiting the lover who purchased her favors.

She opened her eyes, and Sandro nearly drowned in the iridescent lavender blue color of them. "In my opinion," she stated, "no wine can be too sweet." She touched the rim of her goblet to his. "*Salute,* my lord?"

"*Salute.*" He drained the cup in one gulp. God, the stuff was as sweet as clover honey and nearly as viscous. Not at all to his taste, but he found himself holding out his cup for more.

"Slowly this time," she teased as she refilled his glass. "Wine—like all of life's pleasures—should be savored."

Sandro savored nothing these days except his job—the dubious thrill of apprehending criminals, taking thieves, and censoring fatted nobles.

"Are you here on official business, my lord?" she asked.

"Yes."

She laughed. "I take it from the brevity of your response that you don't care to elaborate."

There was a strange, shimmering quality about her, he noticed. She never seemed to stand completely still. She was constantly in motion, smoothing back a lock of hair, flicking the hem of her robe, drawing her fingers along the windowsill. He wondered how Titian had managed to capture her on canvas.

"No," he said after a pause. "It's necessary for a man in my position to be discreet."

"Discreet." She tasted the word as if it were the wine on her tongue. She placed her hand on her hip and good-naturedly mimicked his tone. "A woman in my position can hardly be expected to be discreet. Sister Lucia was always admonishing me about discretion."

Sandro told himself he had no business inquiring about the life of this engaging wisp of a girl. Yet her ineffable charm seemed to draw words from him. "Sister Lucia?"

"How thoughtful and well-bred of you to inquire." Her tone and her eyes teased him with merciless irreverence. "At the Convent of Santa Maria Celeste." She turned her gaze out the window and contemplated the canal crowded with gondolas bearing merchants and patricians about their daily business. Yellow *caorlini* bore food supplies from the mainland. Opposite Titian's house stood other grand palazzi, their lacy façades carved of Istrian stone. "It's where I grew up," she explained, rubbing her hands up and down her arms as if to chase away a chill. "I never knew my father."

As a well-bred and thoughtful man, he could do no less than ask, "And your mother?"

"She gave me to the convent. Sold me, actually." Her voice had the matter-of-fact quality of a shopper giving an order; she seemed not to notice Sandro's sharply indrawn breath.

"Sold you?"

Laura turned to him, and he saw the melancholy in her eyes, saw that she was trying to hide her vulnera-

bility. "The sisters needed laborers more than dowries."
As if sensing the storm brewing in Sandro's eyes, she
added, "We were homeless, destitute. My mother used
the money to leave Venice." Laura's gaze drifted out of
focus, and her eyes filled with the diffuse light of old
dreams. "She said she'd send for me, but . . ." Her
shoulders lifted and fell in a graceful shrug. "I've had no
word of her since I was seven years old."

Sandro rubbed his jaw to ease the tightness there. He
hated to think of this beautiful woman as a frightened
little girl, abandoned by her mother to the care of
strangers. "You decided not to take vows," he observed.

"There was never any decision to be made." She
crossed to a table that held a bowl of wrinkled winter
apples. She held one out to Sandro. He hesitated
before taking it, thinking, *Eve.*

Laura seated herself on the low red couch. "I had
no ambition whatever to be a nun. I intend to be a
great painter."

Sandro stopped in the act of lifting the apple to his
lips.

Laura burst forth with gales of laughter sweeter
than birdsong. "My lord, you're staring at me as if I'd
just said I intend to drive a chariot to the underworld.
Is it so very odd for a woman to want to be a
painter?"

"Indeed it is. I find it . . . inappropriate."

She leaned forward, her mouth bowed in a devilish
smile. "You disappoint me, my lord. I should think a
man in charge of keeping the peace in Venice would
be open-minded. Women have only three choices: to
be a wife, a nun, or a whore. Do you blame me for
wishing to broaden my options?"

His gaze swept down the length of her, and he

couldn't help saying, "Two of the choices will broaden you somewhere."

She slapped her hands on her knees. "Ah, so you do have a sense of humor."

"On rare occasions." He took a bite of the apple, finding it surprisingly sweet and well preserved. "I must wonder if you have the ability to stand the heartbreak, the struggle of a painter's career."

She arched a dark eyebrow upward, rose from the couch, and held out her hand to him. "Why don't you judge whether or not my work is worth struggling for."

Sandro did not want to hold her hand, did not want to allow her to pull him toward her. But his mind bowed down to long-suppressed desire, and he took her hand in his. Her skin was soft, her bones beneath the delicate flesh as fragile as a bird's. She perfumed her hair with jasmine, he noticed, a scent so subtle and enticing that one felt compelled to pause, to close one's eyes, and inhale deeply.

Sandro resisted the urge. He followed her to a side alcove of the studio. Pale sea light, the misty glow of Venice, poured through a semicircular bank of windows. In the middle of the small area stood an easel.

He dropped her hand and looked at the painting. It was an unusual scene, neither sacred nor mythological as most pictures of the day were. This depicted a family. The artist's love for the subject shone in every brush stroke. The family was gathered in a garden fashioned after the lush estates of the nobility along the river Brenta. The woman sat in grass that glistened with the subtle sheen of morning dew, her simple white gown spread out like the petals of a flower around her. She held a book with gilt-edged pages in her lap, and reclining beside her in the grass was a small boy with a face that reminded Sandro of a mischievous cherub. Behind her, his hand lifting a curl of her hair from her neck, stood a gentleman dressed in the finery of a *condottiere*.

The fourth figure in the painting left Sandro feeling vaguely unsettled. Dark clothed, she stood off to one side in the shadow of a flowering chestnut tree. Her face was turned so that only her profile was visible, and this, too, lay in shadow. Her tense pose suggested the urge to flee. So real was she to Sandro that he had an impulse to reach for her, to pull her back into the light. So real were the others that he longed to join them, to hear the story the woman read, to touch her soft, light-kissed hair just as the gentleman was doing.

"It's wonderful," he heard himself saying.

"I'd be complimented, but you said you didn't know anything about art." Though a teasing note chimed in her voice, her cheeks were flushed with pleasure. Sandro had never associated pleasure with color before, but now he likened it to the tint on a new rose.

He cleared his throat. "I was an indifferent scholar and woefully inadequate in the arts. However, I know when something . . . affects me."

She grasped his hand and, before he could defend himself, clasped it to her breast. Her heart beat fast; her flesh was warm beneath the silken robe. "My lord," she said, "either you are a shameless flatterer, or a very kind and sensitive man."

He drew his hand away. "I never flatter people. That is like lying, and I despise liars. Nor am I kind or sensitive. I know of people who would fall down laughing if they heard me described thus. I am simply a man who speaks his mind. You have uncommon skill as an artist."

"No," she said. "You're confusing craft with talent. I need to improve my skill, so I work with Maestro Titian. He gives me lessons in exchange for modeling." Troublesome shadows darkened her eyes. "Painting's an expensive proposition, and I can't work for pay until I'm accepted by the Academy. An unlikely event, alas, since females are not welcome there." She gestured at the painting. "You'll notice I placed the man behind the woman."

"To show his reverence for her?"

"To hide the fact that I can't draw men." She grinned at his startled expression. "You see, as a woman, I've been barred from lessons involving male nudes."

"Excellent. I'm pleased to hear it."

"Spoken like a man," she said. "It's most frustrating." She took a folio from a shelf and flipped through the pages. "His tunic, for instance, looks like it's been folded away in a chest. In addition to male anatomy, I have difficulty with perspective and my composition is—"

"Let me see that while you enumerate your faults." He took the sketchbook and perused a drawing of a budding almond tree, a black-and-brown terrier crouched in a playful pose, a washerwoman hefting a wicker basket, the unique inverted chimney pots of Venice, and a lovely and haughty African woman.

He was struck by Laura's keen eye, the way she seemed to capture the slightest movement or subtlest emotion, to give the subject life like a sorceress sparking a fire.

He paused at a drawing of a young woman bent over a desk, pen in hand. She was deformed, her back humped and her face pinched with pain. And yet the subject seemed to glow from within, her attention focused on the stacked pages in front of her. Laura had neither exploited her unnatural appearance nor oversentimentalized it. She had simply depicted her with authority and compassion.

"That's Magdalena," she said. "She's a postulant at the convent. We grew up together." She lifted the page to reveal a strangely handsome older woman in a nun's cowl. "That's her mother, Celestina."

"A nun? Is she a widow?"

"I don't think so. She's never revealed who Magdalena's father is. Some say it was her own father confessor."

"What are all these glass containers in front of her?"

"In painting, we call them vanities—we surround the subject with objects that indicate her metier. Sister Celestina is an alchemist."

"An unusual occupation for a nun," Sandro said.

"You're not comfortable with the unusual, are you, my lord?" Laura asked. Without waiting for an answer, she went on, "Celestina spends her days mixing pigments for the maestro. Sometimes she makes the oddest concoctions. Once, she caused an explosion that set fire to a whole wing of the convent. She would have been banished, but she has an anonymous patron whose generosity supports the convent."

"When did you leave there, Laura?"

She looked pleased to hear him use her given name. "About six months ago. It was past time. I had frescoed nearly every inch of the convent and illuminated reams of manuscripts. The abbess was starting to complain of the sums I spent on supplies, and I was beginning to weary of depicting only sacred subjects."

Sandro frowned. "You painted the convent?"

She nodded vigorously, her black satin hair rippling like a veil on a breeze. "When I was ten, they set me to work illuminating manuscripts. A book of hours I painted was sent to His Holiness himself, and he praised it. His approval convinced the sisters to supply me with more paints. Then I moved on to altarpieces, triptyches, murals. I spent an entire year on the stations of the cross."

"A peculiar apprenticeship," he mused.

"Yes, and one I'm afraid I outgrew."

"And so you left."

She averted her eyes, a signal Sandro recognized and disliked. "What aren't you telling me, madonna?"

"Why do you think I'm holding something back?"

"Your forte is in painting pictures. My chief business to dig for the truth. What's the real reason you left?"

"I . . . did not want to be party to some of the activities at the convent."

An uncomfortable scratchiness rose in Sandro's throat. He should have trusted his instincts when he'd first laid eyes on her. To his methodical mind and well-ordered life, she was trouble. "You mean you didn't care for the masses and fasting, things of that sort."

She gave an airy wave of her hand. "I can see you'll question me until I tell you. Some of the sisters had . . . unhealthy relationships with visiting priests. There was one—Fra Luigi—who had a taste for the younger postulants. All he got from me is my knee in his . . . well, I refused."

"Brava," Sandro burst out, and already he was planning an extended pilgrimage to Jerusalem for Fra Luigi—aboard the most rotten, hulking roundship he could find.

She sent him a sparkling smile. "It's my earnest

belief that a woman should engage in intimacy with a
man only for the sake of—"

"Love," Sandro finished approvingly, his esteem
for her rising. "I quite agree."

Her shoulders shook with laughter. "A noble sentiment, my lord. However, I wasn't going to say love,
but money."

Sandro's heart chilled. He slammed the sketchbook shut and stalked back into the main studio.
Damn her.

Years ago, his illusions had been stripped away,
but for this brief time she had given him back a taste
of innocence. He shouldn't be angry, he told himself.
She had been raised by women who knew nothing of
love and honor.

She returned to the studio, moving with an elegant, gliding walk. She seemed unperturbed, which
surprised Sandro Cavalli. Few people, after tasting
his legendary temper, managed to smile, and none of
them so dazzlingly.

"My lord," she said. "I've annoyed you. Let us
speak of you instead."

"I don't wish to speak of me."

"I shall badger you until you do." She tossed her
head, and blue highlights flashed in her obsidian
hair.

Suppressing a surge of admiration, Sandro ran a
hand around the collar of his batiste shirt. "I have a
daughter, Adriana, who recently married the heir to
the *capo* of the Council of Ten."

"The head of the Council?" Laura's large eyes
widened, and she gave a low whistle. "I'm deeply
impressed."

Mocking. She was mocking him. He scowled. "My

son, Marcantonio, manages the family shipping concerns and will soon have a seat in the Senate."

"You must be very proud of them both." Now she sounded not mocking but wistful. Sandro wondered if she ever dreamed of her unknown father, her absent mother. "And your wife, my lord?"

"She's dead." Sandro's voice was flat.

"Oh. I'm sorry . . . Did you love her very much?"

"We were wed at fifteen, an arranged match, of course." He grimaced at the memory. All his choices had been made for him—first by his family, then by his own relentless sense of duty. "I married her Persian spices and she married my Murano glass."

"Have you been alone long, my lord?"

"She died twenty years ago." He scuffed the toe of his soft leather boot on the marble floor. "I don't know why I'm telling you this," he mused aloud.

"Everyone needs to say the things that are in his heart."

"There is nothing in my heart, madonna."

Laura laughed a little uncertainly. "What a strange thing to say, my lord. How did she die?"

"You mean was it childbirth, drunkenness, or suicide?" he asked nastily, wanting to lash out at her for reviving a long-buried shame. "Was I too tight with my pursestrings, too loose with other women?"

"My lord, if you don't wish to speak of it—"

"It was in the Arsenal explosion of 1512. Someone sparked a gunpowder magazine adjacent to the shipyards." He looked out the window at the east end of Venice where the Arsenal lay and felt again the panic, the horror, the pain.

"I don't understand, my lord. What was your wife—surely the noblest of ladies—doing at the Arsenal?"

He fixed her with a hard stare. "She had gone to meet her lover, a *galleoto*."

Laura caught her breath. "Her lover was a galley oarsman?"

"Indeed. You look quite shocked, madonna. I suppose it is disturbing to learn of a woman's betrayal."

She sent him an arch look. "On the contrary, I was wondering, my lord, about the nature of your inadequacy."

"My . . ." Anger rose in a flush from the neck of his shirt to the tops of his ears. "What makes you think I have some sort of inadequacy?"

"Well, your wife must have had some reason to turn to another man for . . . comfort."

For a moment Sandro was too shocked to reply. Never, ever, had anyone dared suggest such a thing. But in the hidden depths of his heart, he suspected a grain of truth in Laura's observation. Irritated by her comment and impatient to question Titian, Sandro fell into stony silence.

"I apologize for prying," Laura said.

But it seemed to be her nature to pry and so, with unflagging cheer, she moved on to the less personal subject of murder. "I do wish you'd tell me more about the crime you're investigating."

"What possible interest could you have in my business?"

"As an artist, I'm interested in all facets of humanity. I cannot portray my subjects honestly unless I understand their emotions. Now, this crime. Is it—"

"No." Sandro made a slashing motion with his hand. "You'd not stay so young and beautiful if I told you."

She stopped in the act of pouring more wine. He realized it was the first time he had seen her completely still, like the creature Titian had depicted so masterfully—lush and ravishing, a spiritual entity of inhuman loveliness.

"My lord," she whispered, breaking the stillness to set down the wine cups and rush forward. Before Sandro realized what was happening, she cupped his neck with her hands and raised up to kiss him lightly on the mouth.

His response was as swift and violent as a bolt of lightning. Raw, unreasoning desire took hold, and only the power of his will, honed by years of unrelenting self-discipline, gave him the control to step back and hold her at arm's length.

Her mouth was moist and full, her eyes wide and bewildered. "My lord, forgive me, but I forgot myself."

"Indeed you did." Hoping she would not assault him again, he dropped his hands.

"It's just that no man has ever been concerned with my sensibilities before." She pressed her delicate hands to her breast. "I was touched, my lord. You're a kind and car—"

"No." His response came too quickly. "I'm a man who prefers to do his job without interference from flighty young ladies."

"Charming as ever, aren't you, Sandro," said a jovial voice from the doorway. "Truly, you have a way with women."

"Maestro." Ignoring the gibe, Sandro crossed the studio and extended a hand to Tiziano Vecellio, the most celebrated artist in Venice. "I've been waiting for you."

"I see you've met Laura."

"I see you've taken to robbing convents for your models."

"His lordship was just telling me about the death of his poor wife," Laura said.

Titian's wiry black eyebrows lifted in astonishment. The artist knew Sandro for a private man. Sandro already regretted all he had divulged to the lovely stranger and wondered how she had compelled him to reveal himself.

"Did you get the dove?" Laura asked, lifting the hem of her robe and hurrying forward.

Titian gave her an indulgent smile. With his dark hair and pointed beard, his imposing physique and unconscious grace, he resembled a satyr contemplating his next conquest. "Better than that," he said, summoning his servant with a wave of his hand.

A chubby, eager-eyed youth of about twelve stepped into the studio. Under his arm he held a small brown mongrel.

"He's wonderful," Laura exclaimed, sinking to the floor and patting her knees. The dog squirmed free of the boy and trotted to her, its tail whipping the air as it clambered into her lap and began licking her face. "I think I'm in love."

Sandro looked away in disgust.

"Oh, you," Laura scolded good-naturedly. "Come and meet him. He's enchanting."

Unable to recall the last time he had petted a dog, or if he had ever done so in his life, Sandro walked toward her. The dog twisted from her grip and flew at Sandro, latching onto his high *fisolari* boot. Tiny sharp teeth pierced the fine Cordovan leather and then Sandro's flesh.

"*Corpo di Bacco,*" he swore, lifting his foot. The dog's feet left the floor but it hung on, making low ominous sounds in its throat. "For Christ's sake."

Sandro gave his foot a shake and earned a growl in reply. "Somebody get the beast off me."

"Don't hurt the poor little thing," said Laura.

"Poor little—"

"Hush. Let me." Crooning like a mother to her babe, Laura took hold of the struggling animal and with her hand eased its grip on Sandro's boot. The dog trotted to his cloak, casually lifted its leg, and aimed a stream at the fine crimson lining.

Sandro rolled his eyes. "I knew this was going to be a bad day," he muttered.

Titian wiped tears of mirth from his cheeks. "What's that, my lord?"

"Nothing." Sandro held his jaw so tight that his head ached. "Look, maestro, I've come on a serious matter."

Titian hesitated, the humor leaving his face. "Of course. We'll go to the gold salon." As they started out of the studio, Titian offered, "Some wine?"

Sandro nodded. "I like a good, sweet raisin wine." His voice echoed down the hall.

"My lord, I thought you knew nothing of fine wine," said Titian.

"What man of our age can afford to be ignorant of such things as wine?"

Laura stood in the doorway, smiling as she watched them go. Sandro Cavalli was an interesting— if conservative—man. Very interesting, she decided, turning back to the studio. Never had she seen a face with such rugged, well-worn appeal, a body so mercilessly honed to fitness.

"Keep the dog with you, Vito," she said to the apprentice. "Whatever you do, don't let it follow me."

Vito gazed at her with the familiar worshiping look she sometimes wanted to slap off his face. "Where are you going?"

"To follow them, and I don't want the dog giving me away."

"Laura!" Vito's face paled. "You really shouldn't. People who listen at doorways seldom hear good news."

Laura ignored him. Swiftly and silently, she moved down the hall and pressed her ear to the door of the gold salon.

"I couldn't believe what they said," exclaimed Laura, blinking in horror and wonderment.

"Drink first. Then we talk." Gliding across the *altana* on the roof of the house, Yasmin poured a cup of wine and handed it to Laura. For herself she prepared water sweetened with honey. As a Moslem, she abstained from spirits.

Sitting on a leather-covered bench with her knees drawn up to her chest, Laura watched her friend with unabashed fascination. Yasmin's elegant height, her inborn grace, and her stark, perfect bone structure gave her a striking, almost forbidding appearance. The lovely hue of her skin was a colorist's dream—deep, polished mahogany enriched by golden highlights.

Laura drained her cup and eyed the other women on the *altana*. The softness of the mild winter afternoon induced a natural indolence in them as they sunned themselves. To preserve their pearly complexions, some sat motionless, their faces covered with slices of raw veal dipped in milk. Others nibbled on *buccheri*, the latest Portuguese sensation. Laura grimaced; she had not yet developed a taste for the perfumed bits of clay. The ladies wore crownless, wide-brimmed straw hats so that the sun would bleach their hair. Laura had never bothered with a *solana*, as no amount of sunshine or tincture could alter the color of her night-dark hair.

"Well?" Yasmin prompted, sipping her drink. She held herself very still, a quality Laura had never mastered.

Pulling her attention away from their companions, Laura drummed her fingers on the stone rail and whispered, "He's investigating a murder that happened last night."

Yasmin blinked her wide almond-shaped eyes. "Isn't that the chief business of the Lord of the Night and his *zaffi*?"

"I assume so, but this was . . ." Laura bit her lip, wincing as she recalled Sandro Cavalli's vivid, dispassionate description. ". . . more sinister than an ordinary murder."

"In what way?"

"Well." Laura stood and looked across at the V-shaped chimney pots and tiled roofs. "He was stabbed through the heart. Sandro said a poisoned dagger had been used. I think"—she shivered—"he could tell by the scent."

"Sandro? You call him by his given name?"

"Not to his face—and what a wonderful face it is. He'd probably throw me in the Gabbia. But the killer didn't stop at mere murder. The victim's testicles had been cut off."

Not a single tic marred Yasmin's composure. "Interesting. I can think of several men I would like to introduce to our assassin."

"Oh, Yasmin, you can't mean that."

"Can I not?" Moving like a panther, she stood and prowled the *altana*, brooding down at the patio garden where a trio of musicians strolled among the guests of Madonna della Rubia.

Yasmin turned back, bracing her arms on the rail and thrusting out her chest. "Look at me, Laura. Men kidnapped me from my native land. Men sold me as a slave to Madonna della Rubia. Six nights a week, strange men come to share my bed. Have I ever had reason to wish any man well?"

Laura sighed. "I understand your bitterness, Yasmin."

"What else do you know about this murder?"

"The victim was the personal secretary of the doge," Laura said. "That's why Sandro is so concerned. His name is—was—Daniele Moro."

Yasmin's beautiful composure slipped; her eyes widened and her long, slim body tightened into a predatory stance.

"What?" Laura sprang away from the stone railing. "That name means something to you, doesn't it?"

Yasmin curled her elegant fingers into the folds of her silk lounging caftan. A procuress of the highest order, Madonna della Rubia didn't skimp when packaging her wares.

Yasmin drew a deep breath. "Daniele Moro was *here*, Laura. Last night."

2

Laura hurried across the crowded Rialto bridge. The wide waterway below teemed with gondolas draped in silk, barges from the mainland sunk low with cargoes of fresh water, bread, and vegetables, little skiffs and fishing boats plying out to the lagoons, barcas and flat-keeled galleys laden with goods.

Lined with shops and teeming with merchants and buyers, the famous arch over the Grand Canal tempted her to stop and absorb the color and motion. Her fingers itched to draw the elegant contessa contemplating a bolt of azure damask silk, the self-important Flemish merchant perusing a jeweled headdress, the *gentildonne* tottering on their high chopines and peering into screened shop doorways at mannequins draped in finery.

A beggarwoman crouched on a stoop, her grimy hand extended for alms. Laura had no money, so she untied her Burano lace fichu and dropped it into the woman's hand. It was the third one this month, she thought as she smiled to acknowledge the woman's thanks. Her excuses to Madonna della Rubia were wearing thin, and she was already appallingly in debt to her patroness.

Young gallants in their tight-fitting hosen and jaunty red birettas hooted and pinched; she slapped aside their advances with jaunty good humor.

Laura had never been away from Venice, but visitors from abroad claimed there was no other city like it in the world. She believed this fervently. She loved La Serenissima with the same passion with which she loved painting.

And yet, like many great beauties, the city of water, glass, light, and lace concealed a darker side, high-walled calli where bands of *bravi* lurked with their daggers and stilettos. Thank God for men like Sandro Cavalli who were dedicated to fighting crime.

Shivering in the February chill, she recalled Sandro's conversation with Titian. While conducting the business of the doge, Daniele Moro had been murdered. He was supposed to deliver materials to a printer regarding the Sposalizio del Mare, the annual rite of Venice's symbolic marriage to the sea. After visiting the printer, Moro was to have gone to Titian to schedule a portrait sitting for Doge Andrea Gritti.

The secretary had not kept either appointment. Sandro Cavalli believed the doge was the last person to see Moro alive.

Laura knew better. Duty compelled her to tell Sandro all she had learned from Yasmin.

Leaving the busy mercantile district behind, she found her way to the Fondaco Cavalli. The massive palazzo, pillared in white marble, rose before her. Bright blue-and-gold *pali* thrust, lancelike, against the sky and caught the light. Rich frescoes arched over the massive main door to the street. She recognized the work of Bellini in the painting, and the sculpting of Sansovino in the lyrical carvings that graced the tops of the pillars and windows.

With growing apprehension, she approached the grand house. She had expected the Lord of the Night to be wealthy. Yet she was unprepared for the sumptuousness of the Fondaco Cavalli.

Her artist's eye absorbed the soaring columns and fluted chimneys. Malevolent gargoyles glared from the cornices. Guarding the grand doorway was a stoic civil policeman in a cloak of dark blue. The guard was armed with shortsword and tipstaff.

He peered at her with frank interest. Her smile came automatically. "I'm here to see Lord Sandro Cavalli."

The *zaffo*'s gaze sharpened. "I didn't know the master's tastes ran to one so young."

Laura had long since learned not to be surprised at lewd remarks. She squared her shoulders. "This is a police matter," she informed him. "It's very urgent."

"I'll have to search you for concealed weapons."

"Search me?" She scowled in annoyance. "It's hardly nec—"

"Can't be too careful, madonna." The guard put out a hand and drew it along her arm. "Assassins come in all sizes"—he ran his fingers down her side from rib cage to waist—"and shapes."

Laura held herself as still as she could manage. Soon the day would come that she would not only have to experience a man's caresses, but enjoy them—or pretend to.

But when his hands reached her hips, when his breath blew hot upon her face, she decided the training could wait. He was a commoner; her lovers would be noblemen. There was a world of difference, she told herself.

She put on her most charming smile. "Dear sir, I can't help but wonder something."

The *zaffo*'s face darkened with lust. "What's that?"

"I wonder if Lord Sandro would be pleased to hear of your thoroughness."

The guard released her as if she were a live coal. "Be about your business, then." He pointed. "Through there."

As she walked through the door, Laura felt pleased that her instincts had been correct. Sandro Cavalli treated women with respect and insisted that his subordinates do the same.

A short passageway led to an open garden. An impression of ruthless order struck her. Flagstones in tessellated patterns laid out the pathways. A fountain with a small likeness of Neptune burbled into a pond with mosaic walls. Potted myrtles groomed into perfect orbs marched in a semicircle around the periphery of the patio. Even the fig ivy that climbed the walls had been clipped to a razor edge. Laura imagined that if she were to look into the pool into which the fountain sprayed, she would see fish swimming in synchrony.

To her right was a large doorway that she guessed would lead to the warehouse, for the merchants of Venice stored their goods below their dwellings. To her left, a bank of windows revealed rows of clerks laboring over slant-topped desks.

She was about to inquire within when the center door, flanked by two Grecian urns, swung open.

Out stepped a young man so mythically handsome that Laura could only stare. She had never seen Donatello's whimsical David, but she had heard it described, and for a moment she believed with all her heart that the Florentine masterpiece had come to life and was standing a few feet away, smiling at her.

"Welcome," he said. "To what do I owe this pleasure?"

She managed to find her voice. "I am Laura Bandello. I've come to see Lord Sandro Cavalli."

The handsome features pulled taut, and the resemblance to the statue grew stronger. "Is my father expecting you?"

"No, I—he's your father?" She searched for a resemblance, but found none. Sandro's features were harder, lined by maturity and experience, wisdom and weariness. The father, she decided, had character. While the son, inhumanly handsome as he was, merely had beauty. Given a choice of painting one of them, Laura knew which man she would prefer.

"You must be Marcantonio." Smiling, she dropped into a curtsy that would have made Madonna della Rubia proud.

"He's told you about me?" Marcantonio shook out his glorious hair. The color reminded her of pale polished oak. Sandro's was a rich dark chestnut, threaded with silver filaments. "That's odd," Marcantonio continued. "Father rarely speaks to anyone of the family."

Laura laughed. "I'm afraid I badgered him relentlessly."

Marcantonio subjected her to a long, lazy glance that drifted from the top of her head to the toes of the slippers peeking out from the hem of her brown fustian day dress. His hand rested indolently at his waist, drawing attention to a well-padded silk codpiece tied with golden lace points to his trunk hose. His pose and the expression on his face disappointed Laura. In a man of such beauty, she wanted to see great intellect as well. All she saw in his eyes was simple male lust.

"Please, is your father in?" she prompted. "This is a matter of some importance."

He gave an arrogant toss of his head. Pale, Adonis-like curls spilled over his brow. "This way."

He led her up a winding marble staircase that smelled of lemon oil. They stepped out into a broad hall lined with paintings. Laura wished to linger there, to study the masterpieces. For a man who claimed ignorance in the arts, Sandro Cavalli possessed an impressive collection. She recognized a bucolic scene by Bellini, a Carpaccio allegory, a few decorative works by Zacchara.

Marcantonio took her to a door at the end of the hall and knocked, then pushed the door open without waiting to be summoned.

Muttering a rare oath under his breath, Sandro looked up from his desk. Annoyance turned to surprise—and reluctant pleasure—when he recognized Laura Bandello. Her radiant smile shot him through with a sensation that in any other man would be called warmth. She looked very different from the day before. Instead of a sensuous nude, she resembled a schoolgirl in a demure dress of light brown adorned with a tidy white apron and cuffs. Her hair was caught back in two dark, shining braids.

Her aura of innocence made Marcantonio's hungry regard all the more disturbing.

Clearing his throat, Sandro placed his palms on his leather-topped desk and stood. "Madonna Bandello," he said. "I didn't expect to see you again."

He watched her study the piles of documents, bills of lading, and reports on the desk. Each stack was perfection itself, the edges and corners of the papers precisely aligned. Sandro liked things that way. Yet oddly, her presence made the flawless order of his office seem somehow overly fussy.

"It's your lucky day," she said. "I hope you don't mind."

"Laura has a matter of importance to discuss with you," said Marcantonio. His hand pressed gently at the small of her back, and she sent him a bright, grateful look.

Sandro didn't care to hear his son call her by her given name, to see him touching her. What a small, selfish man I am, he thought. Yet the admission did not soften his tone when he said, "Then I'm sure you'll wish to leave us, Marcantonio, so we can get to the matter at hand."

A faint hint of rebelliousness raised the color in Marcantonio's cheeks, but he bowed curtly. "Yes, I must make ready for my nightly visit to the Ponte di Tetti."

Sandro gripped the edge of the desk and fought for control. Marcantonio enjoyed annoying his sire by flaunting his iniquities; the Ponte di Tetti was the haunt of the lowest of street whores.

As the sound of the slamming door reverberated through the room, Sandro breathed a sigh of relief. There was enough suppressed tension between Marcantonio and him to spark another explosion at the Arsenal and turn the Cavalli fortune to dust.

"Please," he said, gesturing at a pair of chairs angled toward the marble hearth, "do sit down."

"Thank you." Laura glanced at one corner of the room. "My lord, this concerns the business of the *signori di notte.* May I speak candidly?"

"Absolutely." Taking her hand, Sandro led her to

the small desk where his assistant sat impassively, his pen idle upon a letter he was copying. "Madonna Bandello, I'd like you to meet my personal secretary, Jamal."

Sandro savored Laura's wide-eyed stare as Jamal rose to his feet and bowed formally. With skin as dark as the ebony trees that grew in his native Africa, his face and body as glossy and muscled as an Andalusian stallion's, Jamal cut an impressive figure. He wore loose trousers of Egyptian cotton, and despite the cool weather, sported a sleeveless brocaded vest. His taut upper arm was adorned with a wide gold band; a matching hoop hung from his left ear.

Jamal gave Laura a slow, regal nod. He glanced from her to Sandro, and Sandro cringed at his long-time friend's knowing look. Laura held her charming smile, waiting for Jamal's response.

"He can't speak," Sandro said brusquely.

Laura's smile fled. "Messere Jamal, how awful for you."

He spread his huge hands, then pointed at his mouth.

"His tongue was cut out by the Turks," Sandro explained.

"My God," Laura whispered, "why?"

"He was enslaved—it was the sultan's notion of loyalty."

"How did the two of you meet?" she asked.

Sandro was adept at dodging personal questions, but for some reason he could deny this woman nothing, not even long-kept secrets. "I had some unfinished business with the sultan a few years back, and took Jamal as part of the payment."

A troubled frown creased Laura's brow. "So in

other words, Messere Jamal passed from one sort of bondage to another."

Jamal signed an emphatic denial. His onyx eyes commanded Sandro to explain.

"I offered him freedom and the means to return to his native land," said Sandro. "Jamal chose to stay with me." He refused to divulge that Jamal had begged to stay, swearing that he could not bear the shame of returning maimed to his people. "You may speak freely in front of Jamal," he continued, taking her arm and guiding her to the chairs at the hearth. "I keep no secrets from him."

Laura seated herself, and Sandro took the opposite chair. The fire crackled cheerily in the marble framed grate. "Have you run afoul of the law, madonna?"

"Of course not." She folded her hands demurely in her lap. "My lord, I have information about Daniele Moro."

Her words pounded in Sandro's head. Disbelief made him fierce. "How do you know of Moro?"

"Well." She ran her tongue over her lips. Sandro knew women who spent fortunes to achieve that beautiful shade of crimson, but he saw no trace of rouge on Laura. "I have a confession to make, my lord."

A denial leapt in his throat. No. She could not be involved in the butchery of Moro. Not her. Anyone but her. "Go on," he said thickly.

"I heard you speaking of Moro to Maestro Titian." She leaned forward and hurried on. "Please forgive me, but I was so curious, I couldn't help myself. Besides, this might be for the best. I can help you solve this case, my lord."

He didn't want her help. He didn't want to think of this innocent lamb sneaking in the dark, listening at doorways, hearing of the atrocity that left even him feeling sick and soiled.

Without thinking, he jumped up, grasped her by the shoulders, and drew her to her feet. Although he sensed the silent censure of Jamal, he ignored it and sank his fingers into the soft flesh of her upper arms. He smelled her scent of sea air and jasmine, saw the firelight sparkling in her beautiful, opalescent eyes.

"Damn you for your meddlesome ways," he hissed through his teeth. "You have no business poking your nose into the affairs of the *signori di notte.*"

She seemed unperturbed by his temper, unscathed by his rough embrace. She lifted her chin. "I'm well aware of that, my lord, but remember, I did warn you of my inquisitive nature."

"Then I should have warned you that I have no use for women—inquisitive or otherwise."

She lifted her hands to his chest and pressed gently. "Your fingers are bruising me, my lord."

He released her as abruptly as he had snatched her up. "My apologies."

"I wouldn't worry about it, but Maestro Titian will question me about any bruises when I model for him."

Sandro despised the image of Laura laid out like a feast upon the artist's red couch, lissome and sensual as a goddess, while Titian rendered her beauty on canvas.

"Do you truly have no use for women, my lord?" she asked. "That's unusual, especially in so handsome a man as you."

Sandro ignored her insincere compliment and paused to consider his four mistresses. Barbara, Arnetta, Gioia, and Alicia were as different and yet as alike as the four seasons. For years they had fulfilled his needs with the discretion and decorum he required. In exchange, he housed each in her own luxurious residence.

"It's my choice," he said stuffily, settling back in his chair. He did not need to look at Jamal to know that he was grinning with glee.

"Well, I believe my information could be useful to you." She sent him a sidelong glance. Not even the demure brown dress could conceal her lush curves. "That is, if you're still interested, my lord."

As she sank gracefully back into the chair, he stared at the shape of her breasts, ripe beneath their soft cloak of linen. "I'm interested."

She smiled, the open, charming expression that was fast becoming familiar to him. "I happened to mention the murder of Daniele Moro to my friend Yasmin—"

"By God," he snapped, "don't you understand? This is a sensitive matter." He gripped the chair arms to keep himself anchored to his seat. "You can't go airing police business all over the city."

"I didn't." She seemed truly bewildered. "I told only one person."

"You could endanger yourself, madonna. The killer is still at large."

"Oh. I'm not used to having someone worry about my welfare."

"It is my vocation to worry about the welfare of every citizen of the republic."

She shifted impatiently. "Never mind all that. I found someone who saw Daniele Moro on the night he was killed."

Once again, Sandro came out of his chair. *"What?"*

"I'll take you to meet this person, my lord."

"Do that, and I'll think about forgiving you."

"A brothel?" Sandro stood in the gondola, causing the low, sleek craft to list in the canal. The gondolier dug in his pole to bring the boat to the water steps. "Your witness lives in a brothel?"

"Yes." Laura, who had been thoroughly enjoying the voyage in a nobleman's luxurious conveyance, gave her hand to the gondolier and alighted on the steps of Madonna della Rubia's opulent manse, the finest house in the *sestiere* of Castelletto.

She waited at the door while Sandro and his burly secretary joined her. As a footman in ornamented livery bade them enter, her stomach fluttered in apprehension, for she knew the madonna would not be pleased. Squaring her shoulders, she stepped into the foyer. The sumptuous room was decorated with pink variegated marble and alabaster statuary. The windows were glazed in amber and violet. The sounds of music and laughter drifted from the central garden.

Laura reached up and rang the glass bell patrons used to announce their arrival.

Moving like an argosy with all sails unfurled, Madonna della Rubia emerged from a gold-draped doorway. Her smile of welcome crumpled into a scowl when she saw Laura. "Child, don't tell me you've lost yet another fichu. And you know better than to use the front—" She broke off as she spied Sandro and Jamal. Recognition softened her features; as the leading *ruffiana* of Venice, in charge of two dozen courtesans, she made it her business to know every patrician in the republic. Her rouged lips slid back in a smile, and she lifted her hand to touch her fluffy yellow hair.

"My lord," she said in her most refined voice. "Welcome. What is your pleasure?"

To Laura's amazement and delight, a red flush crept out of Sandro's collar. Truly, he did have uncommon appeal. He was so utterly *human* that one couldn't help but like him.

He bowed decorously. "Police business. I'm here to question one of your . . . of the . . . residents."

Madonna della Rubia's ruthlessly plucked eyebrows shot up in outrage. "My girls and I follow every regulation, my lord, and pay all our taxes. I assure you, you'll find nothing untoward here." Laura watched the procuress with an artist's appreciation. She had started a portrait of her benefactress and enjoyed the chance to see a new facet of her subject. If the painting pleased the madonna, she might reduce Laura's swiftly mounting debts.

"I don't expect to," Sandro said, strain tugging at his polite smile. "I merely need to ask some questions." With graceful discretion, he touched the coin purse tied at his waist. "Of course, I understand the value of your time, madonna."

She shot a warning glance at Laura. "Whom do you wish to see?"

"Florio," said Laura. "I'll show them up." Letting the tension ease from her shoulders, she congratulated herself for passing the first obstacle. She would have hell to pay later, but Madonna della Rubia had invested a great deal in her and could not afford to throw her out just yet. Besides, the portrait of the *ruffiana* was unfinished; vanity would not allow her to leave it half done.

Sandro caught himself eyeing Laura's swaying hips as she led him up a narrow back staircase. He seemed to lose all self-discipline when he was around her. He found the changes in himself startling, frightening. In her presence, he was hard-pressed to cling to his strict code of honor and rectitude.

And how the devil had she made the acquaintance of these people? he wondered. Portrait commissions, he assured himself. So early in her career, Laura could not afford to be particular about her clients. Yet, he realized with distaste, she seemed uncannily familiar with the household.

When they reached the upper living quarters, Sandro smiled wryly. The brothel was not unlike his *fondaco*, with the goods below and the residence above.

Laura stopped at a door and knocked.

"Come," said a low voice.

She pushed the door open and motioned Sandro inside. Jamal planted himself in the hall, his brawny arms folded across his chest and his gaze trained straight ahead.

The small, tidy room held the funereal smell of dried gardenias. A lute, a *spinettina,* and a flute were arranged on a table in the center of the chamber. At the window stood a tall figure clad in a black cloak. A mane of blond hair streamed from beneath the brim of a dark biretta.

"Florio," said Laura. "We're so sorry to intrude."

The figure at the window turned. The face was shadowed by the brim of the hat. "Yes?"

The deep voice startled Sandro. Then awareness rushed over him. A man residing at a bordello? Battling a sense of outraged astonishment, Sandro put on his most professional façade. "I am Sandro Cavalli of the *signori di notte*. I've come to ask you some questions about Daniele Moro."

Florio took a deep, shaky breath. His broad shoulders and thick arms parted the voluminous cloak as he reached up to remove his biretta. Without the ornate costume, Sandro thought, Florio might be a well-favored man, for he had a strong cleft chin, high cheekbones, a sculpted mouth. But the woman's garb gave him the look of a popinjay. "What would you like to know?"

Sandro caught Laura's eye. He jerked his head in the direction of the door.

Making a grand show of ignoring him, she stepped farther into the room and indicated a dainty Tuscan chair. "May I?" she asked Florio.

He nodded. "Laura is my friend, and I need her in my time of grief. I have nothing to hide from her."

"I must insist," Sandro said.

"No," Florio countered, his implacability at odds with his appearance. "*I* must insist. She stays, or I tell you nothing, my lord."

Sandro ground his teeth. Laura was distracting him from his purpose. He needed to focus all his attention on Florio, to probe the hooded eyes, to search for a killer. Still, he had questioned suspects and wrung confessions in worse circumstances.

"I understand Moro came to see you on the night he died."

"He did." Florio made an impatient gesture with his hand. "Look, my lord, I'll spare you the probing. My official purpose in this house is to perform as *mezzano*. I regale the patrons with love songs, write ardent letters for illiterate gallants."

"You say your official capacity is *mezzano*," Sandro said. "Have you another role here?"

Florio sighed mournfully. "Daniele and I were lovers. At first he was merely a client, but in time we developed a genuine affection for each other. It was difficult for us to be together, for the doge made many demands on his time, and I . . ." Florio faced him defiantly. "I loved him."

Sandro glanced sharply at Laura; surely she could not understand this. Yet she sat gazing in heartfelt sympathy at her strange friend. "I see. So two nights ago, you found time to renew your friendship."

"We did. He was on an errand for the doge, but he came to me first. He had promised to appeal to the doge to let me perform on Ascension Day. It is my fondest wish to sing a barcarole during the marriage to the sea."

"Florio's a wonderful singer," Laura chimed in. "Singing at the Sposalizio del Mare would make him the envy of all the performers in Venice."

"I don't doubt his talent," Sandro said impatiently, then turned to Florio. "And how did the doge respond to Moro's appeals?"

Florio's smile was full of mournful pride. "I've been invited to sing aboard the state galley during the event."

Laura gasped. "Florio, that's wonderful! It's what you've always wanted."

He touched her cheek, drawing his thumb along the dainty line of her jaw. As Sandro watched the tender gesture, something dark and ugly reared to life in a hidden place inside him.

"Ah, but there is always a price, is there not, *bellissima?*" Florio grimaced. "Daniele won't be there to witness my triumph."

Sandro had to remind himself that the man had a talent for deception. He was such an obvious suspect

that Sandro's mind quickly made a neat case. Florio
and Moro might have had a lovers' spat. Florio,
already ambivalent about his own manhood, was
possessed by the sick impulse to emasculate his lover.

"I know what you're thinking," Laura burst out.
"You're wrong. Florio would never hurt anyone."
She leapt up and took Florio's hand. "I know him,
my lord."

Florio drew her hand to his lips. "Hush, sweet
one. He's only doing his job."

Filled with annoyance, Sandro continued the questioning. He established the time of Moro's arrival.
Eschewing the entertainments in the salon, Moro had
retired with Florio to this room. They had shared wine
and companionship for approximately two hours; then
Moro had gone, taking his satchel with him.

"His satchel?" Sandro kept his voice calm while
suspicion surged inside him. "You're certain he had a
satchel with him?"

"Quite certain. It was made of tooled leather and
had a seal on the flap. The winged lion of San Marco,
it was."

No satchel had been found with the body.

By all rights, Sandro could take the man into
custody and detain him in the Gabbia, but he hesitated
to take that measure on such thin evidence. And then
there was that unexpected tenderness between Florio
and Laura, the look of affection in his eyes when he
had kissed her hand. Was he a strange but innocent
man, or a twisted killer with a knack for deception?
And why did Laura like him?

Discomfited by frustration, Sandro left Florio. In
the long, bright hallway, Laura cried out, "Yasmin!
Wait!" Lifting her skirts, she hurried down the hall.

Sandro recognized the beautiful African woman from Laura's sketchbook. Though Laura was tall, Yasmin towered over her. In contrast to Laura's incessant fidgeting, Yasmin held herself still, grave faced with a subtle danger lurking in her black eyes.

"Yasmin, come and meet Lord Sandro and Jamal." Laura spoke rapidly as she led her friend down the hall.

Sandro glanced at Jamal, then looked again. Jamal had stopped in his tracks and was staring at Yasmin with a painful mixture of longing and panic that tore at Sandro's heart. Jamal's hand went to his throat, and his face contorted with the agony of his silence. Never, Sandro knew, had Jamal wished more fervently for the faculty of speech. Never had he been so ashamed of his inadequacy.

"Come, my friend," said Sandro. "Let us meet this lady."

Yasmin greeted them like a cat, her nose twitching delicately and her face filled with cool disdain. She had thirsty eyes; in a single glance they drank in the essence of a man and, judging from the expression on her face, found him lacking.

"How do you do?" Her voice was rich and velvety with the melody of her native Africa.

"Jamal doesn't speak," Laura explained. "He was in the service of the sultan."

Yasmin's eyebrows lifted. "A man who does not speak?" She put her hand on Jamal's forearm. "What a vast improvement you are over other men."

Alarm flashed in Jamal's eyes, but one look from Yasmin seemed to calm him. The air between them crackled with unseen lightning. Laura, too, seemed to sense the alchemy. "Why don't we show them your garden, Yasmin?" She turned to Sandro. "She has the most marvelous plants, my lord. Myrtle, jasmine, aloes, unusual spices. She persuaded Madonna della Rubia to import some rarities from the East."

Sandro thought fleetingly of all his vital business, yet he succumbed to the urge to linger. They descended together to the main level of the house. Her embroidered velvet caftan flowing in her wake, Yasmin led them out to a broad courtyard bordered by a shadowy cloister. Birds in wicker cages chirped, while a tiny monkey huddled, miserable with the cold, on a perch.

A woman sat on a stool, plucking a melody from a lute. Her companion, a man Sandro recognized from the Senate, sat nearby, eating dried figs from a silver bowl. Around an iron-legged table, two courtesans and two men bent over hands of painted tin cards, intent on a game of La Trappola. The occupants of the courtyard offered polite sounds of greeting. Within hours, all of Venice would know that the Lord of the Night had been seen at a brothel. Sandro did not care. He knew he was a man of honor; he knew why he was here.

What nagged at him was that Laura consorted with people of such low moral fiber. Someone ought to find her better patrons.

Yasmin led the way beneath an archway to a garden. A profusion of vines, herbs, and small trees grew there.

"It is not so prolific in winter," Yasmin explained. She took Jamal's arm. "Come. Let me show you a new nutmeg tree." Glancing at Sandro, she said, "It's illegal, I know. But I do not trade my spices."

As they walked off, Laura smiled up at Sandro. "I knew she'd like him."

To her surprise, Sandro's face was filled with the

dark thunder of anger. "Damn you," he said under his breath. "Don't you realize what this will do to him?"

She drew back, stung by his displeasure. "My lord, what is the harm in introducing him to a woman from his own country?"

"Jamal wants nothing to do with his own country, not after what the Turks did to him. He would rather live out his life in exile than face his people again. To me, his lack of speech is a small inconvenience. But to him, it's an unforgivable flaw. And now you're waving that flaw in the face of an incredibly beautiful woman. A woman he can never have."

"Can't he?" Laura glanced at the couple across the patio. Yasmin kept up a steady, murmured narrative, showing him the buds on a cassia branch, a flower gone to seed. Jamal looked on, but his fascination was clearly for the woman, not the plants.

"Don't be naive," Sandro snapped. "Of course he can't."

"I won't believe that," Laura said stoutly. "He likes her."

"The man can't speak."

Laura leveled a gaze at Sandro. He was so wise, with his craggy, arrogant face and deep, intelligent eyes. And yet in some matters he seemed as ingenuous as a child. She put her hand on his sleeve, enjoying the hardness of his muscles. "My lord, sometimes the most important things are not spoken in words."

He glared at her, then turned and stalked to a figured marble bench. "That's ridiculous."

Without waiting for an invitation, she sat down beside him. "I did this for Yasmin as well as Jamal. She hates m—" Laura clamped her mouth shut, berating herself for a fool. Sandro Cavalli trusted no one; he would suspect his own mother.

"She hates men?" He turned to her, lifting one eyebrow so that he looked like the devil himself.

"Stop it," Laura said. "Yasmin had nothing to do with the murder. It's because of her that you found Florio anyway. She didn't have to tell me Moro was here only hours before he was killed. If not for her, you wouldn't have found out about the satchel." Laura savored his expression of surprise. "I saw your face when Florio told you about it, my lord. The satchel is significant, isn't it?"

"It's none of your business." Filled with shifting measures of anger, frustration, and untimely attraction, Sandro ran a hand through his hair. From the start, he had known the motive was not robbery. The corpse had still worn the gold chain of office and the sapphire ring Doge Gritti had given Moro. But Florio had been certain Moro had taken the satchel with him. Obviously the assassin had stolen it. But why? What was in it?

Eager to get on with the investigation, he started to place his black velvet biretta on his head, but one look at Jamal stopped him. As the beauteous Yasmin spoke on in Arabic, Jamal drank in every word. A few moments more, Sandro allowed, settling himself back on the bench. His gaze took in the array of plants and froze when he recognized a monkshood root drying on a table. Monkshood yielded the poison, aconite. Poison, he mused, in the hands of Yasmin, who had known the victim.

"It's kind of you to give them more time together," said Laura. She had the most uncanny and annoying knack for reading his thoughts.

"I wish you'd quit accusing me of being kind."

"I wish you'd quit insisting that you aren't."

He scowled at a lifeless tree. "Where would you like to go when we leave here?"

She tilted her head to one side. "I don't understand."

"As a gentleman, I cannot leave you in this iniquitous place."

Her laughter chimed in his ears. My God, he thought, she's exquisite. Beautiful women were as common as pigeons in Venice, but Laura had a special quality about her. Magic and allure seemed to shimmer around her. She embodied innocence; it radiated from her like jasmine perfume and floated like her laughter on the wind. She was purity itself—the very essence of unspoiled purity.

"I am home," she said. "I live here."

He felt as though a giant fist were squeezing the breath from him. "Here? In this—this brothel?"

"Yes. I'm sorry, I should have explained before—"

"You're just here doing some portraits." He rushed out the words, driven by the need to reassure himself.

"Of course. I'm working on one of Madonna della Rubia, and there's no end to subjects for sketching." Laura sighed. "But I can't take money for painting until I'm elected to the Academy, for the guild prohibits it. And after Carnival time, I'll have less time to devote to my art."

Sandro's mouth dried. "Why will you have less time?"

"Well, I'll be busy entertaining clients."

"Clients. You mean people who come to sit for portraits."

"Eventually I hope that's what it will mean." Laura turned to faced him. She placed her hands on his knees, and her touch was warm, disconcerting. "My lord, I can see you don't want to hear this. But it's silly to keep dancing around this. I am a courtesan."

Her words thudded like a death knell in his head. Deep down, he knew he had willfully blinded himself to the truth. He had not wanted to see the obvious, had not wanted to think of Laura—airy, talented, achingly young—selling her body to strangers. She triggered in him a protectiveness all out of proportion with mere duty. And even deeper down, Sandro found an equally awful truth: He was deadly jealous of the men she took to her bed.

"I've disappointed you," she stated.

"By your own foolishness, yes. Laura, you're a gifted young woman. Why would you enter into this degrading trade of the flesh? Have you no shame?"

Color stood out high in her cheeks. She left the bench, pacing restlessly. "Aspiring to be an artist is an expensive enterprise. And Madonna della Rubia charges a hundred *scudi* a month for my room and board, and then there's the pigments and canv—"

He stood and planted himself in her path, his arms akimbo and his face set. "Find other means to finance your career."

"Such as?" She waited. He said nothing, so she went on, "The women who stitch sails at the Arsenal earn half what a man makes for doing the same job." With a mocking laugh, she snapped her fingers, feigning inspiration. "I could be a laundress. By the time I reach my dotage, I might have earned enough to buy a few yards of canvas but no brushes or pigments. I have little choice, my lord."

"I hate this trade," he declared. "I've investigated

more crimes that lead to brothels than any other place."

"If you suppress prostitution, then where would men take their lust?" She eyed him with infuriating keenness. "Where do you take yours?"

"I never lust," he lied. "And you're wrong in thinking that if we were to take away the sewer, the whole city would be polluted with corruption."

"That's a crude way of putting it, my lord. But it's like the misty weather of Venice. You can curse it all you wish, but you can't make it go away."

He crumpled his hat in his hands. "Why you, Laura?"

"What else would you have me do?"

"You could get married."

"Oh, that's fine. Marry some crude *arsenalotto* who'd put a babe in my belly every year. I could work on my paintings between night feedings."

"He doesn't have to be a common laborer. You're a lovely woman. You could marry—"

"Your son, my lord?" she asked, a sharp edge to her voice. He felt his face pale, felt his tongue go thick.

She gave a harsh laugh. "Ah. I see. Standards, and all that."

Her cynicism dug at him and destroyed the aura of purity with which he had mistakenly endowed her. Half to himself, he muttered a line from Petrarch: "'Rarely do great beauty and great virtue dwell together.'"

She thrust up her chin. "If marrying some bumptious merchant is your idea of virtue, my lord, then you can keep it, along with your stuffy interdicts about noblemen."

"I just enforce the laws. A patrician who marries a commoner is stripped of his nobility and his place in the Great Council."

"Heaven forbid!"

He grabbed her shoulders, forced her to look at him. "A man's nobility means as much to him as your painting does to you. Would you have him give it up?"

Subdued, she said, "No. Of course not."

He relaxed his grip on her and stepped away. "Find yourself some likely merchant, Laura."

"Why? What does it matter to you?"

Because I want you for myself.

Banishing the thought, Sandro pivoted sharply away from her. "I find it . . . worrisome. How old are you, Laura?"

"Eighteen, but—"

"You are the same age as my daughter, Adriana. Perhaps that's why I feel protective toward you."

"Well, you need not. I know exactly what I'm doing."

"Oh? Then you know of the physical danger, the unspeakable diseases. And when time robs you of your youth, what will you do then?"

"If it's any comfort to you, I don't intend to do this forever. Only until I'm able to support myself as a painter."

He rounded on her, his eyes fierce. "How can you be a painter if you have no self-respect?"

She recoiled as if he had struck her. "I have plenty of that, my lord."

"Do you? What's it like, Laura, lying on your back while a stranger uses you in the most intimate way possible?"

"I don't know yet."

Hope filled his chest to the point of pain. "You mean you're not—you haven't—"

"Madonna della Rubia's customers expect only ladies of the highest refinement. I have much to learn before I entertain men. My career will commence on the eve of Lent. The madonna always puts on a grand masque."

Sandro's tight chest relaxed by inches. Perhaps, then, there was still time. Time to teach her to cherish her innocence, to honor her body. Time to turn her from the path of danger. Time to learn why in God's name she made him feel like an eager green youth contemplating his first conquest.

3

The next day, Laura still felt out of sorts. Damn Sandro Cavalli. He had no right to judge her, to fill her with apprehension about her carefully laid plans. She would sacrifice anything, everything for her art. No price was too high to pay.

Trying to free her thoughts of a stern, craggy face with an unsmiling mouth and penetrating eyes that pretended to be cold, she knocked at the door of Magdalena's room in the Convent of Santa Maria Celeste.

Shuffling footsteps approached, and the door swung open. Laura looked down into Magdalena's shy face. She always brought to mind a child hiding a gift behind her back. Sandy hair peeked from beneath her wimple. She had sad eyes the color of Venetian rain, and an air of sweetness that only Laura seemed to notice.

"Laura." Magdalena reached for her shoulders and stood on tiptoe to kiss each cheek. "I haven't seen you in a while."

"I've been busy with my lessons . . . and other things. May I come in?"

"Of course." She closed the door behind her.

Although most young women shared the dormitory, Magdalena enjoyed a private chamber due to the generosity of an anonymous patron. Her room was cramped and windowless. A candle atop a mound of old wax illuminated a writing desk. Aside from the desk, she had only a low bed, a tall armoire, and a tiny brazier filled with glowing olive stones, which gave off a smokeless heat. The room smelled of candle wax and dampness.

"I don't see how you work here," Laura said. "I can't imagine never feeling the warmth and brilliance of sunlight."

"That's your nature. You're more attuned to the senses. My light is here." She touched her temple, giving Laura a familiar sidelong smile.

"Messer' Aldus would give you an office at his print shop." Laura sat on the bed and eyed her friend. The two had grown up as sisters, yet Magdalena was ever protective of her own privacy.

"We've been through this before, Laura. This is where I want to be. I'm . . . safe here."

"Oh, Magdalena." Laura's eyes misted with sympathy. Here, in darkness, she was safe from eyes that stared at her deformity, the unnatural rise of her back that no rough-spun habit could conceal. Safe from the jeers of children who ran in fright from her; safe from the fiery regard of state inquisitors who believed her imperfection was the work of the devil. "Once I join the Academy, my commissions will pay for a decent house. You could live with me there."

Just for a moment, yearning shone stark in Magdalena's eyes. Then, with a weary sigh, she moved aside the manuscript she was editing for Aldus. "I'm content here. Don't worry about me."

"I always worry about you, Magdalena." Though a

year Laura's senior, Magdalena depended on Laura to be her champion. Laura had consoled her when other postulants teased her. Laura had encouraged her when Magdalena had expressed a desire to work as a printer's proofreader, had celebrated with her when Aldus had given her a manuscript to edit.

"You have your painting now, and your life at Madonna della Rubia's." Disapproval hardened Magdalena's words.

"Not you, too," Laura said.

"What do you mean, me too?"

"Lately people have been wanting to save my soul." Laura did not wish to think about Sandro Cavalli. "Never mind, Magdalena. What news?"

Magdalena toyed with the rope scourge tied around her waist. "Fra Luigi has gone on a pilgrimage to Jerusalem."

"Good." Laura frowned, remembering that she had mentioned the lecherous cleric to Sandro. Could the Lord of the Night have . . . She tossed away the thought. Surely not.

She strolled over to the desk. "What are you working on?" She reached for the top page, but Magdalena snatched it and turned it face down.

"It's not fit for anyone's eyes yet," she said, scurrying to the armoire and jerking open the door. "The author's ideas are admirable, but he butchers the language." She placed the manuscript atop a pile of new, ragged-edged paper, then closed the door and turned. Her lips curved in a seraphic smile. "I'll show you once I finish editing it. What about you, Laura? Has Maestro Titian finished the Danae painting?"

"Almost. Why don't you come and see it?"

Magdalena picked up an ink bottle and twirled it

between her fingers. "I see it already, Laura. In my dreams."

"Oh, you." She sat back down on the bed. "I think it's appropriate that Danae will be the last portrait I pose for before I actually join her in trade."

Magdalena's face fell. "I hate to think of you as a courtesan, Laura."

"Hush. You sound just like Sandro Cavalli."

Magdalena's jaw dropped. "You know the Lord of the Night?"

Laura grinned. "I probably wore the same expression on my face when I met him at Titian's studio." She leaned forward, telling herself there was no harm in relating the story to her friend. Magdalena saw no one save Laura and her mother, Celestina. "He was investigating a horrible murder. The poor man was stabbed through the heart and then . . . then mutilated."

Magdalena's gaze darted about the room. "Mutilated? In what way?"

Laura's throat suddenly burned, and she swallowed hard. "I believe it was a—a castration."

The ink bottle hit the floor and exploded. Splinters of crystal scattered in all directions. Magdalena's face was as pale as an unpainted canvas. "That's horrible. Why would Sandro Cavalli question Titian?"

"That's the interesting part. Titian knew the victim. I'm afraid I've said too much already."

Muttering under her breath, Magdalena scurried to a corner and fetched a broom.

"Here, let me," said Laura, reaching for the broom.

Magdalena jerked it away. "I can manage. I'm not an invalid, Laura."

She subsided to the bed. "It's only a broken bottle, Magdalena. Why are you so upset?"

She swirled the broom over the stained floor, made a pile of the glass, then stooped to brush it onto a piece of paper. "Ouch!" she yelped, staring at her finger. A ruby drop of blood stood out on the tip.

"Here, I'll get a rag." Laura moved toward the armoire.

"Don't!" Magdalena almost shouted.

"Really, Magdalena—"

"Stay out of it, Laura. The business with the police, I mean. It's dangerous, and none of your business."

Magdalena's agitation confused Laura. "Magdalena, what possible danger could I be in?"

The door to the chamber swept open. In walked Celestina, her robes swishing on the stone floor. Laura heard Magdalena's quick intake of breath. "I heard a crash," Celestina said, her voice thin with anxiety. "Did something break?"

"Just an ink bottle," Laura explained. "How are you, sister?"

Celestina's face was not merely handsome, but regal. Her smile was the smile of a queen bestowing unfelt good wishes on a lowly subject. Laura was accustomed to Celestina's cool remoteness; she was comfortable with the distance.

"I am well, thank you. I must come by Maestro Titian's studio soon," said the nun, her large, strong hands folded at her waist. "I've made a new ochre pigment I know he'll want to try."

"I could come to your laboratory and get it," Laura said.

Celestina smiled. "That won't be necessary. I enjoy getting out, visiting the infirm in the hospices, distributing alms." She glanced at Magdalena and noticed the girl's bleeding finger. "You've cut yourself!"

She rushed to her daughter, grasped her by the wrist.

"Mother," Magdalena protested, "it's only—"

"I must put something on this so it won't fester." As she pulled Magdalena from the room, Celestina sent Laura a tight, manufactured smile. "Another time, then, Laura?"

Shaking her head, Laura closed the door behind them. "Another time, sister," she said to the empty room.

In the ducal palace, Sandro closed his eyes and pinched the bridge of his nose. The Sala del Gran Consiglio was empty now, but only a short time earlier the huge gold-and-marble hall had teemed with senators, prelates, and Night Lords. Sandro savored the silence. It was a good time to collect his thoughts, to sift through the evidence he and his men had amassed, to make sense of the puzzle of Daniele Moro's murder.

The problem was, his conclusions led him nowhere. Feeling weary, he winnowed his fingers through his hair. A silver strand fell over his brow, and Sandro shook his head in disgust. He was getting old and doing it ungracefully.

He leaned back in his chair and scowled into empty space. He had no time for vanity when a murderer was on the loose. His mind was like a blank page, ready to be filled with facts, then processed with cold dispatch.

First item: A team of *zaffi* had been following Florio for two days. So far, the poor *mezzano* had left the brothel only to make his way to the Church of San Rocco. There, he had lit vigil candles and wept, then returned home. Yasmin, also under observation, never once left the brothel.

Second item: Sandro's deputies had investigated

the murder weapon. On the nearby island of Murano,
the center of Venice's glassmaking trade, glass stilettos were manufactured by the thousands. The splinters found in the victim's chest were amber, the most
common of colors. Worse, the glassmakers were a
suspicious lot, immune from police, and they guarded
the secrets of their trade like holy relics.

Third item: Doge Andrea Gritti could not be certain
of the contents of Moro's folio. He had given Moro
many messages, some to the Arsenal shipyard where
Bucentaur, the great state galley, was moored; some
to the printer who was to create programs and invitations for the upcoming Ascension Day ceremony; and
a promissory note for Titian, who had been commissioned to paint the doge's portrait. There might have
been other items the doge did not know about.

A sigh rushed from Sandro. The evidence was
thin, the possibilities innumerable. He was troubled
that someone so close to the doge was involved.
Sandro suspected, with instincts honed by years of
service to the republic, that events were driving
toward a plot against the supreme head of Venice.

The last item he pondered had nothing to do with
the grisly murder: Laura Bandello.

Like a haunting melody, thoughts of her stayed
with him night and day, appearing at the most inop-
portune of moments. During the morning's audience
with the doge, he had remembered her as he had first
seen her—lush, soft, unconsciously inviting. When he
had gone to the archbishop to order the banishment of
Fra Luigi, he had thought of her hair, defiantly black in
an age that revered blondes, a river of onyx with the
scent of a garden at evening. During his supper with
Marcantonio, Sandro had recalled her laughter—the

musical sweetness of it, the sparkle in her eyes and the graceful way she moved.

If Sandro didn't know himself better he'd say he was obsessed with her. But that was ridiculous. Sandro Cavalli didn't obsess about anything except his job.

Still, she lingered around him like the essence of fine perfume after the wearer has left the room. Because she was so young and full of promise, he told himself. He didn't want to see her sucked into the netherworld of the courtesans of Venice, to think of her in the arms of strange men, yielding her—

"Stop it," Sandro commanded himself. He steepled his fingers and scowled into the gathering dimness. She claimed she needed money. Very well, he decided abruptly. He would give her money. It was not unheard of for a wealthy patrician to patronize a promising young artist.

Satisfaction eased the frown from his face. Money was so neat, so simple, a solution he understood and respected. She would appreciate his generosity.

"Lord Cavalli." A whisper broke the silence of the chamber.

Sandro's head came up. He looked around. He was alone.

"Listen carefully, my lord, for I will only say this once."

Sandro rose swiftly from the table. The voice was coming from the mouth of the lion's head on one wall of the chamber. Installed to allow anonymous citizens to report crimes against the state, the *bocca di leone* was used less often now that Venice enjoyed a time of peace. The normal means was to drop a letter through the gaping mouth, but more cautious informers spoke directly through the opening.

Scratching the back of his neck, Sandro walked slowly to the bas-relief lion. He bent toward the small, dark opening. "I'm listening."

"You must watch over Laura Bandello. She is in danger."

Sandro's blood chilled. "What sort of danger?"

"Mortal danger. Watch over her, my lord. Keep her safe."

"Look," Sandro snapped, "your warning is too vague."

"Heed me well, my lord. I can say no more. Farewell."

"Wait, I—" Sandro had received a good many dire messages through the mouth of the lion. But never had one affected him as this did. He felt the cold, clean fear that uncluttered his mind and propelled him into action. Racing to the exit of the hall, he entered the passageway behind the *bocca di leone*.

The passageway lay in empty gloom. Sandro pounded down a flight of narrow stone stairs and burst out into the crowded street. The end of the *calle* opened out to the Piazza San Marco, bordered by lacy arcades and the gold bubbles of Byzantine domes. Citizens thronged the plaza. An overdressed *bravo*, a black-robed judge, a flock of nuns, an age-bent man in a cloak, a courtesan dressed in red and tottering on her *chopines* . . . Any one of them could be the anonymous whisperer.

Clenching his jaw, Sandro went to find Jamal. He would assign his most trusted *zaffo* to watch over Laura.

Fear overtook his decision. What if he was already too late?

* * *

Laura had stayed out too late again; she could tell by the arc of light on the mainland horizon. Madonna della Rubia would scold her, but she didn't care. Her excursion had been a failure anyway.

She hugged her sketchbook to her chest. The jars of ochre paint and turpentine, which she had fetched from Sister Celestina earlier, bumped in a cloth bag against her leg.

Laura had gone to the Lido today, hoping to practice drawing men, the greatest weakness in her art. Here, at the Lido, where the waters of Venice joined the vast Adriatic, workmen were busy erecting a grand archway. On Ascension Day, when la Serenissima made her annual vow to the sea, the doge and his entourage would pass beneath the archway.

Carpenters and stone masons manned the scaffolds, seemingly oblivious to Laura's scrutiny. Yet as intently as she studied them, she made no new discoveries about the masculine form. To protect themselves from the chill February air, they wore rough working garb, their sleeves and leggings long and concealing. Frustrated, Laura had accomplished nothing but a few inept pencil strokes.

She thought it a maddening irony that she lived in an establishment where men spent more time out of their clothes than in them, yet the standards for modesty kept them securely behind closed doors.

In a few short weeks, though, she would be entertaining gentlemen, too. The male physique would no longer be a mystery to her.

The thought troubled her even more than usual, for she couldn't get Sandro's words out of her mind: *How can you be a painter if you have no self-respect?*

It was ridiculous, she concluded mutinously. He

had no right to cause her to doubt herself and the choices she had made.

Lost in thoughts of a bossy, judgmental man who intrigued her for reasons she could not name, Laura turned down a narrow *calle* that led to the plaza near the brothel. Her footsteps echoed softly on the timeworn stones. The smell of onions frying in olive oil mingled with the ever-present sea breeze. When she was halfway between the walkway and the plaza, she noticed that other footsteps joined with the sound of her own.

Turning, she saw two men coming toward her. They were *bravi,* she could tell by the mode of their dress. The hired ruffians favored elaborately patterned hose, slashed pantaloons, codpieces of a misleading size, and hats decked with heron feathers dyed in gaudy colors.

"*Buona sera,*" she murmured, her hands tightening instinctively around her sketchbook.

"*Buona sera, madonna.*" One man bowed. He wore a black mustache as thin as a single stroke of a paintbrush. "You are Laura Bandello?"

"No." Her denial was swift and automatic. "I don't know of anyone by that name." As she spoke, she searched the alley for a way out. One end led to the walkway along the canal; the other to the plaza. She could see no one in sight. No lights glowed in the windows of the warehouses that lined the street.

The *bravi* exchanged a glance. With a movement as fluid as a master's brush stroke, one man reached into his hip sheath.

Laura gaped at the glittering glass stiletto. A milky liquid filled it. Poison, as deadly as snake's venom.

She edged backwards. The bottles clinked in their cloth bag. "This is a mistake," she said. "You can't mean to hurt me. I—I'm nobody."

The man took a step forward. His silence chilled her.

"I have nothing you could possibly want," she said, trying to think. Her free hand delved into the bag, and her fingers found the cork in the jar of turpentine.

The *bravo* took a step forward. One hand reached for her; the other lifted the dagger. Laura stumbled back. She turned to run, but his hand streaked out and caught her arm.

The stiletto descended toward her chest. Laura brought up her sketchbook like a shield. The glass weapon shattered against the hardwood surface. Wetness drenched her arm. Seizing her advantage, she kicked him in the groin. Yasmin had taught her the move; Florio had made her practice until her foot was a deadly weapon.

As the mustachioed man doubled over in pain, the other *bravo* started toward her. Laura dropped her sketchbook, yanked the cork from the turpentine bottle, and flung the contents in his face. Roaring out an oath, he fell against the wall, his hands clawing at his eyes.

Laura raced to the end of the alley. She looked up and down for a sign of someone, anyone. In the distance rose the Ponte di Tetti, where common prostitutes gathered to lure men into doorways and under bridges. As always, a few gondolas bobbed below the bridge.

Dragging gusts of air into her lungs, Laura raced toward the bridge. Madonna della Rubia denounced the streetwalkers as leeches who stole business from honest courtesans, but Laura welcomed their company. Risking a glance back, she saw one of the *bravi* emerge from the alley. Staggering, he clutched his codpiece.

The sight of the assassin gave her a fresh burst of speed. Sobbing in panic, she reached the bridge. A stout woman, her breasts bobbling over a neckline that barely contained them, planted herself in front of Laura.

"Not so fast," the woman snapped. "This is our territory, and we'll not have the likes of you stealing our trade."

"Please," Laura gasped, fighting to catch her breath. "I'm in trouble. I need help."

"Who doesn't, in this city?" The woman gave her a shove back. "Now, don't bother us when there's work to be done."

Laura almost screamed in frustration. Both of the *bravi* were coming now, their awkward shadows reflected in the canal. She looked longingly at the gondolas moored below the bridge. A gondolier could move a boat swifter than a man on foot could run.

"Go on with you," the fat whore screeched.

"Stop her," one of the assassins called. "She's a thief!"

The whore reached for Laura. Laura grabbed the bridge rail. In a second, she vaulted over the top and splashed into the icy canal water.

Her skin contracted with a chill that seized her whole body. Saltwater rushed into her mouth. Her skirts dragged her downward. Battling the heaviness, she managed to surface, to reach her hand toward a gondola.

The current tore at her sodden skirts. She managed a choking cry. Her hand touched the hull of the gondola; then she slipped away. She tried one more time, her legs scissoring even as she sank. The water closed over her head. Her eyes stung and burned. She was swirling, savoring a sense of weightlessness, beyond thought, beyond caring. . . .

A strong hand reached out and dragged her into the boat.

* * *

An hour later, she sat in the grand solar of the Fondaco Cavalli. She wore a velvet robe several sizes too large, with nothing but damp skin beneath. Her bare feet were submerged in a basin of hot water, and her hands cradled a mug of mulled wine.

Feeling as if she had been snatched from the jaws of death, she smiled at her savior. "Thank you."

Marcantonio Cavalli sent her a lazy, charming grin. "The pleasure was all mine. It's not every day I have the privilege of fishing a beautiful woman out of a canal." He knelt and lifted her bare feet from the basin, setting the water aside and drying her feet with a soft, snowy towel. He lingered over the task as if it pleasured him, and Laura gave an involuntary sigh.

"Better?" he asked.

She took a sip of the warm wine, letting the sweet spices run over her tongue. "Much."

He sat beside her on the divan, moving close so that his shoulder brushed hers. "Now, *bellissima.* I think you should explain how you came to be floundering in the canal under the Ponte di Tetti."

Laura pressed the rim of the wine cup to her bottom lip. During the swift gondola ride, she had evaded Marcantonio's questions, busying herself with her endeavors to avoid ruining the crimson velvet cushions of the Cavalli gondola. She knew the *bravi* had been motivated by something more sinister than general villainy, for they had spoken her name. Something told her that Sandro, not his too-handsome, too-solicitous son, should be the first to hear her account.

But Marcantonio was waiting. He had literally saved her life. He had brought her to his home and

made her comfortable. The least she owed him was
an explanation.

"I was . . . accosted by *bravi.*" She set down her
wine and shuddered.

His arm went around her, and his hand stroked
slowly up and down her back. "Poor lamb. Are you
certain they were hired assassins?"

She laughed nervously. "They didn't exactly show
me a letter of marque."

"Why would anyone want you dead?" His finger
came up to toy with a stray lock of hair at her temple.
"Have you a rival in your art?"

"How did you know I'm an artist?"

"I was curious about you. I asked around. Now,
what about this rival?"

The idea had not occurred to Laura. She frowned,
thinking of the apprentices who trained in Titian's
studio. "Surely not," she said. "They tolerate me
rather well. They know that, as a woman, I struggle
harder than they do." She gave him a wavering smile.
"Besides, none of them can afford to hire assassins."

Saying the word brought the horror back to her. The
color dropped from her face. Her head felt light, her body
weak. Before she knew what was happening, she swayed
toward Marcantonio. He caught her against him, whispering into her hair, "There, there. You're safe now."

"But when I walk out of here, will they be waiting
for me?" She pulled back, probing his face for
answers he could not give. From the hallway outside,
she heard the ringing sound of boots on marble. Sandro, she thought, going limp with relief.

Marcantonio's face hardened. Swiftly and without
warning, his lips captured Laura's. He held her tightly
with one hand behind her back and the other buried

deep in her hair. Surprised and disoriented, Laura put her hand between them and gave a gentle push. He kept up the pressure, moving his mouth against hers, ignoring her muffled sounds of protest.

She pushed again, harder this time, hard enough to break free. They came apart. He grabbed her shoulder, and somehow the overlarge robe slipped down one shoulder.

"I see your manners haven't improved, Marcantonio," said a voice from the doorway. "But at least your taste in women has."

Yanking up her robe, Laura stood to face the Lord of the Night. He did not look at her, but glared at his son. "Out," he said.

Laura glanced from one man to the other. If Marcantonio was a delicate Donatello sculpture, Sandro was a heroic Michelangelo. For all his brilliant male beauty, Marcantonio seemed somehow diminished in the presence of his father. Even so, she expected Marcantonio to balk. But Marcantonio merely swore under his breath, snatched up his biretta and stormed out of the room.

Sandro's eyes were as cold as driving sleet as they swept from her tousled head to her bare toes. "And is this part of your training?" he demanded. "Or have you already progressed to selling your favors?" He took the pouch tied at his waist. "What does my son owe you, madonna?"

"My lord," she began, dredging the words from the depths of her mortification. Sandro Cavalli possessed the unique ability to make her feel shame. "I have something to tell you."

His back straightened as if he had been whipped from behind. "And I have something to tell you, you little slut. My house is not to be used for carnal activities."

Laura bridled. "Tell your son that, my lord, for I—"

"My son knows that. I can reprimand him. You, I can arrest."

Shame gave way to fury. She took a step back. "You wouldn't dare."

He came toward her, cornering her between the divan and a Sansovino statue. He placed his fingers beneath her chin, his touch gentle yet deadly. Unbearable tension tightened her chest as he drew her gaze to his. "You'd be amazed at what I would dare, madonna."

She jerked away. "Will you kindly listen to me?"

"That little scene I witnessed speaks for itself." He jingled the coins in his purse. "Come now, what do you charge? One *scudo* for you and one for the procuress?"

Laura watched her own hand as if it belonged to someone else. It flashed out in a swift arc and cracked against his jaw.

He stared at her with fury and hatred in his eyes. A red handprint blossomed like a flower on his cheek. "You're not worth saving," he muttered, then flung a pair of coins on the table beside the statue and stalked out of the room.

Through the next week, Sandro was plagued by memories of the scene. He was supposed to be carrying out the investigation of the Moro murder. Instead he found himself, with maddening persistence, thinking of Laura Bandello.

Striding along the main street of Murano, he felt his face flush red. Not from the heat of the glassblowers' furnaces that lined the street, but from remembrance.

He could not shake the image of her locked in a passionate embrace with his son, her hair a wild midnight tumble, her ruby lips bruised by kisses.

She was a lying, manipulative, immoral woman, he told himself. A far cry from the vulnerable, wide-eyed budding artist he had encountered in Titian's studio. No doubt she had schemed to insinuate herself into Marcantonio's good graces, thinking his son easier game than the Lord of the Night. Or perhaps younger, comelier game.

Sandro paused, watching a craftsman lift a glowing gob of molten glass from a foundry. A snip and a twirl of pincers rendered the stream of glass into a vase.

But again, his thoughts returned to Laura. She had created a rift between father and son. Their relationship had always been tenuous; Marcantonio was not the civic-minded merchant Sandro wanted him to be, and Sandro was not the indulgent father Marcantonio seemed to crave. Following the scene with Laura, Marcantonio had left without a word, no doubt to go carousing with his friends. He was probably staying with the heir to the duke of Otranto, and would only return when his allowance ran out.

A velvet-lined box opened in front of Sandro. Startled, he looked up to see Jamal, holding an array of glass daggers. Sandro dragged his mind back to business. "Your assistants have questioned all the glassmakers?"

Jamal nodded. His mouth was a grim line.

Sandro recognized the expression. "No answers? Not even one scrap of information?"

Jamal shook his head. Sandro rested against the corner of a building. The stone was warm, heated by the furnace within. He gritted his teeth in frustration, telling himself he had not really expected to trace the murderer through the glass stiletto. The weapon was too common, as Jamal's array proved.

Jamal held out the slate he always carried with him.

Taking it, Sandro read the message: *Go and see her and be done with it.*

He scowled. "I have no idea what you mean."

Jamal's look annoyed Sandro. "The girl is nothing but trouble. I'm well rid of her." But he kept remembering something: She had not taken the coins.

Jamal lifted his gaze and pretended to study the frescoes over the entranceway of the building.

"If I see her again, she's certain to provoke me."

Jamal nodded emphatically.

Sandro pushed the slate back into his friend's hand. "You have a strange sense of humor, Jamal."

Jamal gestured pointedly at the barge moored at the end of the street. He pantomimed the action of putting on a cloak.

"What's that?" Sandro asked. "Oh, my black-and-red cloak. I did leave it at Titian's, didn't I? After that beastly dog soiled it. The maestro promised to have it cleaned." Sandro rubbed his chin, an idea forming in his mind. "Yes, I should go by and fetch my cloak."

He would not look at Jamal's expression of triumph.

An hour later, Sandro presented himself at Titian's house. The master had released his apprentices for the day, and the antechamber to the studio was quiet. Except for the familiar trill of feminine laughter that drifted from beyond the closed door and raked over Sandro's nerves like talons of steel.

He started to stalk across the room when he realized he was not alone.

4

Pietro Aretino. Of all the ill luck, thought Sandro, stopping in the middle of the antechamber. Self-proclaimed censor of the proud, and prophet of the truth, Aretino was the darling of princes who both adored and feared him. Sandro tolerated him—reluctantly.

Aretino's gown was of black velvet, lined and braided in gold; his doublet was silk brocade, and a damascened dagger in a jeweled sheath rode at his hip.

Before Sandro could duck out, Aretino strode forward, carrying his corpulence with bouncing vigor. *"Ecco!* Lord Sandro!" the huge man boomed, a smile splitting his long, thick beard. *"Divinissimo! Onnipotente!* You've come to illuminate our dull afternoon with your august presence."

"Shut up, Pietro," Sandro muttered in annoyance. "I haven't the stomach for your hollow flattery today."

Aretino pressed a large hand to his chest. "My man, you cut me to the quick. My sincerity runs as deep as the waters of the lagoon. Have I not hallowed a hundred princes with my golden pen? Have I not lifted them to the realms of immortality with my poems?"

"You've dragged a few through the mud, too."

"Ah, but never you, my lordling. For you, I would write an epic. A hero tale to surpass even my deathless tribute to the Pope."

"Modesty must be one of your hidden virtues," Sandro said wryly. "No thanks, Pietro. Save the heroics for your willing patrons."

"A sonnet, then?" His eyes glittered with interest. "A mere fourteen lines, when my heart cries out to write a hundred times that many."

Sandro fought a smile. He alone had no interest in commissioning Aretino to chronicle his deeds—real and imaginary—in poems and pasquinades. The massive poet took Sandro's constant refusals as a personal challenge and pursued him relentlessly.

"I'll not give up my quest, *superbossio*. I'll pursue you until you yield," Aretino promised.

"Go sharpen your claws on someone else," said Sandro.

Aretino threw up his hands. His leonine mane of hair drifted about his shoulders when he moved. "*Ecco!* What manner of man are you? Surely you have some vanity I can pander to in prose."

"I'm too busy for vanity."

Aretino's eyes narrowed speculatively. "Still haven't found any leads in the Moro investigation?"

Sandro snapped to attention. "How do you know about that? Did Titian—"

"Of course not. You swore him to secrecy, didn't you? The man has more integrity than the college of cardinals. You know me, Sandro. The only thing I love more than women and food is gossip. You can't expect to find a corpse with its love nuts cut off and keep it a secret." He selected a sweetmeat from a glass bowl and popped it into his mouth.

Sandro made a mental note to reprimand the Night Lords involved in the case. If Aretino knew, the facts of the case might as well be shouted from the Piazza San Marco.

"I assume you've already established a connection with the doge," said Aretino.

"That's none of your business."

"My business is life itself, old friend, and also death when it's as interesting as Moro's." He chewed slowly and stroked his beard. "The murderer obviously had a particular hatred for poor Moro."

Sandro had concluded that the moment he had seen the corpse.

"So it could be a woman," Aretino went on. "Yes, that would explain the use of the poisoned stiletto. A woman's strength does not match that of a man, but a good potent poison is a great equalizer."

"If you want to keep your manhood intact, Pietro, you'll keep your speculations to yourself."

Aretino winked. "Easier to keep the tide from rising in the lagoon, *divino.*"

Sandro released the smile he had been holding back. As exasperating as Aretino was, he never failed to amuse, and generally reserved his malice for professional purposes.

"Is the maestro inside?" Sandro asked, jerking his head toward the studio door.

Pietro nodded. "Working. We'd best not disturb him."

"Who are you, his watchdog?"

Laughing, Pietro poured two glasses of wine.

"Keep me company, Sandro. I don't see nearly enough of you at Ca'Aretino."

Sandro accepted the wine in spite of himself. "I'd injure myself tripping over all your guests. Pietro, you've turned your house into a hospital."

Aretino gulped his wine. "One wing of it, anyway, poor wretches."

For all his blustering and grasping, Aretino opened his home to beggars as readily as to princes.

"The other wing," Pietro went on with a wink, "is for my harem. I have six mistresses now. Did you know, people are calling them Aretine?"

Sandro had no doubt as to who had coined the term. "Are congratulations in order?"

"Old friend, there is always something to congratulate me for." Aretino tossed back his wine and slammed down the cup. "Come. I want to show you something."

Throwing an impatient glance at the studio door, Sandro resigned himself to Aretino's company. He followed the bulky velvet-wrapped form through a passageway and into a long, darkened room.

"Titian's private gallery," Aretino explained.

"Then what are we doing here?"

"Nothing's private in my book." Aretino lumbered over to a window and threw open the shutters. White sea light flooded the room, empty save for a U-shaped bench. A series of unframed paintings hung on the walls. Each painting depicted the same subject.

Laura.

Sandro used all his control to keep a reaction from his face.

Aretino used all his wiles to interpret Sandro's stony expression. "Ah, I thought so. Not even the

Lord of the Night is immune to her. Titian told me so, but I didn't believe it."

"Titian told you what?"

"That you were . . . affected by Laura."

"Laura who?"

Aretino grinned and wagged his finger in Sandro's face. "My friend, I measure your interest by your insistence on your lack of interest. I can read you like a printed page. You're mad for her, Sandro."

"Don't be ridiculous. She's a child."

"But a most intriguing and alluring child, no? Come, I know you're burning with questions about these pictures, so I'll spare you the indignity of asking." Aretino slapped his palms on his barrel belly. "Still hard as a melon," he applauded himself, then strode down the length of the hall. "What Petrarch did for his Laura in verse, Titian is doing in paint. He's been working on this series for months. As you can see, she affects him in a way that no other model ever has." Aretino paused before a lush Venus. "Makes your mouth water, doesn't she?"

The nude goddess, lying in languid indolence upon a swirl of fabric, evoked a much stronger reaction in Sandro. He tore his gaze from her only to find himself staring at a startling portrait of Flora, ripe as a sun-warmed peach. Next to her was Leda, making love with a human-sized swan; the expression on her face reminded Sandro uncomfortably of the way Laura had looked that day in Marcantonio's arms. Clearing his throat, he turned his attention to Circe using her power to turn animals into humans. On canvas, Laura was all of these women of myth and legend. In life she was none of them.

In each picture she breathed from the canvas like a

goddess come to life. In image after image, she was substantial yet ethereal, her brilliant eyes candid, yet at the same time hooded with secrets.

"They're . . . quite lovely," said Sandro.

Aretino brayed with laughter. "What a poor actor you are, and a poorer critic. By God, Sandro, admit it. Titian has reached his genius with Laura, can't you see it? These pictures are so compelling that they're scary."

"What does he intend to do with them?" Sandro winced as he speculated. He envisioned hordes of patrons clamoring for these masterpieces.

Aretino sighed. "I'm not sure yet, and the maestro hasn't decided. Being the man of business that I am, I should urge him to sell, for these pictures are worth a fortune. Still, I hesitate."

Sandro lifted one eyebrow and put on a sardonic expression. "Growing a conscience, old friend?"

"Never!" Aretino snapped. "It's just that Titian isn't satisfied with the pictures."

Sandro gazed into the eyes of the winsome, self-conscious Circe. He had seen that expression on Laura when she was introducing him to her friends at the brothel. "Impossible. What more could he want?"

"He knows he hasn't plumbed to the bottom of her soul. He hasn't been able to reveal her haunting secrets."

"What makes you think the girl has secrets?" Sandro asked.

Aretino swept his arm wide to encompass the paintings. "Use your eyes, man."

Sandro had to agree. As compelling as these pictures were, there was an elusive quality about the subject that not even the most probing eye could touch. As deeply as Titian had revealed her, there were still hidden facets the artist had not reached.

"You know what's wrong with these paintings?" Aretino asked, clasping his hands behind his back in scholarly fashion. "He's painted everything but her smell."

"Of course he hasn't painted her smell," Sandro snapped. He was disturbed by the intensity of his reaction to her. "A smell cannot be seen."

"Just like her soul," Aretino said. "You know it's there, but you can't capture it. Her scent is like her soul—lush, provocative, and elusive."

Sandro recalled the ineffable floral fragrance of her hair. Even now he could smell her, just on the strength of a memory. And yet a fresher memory corrupted it: the image of Laura, tousled and wanton, in his son's arms.

"Are you in pain, my lord?" Aretino asked. "You look as if you are."

"Shut up, Pietro."

"I never shut up. The Pope and Emperor Charles have both tried to shut me up, and they failed." He gazed again at the picture of Venus.

"You know, I'd take her for myself, make her a part of my little harem of Aretine."

Sandro bridled, clenched his hands into fists.

Aretino chuckled. "Peace, old friend. Taking Laura would be a mistake."

"Amazing," said Sandro. "You actually have some common sense."

"Yes, I'd tend to favor her, and to choose a favorite is out of the question. All my Aretine are charming. Their variety keeps me in love with life and with myself. To Laura, I would become exclusively committed. A dangerous thing, no? A wife, bah! Happy the man who enjoys her metaphorically and keeps his distance in fact."

Sandro thought fleetingly of his own mistresses. Somehow, they had lost their appeal, and that bothered him. Being a just man, he determined to pension them off comfortably, find them husbands and dower them if they wished. That bothered him, too. "For once we agree, Pietro. But I'll delay no longer. I must see Titian."

"You go. I'll spend a few more moments with Laura." He sniffed the canvas and chuckled. "Ah, jasmine. I prefer the child on canvas. In person, she's such a gadfly. Getting her to be still is as futile as trying to pin down the mist off the lagoon." Aretino sent Sandro an arch look. "But if any man can accomplish the task, you can, *divinissimo.*"

"What the hell do you mean by that?" Sandro demanded.

"Maybe she's the one who'll make a human being out of you, *superbossio.* Maybe then you'll beg me to write your history." He smiled beatifically. "And hers."

Shaking his head at the poet's whimsy, Sandro left the hall and knocked at the door to the studio, then stepped inside.

A ball of brown-and-black fur flew at him.

"Jesus!" Sandro glared down at the small dog that had latched onto his boot. "Get him off me, maestro!"

Titian paused in the act of wiping his paint-stained hands on a rag and regarded Sandro with amusement. "If you'd barged in one minute earlier, I would have flown at you myself." He crossed the room and disengaged the dog, tucking it under his arm and smoothing his large, powerful hand over its head. "You know how I hate to be interrupted at my work."

Sandro glowered at the new puncture wound in his boot. "Your other watchdog held me off."

"Is Pietro still here?"

"All fifteen stone of him. Honestly, maestro, I don't know how you tolerate the man."

Titian shrugged. "He finds me commissions. Besides, I admire his philosophy. For Pietro, life is enough. It's important for me to remember that." He scratched the dog behind the ears. "Isn't it, Fortunato?"

The scruffy dog glared at Sandro. Sandro glared back. "Fortunato?"

"I named him." Dressed in her demure street clothes, Laura stepped from behind a screen. Her look was cool, resentful, and accusing.

Her attitude dug at Sandro's pride. She was the one who had wronged him, and yet she was looking at him as if he were an insect on the end of her nose. Worse, he was starting to feel guilty about berating her.

He found himself at a loss for words. Titian handed her the dog. "Take him to the garden, Laura. And listen for the bell. I'm expecting Sister Celestina with some pigments."

"Yes, maestro." She aimed a last, chilling look at Sandro and left the studio. Her angry footsteps rang on the stairs. Her departure left Sandro feeling desperate and incomplete and at last he admitted it: He had come to see her, had waited for her.

"Now," said Titian, "how can I help you, my lord?"

"I've come to fetch my cloak," Sandro lied.

"Ah, yes." Titian picked up a bundled parcel from a work table. "I've had it laundered. I was going to send it with one of the apprentices, but you've saved me the—" He broke off, staring at Sandro, who was gaping at the Danae portrait. "My lord, you've not heard a word I've said."

Sandro could not deny it. The picture of the virgin goddess basking in a rain of gold had new meaning for him now that he knew what Laura was. She, too, was a virgin, her prison a brothel, her future lover the highest bidder for her favors.

"Damn it, Titian," he burst out, "how can you let her?"

"Let her what? Model for me?"

"I can't object to that, for you're a man of honor. But the other . . . Surely you know she means to sell her body in order to finance her career."

"She's not kept it a secret from me."

"And you approve?"

Titian's face pinched in a frown, and he stroked his narrow beard. "It's not my place to approve or disapprove. The choice is Laura's, and she's plucked it from a number of rather unpleasant alternatives. She's an independent soul, my lord, and doesn't take kindly to unsolicited advice."

"Prostitution is a dangerous profession."

"For some. For others, it's a godsend. Laura owes money to Madonna della Rubia, because her supplies and her keep cost a small fortune. The woman is a criminal for what she charges the girls." Titian enumerated the reasons on his fingers. "Laura can't paint for pay until the Academy admits her. And then, she must pay for a studio. On top of that, she buys her own canvas and pigments, her oils and paper. She pays her own models."

"Then let her"—Sandro started to pace—"I don't know, let her borrow money. From you or Pietro, or even I could—"

"Sandro," Titian interrupted calmly, "your trouble is that you don't understand the soul of an artist or the plight of an independent woman."

Sandro contemplated the colorful disorder of the studio, the harsh scents of paint and oil. "I never said I did."

Titian pressed his broad hand to his chest. "A true artist's devotion burns like a fire in the heart. Our art consumes us. When Laura first came to me, I didn't want to have anything to do with her. I subscribed to the view of that second-rate scribbler, Albrecht Dürer, who said women lack the intellectual capacity and the persistence to create great works of art."

"An altogether admirable point of view." Sandro nodded in approval. "So what changed your mind?"

"When Laura told me her plans, said what she was willing to sacrifice, I was convinced. A true artist will go to any lengths for the sake of art. In her position, I would have done the same."

"Prostituted yourself?"

"Exactly. Luckily, I had the means to launch my career. Look, Sandro, don't tear yourself to pieces over this. Laura has true talent. In six months, she's learned what most apprentices spend years to master. If she wins election to the Accademia, her career as a courtesan will be brief indeed. The commissions will come pouring in."

"And do you think the Accademia will accept her? Christ, a prostitute? Don't they have standards?"

Titian grinned. "They've accepted lower life forms than Laura, believe me." He stared at his painting in progress. Satisfaction suffused his face. Sandro wanted to hit him, for he had managed to capture Laura's heartbreak as well as her determination.

"Well?" Sandro prompted.

Titian took off his smock and hung it from a peg. "If it were only a question of talent, I'd say yes without hesitation. That child has more raw talent than the sum of all my students combined. Of course, there is the matter of her sex."

A matter Sandro could not forget, no matter how hard he tried. "They might reject her because she's a woman."

Titian nodded grimly. "My lord, there is nothing more frightening to men than a woman who is their superior."

Sandro shook out his cloak in frustration and put it on. "That's ridiculous."

"Is it?" Titian's satyr eyebrows lifted. "She scares you to death, my lord. Though not for the same reason."

Sandro could not bring himself to dignify the comment with a reply. First Pietro, now Titian delving into his feelings. Before long, half of Venice would know the trials of the Lord of the Night.

"Have you caught the men who attacked her?"

The cloak dropped from Sandro's shoulders and pooled at his feet. A cold iron fist seized his heart and stopped his breath. "Laura was attacked?"

Titian blinked. "I thought you knew. My God, it's impossible that you don't. I've been so concerned for her safety that I now send a footman to accompany her home each day."

"How?" Sandro demanded, clutching the front of Titian's batiste shirt. "When?"

Titian drew back and shook his head in surprise at Sandro's hands. "I thought you'd be the first to know. It was Tuesday last. Two *bravi* threatened to kill her. She escaped by jumping into the canal."

Tuesday last. God. That was the day he had caught her with Marcantonio.

"Your son pulled her out," Titian explained.

Sandro swept up the cloak. Leaving a trail of uncharacteristically vile curses in his wake, he raced out of the studio and toward the garden. He cursed Laura for placing herself in danger. He cursed Marcantonio for failing to offer an explanation. Most of all, he cursed himself for lacking the patience and presence of mind to listen. He was a policeman, for Christ's sake. Ferreting out information and seeking the truth were supposed to be second nature to him. Laura's unwelcome arrival in his life had robbed him of his rationality.

He pictured her bedraggled state that evening: the borrowed robe, the bare feet. She had not been trysting with Marcantonio, but waiting for her clothes to dry. Waiting to tell Sandro. And he had been as blind and stupid as a man in his dotage, as angry and rash as a jilted lover.

Damn, damn, damn.

He paused at the entrance to the garden to collect his wits. Beneath a winter-bare vine pergola, Laura stood talking to a nun in a long black robe. A voluminous cowl hid the nun's face, and her arm was threaded through a large willow basket.

Laura tipped back her head and laughed at something the nun said. The silvery chime of her mirth infused Sandro with a fresh dose of guilt. She had begged for a chance to speak. He had ordered her from his house.

More than anything, Sandro Cavalli hated himself for failing one of the citizens he was sworn to protect.

He stepped into the garden, ducking his head beneath a trellis. "Madonna Bandello?"

She lifted her chin, aiming a bored stare at him. What a fool he must look to her, a grayling acting the groveling suitor.

"Yes?"

He approached the two women and bowed before the nun. "Sister. I am Sandro Cavalli."

The figure stirred, a barely discernible stiffening of the shoulders. One pale, slim hand came up and pushed back the cowl. Sandro found himself staring into a remarkably handsome face, one he recognized from Laura's sketches. Framed by a crisp white wimple, the features stood out in sharp relief. Topaz eyes assessed him with polite regard.

"God's blessings on you, my lord. I must leave now." She glanced into her basket, which contained clay pots sealed with wax, glass jars and vials stoppered with corks, and small pouches tied with leather thongs. "I have deliveries to make."

"Deliveries, sister?"

"Sister Celestina makes pigments for the maestro. She also concocts the most wondrous cosmetics," Laura explained.

Celestina smiled serenely. "The Lord has chosen an unusual means for me to serve Him. My lord, I have a fine henna tint that would bring your hair back to its natural chestnut color."

Sandro felt heat rise to his ears. His hair, silvering at the temples, had never been of much concern to him. Still, the mention of his age made him wince.

Before he could think of a graceful reply, Laura said, "No, sister. It would be a horror to tint his lordship's wonderful hair. Why, I find it—" She snapped her mouth shut, apparently remembering that she was vexed with him.

"I'll take my leave now," said Celestina.

"Thank you for the beauty creams, sister." Laura leaned down to kiss Celestina on each cheek, and the nun departed.

Sandro had much to say to Laura, but the words tumbled incoherently through his head, and all he could think of was a question. "Beauty creams?"

"Sister Celestina has taken an interest in supplying me with cosmetics."

Against his will, against all his principles, he found himself touching her chin, drawing her gaze to his. "Cosmetics, Laura? Wouldn't that be gilding the lily?"

She pulled away and dusted her hand over a statue of Venus. "I won't use them. They're such a bother. My lord, if you don't mind, I must go home."

To hear her refer to a brothel as home grated on his nerves.

"Laura. I came to tell you I'm sorry. Titian told me you were attacked."

She toyed with a lock of her hair. "I intended to tell you myself last week, but you were in no mood to listen."

He took both her hands, drew her down to a bench beneath the trellis. "I'm listening now, Laura."

She began to speak, and her tale of terror hit him like a ramrod to the gut. Her resourceful defense filled him with admiration. Her dramatic escape choked him with shame.

When he could find his voice, he said, "Have you any idea why, Laura?"

A soft mist clouded her blue eyes, and she plucked a dry leaf from the vine. "None at all. Marcantonio thought the *bravi* might have been hired by a rival artist."

Marcantonio. He had been the one to rescue her from the assassins, to comfort her after her ordeal, to speculate with her on why someone would want to murder her.

Sandro knew he would be apologizing to someone else before the day was done.

God. Marcantonio. Still, he had taken advantage of her vulnerable state and kissed her.

"Could he be right?"

Laura shook her head, and her midnight curls bounced vigorously around her shoulders. "No male artist would see me as a threat. Even the mediocre ones have the advantage over me."

"Can you think of any other reason someone would want you—" He could not bring himself to finish the thought.

"Dead?" She shivered and crumpled the dry leaf in her hand. He longed to put his arm around her but stopped himself. This was a professional matter. He must keep their dealings on an impersonal level.

"No," she said. "I just don't know."

"I do," he said, anger rising within him. "You asked too many questions about Moro. Damn it, girl, you were a fool."

She glared. "I was acting the responsible citizen. Will you censure me for doing my civic duty?"

"You should have left it to the *signori di notte*."

"It's not my way to leave anything alone."

"That's precisely what I fear. Here's what you'll do. I'll send Jamal to the *ridotto* to collect your belongings. You'll take my barge to the mainland."

She looked at him as if he had grown horns. "To the mainland?"

He gave a curt nod. "I have an estate on the river

Brenta, a staff of servants and stewards whom I trust implicitly. You'll stay there until I apprehend the killer."

She folded her arms across her chest. "No."

"I give you no choice."

"I make my own choices."

He battled the urge to shake her. "Look, I'll pay you to—to paint frescoes. That should satisfy your creative urges."

"If I liked painting solar walls, I'd be doing it. I don't wish to be an unsung decorative artist. I did that in my convent days. Besides, I need the guidance of Titian for the work I'm submitting to the Academy."

His lips thinned in annoyance. "God, you give me a pain."

With familiar capriciousness, her mood changed from stubborn anger to pure delight. "Why, my lord! I never thought you capable of feeling anything!"

An hour later she walked toward home, her footsteps dogged by a tall, stoop-shouldered *zaffo* with a long, narrow face and the nose of a hunting hound. As they started up a crowded walkway toward the Rialto bridge, Laura said, "Messere Lombardo, this really isn't necessary. I told Lord Cavalli I can look after myself."

"Sorry, madonna, but I have orders to watch you at all times. I mean to obey those orders, for I owe a debt of honor to Sandro Cavalli."

Curious, she studied Guido Lombardo's melancholy face. He had pouches of weariness under his eyes, lines of strain around his mouth. Beneath his red Frisian cap, his wiry gray hair strained against confinement like weeds in a garden.

Laura negotiated her way past a pair of ladies

tottering on their twelve-inch-high chopines. "What sort of debt?" she asked.

His humble expression turned to a smile. "I was once like Sandro myself. A patrician. A member of the Senate."

"What happened?" she asked, touched by his candor.

"A disaster." Humor pulled up his sagging jowls. "I fell in love."

She smiled. "A disaster indeed."

"In my case, it was. Serena is a commoner. When I met her, she was a sailmaker at the Arsenal. My family urged me to make her my mistress, but I couldn't dishonor her. I would give Serena nothing less than marriage."

"How very noble of you, Guido."

He rubbed his lantern jaw. "Actually, it wasn't a good thing. I was stripped of my nobility, my seat in the Senate. I lost everything."

"But was she worth it?"

"Yes. Oh, yes, even though we nearly starved that first year. I was shunned by merchants and manufacturers alike. Being a patrician, I knew no trade save commerce. Then Sandro offered me a post as a *zaffo*. My family was appalled that I agreed to work as a common policeman, but at least now I can earn a living for our children. I'll always be grateful to him."

Laura hid a smile. Sandro's misogyny was only skin deep. Beneath the façade of cold command lay a heart ruled by compassion, though he'd rather die than admit it. Laura thought it a shame that no one had ever been able to touch the soul of the Lord of the Night.

"Make way," someone shouted. "Make way for the Soldiers of Christ."

Guido swore under his breath as a contingent of inquisitional soldiers formed a column that filled the width of the bridge. Long pikes shoved the people to each side. The marching soldiers rived the crowd in two. Laura was jostled by bodies that smelled of damp wool and stale perfume.

Suddenly finding herself separated from Guido, she pushed back against the throng, trying to fight her way toward her protector. She lost sight of him as the soldiers, their helms creating a forest of plumes, blocked her view.

A hand closed around her wrist and pulled.

Laura screamed, expecting to feel the sting of a dagger. "Hush," someone said. The voice was mellow with an undertone of laughter.

Laura twisted around to find herself nose to nose and breast to chest with Marcantonio Cavalli. He smiled into her eyes while she swayed against him in relief. He was extravagantly dressed in a velvet doublet, parti-colored silk hose, and a short jacket with deep, satin-lined sleeves. He looked more comely than one of Raphael's archangels.

"How did you find me?" Laura asked.

"I've been following you. I was worried about you," he added quickly. "Come on, let's get out of here. This is no place for a lady."

"But—" A stout matron plowed into Laura, and the surging crowd nearly engulfed her. Clinging to Marcantonio's hand, she followed his sinuous lead to the end of the bridge. The crowd thinned there, and she blew out a breath of relief.

"Thank you, Marcantonio. I'd best start looking for Guido."

"Lombardo?" Marcantonio's eyebrows lifted with

sardonic humor. "You're with that old mule? He couldn't even hang on to his title after he got involved with some slut from the Arsenal."

Instantly, Laura remembered why she preferred the father to the son. Marcantonio pretended to be kind, while in truth he was petty and mean. Sandro pretended to be cold, while in truth he was soft as a lamb.

"This way." Marcantonio pulled her down a flight of water steps under the bridge.

Laura resisted. "I'm supposed to stay with Guido."

A flash of annoyance glittered in Marcantonio's eyes. "Already taking orders from my father, are you?"

"I wouldn't want Guido to think he's failed to protect me."

Marcantonio drew her close. With a gentle shove, he helped her into a waiting gondola. As she plopped down on the velvet cushions, he pulled her into his arms. "What the devil do you need with Guido when you've got me?"

The gondolier poled out into the canal. Laura twisted around to see Guido, but the shop-lined bridge obscured her view.

She scowled at Marcantonio. "That wasn't very nice of you. Guido will have to tell your father he's lost me."

His exquisite eyes dark and intent, Marcantonio leaned forward and said, "What does it matter, when I've found you?"

Laura cast a glance at the gondolier, but the oarsman gazed impassively at the Grand Canal. "I wish you'd take me home right now," she said.

"Not until you make me a promise."

"What promise?"

He took her hand in both of his and pressed it to his chest. His beautiful face was soft with an ardor that Laura found disturbing. "I want you, Laura."

She gasped, and he kissed her long and hard, coming up for air to add, "I mean it, *bellissima.* I've thought of nothing else since we met."

She tried to pretend it was a joke. "Don't be ridiculous, Marcantonio." But as preposterous as his offer was, the possibility flashed through her mind. She imagined being Marcantonio's lady, seeing Sandro every day and wondering. . . . The brief fantasy left no doubt in her mind. "I can't."

"You must."

"I won't."

His hands clutched her shoulders. "Damn it, Laura, I love you!"

The declaration, made in angry impatience, had the ring of a little boy wheedling for a sweet. "How can you love me? You don't even know me."

"I'll come to know you once you give me a chance."

"You won't like what you learn."

"How could I not, *bellissima?* I love everything about you."

"Including the fact that your noble friends will gossip, perhaps shun you?"

"My father would find a way to prevent that."

"He's the Lord of the Night, not God."

Marcantonio's face hardened into a scowl. "Someone ought to remind him of that. Laura. It's true. I do love you."

"Could you love the fact that I was abandoned to a convent by a woman who was never married to the man who sired me?"

"I'll love you all the more for your lack of family."

Relentlessly she went on, "Could you love the fact that I'm a courtesan?"

His grip on her shoulders slackened, and his hands fell to his sides. Shock blazed across his features. "You lie, Laura."

She told herself she should not be surprised at his horror. Hypocrites that they were, Venetian men dallied endlessly with prostitutes, all the while thinking them the lowest creatures of humanity. "It's true, Marcantonio."

His handsome face froze into a mask of fury. He signaled the gondolier to dock at the first available landing. Within seconds, the craft bumped against the steps beneath the Bridge of Straw.

"Get out," Marcantonio said. His face was as hard as an alabaster statue's.

His youthful petulance made Laura feel old. "You're disappointed, Marcantonio," she said softly, then stepped from the boat. "But it's for the best."

She stood watching as the gondola drifted back out into the canal. Marcantonio sat in the hull, watching her, his eyes as cold and beautiful as sapphires.

Laura turned away and trudged up the steps, finding herself completely alone. Just as she had been when the *bravi* had attacked her.

5

She was but a short walk from the Convent of Santa Maria Celeste. Relieved, she entered through the front gate and crossed the cloister to Magdalena's tiny room. She knocked at the door. Getting no answer, she passed through the refectory and climbed the steps to Sister Celestina's chambers.

The alchemy room reeked of strange metallic smells, burning sulfur, and alcohol. A light yellow fog hung in wispy layers over the chamber. In the middle stood a narrow table crowded with vials and bottles, copper tubing and glass siphons. The hearth had been converted into a forge with heavy iron doors and a stoking hole in the bottom.

"Sister Celestina?" Laura squinted through the fog. "You finished your deliveries rather quickly."

"Shush!" came the nun's annoyed voice. "I'm counting."

Bemused, Laura went to the corner where Sister Celestina crouched beside a marble-topped table, counting rhythmically in Latin under her breath. Her cowl was thrown back to reveal her wimple, limp and yellowed with chemical smoke. Beads of sweat stood out on her face. Her gaze was fixed on a length of twisted rope. The end of it burned with a steady hiss.

Laura watched, fascinated, until the rope spent itself.

Celestina gave a satisfied grunt. "Six seconds to the handspan," she muttered. She made a swift calculation on a scrap of paper, then straightened and wiped her hands on her stained apron. "I'm sorry, child. I was in the middle of a test."

"I didn't mean to interrupt," said Laura. "I was looking for Magdalena." She studied the nun's sweat-streaked face, the large strong hands clasped in rapture. Celestina's wide gray eyes seemed brighter than usual today. "Have you made some sort of discovery, sister?"

"Oh, yes. I've developed a candle wick to burn away the hours exactly."

Laura smiled. Celestina had always been a puzzle, a mixture of incomprehensible genius, religious passion, and obsessive devotion to her work. "Do you know where Magdalena might be?" Laura asked. "She's not in her room."

Celestina poked a sooty finger into the trail of ash left by the burned rope. "I believe she had an errand at the printer's, my dear."

"Magdalena went out?" Hope crested in Laura. "That's wonderful. I worry that she keeps too much to her room."

The light in Celestina's eyes dimmed. "Can you blame her?"

"She must learn to hold her head up, sister."

Celestina tucked a strand of hair up into her wimple. "You're still so naive, child."

Laura laughed. "You sound like Madonna della Rubia."

"I try not to judge the path you've chosen, child. Perhaps, in a way, it's better to choose the scarlet cloak of the courtesan than the black veil of a nun. Here in the convent, we hide from men. But a good courtesan controls them."

Surprised at Celestina's insight, Laura said, "I'm not entering into it for the purpose of controlling men." For some reason the notion brought Sandro Cavalli to mind. If ever a man neeeded controlling, he did.

"I'd best be going, sister." She kissed Celestina and stepped out, savoring the fresh cool air after the sulfur smell of the laboratory.

Reluctantly, she started back toward the *ridotto*. Lately the atmosphere of lazy indolence and sensual indul-gence dragged at her spirits and gave her a leaden feeling in her stomach, as if she had eaten too many sweets.

Looking around her, she remembered the danger she was in. The back of her neck prickled. Following the sweep of foot traffic through broad walkways, she approached the printers' quarter. Magdalena was a good listener, and Laura felt a need to speak of her trouble with Marcantonio.

In the Street of Ink, she spied a shop front with a large illuminated A carved in bas relief in the stone. A sign hung out over the street. It showed a dolphin and anchor, the colophon of the printer, Aldus.

The narrow windows facing the street were coated with the dust of ink powder. She knocked at the door and waited, then stepped inside. The shop seemed deserted, lit only by the windows and a tiny square skylight.

Stacks of paper lined shelves along one wall, and below the shelves were shallow boxes of type-setters' characters. Books bound with gilt calfskin or parchment-covered boards were stacked on a counter, ready for sale.

The huge printing apparatus, supported by jacks and timbers from floor to ceiling, dominated the room. The giant screw was fully lowered, forcing the platen down upon the bed, as if the pressman had just begun an imprint.

The smell of ink and vellum were familiar to Laura, but as she walked closer to the massive press, she sensed something else, a faint rusty-sweet odor that made her grimace.

Apprehension drummed in her breast. "Is anyone here?" she called. "Magdalena?"

Laura stepped around the printing press and glanced at the floor.

She took one look at what lay at her feet and started to scream.

In a foul mood, Sandro paced the Council Chamber of the ducal palace. Behind him opened the gilded maw of the Golden Staircase; on each side were pink marble walls decked with tapestries.

Seated in front of Sandro, upon a huge chair uphol-stered in purple velvet, Doge Andrea Gritti shifted in impatience. "Damn it, can't you be still, Cavalli?"

Sandro stopped and faced his prince. The echoes of his footsteps on the inlaid floor died. "Sorry, Your Serenity." Sandro had known Andrea Gritti for a quarter century; Gritti had been his commander some twenty years earlier in Padua. When Sandro had distinguished himself in that battle, Andrea had sponsored him to become a *condottiere* in his own right.

"I just wish you'd trust my instincts and not require so much evidence about this plot."

Gritti stroked his long, double-pronged beard. His red ducal *corno* shadowed a heavy brow and a prominent, patrician nose. "The plot against me seems to be in your head."

Sandro's hand cut the air in frustration. "Then why Daniele Moro? Why was he killed in so savage a manner, for the sake of a cache of papers? Andrea—" Sandro dropped the formal address. "Moro was close to you. He might have been killed for the documents he was carrying."

Gritti gripped the carved arms of his chair. "Then he was killed for nothing. Those papers weren't important. They were simply invitations to our annual marriage to the sea, and a roll of the dignitaries who will be present for the event."

Sandro planted his boot on the lower step of the dais and leaned toward the doge. "Are you certain? Think, Andrea. State secrets pass through the channels of Venice like water through a spillway."

"Then I assume you've set investigators on all the foreign ambassadors and their staffs."

"Of course." Sandro pinched the bridge of his nose. The investigation had yielded nothing. Even the wild Turks were behaving themselves for a change. "Could Moro have had other . . . associations like the one with the singer, Florio?"

"I don't know. I had no notion of his aberrant sexual behavior. That's the key, Sandro. You're wasting time nosing around in state affairs. This was obviously a crime of passion. The man Florio is the culprit."

Sandro's well-honed instincts leapt up in denial. But his well-disciplined tongue stayed silent, for he had no hard evidence yet. "Florio's under constant secret watch. He's done nothing but light candles to Moro's memory and practice his singing." He did not bother to mention Yasmin and her garden of herbs and poisons, for she was an even more unlikely suspect than Florio.

With a sudden chill in his heart, he thought of Laura, then admonished himself not to seek out more trouble than he had already located. She was safe with Guido Lombardo.

"Keep watching, then," Gritti said. "I'll wager the culprit will slip up, and—"

"My lord!" A *zaffo* burst into the room and skidded to a stop, followed by Jamal. Snatching off his hat, the policeman made obeisance to the doge, then said to Sandro, "It's happened again, my lord. This time in the printers' quarter. Another murder."

A small crowd of printers and apprentices gathered beneath the Aldus colophon of the dolphin and anchor. One man had his arm around a weeping woman; he had covered her head and shoulders with his brown cloak.

"Clear the way," shouted one of Sandro's deputies. "Make way for the Lord of the Night."

With Jamal and several assistants, Sandro entered the shop. This should be a place of noise and activity, alive with scurrying apprentices, binders, and press operators, ringing with the rhythmic thud of the press. Instead, a murderer had made it a place of death. Silence, and the smells of the printer's trade, filled the large room.

As always, Sandro looked first at the face. As always, he was sorry he had. It was a nice face, mild even in death. Freckles stood out against the unnatural pallor of the young man's cheeks. A wispy fringe, the youth's first proud attempt to raise a beard, lined the soft jaw and chin. The victim had been well fed, his plumpness accentuating the boyish impression.

His hands bore black smudges of ink and a smattering of his own blood. Other than that, Sandro observed no sign of a struggle; all the furniture and papers were in place. The printing press platen was screwed down upon a document.

The culprit had been someone the printer had trusted, someone he knew, perhaps, or someone who showed unimpeachable credentials. A sinner masquerading as a saint.

Sandro squatted beside the body to examine the wound. Dr. Carlo Marino, coroner of the republic, joined him. Together they gazed at the clotted gore of the injury. With a pair of tweezers, Marino extracted a sliver of amber glass from the chest wound.

A grim sense of his own accuracy struck Sandro. The second murder proved the crimes were not committed by a lover in a jealous rage. Still, he would try to find a connection between Florio and the latest victim.

"Same as Moro," Marino pointed out.

Sandro forced his gaze down along the body to the livid wound in the victim's groin. As with Daniele Moro, the victim's codpiece and hose had been cut away. A clean-edged instrument had performed the ultimate horror. This job was even neater than the other. The killer was honing his craft.

"At least the poor fellow was dead before this was done to him," the coroner commented. "I can tell by the lack of bleeding."

Sandro shivered. His bones ached with cold. He

was getting too old for this, too old to look at promising young men cut down in their prime. Wearily he straightened. His dark face grave, Jamal handed him a stack of printed matter.

The ink had barely dried on the papers; they had been carelessly stacked so that some of them were smudged.

The few sheets on the top off the stack were a list of dignitaries who would accompany the doge on the state galley during the marriage to the sea. Beneath this list were invitations to the annual event, to be held on Ascension Day as tradition dictated.

"The doge's business," Sandro muttered.

Jamal lifted the platen off the press. Sandro studied the type. The letters were backwards, but he was able to decipher the words.

"These were the last documents printed," he said, taking some samples from the stack. "Damn. They were obviously set from the papers stolen from Moro."

Jamal nodded, then spread his hands. Sandro agreed with the gesture of futility. They had more pieces of the puzzle, but still could not see the whole picture. Had the murderer set the type himself? But why? These were hardly state secrets, but someone was willing to kill for them.

Sandro looked at the pale, worried men crowding in the doorway. "Who was he?"

A red-faced man clutching a black hat in his hands edged inside the shop. "His name was Gaspari, a typesetter."

Sandro studied the watery eyes and trembling chin of his informant. The man was young, dressed in merchant's finery. "And you are? . . ."

The man bowed. "Valerio, eldest son of Aldus, who established this shop."

The master printer, Aldus, had risen to promi-
nence through his staunch conviction that printed
books should be available—and affordable—to all. So
famed was he that he enjoyed ducal patronage—and
now the sinister sponsorship of a murderer.

"When did you last see this man alive?"

"Less than three hours ago. I left to meet with a parchment factor. Gaspari was working on materials from the
doge." Valerio gave Sandro a handwritten manuscript.

Sandro saw Daniele Moro's mark at the bottom of the
paper, and the doge's seal of office. "Who delivered this?"

"I don't know. Gaspari himself must have received
additional documents after I'd left."

"Is he usually alone in the shop?"

"No. Most of my workers are Jewish. I know the
Church frowns on it, but I give them their Sabbath
day off."

The murderer was no fool, then. Methodical as a
spider spinning a web, the villain had waited patiently
for a chance. Someone who knew the schedule. This
was no rash act, but a crime planned with cold-blooded
care over a period of time.

"You discovered the body?" Sandro asked, battling
a burning rage. These violations were a cancer on the
fair face of his city, and he felt as powerless as a doctor
whose medicaments had no effect on a dying patient.

"No," said Valerio. "It was—"

"It was me," said a small, feminine voice. The
cloaked woman who had been weeping stepped
inside and lowered her hood.

Sandro's rage burgeoned into horror. He took a
step forward and grasped her hands, jerking her
toward him. "Laura!"

Even streaked and puffy from weeping, her face

was lovely, soft and childlike, bewildered with grief. Her hands felt stiff and icy inside his own.

"What the hell are you doing here? Where's Guido?" Sandro demanded.

She drew a deep breath and pulled her hands from his. He resisted the urge to grab them back. "We were separated in a crowd at the Rialto," she explained. "I came here looking for my friend, Magdalena."

Sandro recalled the young woman in Laura's sketchbook. "The editor."

"Y-yes." She stared at the floor. Instinctively Sandro stepped into her line of vision so she would not be able to see the body. "She was working on a manuscript for Aldus, and had a delivery to make. I must have missed—" Seeing the expression on Sandro's face, she broke off. "No! Magdalena is *not* responsible for this. She's gentle and kind. Only a monster could have—have—oh, God!" She covered her face with her hands.

Sandro's tight thread of control suddenly snapped. "Are you satisfied now?" he demanded, fury lashing from him like a knotted whip. "You wanted to know all about my business, and now you do. 'To intensify my art.'" He mimicked the words she had spoken to him on the first day they had met.

"My lord, I'm sorry." The hurt in her eyes tore at him.

"Ah, Laura." Ignoring the astonished expressions of his assistants, Sandro pulled her into his arms. Unlike shorter women, she fit exactly right, her head tucked against his shoulder and her shaking form pressed close.

"Hush, try not to think about it." Sandro whispered the words into her soft, sweetly perfumed hair. He should not be having such thoughts at a crime scene, in view of his men, but he caught himself disputing the accepted classical ideal of feminine beauty.

Golden tresses were nothing compared to the midnight silk of Laura's hair.

"I'm sorry," he said, and fancied that he could actually hear the dropping of jaws all around him. "I'm sorry you had to see this, that I spoke sharply to you."

Her tears poured onto his black cloak, probably ruining the fabric forever. Sandro didn't care. For this insane moment, he cared only about comforting the woman he had hurt.

As his assistants searched and catalogued the print shop, and the coroner's team shrouded the body, Sandro helped Laura outside. He kept his arm around her because she needed comforting. Then he admitted to himself that he kept his arm around her because he wanted to hold her.

The crowd had dispersed and the street was empty. Sandro brought Laura around to face him. He brushed a dark curl from her brow, then dabbed at her cheeks with the corner of his cloak. "You know," he confessed, "the first moment I saw you, I knew you were trouble. I was right."

A smile trembled at the corners of her mouth. "The first moment I saw *you,* I knew you were a kind man. I, too, was right."

He stiffened, uncomfortable under her knowing regard. He dropped his arms and cleared his throat. "Yes, well, it is the business of my office to aid citizens in distress." Her smile widened. He ran his finger around the inside of his collar and cast about for a suitable excuse for his unconscionable behavior. "Had my daughter, Adriana, found herself in similar circumstances, I would hope someone would offer her comfort."

She lifted a dark eyebrow. "So you were just playing the fatherly part?"

"Precisely." His ungovernable body jeered a denial.

She seemed about to reply when the coroner's team brought out the shrouded body on a litter. Her delicate fingers touched her lips. "Who is going to tell that poor boy's family?"

"I'll send a priest. I always do." He caught her chin and drew her gaze from the corpse.

"You don't go yourself?" she asked, her deep blue eyes searching his face.

"No, of course not," he said, dropping his hand. Her skin was too soft; it was impossible to resist stroking his thumb along her jawline, her throat, her breasts. . . .

"I see." Her eyes misted with sympathy. "Because you're so tender of heart."

Because I'm afraid. He nearly blurted the truth, but stopped himself just in time.

"Now," he said, eager to abandon the topic, "I'm anxious to hear your explanation about getting separated from Guido. Why the devil didn't you stay at the Rialto and try to find him?"

"I would have, but . . . a friend came along."

"A friend." Sandro did not trust a single one of her friends. "Someone you know from the *ridotto?*" Unreasoning anger swept like a fire through him. "Tell me, will you still consider him a friend after he's purchased his pleasure from you?'

"No," she snapped, wincing at his sarcasm. "It was Marcantonio."

As Sandro's blood went cold, she added in a harsh voice, "He found me in the crowd and insisted I accompany him. Having lost Guido, I thought it the safest choice. He is, after all, the son of the Lord of the Night."

In a flash of remembrance, Sandro saw Marcantonio and Laura locked in an embrace. The feeling of rage and inadequacy lashed him once again.

"Obviously it was not the safest choice," he said. Suddenly, an appalling thought struck him. He grabbed Laura by the shoulders, sinking his fingers into her soft flesh. "Did he . . . Laura, did he harm you?"

She flung up her head, and her hair swirled in wild dark tangles around her face. "You hold a poor opinion of your own son, my lord."

She was right, Sandro thought bleakly. "Did he?"

"No." She stepped away from him. "He asked me to be his mistress."

The bottom fell out of Sandro's stomach. It was all he could do to stop himself from lifting his head and howling with rage. "You?" he choked.

"No need to look so disgusted, my lord," she bit out. "I refused, of course. Far be it from me to blacken the hallowed Cavalli name. I know you'd never be able to stomach having a bastard-born whore as your son's special companion."

Sandro tried to deny it, but the words stuck in his throat. He did indeed find the idea of a liaison between Marcantonio and Laura insupportable. But the reasons were not what she thought. The real reason was that the very idea threatened to send him into a howling fury.

"I'm pleased you had the sense to refuse him," he said.

"Oh," she said bitterly, dashing the last of the tears from her cheeks, "I should never like to be the one to besmirch your family honor."

Honor? thought Sandro. Honor had nothing to do with it.

* * *

"What the hell were you thinking of?" Sandro demanded.

Looking away from his contemplation of a sweating, puffy-cheeked glassblower, Marcantonio gave his father a slow, lazy smile. "At the moment, I was thinking of the glassblower's daughter. You know, the buxom one who brought us our lunch. I had the distinct impression that she would have been willing to offer more than antipasto and Tuscany wine."

Gathering his patience, Sandro paused to contemplate the belching chimneys of Murano, the hive-shaped glassblowers' forges, and in the distance, the spires of Venice rising across the lagoon. Much as they had done after the Moro murder, his men were moving systematically among the island artisans, questioning them about whether anyone might have recently bought a stiletto. Sandro awaited the answers without much hope. Nearly all the glassblowers would answer in the affirmative; the hollow glass weapons were as popular as colored beads.

Sandro would not even have come here himself, except that he had been told that Marcantonio was here on the pretext of meeting with the Cavalli glass factor. As calmly as he could manage, he raised the question that had been burning in his mind since the day before.

"I think you know what I'm talking about, Marcantonio. Why did you ask Laura Bandello to be your mistress?"

Color rose in Marcantonio's handsome face, and his clear blue-gray eyes narrowed. "The bitch. She had no business telling you."

Sandro's hand itched to slap his son, but with his usual iron control, he resisted the urge and indulged Marcantonio. What the devil had he done to the lad?

How in God's name had Marcantonio grown into this selfish, small man?

"I made her tell me. She was supposed to be with Guido Lombardo, and they got separated in a crowd. What sort of game are you playing with her?"

"It wasn't a game, Father."

Sandro's blood ran cold. "What do you mean?"

Marcantonio laughed harshly. "It's impossible for you to understand, isn't it, Father? You simply assume I'd choose a woman in the same manner you and all the hallowed Cavallis before you did." Shouldering past Sandro, he paced to the middle of the byway. "Only a woman of impeccable bloodlines will do for a Cavalli, even as a mistress. If her family hasn't been in the Libro de Oro for at least a century, I have no business even looking at her, isn't that right?"

Stark, honest words knotted in Sandro's throat, and he forced out, "The two of you don't suit."

Marcantonio stopped pacing and threw up his arms. "Why do you find Laura so objectionable? She's young and beautiful, vibrantly healthy, well-mannered and accomplished." He laughed. "Or perhaps I should choose a woman who is old and ugly, sickly, ill-mannered and uneducated. One who would spread her thighs for the lowliest of *condannati.*"

Sandro hated these verbal battles Marcantonio always seemed to incite. "I'm thinking of you, Marcantonio. You thrive on the esteem of your peers. What would you be if you lost that?"

Marcantonio stroked his strong, chiseled chin. "An excellent point, Father. But I want her anyway, and I mean to have her."

A hot and powerful denial leapt up in Sandro, and

he had to force himself to speak calmly. "I'd advise against that, son."

"Why? It's not unusual for a courtesan to serve one patron exclusively. You, sire, have four."

Not anymore, thought Sandro. But Marcantonio couldn't know that.

"Leave Laura alone, son."

"Why? What aren't you telling me, Father? Do you want her for yourself, then?"

Sandro snatched off his hat and raked a hand through his hair. "If it's a whore you want, then find another. There are eleven thousand in Venice to choose from."

Marcantonio's face lit with delight. "You do want her. God be praised. Saint Sandro Cavalli lusting after a whore."

"Don't be ridiculous."

"Very well. Henceforth, I shall strive to achieve your perfection, sire." His lazy grin still in place, Marcantonio ambled off toward the *vigna* of his friend Adolfo of Urbino, where no doubt they would pass the day in games and drinking.

Sandro felt raw and battered by the encounter. He always did after he and Marcantonio quarreled. For years he had been haunted by the idea that he had somehow failed Marcantonio, had not loved him enough, or perhaps had indulged him too much.

A wave of weariness swept over Sandro. What bothered him most about the encounter was Marcantonio's obvious fury at Laura.

Sandro knew his son did not take rejection well.

Hours later, Sandro longed to be at home, sitting in his loggia with a cup of wine in his hand and absolutely nothing on his mind.

Instead, he found himself standing at the street gate of the Convent of Santa Maria Celeste, asking to see the postulant, Magdalena.

A stern, silent nun led him to a small garden and bade him wait. He stood gazing at a shrine to Saint Celeste. The kindly saint and her adoring animals were besmattered by pigeon dung. Slow, heavy footsteps drew his attention to the cloister.

Magdalena was smaller than he had guessed from Laura's sketches. An oversized habit of brown homespun cloaked the massive hump on her back. Her cowl lay about her broad shoulders, revealing her wide, pale face.

Sandro greeted her with a bow. She stood staring at the ground, her hands tucked into her sleeves.

"I'm sorry to intrude," Sandro said, studying the milk-pale face. There were some girls, he concluded, for whom the convent had been invented. Magdalena was truly one of them. Despite her strange and beautiful eyes, deep and liquid and thickly lashed, she was painfully plain. Her pudgy face resembled a mass of unformed dough, with bulging cheeks and multiple chins. Laura swore they were the best of friends. If so, Magdalena possessed a remarkable generosity, for most girls would have been consumed by envy of Laura's scintillating beauty.

"How may I help you, my lord?" Magdalena asked. Like her unusual eyes, her voice was uncommonly lovely—well-modulated, deep-toned, clear as a choirboy's.

"I'm sorry to disturb this place of peace," he said, his gaze roving the square garden and straying to the upper cloisters. A thin trail of smoke issued from a high window, and he frowned at it.

"That's just my mother," Magdalena explained. "She does the most wondrous alchemy."

"So I've heard." Sandro took a deep breath. "I must ask you some questions about a crime that occurred at the establishment of Aldus."

Magdalena held herself very still. "A crime, my lord?"

"A murder. A typesetter named Gaspari was killed."

"Gaspari." She made the sign of the cross. *"Ave Maria."*

"You knew him?"

"I did, my lord. I edit manuscripts for Aldus."

"And you were there earlier."

"Yes." She did not question how he knew. "I—I saw Gaspari. He was fine." She swallowed hard. "He told me he was planning an excursion to the Lido with his sweetheart."

"And he was alone in the shop?"

"Yes." She drew her hands from her sleeves and clutched the coral rosary tied around her waist. "My lord, who could have killed him?"

His gaze probed her plain, sad-eyed face, and he saw nothing but grief. "That's what I'm trying to find out."

"In my estimation, the French win out." Portia, whose skills in costume design were surpassed only by her talents in bed, spoke around a mouthful of straight pins.

"The French! Bah!" Fiammetta burst out, measuring a length of gold braid. "Stand still, Laura. You fidget too much, and we'll never get your costume finished."

Laura and Yasmin exchanged a glance. They were in Madonna della Rubia's boudoir, a room of surpassing sumptuousness. The walls were hung with cloth of gold, embroidered in patterns of a Byzantine flavor. The cornices, created by the master Sansovino, were decorated with precious gold leaf and rich ultramarine. On each cornice stood vases made of alabastrine, porphyry, and serpentine. Carved and inlaid tables and chests supported thick, leather-bound tomes of Latin classics. In the far corner sat Florio in his black *mongile,* strumming softly on a viola da braccia.

Laura tried to hold still as Portia and Fiammetta draped her in white silk, the costume she would wear for the carnival masque. "What's your objection to the French, Fiammetta?"

She made a face. "They do disgusting things with their mouths."

"What can that matter?" Portia asked. "They pay us well for our troubles. The ambassador's son gave me twenty *scudi* in addition to the usual fee. And thank God, they don't use us like Thorvald does poor Yasmin."

The women looked at Yasmin in sympathy. Thorvald, a crude Swedish merchant, had a special liking for the African woman.

"In my opinion," Portia went on, "it's the Spaniards you should avoid, Laura."

"The Spaniards are good lovers," Fiammetta objected. "Very passionate, very masterful."

"And what do you have but memories after the passion fades? They're as miserly as the Scots," Portia insisted. "The only payment you'll get from a Spaniard is an overblown account of his exploits in the New World." She drew the white gown to one of Laura's shoulders, leaving the other bare. "Naked savages, rivers of gold, fountains that restore youth . . . Who needs such lies?"

"It sounds marvelous to me," said Laura.

Yasmin, who was working on the headpiece for the costume, glanced at her sharply. "Do you feel quite well, Laura? You look pale."

Laura laughed. "I'm fine. I'm looking forward to carnival. It marks the beginning of my financial independence. I'll be able to pay my debts at last."

"Madonna della Rubia expects a great sum for you," Portia assured her.

Laura nodded, but as she contemplated the future, she discovered a feeling of apprehension. "I suppose I'm a bit nervous," she admitted.

"Nonsense. Lift your foot," said Fiammetta, fitting a sandal with gold straps on Laura's foot. "Madonna della Rubia has prepared you well. You know how to comport yourself, to eat with dainty manners, to eye and flatter a man."

"Your manners still need a little work," said Portia. "When you eat, don't throw yourself on the salad like a cow on its hay."

"And never have your glass more than half filled," Fiammetta said.

"And for the love of God," Florio chimed in, "don't belch."

Laura giggled. "And if one escapes me?"

Florio pursed his lips. "Then you will be regarded as disgusting."

Laura tried to let herself be teased out of her mood, but misgivings still shadowed her thoughts.

"Don't worry," said Florio, setting aside his viola da braccia. "At the price our good mother anticipates, only a wealthy and sophisticated man will be able to afford you."

"Wealth and sophistication do not govern a

man's behavior in the bedchamber," Yasmin pointed out.

"Hush, you," said Portia. "Laura, at worst, you've only to look forward to a night of witty conversation and flattery. You'll have good wine, perhaps a game of two-handed cards."

"The coupling will be over before you know it." Fiammetta sighed. "It always is."

"I suppose you're right," said Laura, wiggling her toes in the dainty golden sandals. Yet melancholy filled her. Many years earlier, she had dared to dream of falling in love. But time and disappointment had laid waste to dreams. She was a daughter of Venice, La Serenissima, a city of hard men and submissive women. Only as a courtesan could she enjoy relative liberty. She would be limited only by herself, not by any man.

Unbidden came thoughts of Sandro Cavalli, exhorting her to turn away from prostitution.

"What?" Yasmin asked, stepping forward. "You're troubled."

"It . . . seems dishonest to take advantage of a man."

Yasmin took Laura's hands. "My friend, they are rich men in an unjust world. They were born to wealth and privilege while you were born with nothing but your beauty and your wits. A man uses every advantage to make his way in the world. It is no crime for you to do the same."

"A mercenary commits far greater crimes for money," said Portia, "and he is lauded for his deeds."

"I just wonder if I'll be able to keep up the pretense," said Laura.

Florio struck up another soft melody. Portia and Fiammetta took the costume from Laura and started sewing. Yasmin helped her into her smock.

"You will," Yasmin told her in a voice deep and rich with feminine wisdom. "My friend, you will know times when you must force yourself to laugh although you feel like crying, and times when you must weep to hide your laughter. You will do both and more because you have to, Laura. Trust me."

But Laura could not forget the wonderful, craggy face of Sandro Cavalli, the solid support of his embrace, and his utter certainty that she was making a terrible mistake.

"I wish," she said, thinking aloud, "that he would come to the masque."

Yasmin frowned. "Who?"

"The Lord of the Night. I feel . . . safe with him. But he never frequents brothels."

Yasmin curled a lock of Laura's hair around her finger. "Would he break his principles for you?"

Laura sighed, and an ache started in her chest. "Sandro Cavalli would not break his principles for his own mother."

Yasmin gasped. "Don't do it, Laura," she implored.

"Don't do what?"

"Don't fall in love."

"How ridiculous, Yasmin. Of course I won't fall in love."

6

The incredible thought dogged her footsteps all the way to the convent. In love? she thought in disbelief. With Sandro Cavalli? The proper, dutiful, straitlaced, agonizingly correct Lord of the Night?

"Ridiculous," she muttered, yet her feet barely touched the cobbled walkway she had tread so often. If she were going to lose her heart to a man—which, as a sane woman, she had no intention of doing—she would not choose Sandro Cavalli, but an amenable man who appreciated whimsy, adored unconventionality, treated her like a goddess, and flamed with desire for her alone. She tried to conjure an image of Sandro Cavalli lying with his head in her lap while she fed him figs, or taking her in his arms and burning up with wanting her. But try as she might, Laura could not imagine the Lord of the Night on fire with passion.

At the entrance to Magdalena's chamber, she raised her hand to knock, then hesitated at the unusual sound of angry voices.

". . . twenty years ago. Let it pass, mother," Magdalena was saying in that husky voice that spoke of impatience.

"Better I should relinquish my claim on life itself, child," Celestina shot back. Then she murmured something indistinct.

"I won't take my vows, Mother," Magdalena snapped. "How can I, when—"

Feeling guilty, Laura knocked loudly. The last time she had listened at a door, she had gotten herself in serious trouble. Her friends' argument did not concern her. Yet she admitted to surprise. She had not known that mother and daughter ever argued.

Magdalena opened the door. Lines of worry pulled at her pale face, but she smiled. "Come in, Laura. Mother's here."

Laura greeted Celestina with a kiss. As always, the nun smelled of sulfur and herbs. "You're looking tired, Laura," said Celestina. "Have you been using the cosmetics I gave you?"

"I have so little time," Laura said evasively.

"You should avail yourself of those sleeping powders, then."

"Please, Mother," Magdalena said, "Laura doesn't need your preparations."

Celestina's handsome features hardened. "I merely want to see her succeed. My efforts will come to naught if you don't take my advice, Laura."

Celestina's worldly-wise tone startled Laura. "It's not that I'm ungrateful, sister. And you're right. Madonna della Rubia claims I spend too little time on my toilette. I'll try to remember your potions from now on."

Celestina touched Laura's cheek and smiled. "We—both my daughter and I—only want your success in all your endeavors, Laura. I must go now."

After she had left, her harsh scent lingered in the air.

Laura turned to her friend. "I would have come sooner, but I had no time to get away. The carnival masque is nearly upon us, and Madonna della Rubia counsels me constantly on table manners and deportment."

Magdalena eyed her from beneath her long eyelashes. "I wish you'd change your mind and come home, Laura. I hate to think of you consorting with courtesans and immoral men."

Laura blew out a sigh. "Don't worry about me, Magdalena. I know what I'm doing. The *ridotto* is a place of luxury and refinement, and I don't plan on staying long. In fact, I'm looking forward to having done with it."

"You're not afraid?"

Laura smiled. "Nearly every woman loses her innocence and survives. It just so happens that I'll be losing mine to a total stranger." She took her friend's hands. "It's you I'm worried about. There was a murder in Aldus's shop."

Magdalena extracted her pudgy hands and took hold of her crucifix. "I know. The Lord of the Night came to question me about it."

Surprise and anger stormed through Laura. How dare he intrude on Magdalena's solitude, sully her with his questions? "Sandro Cavalli was here?"

"Yes."

Laura drove her fist into the palm of her hand. "Damn him. He had no right to upset you."

Magdalena lowered herself to a chair. For a moment, her faced pinched with pain; then the spasm passed. "He was only performing his duty. I'm sorry I couldn't help him." She shook her head. "So very, very sorry."

"At least you didn't see the body." Laura shivered.

Magdalena bit her lip. "Was it horrible?"

Laura drew a shaky breath and stared at the guttering candle on the desk. "Remember the painting I did of Judith slaying Holofernes?"

Magdalena nodded. "It's always been one of my favorite stories. How brave she was, holding up his severed head by the hair, challenging the men of her city to drive out the invaders. But what does that ancient tale have to do with the murder?"

"Well, I thought I had captured the horror of unnatural death. But my art pales before the reality." Laura stopped herself from saying more. She did not want to trouble Magdalena with the details of the butchery; she prayed that Sandro, too, had been discreet.

Magdalena opened a drawer of her desk. Turning, she handed Laura a velvet sheath. "I want you to have this."

"What is it?" Laura felt a hard object the length of her forearm.

"Open it."

Laura withdrew the object and gasped. With an unsteady hand, she held a sharp stiletto made of glass. It was curiously light, cold and delicate to the touch. A deadly weapon that weighed no more than a paint brush. Inside, a pale, cloudy liquid slid to and fro. Poison, she realized, resisting the urge to throw it down and run.

Magdalena was concerned, she told herself. Her friend. The sister of her heart. "Where did you get so lethal a weapon?"

Magdalena leaned forward in a conspiratorial posture. "From a shop on the Rialto. I know it's distasteful to you, Laura, but I want you to keep it with you at all times."

"A shop at the Rialto," Laura echoed dully.

"Of course. They're as common as glass bells. The proprietor says visitors to the city love them. This weapon is specially favored by papal legates."

"Why are you giving it to me?"

Magdalena put the stiletto in its sheath and tied the strings to Laura's sleeve. "I know you're in some sort of danger."

"How did you find out?"

Magdalena stood and shuffled restlessly across the room. "I'm not so cloistered as you think, Laura. That long-faced *zaffo* who's waiting for you outside is a bit obvious. I worry about you. Please. Do this for me." She stared steadily at Laura, her beautiful rain-colored eyes full of love and concern.

Laura managed a smile. "Very well, I'll carry it. But I can't imagine myself killing anyone."

"This second murder is atrocious, my lord," said Doge Andrea Gritti, fingering the tassels on the cushion of his throne. "But I see no reason for placing extra guards on me."

Sandro felt a tic of annoyance start in his jaw, but he put on his most respectful façade. "Indulge me, Your Eminence. If I'm to devote my full attention to solving the murder, I must have peace of mind."

Doge Gritti inhaled dramatically, his nostrils narrowing in disdain. "How the devil can you link the foul murder of a young typesetter to me?"

Sandro motioned to Jamal, who came forward and laid a bundle of papers on the table in front of Andrea Gritti.

"What's this?" the doge asked.

"The job the printer was setting—probably moments before his death."

Gritti picked up the top sheet, angled the page toward the light, and squinted at it. "Why, these are only invitations to the Ascension Day ceremony. I ordered hundreds. There's nothing suspicious in that."

Sandro rubbed his jaw. The centuries-old tradition of Venice's symbolic marriage to the sea was her most popular and auspicious water pageant. Each year at Ascension Day, in honor of the great city's debt to the sea that made her existence possible, the doge and all the princes of the republic went out on the lagoon in *Bucentaur,* the great state galley, and tossed a golden ring into the water as a symbol of their covenant.

"What about this?" Sandro handed Gritti another document.

"It's the programme of the ceremony with a list of the dignitaries who will accompany me aboard the galley." The doge scanned the printed page.

"Florio's name is here." Sandro pointed.

The doge frowned, leaning closer. "It says that he's to perform a barcarole. I don't remember approving that."

Sandro's instincts took aim at Florio, the strange blond man in woman's clothes. He had sworn that Moro had secured him a position on *Bucentaur,* yet the doge claimed no knowledge of the agreement.

But Florio's whereabouts during the second murder were indisputable: Sandro's *zaffi* had seen him go to confession and mass at the Church of San Rocco. Still, he might have acted in concert with someone else.

"Then how," asked Sandro, "did his name come to be here?"

Gritti scratched his chin. Suddenly sadness flooded

his eyes. "I remember now. Daniele recommended him to me, told me the man is a talented singer. At first I was hesitant to break with tradition and allow a commoner on the voyage, but I do believe I gave my approval. Then again, maybe I didn't. Now I'm confused."

"What about the other names on the list? Are any of them suspect?"

"They are in order. A beautiful job of typesetting, don't you think?"

Sandro bit back his impatience. "My prince, the names are important. Moro carried the drafts the night he was killed. Somehow, the papers appeared at the printer's and were set in type. Moro is dead. So is the printer. We must determine whether or not the documents were altered."

Andrea sighed, slouched in his chair, and toyed with his chain of office. "I'm not adept at intrigue and manipulation," he said, then grimaced. "Such things were my father's forte, God rot his soul. He was always a man to plan the most ruthless of conspiracies."

"The list, Your Serenity," Sandro prompted, trying to quell his impatience.

"Very well." Gritti scanned the list of dignitaries, keeping his place with a beringed forefinger. "Nothing amiss here . . . Otranto, Urbino, Mantua . . . the Spanish ambassador. . . . Lord, they'll be spilling over the rails." Gritti frowned. "What's this?"

Sandro leaned over the table. "What?"

"Giorgione della Brenta. Now, there's a name I haven't heard in years."

"You didn't include his name in the draft?"

"I don't think so. . . . But then again, I might have. My memory fails me sometimes, you know."

"Who is he?"

"He was my father's chief groom. About twenty years ago, my sire promoted him to master of horses, probably as a reward for some bit of wickedness done on my father's behalf."

A spark of suspicion came to life inside Sandro. "Does Giorgione have any reason to plot against you, Andrea? Any at all?"

"None that I can think of."

Sandro vowed to see that someone questioned Giorgione anyway.

"Ah, here's another. . . . " said the doge.

In all, Gritti found nine names he did not remember telling Moro to include on the document. Those nine had something very interesting in common: Andrea had seen none of them in at least two decades; all had some association with Gritti's unmourned father, the formidable and ruthless patriarch of the family.

Sandro's mind embraced a host of dark possibilities. Had Andrea committed some slight against his father's men? Did they mean to conduct their conspiracy aboard *Bucentaur*?

"I can't imagine that I offended any of them," said Andrea. "My father and I never got on. He was a cruel man. But my quarrel was never with his minions. Why would Daniele include these men?"

"Perhaps Daniele Moro was not the one who altered the list."

"My lord!" A *zaffo* dashed in. A sense of déjà vu rose in Sandro; just days earlier he had been interrupted with similar urgency.

Nervous excitement shone in the policeman's eyes. "There's been another attack with a poisoned stiletto. We're holding the culprit in the Gabbia."

*   *   *

Marble-and-gilt halls sped past in a blur as Sandro raced through the ducal palace. The Gabbia had been designed to house prisoners of all ranks. Sandro could not wait to get a glimpse of the assassin, to see the villain he would delight in bringing to justice.

He drew himself up short in the antechamber of the Gabbia. A clerk shot to his feet and bowed. Sandro flung his biretta on the desk and winnowed his fingers through his hair. "Which cell?"

"First on the right, my lord. But I think—"

"You're not paid to think." Sandro jerked open the door. A long, dim corridor loomed before him, a tunnel of darkness leading to the bowels of the palace. Smells of mildew and waste mingled with the harsh stink of pine torches.

"Bring a light," Sandro said over his shoulder.

The clerk placed an oil lamp in his hand. "My lord, if I could just explain before you—"

"Shut up," Sandro said, throwing the iron latch and yanking open the cell door. Ducking beneath the low stone lintel of the doorway, he stepped inside and held the lamp high.

A lone figure, hooded and cloaked, sat huddled on the straw pallet, knees to chest, pale hands linked.

"We have some serious business to discuss," Sandro said.

The culprit looked up and the hood fell back. Golden lantern light illuminated wide, frightened eyes set in an impossibly lovely face.

"Laura."

She rose and crossed to him. Before he could mount a defense, she flung herself into his arms. Her body felt both frail and bountiful at once, and the sensation disconcerted Sandro to the tips of his booted feet.

"Thank God you've come, my lord," she cried. "Those men out there think I'm a murderer."

Sandro stepped away from her. He held himself very still while his thoughts raced. Frantic denials clawed at him; then he forced himself to face the possibility that this fragile, captivating girl was a killer.

"Are you?" he asked coldly.

Her mouth formed a perfect O of surprise. Hurt shone in her eyes. "I can't believe you would ask me such a thing," she whispered.

Neither could Sandro, but circumstances pointed like accusing fingers at her heart. He enumerated them aloud.

"You live at the house where Daniele Moro was last seen."

"Yes," she said in a small voice. "But—"

"You found the body of the printer."

"To my great mortification, yes."

"And you attacked a man today with a poisoned stiletto."

"Defended myself," she amended.

"That remains to be seen. Where did you get the weapon?"

Her gaze slid away. "At—at a shop on the Rialto. Really, my lord . . . "

Sandro's blood chilled as he envisioned her piercing a man's heart, mutilating his body. Could it be that behind her blithe, lovely façade, she harbored a fierce hatred of men? The idea gripped his heart like a steel vise.

Sandro had always prided himself on his professional ability to detach himself from the most heinous of crimes, the most vile of perpetrators. Now he felt sick, violated. For him, Laura had personified youth and hope and beauty. Her actions shattered that pristine image. She could have wielded the knife, he thought dully. But why?

Florio. She adored him. But would she have done murder for Florio's sake? How well did he truly know her?

He vowed to find out more about this confounding woman. A dark thought took shape in his mind. He would take his time learning her secrets. If she were detained as a suspect, she would miss the masque that would launch her into the world of the courtesans. The notion brought him a surge of satisfaction.

"Keep her locked up," Sandro ordered the clerk.

Laura propelled herself forward. "Here?"

"You gave up all right to object when you snuffed out the lives of innocent men," Sandro shouted, his blast of anger as frigid as the winter wind. Seeing the horrified expression on her face, he relented, but only a little. "You'll stay in better quarters than this," he promised. "I'll assign you a servant, and you'll have every convenience."

The words thudded painfully in Laura's head. She could not believe this was happening to her. "But I'll still be your prisoner," she squeaked. "Why, my lord?"

"I mean to bring you up on charges." Sandro enunciated each word as if he were speaking to an idiot.

She flung up her head. "I don't believe you."

"Then you're a fool."

"I didn't do anything. Won't you at least let me explain what happened?"

"You'll have that chance later—before the Council of Justice."

He turned to go and nearly collided with a dripping wet and highly agitated Guido Lombardo.

Laura stared at the *zaffo* in confusion. After leaving Magdalena, she had not seen Guido at his post outside the convent. Presuming that he had wandered down the street to one of the wine shops, she had gone on her own toward Titian's house.

Only a block away from the convent, she had been grabbed by a *bravo*—one of the men who had accosted her earlier. In unthinking terror, she had drawn the stiletto and stabbed out blindly. The man's scream of pain still echoed in her ears.

The rest happened in a blur. Alerted by the scream, two policemen had pounced on her, taken one look at her broken weapon, and hauled her away to the Gabbia.

"Been for a swim, Guido?" Sandro asked sarcastically.

God, she hated the Lord of the Night, hated his sanctimonious superiority, his indifference to Guido's shivering, hand-wringing distress.

"I tried to stay with her, my lord, just like you said. But a man hit me over the head and threw me in the canal. By the time I hauled myself out, she was gone."

"Oh, well done," Sandro said, then turned to Laura. "Tell me, did you bash Guido, or do you have an accomplice?"

"You horrible man," she said. "How dare you think me capable of these crimes?"

Laura could see the moment Sandro's anger fled, leaving a bleak, weary man in its wake. She steeled herself against feeling any sympathy for him.

"You're a remarkable young woman, Laura," he said tiredly. "I think you capable of anyth—"

"My lord, if I may speak." Guido wrung out his tunic and eyed Sandro angrily. "The man she stabbed is well known to us all, for he's never far from trouble. Vincente la Bocca."

Sandro's face changed, hardened. "That scum?"

Guido glared at the water pooling at his feet. "In truth, my lord, His Serenity should give the lady a medal of honor for removing garbage from our streets."

Laura regarded Sandro smugly. "You see, I told you—"

"This only means that your victim was not of the highest character," Sandro interrupted.

"I found someone who witnessed the entire incident," Guido pressed on. "I believe he can vouch for the lady's innocence."

Sandro's mouth pulled into a tight, skeptical smile. "A witness? What did he cost you?"

Guido gestured toward the door. In walked a solemn, moon-faced priest, leaning on a cane. "I am Father Rizotto of San Rocco."

Sandro leaned back and crossed his arms. Laura longed to scratch the dubious look from his face. "And you say you witnessed this incident."

"Indeed so, my lord. I happened to be in the bell tower, preparing to ring for midday mass when I heard shouts and screams. The ruffian attacked her. I don't think he was expecting her to fight back. She stabbed him—some sort of knife, I think. He fell, bleeding from the arm and hitting his head on a water marker."

Sandro lifted one eyebrow. "An admirable account, but I must wonder why a man of mercy such as yourself did not rush to the lady's aid."

"I . . . tried." The priest's face flushed, and he lifted the hem of his brown robe, revealing a rag-wrapped club foot. "It is a hundred steps from the top of the tower to the street level. I reached the bottom in time to see the *zaffi* taking the lady and her wounded attacker away." He gestured at Guido. "This good gentleman was engaged in a frantic search, and came to question me. When we realized the truth, we came straightaway."

A deep red flush sneaked out of Sandro's collar and rose slowly, staining his strong neck and craggy cheeks, rising to the tips of his ears. Laura watched the phenomenon with undisguised delight. She put on a self-righteous expression. "What have you to say to the good father's account, my lord?"

He said nothing, but took her hand and drew her out of the cell. In the antechamber, a pair of Sandro's aides waited.

Laura expected stammered excuses, insistent justification for his ugly suspicions. Sandro Cavalli offered none.

"You were only doing your duty, my lord," she said, making his excuses for him. No, for herself. She needed to find a reason for his lack of trust. If she didn't, she would break into pieces, for somehow she had begun to care deeply what he thought of her.

He led her to the desk and nodded at the clerk to start writing. "I must hear every detail of your account."

In a slow, clear voice, she told him that the *bravo* had been instantly familiar to her. One look at his face, and she had grabbed for her weapon—a glass stiletto filled with poison.

"The one you got at the Rialto?" Sandro asked.

"Yes," she answered without hesitation, knowing

she would never mention poor Magdalena. "I cut his arm, and the glass broke. Will he live?"

Sandro sent a questioning look to his aide.

"The man's still unconscious, my lord. For now, the head wound is more serious than the cut. But the doctor fears the poison could fill him with bad humors."

"Oh, please," Laura prayed, squeezing her eyes shut, "don't let him die." Twice the unknown man had tried to kill her, but she could not bear the responsibility of causing his death.

Sandro ordered a constant guard on the man, who was at the Hospital of San Vittorio. "Fetch me the moment he regains consciousness."

Drowning in his own foolishness, Sandro guided Laura out of the Gabbia and through the halls of the palace. She walked slowly, and he looked back to see her gaping at the Carrara marble picked out in gold, the luminous frescoes on the ceiling, the ornate plasterwork framing doors and windows.

She gave him a soft smile. A forgiving smile. A smile he didn't deserve. "Beg pardon, my lord. I've never been to the doge's palace."

Her simple statement slammed home the differences between them. To Sandro, the palace was as familiar as his own wardrobe. To Laura, it was as alien as another planet.

The gulf separating them gaped wide and deep. Sandro refused to ponder the fact that their differences bothered him.

He helped her into his gondola. There was no reason to draw the privacy curtains over the inverted shell of the hull, but he closed them anyway. When he lowered himself to the velvet-covered seat, Laura was already there, leaning back, preparing to enjoy the voyage.

The sunlight, filtered through the amber draperies, imbued her features with exquisite rich color. She looked more precious than gold, half lying in her seat, watching him, a smile on her face and a dark curl dangling across her cheek.

Unable to stop himself, he brushed aside the soft lock of hair. "Ah, the resiliency of youth," he said.

She caught his hand and pressed his palm to her cheek. Mischief flickered in her eyes. "Ah, the allure of experience."

Sandro ignored her mocking tone. "You're remarkably calm for a woman who's spent the afternoon at the Gabbia after being attacked."

"It does no good to dwell on past wrongs." She cradled her cheek in his hand. "Tell me, my lord, is it only the young who are resilient?"

He took his hand away. "Only the young."

"I wonder." She shifted her leg, made a face, then lifted the hem of her gown, revealing a worn velvet slipper and a few shapely inches of delicate white calf. The sight transported Sandro back to the first day he had met her, when she had lain naked upon Titian's couch. The image engulfed him in a lust so bright and hot that for a moment he went blind. Then his eyes focused.

"That's blood," he said, grabbing the fabric she had been rubbing. "My God, Laura, you should have told me you were hurt."

"It's not my bl—"

"Damn it." Sandro's thoughts dissolved. In a blur of motion, he pulled her onto his lap and gathered her to his chest. Overcome by relief at her innocence and fear for her life, he crushed his mouth down onto hers.

Soft. Her lips were soft, pliant, sweet as sun-

ripened plums. Her body was soft, too—soft breasts
pressed against his chest, soft hands cupping his neck,
soft thighs moving against his own. He lost himself in
the kiss, the passion, the heat. He dipped his tongue
into her mouth and her teeth bit down, not hard but
sensually, filling him with a taste that made honeyed
wine seem bland. The years peeled away and he was
young again, strong and lusty, unfettered by the mis-
takes that had trapped him in an emotional prison of
his own making. The taste and scent and feel of her
washed his soul clean, scrubbed away the darkness of
his wife's betrayal, and reminded him that he had
once been a dreamer. With a simple kiss, Laura gave
back all that life had robbed him of, and his heart rose
up in wordless gratitude.

His hands moved as of their own accord, pushing
up her skirts, tracing her soft inner thigh. He handled
her with a tenderness that he had never before
believed himself capable of. Something inside him
sprang to life, and he realized it was romance and
poetry and a boundless sense of hope.

Laura was stunned by his sudden kiss, too
stunned, at first, to do anything but feel his firm lips,
taste his mouth, sense his strong, sure hands caress-
ing her. This must be what drowning feels like, she
decided, when a body is caught up in currents beyond
hope of rescue.

Helpless, whirling, she surrendered to a dark, liquid
longing that made her head spin in amazement. When
his mouth left hers, she threw her head back against
the velvet cushions and arched upward. Immediately,
his lips found her throat, blazing a moist trail to the
cleft of her breasts.

She heard the canal water whisper past the hull,

heard the rustle of her clothing as he started to remove it. "Ah, Laura, if I could paint with your genius, I would show you as you are now, still pure and innocent, lovely as a flower. . . ."

His words awakened her reason. She heard the warning as clearly as if someone had shouted it in her ear. If he took her now, she would no longer be of such great value to Madonna della Rubia. The women at the *ridotto* had assured her that her first night with a man would earn her no less than a hundred gold *scudi*, enough to buy her freedom the very next day.

The choice tore into her desire. She could have this man, or she could have her future as an artist. She could not have both.

Weighing momentary fulfillment against years of heartache, she forced herself to choose the future. Her art would sustain her long after this wild passion was but a dim and painful memory.

She tried to summon the will to resist; then his hand reached inside her bodice and slid over her bare breast. Heat rushed through her, and she leaned into him. His other hand moved up over her thigh to her belly and toyed with the drawstrings of her undershift.

Laura made herself think. Sandro Cavalli might fill her belly with his children; he would never fulfill her ambition to to be an artist. Painting would never break her heart.

The thought gave her the strength to drag herself up from the dizzying depths of passion. She pulled out of his embrace.

"San—my lord. Please don't do this."

He looked at her, and for a moment his eyes were

glazed with a hot smoky look that made her want to fling herself into his arms once again. Then his eyes cleared, hardened. "Why not?"

Because if you make love to me, I'll lose everything, including my dreams. She could not tell him so, for he would argue her point, and win. In verbal battles, he always did.

"Because I do not offer my favors for the price of a ride in your gondola," she forced herself to say.

He took a quick breath, and a whispered oath escaped him.

The boat bumped against the water steps of the *ridotto.* Laura glanced away from Sandro, away from the pain on his face which he could not quite hide. She shot to her feet, yanking back the curtain. Unable to face him when she next spoke, she forced a breezy, insouciant laugh. "My dear lord, if you wish to have me, then you'll have to outbid all the others at the carnival masque."

7

"No, no, no," Portia scolded, hiding a giggle behind her hand. "Laura, you cannot simply wander aimlessly into a room. You must make an entrance. Now, try it again."

Smiling ruefully at Portia and the other women, Laura stood in the doorway of the main salon. Sunlight streamed through the colored windows, making rainbow patterns on the marble floor. She did not want to be here, practicing a courtesan's swaying walk. She wanted to be in Titian's studio, trying to duplicate the splash of colors on the floor.

Resigned to her fate, she filled her chest with air and let half of it out. According to her friends, this served to calm the nerves—and also to display the bosom to best advantage. She formed her lips in a charming smile.

"Now remember, this is an entrance," Portia reminded her.

Fiammetta nodded encouragingly. "You want to halt every man in his tracks. You want him to forget what he was saying, to stop his wine goblet halfway to his lips, to see only you. You want to hear jaws dropping all the way to the floor."

"You're asking a lot of me," Laura said.

"It's no more than you're capable of." Portia tapped her foot. "In truth we should all be jealous of your looks and your youth, but for some reason we aren't."

"Because we're friends," Laura said with certainty.

"And because this is all a game," said Fiammetta. "Try it, Laura."

Just a game, she told herself, placing her arms just so, lifting her chin, and sailing into the room. How different these women were from the nuns of her upbringing. Were there winners and losers in the game? she wondered. And who decided the outcome?

The questions brought on fresh memories of Sandro Cavalli's kiss. He had held her, kissed her, as if he had cared about her. Did most men pretend, or only the mannerly ones? And how could one tell the difference between a man answering the call of his heart and a man heeding the desire in his loins?

The women applauded her entrance.

"Brava!" Portia exclaimed. "Where's Yasmin? I want her to see how much you've learned this morning."

"Yasmin's off in her garden," said Bianca. "With him. Again."

Laura enjoyed their knowing looks. Sandro had sent Jamal to watch over her, for one of her attackers was still at large. Taking advantage of Laura's lesson with her friends, the huge, silent man had gone to see Yasmin. Last night, after dark, Laura had lain in her tiny attic room while the two met outside on the *altana* where, by day, the women sunned themselves.

She had heard them—or rather, Yasmin—talking long into the night in the Arab tongue. Jamal's silence seemed to draw out the usually quiet Yasmin, while her talk seemed to nourish his soul.

"Laura, pay attention now. We're almost out of time," Fiammetta prodded her.

Returning her attention to the other women, Laura reviewed the table graces, deftly handling the new utensil called a fork. With studied delicacy, she lifted a goblet by the stem and used the fingerbowl. She had less success when Portia played the gentleman's role, plying her with wine and compliments.

"You have to pretend your heart's in this, Laura. Don't just stand there like a stick. Smile, bat your eyes a little. Let him think you exist for him alone."

Laura complied, then stuck out her tongue. "No man in his right mind would fall for that."

"You overestimate men, my friend. They see what they want to see and follow the dictates of their loins."

A footman interrupted the lesson. "Someone's here for Madonna Bandello."

"She's not ready to receive gentlemen yet," Portia protested. "You know that, Benvenuto."

"It's no gentleman, but Lord Sandro Cavalli," Benvenuto replied.

Laura tamped back a surge of surprise and delight.

"Wonderful," Portia exclaimed. "If you can summon that expression for our clients, you'll soon be a wealthy woman."

"You can practice your conversation skills on him, make him melt in a puddle at your feet," Fiammetta urged.

Laura shook her head. "I'd have more luck melt-

ing a stone." She was certain her parting words to
him had made him despise her for good. Wondering
if he had news on the condition of the assassin, she
hurried to the grand foyer.

Sandro stood like a rough-hewn statue, his features
chiseled but not smoothed by sanding. As he had
before, he looked ill at ease in the brothel.

She started toward him. "My lord—"

"Get your cloak," he commanded. "We're going
out."

"But I'm busy."

"Now, Laura."

Puzzled, she hurried upstairs and fetched her
cloak, fastening it at her throat as she followed him
outside. The gondolier, not Sandro, helped her into
the boat. When she was seated, he drew the curtains—
but stayed on the outside, perched at the stern, talking to the gondolier.

Fine, thought Laura, settling back and trying to
enjoy the ride. She had angered him. Angered the
man who, only the day before, had accused her of
being a murderer. Let him sulk.

Before she had met Sandro, Laura had not even
dreamed of riding in a nobleman's gondola. But
already the novelty was wearing off. She was relieved
when she felt the hull bump against stone and heard
the gondolier toss out the mooring ropes. Without
waiting for Sandro's permission, she drew aside the
curtain.

She found herself staring at the gray stone edifice
of the Hospital of San Giacomo. Sandro pulled her
up the water steps at the entrance.

Apprehension chilled her. "Is this about the
assassin?"

"No. He's feverish now, delirious. His doctors can't say when he'll be well enough for questioning. Besides, this hospital does not treat his sort of ailment."

"Then what are we doing here?"

Sandro pushed her into the foyer. "You'll see."

Laura took a moment to absorb her surroundings. The thick stone walls were impervious to light and heat from the sun. Nuns bundled against the cold bustled past, carrying trays and jars and missals. From a long hallway came sounds of moaning and smells that made Laura itch to grab her fichu and press it to her nose. Instead, she drew her face deeper into the hood of her cloak.

"How awful it must be to lie sick in this place," she remarked.

"I thought you'd feel that way," said Sandro. "It gives me hope that you'll avoid certain . . . complications of your chosen profession. Come." Taking her arm, he led her into a dark, tunnel-like hallway. The sounds and smells were stronger here.

Arches in the hallway opened to large wards with rows of narrow, rope-slung cots. Nearly every cot was occupied. Sandro drew Laura into one of the wards and pulled her along the rows. Some of the women they passed stared blindly at the ceiling; others were covered in skin lesions; two, out of their heads and babbling, were tied to their cots.

Sandro stopped at the last cot, which was below a window glazed in cheap, milky glass. A low curtain concealed the occupant.

"It's me, Imperia," Sandro said. "I've brought . . . the friend I told you about. Laura will be interested to hear about your life."

"My life?" asked a woman's rasping voice. "Ah, there you're wrong." She poked a reed-thin arm through a gap in the curtain. "I am dead."

"That's for God to decide," Sandro said firmly.

"Nicely said, my lord," Laura muttered under her breath. "Your compassion overwhelms me."

"Open the curtain," said Imperia. Sandro did so, and Laura gasped. She clutched at Sandro's sleeve, hissing, "Is this a lazar house?"

"No." The muscles of his arm tightened beneath her hand. "These women aren't lepers."

"It's the French pox," said the woman on the bed. "Or so we in Italy call it. In France it's the Italian scourge, and in Spain . . . never mind. Sit down, dear."

Numb with shock, Laura sank to a low, three-legged stool. Sandro left the ward, and she wanted to call him back, but did not wish to appear rude. "Coward," she said half to herself.

"Him? No, not Sandro. Far from it. One day, you'll see." Imperia folded her hands on her chest. "Madonna della Rubia never told you about this place, did she?"

"No, madonna."

Bony fingers trembled on the thin blanket. "She wouldn't, of course. We knew each other, were friends, when we were your age or younger. Both as fair as the morning." She paused to catch a breath. "Both courtesans."

Nodding at Laura's startled look, she went on dreamily, "I was born Aranchia, but I called myself Imperia, so proud was I, so sought after. At my peak, I had a train of a dozen pages, footmen, and lady's maids, my own dwarf, a menagerie of exotic animals,

gowns and jewels beyond counting. Men often fought
to the death to possess me. And if I was not always well
pleased by the men who purchased me, if they sometimes did unspeakable things in the privacy of my bedchamber, I told myself that the rewards were great—
jewels, gold coins; once a man gave me my own *vigna*.
And all this before I reached the age of twenty."

Her eyes took fire. She grasped Laura's wrist. "No
doubt you've heard such tales before, eh?"

"Yes, madonna."

"Ah, they all tell you that part. I can tell you the
rest. The rotten truth that lies beneath the gilded
crust. Whoring is a way of life that seduces the young
and destroys the old. You know the Trentuno?"

"Thirty-one?" Laura shook her head in confusion.

"A vile tradition," Imperia spat. "For sport—or
sometimes for revenge—thirty-one men abduct and
use a woman. I suffered the Trentuno more than
once in my time."

"I swear I won't," said Laura, squeezing her eyes
shut, trying to block out the horror.

"When the time comes, it won't be for you to
decide. I imagine you fancy yourself holding court
while men throw gold and diamonds at your feet. But
what will you do if they refuse to pay? You must cast
yourself upon their mercy, grovel and beg for a single
soldo so you can pay your bills for all that luxury.
And your taxes, or you'll find yourself in jail. Men
give, and they take away. They give you love and
devotion, and take it away when they tire of you. But
there are some things that can never be taken back."

She paused, and Laura said, "I'm not sure what
you mean."

Imperia let go of Laura's hand. "The babies."

Laura's eyes stung. "Babies, madonna?"

"I had six, all daughters. All dead now. Four before they reached their first birthdays. The other two I sold. Yes! I sold my girls to a man who set them up as his mistresses. You think you will never reach that point of desperation, never sink so low that you would sell your own flesh and blood in order to survive."

Laura believed it, for her own mother had done just that. It was yet another reason she had resolved never to have children.

"But you will one day. It's like a madness, burning inside you, eating at you. The desire for more wealth and greater luxury. Ah, and there is another thing your lovers will give you, oh, so sweetly. And that is disease. Perhaps it will be a mild affliction, and you'll lose the ability to bear children. In my case, that would have been a blessing. But I got the pox, and you see what it has made me. A walking corpse, rotting from the outside in. Lord Jesus Christ, take me from this misery!"

Laura's tears drenched her hands, which she held clenched tightly in her lap. "Madonna, if I can do anything to ease your pain . . ."

"Light a candle for me. I am going blind, and crave the light." Imperia's voice was breathy, as if she had exhausted her strength with her tirade. "And think hard about the path you've chosen. Leave me now. I'm tired."

Laura stood, and Sandro returned to them, striding into the ward with his cloak swirling around his torso, his boots ringing on the flagstone floor.

Laura shot him a look of hatred. How dare he bring her here, show her this, exploit these wretched creatures just to prove a point? He was the coldest, cruelest man in Christendom.

"We must be going now, Imperia," he said.

"Until next week, then?"

"Of course."

Laura gaped at him in astonishment as he smiled and leaned down to kiss Imperia's papery cheek. "Until next week," he said, then went out into the hallway.

Laura's rage dissolved into confusion. "You come here each week?"

He paused to deposit an awesome sum into the alms box in the foyer. "I do."

"But why?"

His hard features never changed. "Because no one else will."

She followed him into the sunlight, drinking in the cold, damp air as if she had been dying of thirst. Damn him. *Damn* him. Just when she made up her mind that he was a ruthless cad, he surprised her.

As they stood on the steps of the hospital, she tried not to shiver. "I know what you're trying to do, my lord, and I do appreciate your reformist attitude. However, you will not change my mind."

"By God, did she make no impression at all on you?"

"She impressed me as a careless woman who gained wisdom too late. I shall not end up like Imperia. My career as a courtesan will be brief. And Madonna della Rubia is scrupulous about her patrons."

"The *ruffiana,* I assume, is infallible."

"Oh, shut up," Laura said, turning away.

He grabbed her arm and brought her around to face him. "God, you're a stubborn female. All right, assume you avoid Imperia's fate. Your body might stay healthy, but what about your heart?"

"What *about* my heart?" she demanded, resenting the hard pressure of his fingers around her upper arm. "At least I have one."

"Some man is going to break it, Laura." His face was close, intent.

"I'd like to see you try," she flung at him, only belatedly noticing her slip.

He came even closer, his breath gusting against her cheek. "Shall I, Laura? Shall I try?"

Shock held her riveted, for his question suggested something more than passion, something deeper. "N-no. I mean, yes! That is, you won't succeed."

"I succeed at everything," he countered, pulling her into the shadows of the hospital entrance. He kissed her hard, and despite Laura's best intentions, managed to wring a helpless moan from her throat.

He had an uncanny way of stripping away her defenses, finding her deepest fears and shamelessly exploiting them. Incensed, she broke away and stumbled back. "Stop it!"

A slow, cruel smile curled his lip. "You don't want me to stop."

"You're being ridiculous."

He lifted one eyebrow. "Oh? In what way?"

Laura hesitated. She, too, could be cruel. "You can't use me like this. You can't use me to reclaim your lost youth, or to make up for failing your wife, or to spite your son." She enunciated each word with deadly clarity.

Sandro stood very still, staring at her while she glared back. She saw the storm of agony in his eyes and knew that she had accomplished her goal, that she had hurt him.

"You win, Laura," he said softly. "I learned long

ago when to fight and when to retreat. We should leave each other alone."

Two days later, as he stood on the Rialto bridge, Sandro realized that Laura's words, flung at him after the hospital visit, still stung. Watching the glittering young dandies striding past, he became acutely aware of his age. Their faces were fresh and smooth and handsome, while Sandro's was etched with lines of worry and pain and experience. Beneath feathered caps, their hair flowed loose and gleaming, while Sandro's once proud crown was threaded with gray.

He hated himself for caring. He had never been a vain man, but Laura's cutting words had nearly sent him running to the laboratory of the nun, Celestina, who claimed her potions could restore the color of his hair.

Shaking off the thought, Sandro shouldered his way past a group of brightly clad masked revelers. He glowered at them, for their gay costumes reminded him what day it was.

The eve of Ash Wednesday. The last chance to indulge to excess before the forty solemn days of Lent.

Tonight, Madonna della Rubia would hold her carnival masque. Tonight, Laura would take a strange man to her bed.

The thought felt like talons of cold steel clawing at his chest. He told himself not to care. At eighteen, she was actually years past the customary age that most women marry, take the veil, or enter into prostitution. She had shown herself to be independent and self-reliant.

She had shown herself to be lovely, fragile, and utterly enchanting.

Stop it, he told himself. She thought him a doddering old fool; her words had made that clear enough. She was a born whore, he insisted. Even her virginity was probably a fiction created by Madonna della Rubia; the courtesans of Venice had always possessed the uncanny ability to reinvent their virtue.

But not Laura, a voice whispered in his mind.

The idea of her being sold like a piece of meat on the hoof tore at him. He forced his mind to other worries: The assassin, Vincente la Bocca, still lay senseless, burning up with fever; he had not spoken a coherent word since the incident. Nothing of use had been found to implicate the dignitaries on Doge Gritti's list. And then there was Marcantonio.

A new brand of pain seared Sandro's heart. With each passing day his son had grown more distant. He was secretive, too. Just this morning, when Sandro had entered the house and found Marcantonio with thirty of his young friends, the group had fallen silent. Some of them had flushed as if embarrassed; others would not meet Sandro's eyes.

Feeling tired and troubled, Sandro made his way to the Piazza San Marco. Here, the revelry was intensifying to a fever pitch. Mummers in parti-colored costumes entertained a crowd with a juggling act. The wharves facing the ducal palace were crowded with gondolas and barges decked in bright silk bunting. Masked tumblers cavorted in the palace arcade.

And everywhere, Sandro noted with cold satisfaction, were the Night Lords. He had increased the number of *signori di notte* and *zaffi* for this night. He had cautioned them to patrol with extra vigilance, for the pre-Lenten revelry always spawned riots and looting.

He had assigned a small army of men to watch over the *ridotto* of Madonna della Rubia.

He turned down a narrow street and stopped in front of a blue door. One of his mistresses lived here, and for a moment he forgot her name. Ah, yes. Barbara. She had cool hands and a soft, soothing voice. She knew better than to make demands.

Something stopped him from going inside, from losing himself in a few hours of mindless passion.

Duty, he told himself. He would not abandon Venice on the wildest night of the year.

"God, your integrity makes me sick," said a voice behind him.

Sandro swung around to see two men in elaborate disguises. One, tall and thin, was a satyr, complete with horns sprouting from his brow. The other, tall and portly, wore a grinning Bacchus mask.

"We've been looking for you, *divinissimo*," said Bacchus.

"So you've found me, Pietro." Sandro scowled into the eyeholes of Aretino's mask. "Don't you and the maestro have a variety of pressing sins to commit?"

"We were hoping we'd get you to commit them with us," Titian said, fingering the beard that peeked from beneath the mask.

"I'm on duty," Sandro stated.

Aretino snorted, a hollow sound behind his mask. "You've got every last *zaffo* in the republic on duty," he pointed out. "Surely they can keep the peace without you for a few hours."

"No."

Titian gave an exaggerated sigh. He and Aretino exchanged a glance. "He asked for it," Titian said.

The two men stationed themselves directly behind Sandro. Cursing under his breath, he realized he was about to become a victim of tradition. When, on the eve of Lent, revelers encountered a spoilsport, they followed at his heels, mimicking his every move until the victim relented and treated them to a round of wine.

Furious, Sandro planted his hands on his hips and glanced over his left shoulder. Titian and Aretino planted their hands on their hips and glanced over their left shoulders.

"Some people never grow up," Sandro snapped.

"God forbid that we ever do," said Aretino.

Sandro decided the quickest way to get rid of them would be to get some wine into them as soon as possible. Feeling ridiculous, he strode across the street toward a wine shop. Behind him, making a parody of his powerful strides, were two grown men, giggling like choirboys.

In the dim shop, Sandro found a corner table and called for a jar of cheap, potent wine. Titian and Aretino let down their pretense and removed their masks.

Aretino raised a bushy eyebrow and lifted his cup. "To life!" he boomed. "For us, life is enough."

Titian followed suit. "Life is enough," he repeated, more quietly than his friend. Sandro saw regret steal over the artist's features. Titian had adored his wife, and her untimely death a few years earlier still pained him.

Sandro wondered what it was like to mourn a cherished wife.

"Well?" Aretino elbowed him in the ribs.

Resignedly, Sandro lifted his glass. "Life is . . . enough." He barely tasted the wine. By the time he set down his cup, Aretino was proposing another toast.

"To our own Laura," he said, fixing his keen, merciless gaze on Sandro. "May she be wallowing in gold ducats this time tomorrow." He gave Sandro another nudge. "You *did* know that she makes her debut tonight, didn't you?"

Sandro said nothing. He did not lift his glass.

"Ecco! To her health, old friend," Aretino insisted. "Don't you wish her well?"

Sandro's temper snapped. He slammed down his pewter goblet. "No, damn you. I do not wish her well, and you know it. It is my earnest wish that she fail miserably at her endeavor to be a courtesan."

"But she'll make a perfectly splendid courtesan. She'll outshine those Roman sluts, Tullia and Veronica Franco."

Titian twirled the stem of his goblet. "I wonder who will claim her for the *nozze solenne.*"

"I wonder what it will cost him," Aretino said. He slid a glance at Sandro. "Don't you wonder, *onnipotente?*"

"Not," said Sandro, grating at Aretino's false honorary title, "in the least."

Aretino burst out laughing. "What a poor liar you are. This thing is tearing you to pieces, *superbossio,* that's plain to see." He slapped his beefy thigh and stood. "Well, there's only one remedy for this."

Titian replaced his satyr's mask. "Indeed. Let's go."

Sandro glared at them. "Go where?"

Titian and Aretino guffawed. Gasping, Aretino dragged Sandro up off his seat. "Ah, my man, as if you didn't know."

8

Unseen, Laura sat in a dim alcove of the grand ballroom and watched the masque from behind a silk screen. Through the thin fabric, the salon on the other side of the divider glittered with a thousand candles in wall sconces and chandeliers, turning the room into a world of stars. Costumed guests and graceful courtesans danced the *rosina,* wheeling across the marble floor to the sprightly music of rebec, flute, and harp. Between dances, Florio sang lovers' laments, his beautiful tenor voice throbbing with grief.

Yasmin, intimidatingly beautiful as the Queen of Sheba, glided over to the screen and stood with her back to it. She whispered from the corner of her mouth. "Are we enjoying ourselves yet?"

Laura hugged herself, rubbing her palms over her bare arms. "I'm cold. This costume is ridiculous."

"The more ridiculous, the better. Men love the ridiculous." Yasmin's voice softened in sympathy. "The truth now. Will you be all right?"

Laura thought hard before answering. She had survived an austere existence as an undowered resident

at the convent. She had resisted the demands of a las-
civious priest. She had thrown herself into her career
as an artist. She was prepared to barter her most private self for the sake of her art and her independence.

"I'll be fine, Yasmin."

"You don't sound very convincing, little friend."

*Your body might stay healthy, but what about
your heart?* Unbidden, Sandro's challenge drifted
into Laura's mind.

What about *my heart?*

*Some man is going to break it, Laura. . . . Shall I
try?*

Damn Sandro Cavalli. Damn him for planting
doubts and fears in her mind. Damn him for making
her wish that he was among the revelers, that he
would fling down a fortune to possess her.

To distract herself, she thought about her portfo-
lio of paintings. Before long, she would submit them
to the Accademia. Her paintings were good. But were
they good enough?

Yasmin's regal stare traveled through the room.
"It seems we have guests from every noble house in
Venice."

"I can't tell one from another." Laura scanned the
crowd. The woven silk screen muted the harsh lines
of the scene, giving it a dreamlike quality.

"You're not supposed to be able to," Yasmin said.
"The great lords of Venice are protective of their
reputations. However"—she gestured at a man
dressed as Caesar—"that one's a papal nuncio. See
his ring of office?"

"Charming," Laura murmured, "for a man of the
cloth to be so blithely indifferent to his vows." She
studied a young man tricked out in a glass-beaded

tunic. He stood in earnest conversation with a serpentlike creature whose costume glittered with bright red scales.

"What the devil is that?" Laura asked.

Yasmin shrugged. "Some sort of fish. A herring, perhaps?"

Laura's eyes widened as she noticed a guest in the guise of Vulcan, the swordsmith of the gods. His massive bare shoulders and the confident way he carried himself reminded her painfully of Sandro.

Impatient with her own thoughts, she speculated on the identity of the masked and hooded Priapus, god of male fertility. Surrounded by his fellow revelers, the man was well built and spry, a graceful dancer. Like Vulcan, he had a nagging familiarity about him.

The costumes of the *zaffi* assigned by Sandro Cavalli to guard the brothel were lackluster compared to the glittering garb of the dancers. As a concession to the festivities, the police sported half masks and streamers tied to their shortswords.

"Nothing can conceal the identity of Jamal," Laura said, watching as he scribbled on his slate and handed it to Madonna della Rubia.

"True. Is his costume not beautiful?"

Laura agreed. He was garbed as a genie, wearing a turban, embroidered gloves, loose trousers of pink silk, and a short red vest that revealed his massive chest and arms. Yasmin sighed, and Laura smiled secretly, for her friend was falling in love and no longer bothered to conceal it.

Leaving Yasmin alone with her thoughts, Laura continued perusing the crowd of men dressed as characters from classical antiquity. They all seemed vaguely threatening, even the sprightly

Pan, for once the night was out, she would belong to one of them.

A stir at the entrance caught her eye. For a moment, she stopped breathing. Then she said, "Yasmin, look who's here."

Yasmin turned toward the marble arch over the doorway, and her back went rigid. "The Swede!" she hissed.

Laura shuddered in commiseration, for Yasmin was the giant's favorite. Thorvald was one of the wealthiest, most dangerous foreign merchants of the republic. Twice yearly he came to Venice on business, and each visit left the entire city shaken.

Dressed now as his forebears, in steel tunic, animal skins, and horned iron helm, Thorvald was a throwback to another time, a wild age when barbaric Norsemen swarmed in destructive hordes across the civilized world.

Built like a gothic cathedral, he wore a short skirt of overlapping steel tongues that revealed the pillars of his legs. His primitive sandals were fastened on with long leather thongs that crisscrossed like ivy up his rock-hard calves to his knees.

Pale blond fur covered every inch of flesh that Laura could see. His head was the size of a bullock's, his face like a side of beef, ruddy and unattractive.

Accompanied by two normal-sized servants who appeared as children next to Thorvald, the Viking chief stormed to the center of the room, parting the crowd with his progress. The floor seemed to tremble with each step he took.

No, not him, Laura prayed silently. *Please God, not him.*

The Viking planted his hands on his hips. His

elbows flared out like flying buttresses flanking the walls of a fortress. He threw back his head and bellowed, *"Yasmin!"*

Alarm rose in Laura's throat. "Yasmin, quickly. Come behind the screen!"

But Yasmin stood frozen, helpless. Laura's heart broke for her friend. The last time Thorvald had visited her, she had taken to her bed for a week afterward. "Yasmin, hurry!" Laura urged. "Before he sees y—"

"There you are," Thorvald trumpeted, spying Yasmin. "By thunder, I've missed you!" He tramped across the room, a veritable siege engine of sexual energy.

A collective gasp rose from the revelers as Jamal planted himself between Thorvald and Yasmin.

Laura's heart lurched. Jamal was no match for the Swede. If Jamal was a venerable tree, Thorvald was a column of stone, half a head taller than the African and twice as broad.

"Out of my way, you pagan scum," Thorvald roared in bad Italian. "Somebody ought to geld you and feed you to the fish."

Jamal held his ground and flexed his arms. Laura could not see his face, but she imagined the defiance carved in his ebony features.

Yasmin hissed an urgent message in Arabic. Laura knew she was imploring Jamal to give way. Very calmly, he lifted his hand, peeled off one of his gloves, and tossed it on the floor at Thorvald's gondola-sized feet.

The Swede lifted his huge arms, flung back his horned head, and beat a military tattoo on his chest. "Yes!" he exploded. "A fight before I claim my woman!"

Madonna della Rubia bustled through the crowd and laid her hand on Thorvald's furry arm. "My dear most honored sir," she said, "I cannot have brawling in my establishment. Let this be a night of genteel pleasures. I'm afraid this gentleman" —she indicated Jamal with a nod—"has already secured the company of Yasmin for the night."

Yasmin stared at Jamal. The hard, dangerous lines of her face softened, and a smile lit her eyes.

"He challenged me!" Although Thorvald's voice tolled like a deep-throated bell, it had the whiny edge of a little boy deprived of a treat. "He challenged me!"

"But sir, you cannot—"

"Let them fight, madonna," someone shouted from the crowd. "Lent starts tomorrow, and we'll have forty boring days observing the Lord's peace."

"Fight! Fight!" The cry rang across the room.

Laura hugged her knees to her chest and burned with anger. Sandro Cavalli claimed his mission was to preserve order; so where the hell was he now? She prayed one of his men would have the sense to summon him, but the saucer-eyed *zaffi* merely stood gaping at the two huge men.

"Very well," Madonna della Rubia conceded with a long-suffering sigh. "You may fight, but it must be an arm-wrestling match. The winner takes Yasmin for the night; the loser forfeits his fee."

"Done!" Thorvald bellowed.

In a flash, servants brought a round table and two stools. Thorvald would no doubt break Jamal's arm, but at least he would escape with his life. Broken bones were a small price to pay for his foolish gallantry.

From the screened alcove, Laura had a perfect view of the opponents. They lowered themselves to the stools and faced each other. Jamal planted his elbow on the table.

Thorvald's forearm was inches longer than Jamal's. The picture their clasped hands made was oddly beautiful—gleaming ebony and gold-dusted pale skin.

The papal nuncio played the role of arbitrator. "Left hand behind your back," he ordered. Jamal obeyed. Thorvald looked momentarily confused. The papal nuncio touched his hand. "This is your left, *messere.*"

The official raised his hand. "Ready . . . now!"

His arm swept downward in an arc. The battle was joined.

Thorvald smiled, clearly anticipating an easy victory. As he encountered unexpected resistance, he frowned. Jamal was holding his own.

Yasmin clutched her hands to her chest and whispered a prayer to Allah.

Thorvald's eye-bulging surprise turned to cold determination. He set his lantern jaw and settled in to destroy his challenger.

Muscles knotted; teeth ground. Thorvald swore. Their arms trembled, neither giving way. Jamal seemed a carven image; his eyes were glazed like the unseeing orbs of a statue. The only indication that he was a living, breathing, human being was the sweat that ran in rivers down his face.

Deafening roars of encouragement blasted through the crowd. Coins changed hands as bets were laid. Still the stand-off held.

Then Thorvald's pale eyes burned as he poured new power into his arm. Their clasped hands began to lean.

Tears started in Yasmin's eyes. The crowd hushed, waiting for the inevitable end.

Laura wished she could tell Jamal that the Swede had a single weakness: Not only was Thorvald built like a granite mountain, he was just as dense. That bestial stupidity could be the Swede's undoing.

Jamal's sweat-drenched hand hovered scant inches from the table now. Hope and conviction still flared in his eyes.

Laura drew a deep breath, then whispered through the screen: "My lord Thorvald!"

Thorvald's great head jerked up so quickly that his horned helm toppled to the floor with a metallic clang. His gaze cast about as he sought the source of the voice.

"Careful, my lord, behind you!" Laura whispered.

Thorvald turned to look.

In a blur, Jamal's hand snapped over, neatly pinning Thorvald's to the table. The motion was so swift, so violent, that the Swede's entire body followed the arc.

He loosed an animal bawl as he came out of his stool and hit the floor. The room shook with the impact. Thorvald lay unconscious in the stunned silence.

Madonna della Rubia recovered first. She took a vial of perfume from her bodice, put a few drops on a lace-edged handkerchief, and let it drift down onto Thorvald's face. He coughed, coming to.

Madonna della Rubia leaned over him and said, *"Messere,* you owe me thirty *scudi."*

Yasmin and Jamal came together in a fierce embrace. As he scooped her into his arms and started through the cheering crowd toward the stairs, Laura caught a glimpse of her friend's face.

"Oh, Yasmin," she whispered, smiling through a sudden rush of sentimental tears. "You've broken your own cardinal rule and fallen in love."

Thorvald revived enough to drink a small cask of wine. Complaining loudly of ghostly voices and infidels doing the devil's work, he went to sleep on the floor.

More guests poured through the entranceway of the *salone,* and Laura sensed that the time was drawing nigh for her to make her entrée.

At that moment, the maestro stepped into the room. She recognized his satyr's mask, for Titian had shown it to her earlier. The heavy-set Bacchus behind him was Aretino. Even before he loosed his trademark belly laugh, Laura knew him.

Accompanying them was a third man, this one garbed as the greatest hero of the classics. *"Mars vigila!"* someone shouted, and all heads turned to look at the powerfully built stranger in a white tunic and mask of gold, his head covered by a winged helm. Sansovino, Laura guessed, for the sculptor was never far from his two friends. So famed was their association that people called them a triumverate.

Still, Laura felt an odd, portentous flutter in her stomach. She was costumed as Venus, who took Mars as her lover.

"We're too late," Sandro muttered, his voice muffled behind his golden mask. He had insisted on a concealing costume, for he didn't want the gossips to bandy it about that the Lord of the Night had visited a brothel.

"Don't be daft," Aretino said, "the party's just

begun." He strode into the room and slapped his generous girth. "Ah, Venice," he sighed. "There is nothing so desirable as an evening in la Serenissima, except perhaps a night with a beautiful woman."

Glaring at Aretino, Sandro stepped over the mountainlike body of a sleeping Viking. He did not pause to wonder at the oddity of a man sound asleep in the middle of the floor. At carnival time in Venice, nothing was odd.

Not even the sale of a virgin.

He grabbed a glass goblet from the tray of a passing servant, lifted the glass under his mask, and tossed back the wine. Where was she?

"Patience, old friend," Aretino said, speaking out of the corner of his mouth. "Be patient, and you won't miss a thing."

The idea of purchasing a strange woman repelled Sandro. He felt dirty, degraded, just being here. It went against all of his dearly held principles.

He told himself he meant to win the bid in order to preserve her virtue, to buy time to convince her that she had taken the wrong path.

Ignoring the beckoning look of a whore dressed as a siren, Sandro waited, stiff and silent behind the mask of Mars, for Laura to make her entrance. He felt ridiculous in the white tunic, which he had borrowed from Titian. Around his waist he wore a wide belt studded with iron. The tip of his antique Roman sword nearly brushed the ground as he walked about the room. So far no one, not even his own *zaffi*, had recognized him. Sandro had insisted on complete anonymity, and Titian had artfully complied.

Passing the costumed revelers, he thought he recognized a few of the men present, but Venetians loved the game of concealment and those here gave off few clues. Besides, he lacked the time and the inclination to play guessing games.

A group of young men dressed as fools, troubadours, and heroes of myth laughed raucously. Zeus, with his helm of lightning bolts, drank with admirable stamina. Beside him stood a well-built man in the tasteless guise of Priapus. Romulus and Remus, covered in wolf skins, played chase with a pair of courtesans.

Sandro wondered if his son were among the revelers. A likely possibility, for this was the largest and most notorious masque in Venice. The notion bothered Sandro, for Laura had spurned Marcantonio, and he might have come to witness the sale of her innocence.

From the musicians' gallery came a bright blare of trumpets. The dancing stopped and the crowd parted, making a path across the floor to a raised dais upon which rested a divan shaped like a large seashell and upholstered in gold brocade.

Four footmen entered through a side door. Their extravagant livery violated sumptuary law, but Sandro barely noticed, for his attention was riveted to the burden they carried. It was a litter painted with gold leaf and shrouded in cloth of silver. The musicians played a processional as the footmen bore the conveyance to the dais.

Madonna della Rubia met the litter. She made a practiced speech, extolling the virtues of her famous *ridotto,* the refinement of the courtesans, the loftiness of her clients. She told of discovering a maiden straight from the convent, a young woman whose charms would soon be immortalized in sonnets. "My dear friends and patrons," she concluded, then paused dramatically. "I give you Madonna Laura Bandello."

A whoosh of indrawn breaths accompanied the parting of the shroud. Out stepped a vision that drew groans of longing from the men.

Sandro could do no more than gawk. Here was Laura as he had never seen her, not even in Titian's studio. She wore a filmy white sheath fastened at one shoulder by a golden clasp, leaving the other milk-white shoulder bare. Her raven curls were piled atop her head and crowned by a jeweled coronet. Her pale, slim arm jangled with bracelets, and Sandro realized who she was.

Venus, goddess of beauty and love.

The litter was borne away and Laura stood alone, and for once she held herself unmoving. Her stillness gave the illusion that she was frozen in a living portrait, a solemn, sensual deity painted in glowing tones by the winking candlelight.

Then she reclined on the cunningly designed half shell. More groans broke from her rapt observers. The gauzy costume molded her form, outlining the shapes of her breasts, the curve of her thigh. A dainty, sandaled foot peeked from beneath the garment.

Dragging his gaze from her mouth-watering body, Sandro studied her face. It was expressionless but not blank or dull, simply . . . accepting. What in God's name could she be thinking? What thoughts passed through the mind of a woman about to spend the night with a stranger?

She wore little or no face paint, he noted, probably to play up her chastity. Indeed, innocence was part of her appeal. Yet it was her inner strength and optimism that attracted Sandro.

Despite all his efforts to rein in his rampant thoughts, fantasies arose within him. He imagined touching his lips to her bare shoulder, finding the texture as fine as the skin of a babe. He thought about the buds of her nipples moving subtly beneath the garment, and about the dark, sweet mystery of her womanhood barely concealed by the costume.

Sandro Cavalli, who had always prided himself on his stern discipline and iron will, found himself rock hard and burning for her. He realized, with a sinking sense of disappointment, that he was no more immune to her bewitchment than the next man.

He touched his cache of ducats, which weighted the purse that dangled from his wide belt. The coins had been painted in bright colors for the occasion. And he knew, with terrible certainty, that he would match any offer, top any bid, to possess her.

He was through trying to use words to convince her that a whore's life brought danger, misery, and heartache.

Tonight, he would *show* her.

Laura held her face impassive as she scanned the crowd. The offers started immediately, each man expressing the sum he was willing to part with by stacking painted ducats at the base of the dais. Madonna della Rubia's eagle eye took in the growing stacks.

Awe and dread mingled painfully in Laura's chest. Was her body such a valuable commodity that men would squander fortunes to win a night of her company?

Trepidation chilled her, for she could summon no enthusiasm for the idea of being touched by, invaded by, a stranger. The man who won her would expect a

great deal of entertainment in exchange for so princely
a sum.

To quell her growing apprehension, she searched
the crowd for her friends. Her gaze picked out Titian
and Aretino. The portly writer gave her a thumbs-up
sign of encouragement. Portia, dressed as Spring,
fluttered her ivy-covered fan at Laura. Fiammetta, as
Medusa in a cunning wig of wire snakes, blew her a
kiss. For the most part, Laura could not guess the
identities of the disguised guests.

The clink of coins sounded like thunder in her
ears. One of the tallest stacks belonged to the slim
man costumed as Priapus. The large mask, frozen in
a leer, covered his entire head. The eyeholes were too
small to discern the color of his eyes.

Laura mistrusted a man who portrayed himself as
a lewd braggart. To her relief, each time Priapus
increased his bid of colored money, the amount was
surpassed by the broad, powerfully built man in the
guise of Mars. He, too, was well-concealed, but
Laura clung to the possibility that he was the sculptor, Sansovino, a fellow artist and her friend. As
famed for his dalliance with ladies as he was for his
sculptures, Jacopo Sansovino would surely bring her
no harm.

As Mars, he moved strangely, hesitantly, as if he
found the business distasteful. It probably pained the
poor soul to part with so much money. Still, Laura
was grateful to him for keeping pace with the lascivi-
ous Priapus. She was grateful, too, for the money.
The avid look on Madonna della Rubia's face told
Laura that these sums were unheard of. Sums that
could buy Laura's freedom from debt. After tonight,
she would never have to sell herself again.

That should satisfy Sandro Cavalli, who had tried his best to change her mind.

But then again, he might never forgive her. So strict was his code of ethics that even one lapse was one too many. Sandro Cavalli could well afford to maintain his honor, she thought resentfully. He had never known what it was like to be denied his heart's desire for lack of money. He had never been tempted by an easy way to fulfill his ambitions. He knew nothing of the trials of a woman trying to succeed in a man's world.

After a time, all but two of the men came to reclaim their money from among the steadily growing piles. The bidders had dwindled to Priapus and Mars.

Madonna della Rubia had instructed Laura to take no notice of the transactions, for to show interest in money was crass and detracted from the fantasy.

To mask her interest, she lowered her lashes. Priapus laid a ducat on his stack. Mars added two to his. Priapus bested the amount. So it went, on and on, until the towers of coins threatened to collapse.

So many ducats, thought Laura. Lesser amounts had purchased merchant galleys. Lesser amounts had sent Columbus across the Ocean Sea.

Then she saw Mars hesitate, his fingers buried deep in his leather bag of coins. A muffled curse came from behind the mask.

"Have you exhausted your fortune, *messere?*" Madonna della Rubia asked politely.

The amounts were equal. Priapus added one more ducat and gave a growl of triumph. "She's mine!"

Laura tried not to shiver as his friends began hooting and slapping him on the back.

Amid the hubbub, a gruff voice shouted, "Wait."

All eyes turned to Mars. He stepped forward, lifted his gloved hands, and unclasped a golden chain from around his neck. From the neckline of his tunic came a huge jewel. He laid it on the dais. The cabochon ruby, smooth and rounded, stared up at her like a giant unblinking eye. The jewel had a Byzantine flavor, surrounded by onyx and set off by a fiery border of diamonds.

Priapus stiffened as if he had been struck. His hand moved toward the jewel, but one of his friends pulled him back.

People crowded close to see. "It's beyond price," someone said.

"Not quite," another replied, "but it's worth twice the sum of all the gold combined."

Priapus stormed out with some of his friends in his wake.

Relieved at his departure, Laura turned her attention to the man dressed as Mars. If he truly was Sansovino, he could hardly afford the amount glittering before her. He must be mad.

She was still thinking this as the litter bore her to the opulent boudoir where the assignation would take place. Maidservants descended upon her, freshening her perfume, buffing her nails, untying her sandals, freeing her hair so that it tumbled down around her shoulders, covering her breasts and her back.

Laura endured it all with feigned good humor, forcing herself to laugh at the maids' bawdy jokes, pretending that it was completely appropriate that Venus and Mars, the lovers of myth, should become lovers in fact.

She caught a glimpse of herself in one of the many polished mirrors that graced the room. Outwardly she looked flushed, her eyes sparkling, her lips moist and red from the nervous chewing she had subjected them to.

Inside, she was dying by inches.

She barely noticed when the brigade of servants left, and was surprised to find herself alone. Alone with a sumptuous feast of wine and fruit and nuts on the table, a cheery fire crackling in the hearth, and a host of terrors clawing at her throat.

Like a cat in a cage, she paced the room. When she heard the click of the door latch, she froze.

Mars stepped into the room.

The firelight flashed over his golden mask and glittering winged helm. His shadow, flickering on the wall behind him, loomed huge and frightening, a darkness that threatened to swallow her up.

Laura burst into action. "Welcome, *messere*. Can I pour you some wine? It's a wonderful vintage."

Mars shook his head.

"Some fruit, perhaps." Laura knew she was babbling but could not stop herself. "The dates from Smyrna are large and sweet. Madonna della Rubia had these oranges brought from Jaffa just for—"

"I did not spend my coin for wine and fruit." His voice echoed, alien and hollow, behind the mask.

"Oh," said Laura. "Then what—" Her voice broke, and she cleared her throat. "What is your pleasure? Perhaps a game of chess or la Trappola. I painted the cards myself, and—"

"You, Laura. All I want is you." He reached up and removed his mask and helm.

Laura found herself staring into the hard, handsome, craggy face of Sandro Cavalli.

"My lord!" Her hands flew to her cheeks.

"Don't act so surprised," he bit out. "It was you who invited me to purchase your favors."

"Yes, but . . ." She felt hot and cold at once, clumsy and tongue-tied. And vastly relieved.

"But what?"

"You—you don't patronize brothels. You said so yourself."

His mouth curved into a smile. His ice-cold eyes robbed the expression of any humor or warmth. "In your case, I made an exception."

"Why?"

Setting his hands on his hips, he regarded her as a merchant might contemplate a bolt of cloth. "That's an odd question. When a man buys a whore, people rarely ask why, since the reason is obvious."

The lightness of relief dissipated. Her pride shriveled at the sound of the word "whore" on his lips. "But this is not right. We—we *know* each other."

He stroked his jaw. "I see. And losing your virginity is more proper with a stranger?"

"That's not what I meant."

"Then we should stop talking and get to the business at hand." Without warning, he sprang forward and captured her in his arms. His kiss was rough, demanding. His tongue plunged in and out of her mouth in a wildly suggestive rhythm. Laura's thoughts swirled in her head. She was relieved because it was Sandro. She was appalled because it was Sandro. She was terrified because it was Sandro.

She tried to pull away. He allowed her to step back. The color had risen high in his face. He reached out and unclasped the fastener at her shoulder. The wispy white garment drifted to the floor.

Sandro's breath stopped in his throat, creating a hard, throbbing lump that made it painful to swallow. He had not realized that his lesson in ethics would prove so difficult. He had envisioned a bad farce, with him playing the randy customer, frightening Laura into admitting she had been wrong.

Instead, he stood in front of her like a buffoon in a morality play who had forgotten his lines. He had been the one who was mistaken, thinking himself clever and cold-blooded enough to terrorize Laura Bandello.

She stood naked and unashamed, gazing calmly from her wide, blue-violet eyes. Her courage and her serene acceptance of his callous treatment infuriated him. He would have preferred to see her grow angry, fight, demand that he treat her with honor.

But she seemed to understand that a whore had no right to expect kindness from a man who had squandered his hard-earned money on her.

Sandro's conscience told him he had no business gawking at her. Nonsense, his reason countered. He had just laid down a year's profits for the privilege. Since he had no intention of actually going through with the sordid performance, the least he could do was enjoy the view.

She was even more lovely than she had been in Titian's studio. Her skin had the luster of pearls, glowing in the candlelight. Her legs seemed endless, rising to her gently flaring hips with the grace of an alabaster sculpture. Her breasts were perfection, pale mounds precisely the size of his cupped hands and tipped by the color of the rarest pink coral. Her hair was midnight fire, swirling around her face and shoulders, wafting gently in the heat from the hearth.

She was, he reflected bitterly, the ideal courtesan—
a heady mixture of feminine allure and wide-eyed
innocence. She had the power to drive a man insane.

The silence drew out long, plucking at his nerves
and his resolve.

"Is something . . . the matter?" she asked softly.

Sandro's lips tightened in annoyance. "Nothing's
the matter." *Except that I can't play the villain,
Laura. I want you too much.*

"Oh." Her shoulders lifted in a graceful shrug.
"Well, then . . . shall we retire to the bed?"

The bed. Sandro's mouth dried. His gaze darted to
the grand bed, its soaring posters and elaborate
draperies. The gleaming white satin counterpane billowed like a cloud.

"Ah, yes," he said, honing a cruel edge on his
words. "That's where your talents lie, isn't it?"

She paused, half turned toward the bed. Humiliation flooded her eyes. Her full lower lip trembled,
and she caught it in her teeth. "My talents are in art.
You, sir, purchased a virgin."

Sandro bit his tongue to keep himself from pouring
out apologies. Damn her! He had come here to show
her the error of her ways. Instead he found himself
wanting to gather her into his arms, to whisper endear-
ments in her ear, and to kiss the pain from her eyes.

"Come here," he blurted, and the order sounded
like a command he would give a laggardly *zaffo*.

His imperative tone stiffened her spine. Her show
of spirit pleased him. In Laura, he could abide any
mood except hurt. "Yes, my lord," she said and
returned to stand before him.

"Closer," he said, his gaze measuring the arm's
length that separated them.

She took one step, then two.

"Closer," he said.

She closed the remaining distance between them. Now he could smell her jasmine fragrance, feel the warmth of her bare skin, hear the little gusts of her nervous breathing. A vein pulsed gently in her throat. It was all he could do to keep from tasting her there.

"Kiss me," he said.

She swallowed audibly. "I rather thought it was up to the gentleman to take the lead."

"This gentleman laid down a fortune for you," he reminded her. "Kiss me now, Laura, and make me believe you're worth what I paid for this night."

Color flared in her cheeks. "I'm supposed to make you forget you paid for me."

He forced a laugh. "Ah, yes, all part of the fantasy. But I won't forget, Laura. I couldn't possibly forget."

"Damn you, Sandro," she whispered.

While he was still blinking in surprise at her use of his given name, she placed her hands flat against his chest. She ran them slowly upward, and the heat of her blatant yet curiously restrained caress took his breath away. Relentless, practiced, compelling, her hands slid to the tops of his shoulders and then met at the nape of his neck. She lifted her face to his. Her tongue slipped out to moisten her lips. Then she raised herself on tiptoe and touched her mouth to his.

As gentle and slow as the kiss was, Sandro perceived it as a blistering assault on his senses. Her tongue made a clever pattern of advance and retreat between his teeth. She captivated him with a sensual pull, made him forget his purpose. His arms, which he had held rigidly at his sides, went around her, his hands skimming over her smooth back.

She was Venus come to vivid life, darkly dangerous and knowingly carnal. She was a siren, luring him from his purpose. She was evil, a demon goddess. He had been wrong to think her pure and innocent.

Then he made a shocking discovery. Bitter, burning tears were flowing down her cheeks.

He thrust her away as if he had tasted poison. "Don't," he said. "Don't you dare weep."

She wiped her cheeks with the back of her hand. "I was trying not to."

"That's a lie," he said, knowing it wasn't. "If you hope to avoid the ordeal tonight by playing upon my sympathies, you're mistaken."

"Is that what you would call our night together?" she asked. "An ordeal?"

"You knew you would have to give yourself to some man, Laura, when you offered your body for sale."

"But I didn't think that man would be *you.*"

Sandro drew a sharp breath as if she had struck him. He understood exactly what she meant. She was weeping because she was going to have to give herself to Sandro Cavalli, a man too many years her senior, a battered old warrior who obviously disgusted her.

"That's one of the disadvantages to being a whore," he told her. "You don't get to choose your lovers. If an elderly man wishes to bed you, you have no choice but to submit."

"I suppose you're right." Turning, she walked to the bed. Donatello himself could not have sculpted a more perfect pair of buttocks. Sandro followed her, found her reclining on the white satin. A fallen angel, he thought, cradled on a cloud.

"Another disadvantage," he continued, lowering himself beside her, "is that you have no say in the way things are conducted."

She drew up one leg so that her dainty bare foot touched his calf. "What do you mean?"

Sandro forced himself to remember Imperia, the dying courtesan. He drew cruel words from the well of bitterness deep inside him. "I mean, madonna, that with a whore, a man feels free to exercise the perversities of his nature. With an honest woman, of course, he's honor bound to treat her with gentle respect."

She winced and shrank from him.

He winnowed his fingers into his hair and closed his fist. *Do you know how hard this is, Laura? How hard it is to hurt you?*

Remorselessly, he lowered his head and subjected her to a hard, bruising kiss that drew a small gasp from her. It was for her own good, he told himself as his hands moved over her with a savage possession that shamed him to his core. After tonight, she would never again sell her body to a stranger.

But despite the fact that his bullishness was all a cheap charade designed to show her what she was in for if she stayed in this profession, Sandro felt his body come to life.

Not slowly and predictably, as it did with his mistresses, but with a breath-stealing jolt that made the blood hammer deafeningly in his ears and sent his heart beating like a lustful youth's. The laces of his hose felt suddenly far too tight. His breath came in short, ragged gasps. He dragged his mouth from hers and slid his lips to her nipple, which his fingers had teased to hardness. She was sweet and tender; the taste and texture of her made him want to slow down, to savor her, to bring cries of genuine pleasure to her lips.

But seduction was not his purpose tonight. He bit her—not hard, but the graze of his teeth made her cry out softly. His hand plunged downward to explore her inner thighs. He forced her legs to part, and she offered no resistance.

Beg me to stop, Laura, he entreated her silently. *Please don't let me hurt you anymore.*

She didn't beg; she didn't say a word. In her own perverse fashion, she held to the courtesan's code of honor, which decreed that a man was entitled to what he had paid for.

It was her courage, and the ache of pity she inspired in Sandro, that finally defeated his purpose. In the end, he simply couldn't do it. Couldn't bring her pain, couldn't bring her sorrow. At his core he was a man of principle, and even his determination to prove Laura wrong couldn't shake that.

He lifted his mouth from her breast and raised himself on his elbow to gaze into her face. She was making a brave effort not to cry, her lips swollen and her eyes bright.

"Laura . . ." He meant only to brush his lips against hers as a gentle prelude to explaining what he was about. But somewhere he lost himself, and for the first time he kissed her the way he wanted to.

His tongue traced the full curve of her lower lip. Then he touched his mouth to hers, slowly moving his head from side to side. She sighed, and her body relaxed as if this was the kiss she had been waiting for.

She wasn't supposed to enjoy being ravished, Sandro thought as he gently closed his mouth over hers. Neither was he. But she was very close to achieving her goal of making him forget he had paid for her. Very, very close.

She had an uncanny talent for destroying the best of intentions; there was about her an air of fragility that made him want to deny what she was trying to become, and cherish her for the woman she really was.

The admission seemed to release all the tenderness he kept guarded so closely in his heart. "My God," he whispered, "you tear me to pieces, Laura. You're beautiful. Too much so." He caressed her body lightly, slowly . . . lovingly. Holding her close to his heart gave rise to strange, poetic visions—eating oranges in bed, taking afternoon naps, shirking all his duties and cares to spend a lifetime with her.

"One touch of your lips," he murmured, tasting her mouth, "and my soul turns to kindling. God, Laura! You make me want to fly away with you into a sky of perpetual sunrises. You make me realize that I never truly wanted anything in my life . . . until you."

She made a small sound in her throat and reached for him, and at that moment Sandro felt something burst inside him and take flight, the release of feelings he had kept imprisoned in his heart for years. He wanted to sweep her into his arms, take her away and close her in a charmed bower where no one else could touch her.

A knock at the door rescued him from the madness. Sandro fell still; even in his passion-fevered mind he recognized the three short raps, followed by a pause and then two more. Jamal.

Yasmin's voice was hissing something in Arabic; she was obviously trying to keep Jamal from disturbing them. Then the knock sounded again.

Saved, thought Sandro, half-relieved as he rolled off the bed and drew the drapes around Laura. Jamal had saved him from falling victim to the most dangerous peril of all: love.

He jerked the door open. Yasmin glared at him dangerously. Jamal looked as frustrated as Sandro felt. "What is it?"

Jamal motioned someone forward. Sandro recognized one of the men he had assigned to guard the *bravo* in the hospital.

"My lord." The man bowed. "The assassin had a brief period of recovery."

"Excellent," said Sandro. "I'll question him in the morn—"

"Beg pardon, my lord, but a mishap has occurred."

Fury tightened like a band across Sandro's chest. "What sort of mishap?"

"He's been stabbed, my lord. The doctors don't expect him to survive."

Sandro didn't bother to ask how a murderer had slipped past the guards; he would deal with that later. "Wait for me below," he ordered, then slammed the door. Stalking back to the bed, he yanked the curtain aside.

Laura was sitting up, wrapped in the coverlet, her knees drawn to her chest. She gazed at him with huge, sorrowful eyes. "I never meant for him to die."

Sandro yearned to pull her into his arms. She made every instinct inside him leap up to protect her. "It's not your fault," he said gruffly, then touched her cheek. "Wait for me, Laura. I'll be back."

9

Oil lamps lit the corridor of the hospital. Sandro hurried to the ward where the *bravo*, Vincente la Bocca, lay dying.

A doctor and his assistant, two nuns, a priest, and a police guard clustered around the low bed.

The assassin's face was the color of parchment. His forehead gleamed from the olive oil with which the priest had anointed him. His open eyes stared at nothing.

Sandro felt no pity, no compassion. This man—this murderer—could be the key to unlock the murders. In addition to a lifetime of petty crimes, la Bocca had tried twice to kill Laura. He inspired nothing but displeasure in Sandro.

Coldly eyeing la Bocca, Sandro knelt beside the bed. "Has he said anything? His true name? His purpose?"

"He's been babbling, my lord, calling for his mother." The doctor shook his head. "All dying men call for their mothers."

Sandro touched the man's shoulder. "Vincente. Can you hear me?"

The glazed eyes blinked slowly.

"Can you speak?" Sandro waited. The stench of death was strong, familiar, and unforgettable. The dark smell of a wasted life.

The victim wagged his head from side to side and made a gagging sound in his throat.

Sandro glanced up at the guard. "Where were you when he was attacked?"

"That's the strange thing, my lord. Conti and I were right here." He gestured at a wooden bench. "The poor wretch had just awakened, and we called in the doctor. Not an hour later, I noticed a pool of blood under his cot."

Sandro studied the thick compress on the man's side. "I want to see the wound."

The doctor bent and removed the blood-soaked pad. Sandro stared at the livid, open gash. "A knife wound," he said, thinking aloud. "The blade was small. . . ." Small enough to fit in someone's sleeve or boot. But whose?

"Who has visited this man since he awakened?" Sandro demanded. "I gave orders that he was not to be disturbed."

"Only the usual persons," said the guard. "The doctors and their assistants, nuns and priests. Some of the patients have family members who visit them, but no one has come to claim la Bocca as his own."

Sandro rubbed his jaw, feeling suddenly old. Funny, he hadn't thought about feeling old during his hours with Laura, her disgust at his advanced age notwithstanding. "I'll want the name of everyone who visited the hospital," he said distractedly.

"We don't keep a tally, my lord," the doctor said. "It's never been nec—" He broke off as the patient started to gasp. He wheezed in a sudden effort to speak. An ominous sound rattled in his chest.

The priest launched into the prayer of extreme unction. The nuns added their voices to his. At the same time, the assassin began to speak.

Frustrated beyond control, Sandro roared at the priest, "Be silent!" Stunned into obedience, the cleric stopped his praying. The nuns, too, quieted and shrank into their cowls. Sandro leaned forward, his ear close to the patient's mouth.

". . . all for the cause, but I didn't . . . didn't know about . . . the madness . . . or the others . . ." The death rattle clicked in his throat.

It was over, Sandro realized, staring at the still body. He'd come too late. The assassin had died, taking his secrets with him.

Or perhaps not. Sandro pondered the garbled, whispered words the man had uttered. *For the cause . . . the madness . . . the others.* Every word was obscure.

Sandro stared down at the assassin in his unnatural sleep.

The cause . . . Sandro's instinct told him that this "cause" meant a plot against the doge. Still, he had nothing but the whispered word of a dying murderer.

He gave clipped instructions to the doctor. If anyone returned to visit la Bocca, he wanted to know without delay.

A bell tolled the hour. "Night's still young," the doctor said, rolling down his sleeves.

Sandro snapped to attention. He yearned to escape from this place of death and disease. He intended to finish what he had started with Laura.

* * *

Laura stared at the last candle left burning. The others had guttered and gone out, but one remained, measuring the endless minutes of Sandro's absence. She had not stirred from the bed, and in the slowly passing hours had discovered every lump and ripple in the mattress. Obviously comfort was not the purpose of this bed.

No one had disturbed her; perhaps everyone assumed Sandro was still with her.

Sounds of revelry drifted from the *salone* below, and the laughter only served to intensify her misery. She had wept until she had no more tears. Nothing had gone as planned. The last person she had expected this night was Sandro Cavalli.

Now, hours later, she realized that she could never be a courtesan. Could never let a man touch her so intimately, hold such awful power over her. She should have listened to Sandro, should have listened to poor dying Imperia. Should have listened to her heart, which cried out for love and rebelled against anything less.

As she stared at the guttering candle on the nightstand, the flame shrank to a tiny blue orb, then went out with a quiet hiss. All her soul searching, all her emotion, washed over her in a great wave of fatigue. She pulled up the coverlet and drifted off to sleep.

A sound awakened her from a dream she could not remember. She knew only that it was full of lovely, calm images painted in soft azure and muted gold. Her sleep-fogged mind grasped at it. But the wonderful dream slipped away like dust through her parted fingers, and reluctantly she drew herself to wakefulness.

She heard footsteps and blinked in the dimness. "My lord?"

The bed curtains parted. A black shape loomed before her. Suddenly she knew the answer to her confusion. She did want Sandro, even if one night was all he would give her. She stretched her arms toward him, awaiting his touch.

Instead, she received a stunning blow to the head and a mouthful of fabric. Someone pinned her back against the gulls-down pillows. The rough, smelly rag muffled her wail of terror. She struggled, screaming until her throat burned with the effort.

She tried to make sense of what was happening. Whispered curses and low, sinister laughter. Grasping hands. Cord biting into her wrists. She thrashed her head from side to side; then a pillow smashed down on her face. Her movements slowed, weakened. The color of hopelessness and terror was black. Deep, impenetrable black.

Sandro stood outside the door of the room where Laura waited. The distant strains of music and laughter came from the main hall below. He heard Jamal's retreating footsteps as the African made his way to Yasmin's chamber. On the way back to the *ridotto,* Jamal had explained, with scribbled notes and hand signs, that he had fought a giant for the right to spend the night with the slave woman. Amazing, thought Sandro. After all these years, Jamal had fallen in love. Pity it was with a whore.

His fist closed around the cool glass doorknob. He would never make such a fatal error. He intended to enter the room, inform Laura that she was to leave the *ridotto* at once, and convince her to accept his patronage so she could pursue her career without worrying about money.

It was a neat, cold solution. Sandro tried to feel satisfaction, but felt only bleakness. It was not like the business transactions that brought him so much money and gratification. The notion left him feeling curiously hollow.

He twisted the knob, opened the door, and stepped inside. The candles had all gone out; a heavy silence muffled the sounds of revelry below. A breeze rustled the drapes of the tall window. Laura must have opened the window, and he wondered why, for the night was chilly. She must have helped herself to wine, too, and clumsily; the sour smell pervaded the air. He felt guilty that he had driven her to drink.

He paused at the foot of the bed, loath to part the drapes and awaken her. But perhaps in a drowsy state she would be amenable to his persuasion.

Even as he reached for the edge of the curtain, his body responded with the hard heat of arousal. Surprised and dismayed, he promised himself he would not give in to the pounding urge to take her.

He swept open the drapes and whispered, "Laura."

The dim glow of the dying hearth fire fell upon an empty bed.

Alarm jolted in Sandro's chest. He forced himself to stay calm. Hurrying out to the hallway, he seized a tall candle from a wall sconce and went to search the room.

Linens lay in a trail toward the window. A cup of wine had fallen to the floor. Sandro told himself she had gone to one of her friends, perhaps to the kitchen or the necessary room.

But all signs indicated that Laura had been taken from the room against her will. She had suffered two attempts on her life. Would her attackers succeed tonight where the others had failed?

Keeping his alarm in check, he approached Madonna della Rubia and informed her that Laura had vanished. Within minutes his inquiry was sent out among the guests, whose numbers had dwindled considerably over the course of the evening.

The result was what Sandro had dreaded. Laura was gone. Missing.

In an icy state of fear, he summoned Jamal and the *zaffi* he had assigned to the *ridotto*. Jamal arrived with Yasmin in tow. She wore a beautiful caftan and a look of concern on her face. Understandably fearful of Sandro's wrath, the policemen shuffled their feet.

He vented it quickly, efficiently, upbraiding his men for their negligence, then organizing a search party.

Titian and Aretino, though deep in their cups, offered to help. "What scoundrel could have abducted her?" Titian demanded.

Aretino removed his Bacchus mask. His face was flushed and sweaty. "Were it another of these tarts, I'd say it was too delicious. But Laura . . . Tell me, Sandro. Who was that rival of yours?"

"Priapus," Sandro said with distaste. The man had beggared him earlier in the evening.

"We know that, but who the devil was he?"

Sandro shook his head. "I don't know."

"You do not?" Amazed, Yasmin stepped forward. "After you took Laura off, he . . . used one of the other girls. And not gently."

Sandro swung around to face her. "Damn it, woman, don't play games. Who was he?"

Yasmin's beautifully sculpted nostrils flared. "My lord, he was your son."

Your son . . . your son . . . your son . . . The words pounded in a dirgelike rhythm through Sandro's brain. The horror pursued him as he left the brothel, followed by a handful of men and Yasmin, and headed for his house.

Damn! He should have recognized Marcantonio's scheme earlier. The large sum he had recently drawn from the treasury approached the amount he had offered for Laura. He had planned carefully, Sandro thought. But not carefully enough. He had not reckoned on his father finding out. The abduction had been an act of desperation, perpetrated by a selfish young man. But damn him, it had worked. Sandro forced himself to wonder how low Marcantonio would stoop in exacting revenge from the woman who had spurned him.

He did not expect to find Marcantonio at the house, but wanted to question the servants. They stood before him, rubbing the sleep from their eyes. "I'm looking for Messere Marcantonio," he informed them. "Can you tell me where he went?"

The cook shuffled forward, twisting the ends of his long mustache around his finger. "To the company galley, my lord. He ordered a feast to be taken there."

"A feast?" Sandro envisioned the seduction, and it made him sick.

"Yes, my lord. A feast for thirty-one."

Sandro's blood ran cold. He remembered Marcantonio's recent meetings with thirty of his wastrel friends; including Marcantonio, that made thirty-one. Trentuno.

* * *

"The Trentuno?" Laura whispered in a shaking voice as she stared in horror at Marcantonio Cavalli. He had removed his mask to reveal his cruel, beautiful face.

She tugged at the silken cord that restrained her. She stood on the open deck of the flat-keeled galley. Her arms were outspread, each wrist bound to the midships rail. The cool night breeze plucked at her robe. A ring of leering young men surrounded her. Some of the young men were eating cold roast capon; all were drinking wine at a furious rate.

The dark water of the lagoon slapped against the hull, and the timbers creaked as the galley tugged at its cables. Torches blazed along the rail, reflected in the calm water. In the distance blinked the lights of Venice.

"The Trentuno?" she repeated.

Marcantonio gave her a charming smile. "I assume you understand what that is, *bellissima.*"

His friends laughed and elbowed one another. Now that they were unmasked, she recognized many of them; they were the sons of the noblest clans of la Serenissima and beyond. Titian himself had painted some of their portraits. Others had visited the *ridotto* from time to time.

Noblemen, she told herself. Sons of the republic. The thought brought no comfort. They need not treat a common whore with honor; had Sandro not warned her only tonight?

Marcantonio touched her chin, forcing her to look at him. She saw a comely, smiling man, but now she looked past the beauty to the decayed soul that lay behind it.

"Answer me, darling. Do you, or do you not understand the tradition of the Trentuno?"

Laura did; Imperia had described the act to her. Still, Laura saw feigning ignorance as a way to stall for time. Her head throbbed where she had been struck, and her mouth was dry from the rag that had stifled her screams until the galley had been rowed out and anchored in this isolated spot on the open water. Belowdecks, the galley oarsmen waited on their benches, resting from their hasty voyage out into the lagoon. Laura wondered if she could find help from them; then she realized the foolishness of her hope. Marcantonio and his friends had provided a cask of wine; no *galleoto* would bestir himself to come to the aid of a whore.

"I have never heard of this Trentuno." Her tongue felt thick and dry with fear.

Marcantonio laughed low in his throat. "Then we shall be the first to show you the tradition. Satisfying men is one of the imperatives of your profession, and it's best you understand that."

"I assume," she said, refusing to give in to the panic that clawed at her throat, "that I am privileged to have you noble gentlemen explain it to me."

He ran his hand slowly up and down her arm. She flinched at his cold, feathery touch.

"Ah, but she's charming, isn't she?" Marcantonio glanced over his shoulder. "Show her the broadside, Adolfo."

Adolfo was the heir of the duke of Urbino. Unlike Marcantonio, who masked his malice behind a charming smile, Adolfo wore an expression that was blatantly cruel. He carried himself with the quick, lithe grace of a swordsman. His dark features opened into a grin of lust and triumph. He unfurled a document. "We had these printed up to distribute in the morning," he said. "The printing was done by Aldus, for we only use the best."

Laura's heart skipped a beat. She had discovered a dead man at the shop of Aldus.

Before she could make sense of the thought, the words in large, bold type sprang out at her. What she read would have sent her to her knees had she not been tied to the stout rail. The broadside read: "On 16 February 1531, Laura Bandello satisfied everyone."

Although fright was tearing her apart, she feigned an expression of confusion. "I don't understand."

Marcantonio answered, "You will, *bellissima.* Very soon you will." He leaned close to her ear and whispered, "And you'll wish you'd accepted my offer, bitch."

"Pity Mars had her first," remarked a man Laura recognized as Tomaso, nephew of the marquis of Mantua.

"It's better that way," said someone else. "We won't have to fight for the honor of the *nozze solenne.*"

"Who do you suppose he was?" asked Adolfo, stroking his chin.

Marcantonio squeezed her breast through the fabric of her robe. "And how was he, Laura? I know you have no basis for comparison, but was he good?"

The question touched off a flame of defiance that burned through her terror. She jerked as far away from him as her bonds would allow. "I assure you," she stated loudly, "he was your superior in every way."

The young men burst into laughter. Glass clinked as they saluted her show of spirit and drank deeply.

Marcantonio drew in his breath with a hiss and raised his hand to strike her. Laura refused to give him the satisfaction of making her cower.

As Marcantonio's hand descended, Adolfo caught it. "Not so fast, friend," he warned. "Don't wear her out before we all get a chance."

Marcantonio dropped his hand. "Right."

Some of the young men threw themselves upon the feast of capons and Bologna sausage and bowls of figs. They drank more and more wine, guzzling until most of them were staggering drunk. For courage, Laura thought contemptuously.

"We didn't set a place for you," Adolfo said with mock regret. He tossed a heel of bread overboard. "We didn't think you'd feel like eating."

Laura's mind reeled. She nearly gave in to the terror. Then another man appeared, stepping over the platters of picked-over bones. He wore a shoulder badge bearing the arms of the House of Otranto. In contrast to his leering companions, this man—he was a youth, actually, with only a few sprouts of a beard—looked solemn, almost scholarly.

"Perhaps," he said, holding out a flask, "we should give her some of this opiated wine. T-to calm her down."

Marcantonio regarded Laura speculatively. Never taking his eyes off her, he said, "No, I think not, Giulio. I want her to feel . . . everything."

As he waited for his gondola to be brought to the landing, Sandro kept his gaze fastened on the bobbing line of lights that marked his galley. God. *His* galley.

Bile boiled in his throat. He had known Marcantonio to be lazy and easy in his conscience. But never in his darkest imaginings had Sandro considered his son capable of this brutality.

Shame stole over him. Where had Marcantonio learned his evil? How had Sandro failed him?

"Let's go," he said, leaping into the gondola the second it arrived. Guido Lombardo and Jamal joined him. "Yasmin, you stay here."

With a fluid, feline motion, she poured herself into the gondola. "I am coming with you and Jamal."

"No. It could be dangerous."

"I am certain that it will be. But if what we fear has come to pass, Laura will need me."

The quiet reasoning tore at Sandro's heart. The gondola cut a swift wake through the black water. Sandro demanded silence, for they would need the element of surprise if the rescue was to succeed.

He tried not to think about what might be happening aboard the galley. He tried not to remember other cases of Trentuno that he had investigated. One woman had bled to death; others had turned to the shelter of convents. Still others, Sandro had heard, had gone mad.

What would Laura do if, God forbid, he arrived too late?

He wanted to urge the gondolier to hurry, but dared not speak. They were too close, and voices carried across the water. The air rang with the boisterous laughter of young men in the midst of an adventure.

The sound set him aflame with fury. And fear.

The gondola glided alongside the galley. Lombardo

expertly ran a line through an outrigger on the galley
so the gondola would not drift. Sandro could hear
the voices clearly now, could pick out Marcantonio's
ringing laughter and the good-natured, drunken talk
of his companions.

From Laura, he heard nothing.

With his jaw set in grim determination, he hefted
the weapon he had brought, caught hold of the deck
rail, and pulled himself up the side of the hull. It had
been years since Sandro had performed a rescue in
stealth; such acts of daring were better suited to
younger men. He was surprised by his own agility, by
the lightness of his tread as he dropped soundlessly
to the foredeck.

Laura told herself not to struggle. Fighting them
now would only bring her more pain, more injury.
Still, she could not keep from baring her teeth at a
leering face when it loomed close, from kicking out
at men's legs encased in expensive silk hose.

"Damn it!" Tomaso roared, pitching a chicken leg
over the side. "Hold her still, will you?"

Hands grabbed at her, and her kicking legs were
subdued.

"I want the dress off," said Adolfo. Boisterous
cheers of assent greeted his words.

He reached down and grabbed the neckline of her
garment, giving it a hard tug. "Damn. The thing's
sewn as stoutly as sail cloth."

"Just hike it up," someone shouted.

"*Dio!* Can't you stop her from kicking?" Adolfo
demanded as her foot shoved at his chest. "Let's just
tie—"

"That's enough," Marcantonio said, his voice edgy.

"What? We've not even begun." Adolfo eyed him incredulously.

"Adolfo, we discussed the plan, remember? I only did this to scare the wench. You all agreed! You swore! I just wanted to shame her."

"That's what *you* wanted, friend. What I want, I mean to take right now." Adolfo tugged at the lace points of his codpiece.

"Oh, God," Laura whispered. Sandro would never know she was gone. She nearly begged for mercy, but knew that would only amuse them. She repeated the Pater Noster in her mind but the horror would not go away. Adolfo stood before her, and others lined up behind him, waiting their turn with drunken impatience. A knife appeared from somewhere. The blade descended, razor edge out, toward Laura's robe.

Laura inhaled, gathering her voice in her throat to scream. The blade touched her robe.

"Hold!" A furious voice broke through the ranks of men.

Adolfo straightened, gripping the hilt of the poniard. Laura dragged herself up on her elbows and looked toward the bow of the galley.

"Corpo di Cristo," Marcantonio whispered.

Torchlight flared over the powerful figure of Sandro Cavalli. He stood with his back to the deckhouse, his black cloak fluttering in the night breeze, his booted feet planted wide. In his hands he held a large firearm of some sort, the iron barrel pointed at the group of men.

Laura shrank back against the deck rail. "Thank God," she whispered, tears of relief pouring down her face. "Oh, thank God."

"Step away from her," Sandro ordered, jerking the firearm to one side. "Now."

For a moment, no one moved. Then the Otranto youth shuffled toward the rail. A few others started to join him.

"Cowards!" Adolfo yelled, raising his knife. "Draw your weapons. He's but one man. We'll have him floating face down in the lagoon before he can say Ave Maria."

"Damn it, Adolfo," Marcantonio said through clenched teeth, "he's my father."

"Yes, and it isn't the first time he's interfered in the business of nobles," Adolfo shot back. "Come!" he shouted to the others. "Stand with me if you be true sons of the republic!"

A few others drew dress swords or daggers, some of them defiantly; others halfheartedly. A small knot of men advanced a few steps toward Sandro.

Laura expected him to retreat in fear, but he merely threw them a contemptuous look and said, "It's true, the lot of you could attack, and I'd fall under your numbers. However"—he shoved the stock of the gun snugly against his shoulder—"I'd be compelled to take at least one of you with me. Just out of spite." He gave a dry chuckle. "You see, I'm a spiteful man."

Laura gaped at her furious, cloaked rescuer. She had never thought Lord of the Night a fitting title for so honorable a man as Sandro Cavalli, but now she saw another side of him. A side that was as dark and wrathful as an avenging angel.

The advancing group slowed, then stopped.

"Come on," Adolfo said angrily. "He's bluffing, can't you see that?"

"Maybe I am, my young puppy," said Sandro. "But then again, maybe not. Of course, there's one way to find out." He sighted down the barrel. "This is a military gun, Brescian, I think. German soldiers stake their lives on it. They say it can tear a hole the size of a cannonball in a man."

"Jesus!" said the Mantuan youth, flinging down his dress sword. "No wench is worth that."

Following his lead, the others placed their weapons on the deck. Only Adolfo remained, gripping his knife, feet planted in a combative stance.

"Will you force me to shoot then, my good lord of Urbino?" Sandro inquired politely.

"You wouldn't dare. My father would have you strung up in the piazza if you brought me harm."

"Quite true, my dear heathen cub," Sandro agreed. "However, you'd never live to see my shame, would you?"

Adolfo moved as swiftly as a shadow. In less than a second, he had stepped behind Laura and grabbed a handful of her hair. The cold blade of the poniard pressed into the flesh of her throat.

"Is it a game of bluff-and-yield, my lord?" Adolfo asked triumphantly. "The question is, who will bluff and who will yield?"

Laura saw the change creep over Sandro's torchlit features. He lost the look of the dark avenger; rage and defeat crept over his face. He was going to give up, all because this pup from Urbino was threatening her.

"No!" she shouted. Her foot came up and landed hard on Adolfo's instep. Howling, he hopped on one foot, but did not fall. As he lunged toward her, a hand clamped onto his wrist and hauled him back.

"Enough, Adolfo," said Marcantonio.

The duke's son glared at Marcantonio. He wrenched his wrist free, but Marcantonio plucked the knife from his hand and sent it sailing over the side. Weak with relief, Laura slithered to the deck.

A moment later, led by Jamal, the galley oarsmen appeared from below.

A furious oath exploded from Adolfo.

"Well done," said Sandro, flinging back his cloak and strolling down the deck. Studying his weapon for a moment, he held out the gun to Guido Lombardo. "You know," he mused, "I really must learn to use one of these things someday."

He gave his captives a terrible pirate's smile. "I hope you gentlemen don't mind a bit of exertion." He drilled Marcantonio with an icy stare. Even Laura winced at the cold fury in Sandro's eyes.

Marcantonio flung up his head in defiance. "My lord, what's your intent?"

"I think you gentlemen could do with a stint at the oars."

Protests burst from the young lords, but most went willingly, if sullenly. Laura watched Adolfo, the most hateful of the lot, being marched along by Jamal himself. As they moved toward the hatchway, Adolfo seemed to stumble. Only Laura, lying on the deck, saw him draw a stiletto from his boot.

"Jamal, look out!" she screamed.

He did not apprehend the danger quickly enough. The pointed blade drove upward. At the same moment, a dark, slim shape sprang out of the shadows of the deck saloon and landed on Adolfo's back.

"Yasmin!" Laura whispered in amazement.

The tall woman clung like a cat to her prey. She

sank her teeth into Adolfo's arm while her long, lacquered nails tore into his eyes. He let out a horrible yell and dropped the stiletto. Glass shattered on the deck and the liquid seeped into the planks. Jamal hammered Adolfo with a clublike fist. The young lord crumpled to the deck. Yasmin placed her hands with palms together and laughingly made a salaam.

At that moment, a shadow fell over Laura. Instinctively she strained at her bonds. "Don't touch me! Please don't—"

"Hush, it's me." Sandro knelt beside her.

She understood that he had come to help, but could not stop herself from shrinking from his touch. "Oh, God," she whispered. "No . . ."

"Easy," he said, and his voice broke, surprising her with a show of emotion. He closed his eyes and spoke through clenched teeth. "Thank God," he said. "Thank God you're all right."

Then he seemed to conquer himself and reached for her again. And once again, she remembered the terror, fought her bonds, and tried to elude his touch.

"Please Laura, be still. I won't hurt you. No one will ever hurt you again."

She held herself rigid to still her trembling. The aftermath of horror left her weak and vulnerable.

Keeping up a low, steady murmur of meaningless yet reassuring talk, Sandro cut her bonds and helped her to her feet.

He opened his arms and stood back.

At last she realized the enormity of what he had done for her. Sobbing, she fell into his waiting arms.

10

Wrapped in blankets woven of the softest wool, Laura sat at a window in Sandro's house and gazed out at the dawning day. A thick mist swirled in from the lagoon and snaked along the canals and streets between the tall gray buildings. Church spires seemed to float on the clouds. Street sweepers, wielding twig brooms with curved handles, emerged like ghosts from the fog. A few barges sunk low with water and wood from the mainland slipped along the Grand Canal. The wide-mouthed chimney pots exhaled threads of smoke into the air.

Laura pressed her cheek against the cool stone window embrasure. At this hour, Venice lived up to her name of la Serenissima. The city was serene, a peaceful old woman drawing a cloak of mist around her.

Laura felt an urge to sketch the disembodied spires and chimney pots, but she denied herself. The moment she touched pencil to paper, the turbulence inside her, boiling up like bile in her chest, would turn the tranquil sunrise into an inferno of violence.

She shivered and glanced over her shoulder at

Yasmin, who slept soundly on the bed of the guest room. Laura had yet to close her eyes, for she feared the monsters that were sure to haunt her dreams.

The sound of voices raised in anger drifted from a window below her. Sandro and Marcantonio, she realized. The chief magistrate of the Night Lords had caught his son in the midst of a heinous act. Father and son would never be the same. Laura felt no pity for Marcantonio; he deserved his father's wrath and worse, but her heart ached for Sandro. How it must hurt to know his child was capable of such cruelty.

It was for Sandro's sake that Laura dressed herself in a dull gold damask robe from the chest at the foot of the bed, for his sake that she hurried barefoot down the cold marble stairs toward Sandro's offices. It might comfort him to know that Marcantonio had meant only to frighten her; it was Adolfo who had caused matters to get out of hand. Also, Sandro must be told that Adolfo had gotten his broadsheets printed at the establishment of Aldus.

She rapped lightly on the office door and stepped inside without waiting to be invited. Sandro stood with his palms pressed to the desk. He leaned toward Marcantonio, a furious expression on his face. Both men looked haggard, whiskers sprouting along their jawlines and dark circles under their eyes. Sandro had the look of a wounded man.

Laura spared not a glance for Marcantonio. "My lord," she said, "there's something you must understand about last night."

Sandro's expression softened. "Shouldn't you be abed?"

"I couldn't sleep, my lord. I think you should know, M—" She could not say his name. "Your son did not mean to injure me last night."

Marcantonio huffed out a sigh of relief. "I told you—"

"Silence." Sandro glared at him. "He claims he merely wanted to give you a fright." Then he turned his gaze on Laura, and it was a probing, professional look designed to spot a falsehood.

"It's true," she said. "When . . . matters started to get ugly, he did raise a protest."

"You see, Father?" Marcantonio said triumphantly. "I had only the best of intentions. I believed Laura should be dissuaded from choosing the life of a courtesan."

Sandro's eyes widened in genuine surprise, and she wondered if Marcantonio's intent was truly so noble.

Then she remembered his whispered words: *I want her to feel . . . everything.* He had meant to punish her for rejecting his affections, not save her from life in a brothel. Still, if the lie would banish the agony from Sandro's eyes, she would raise no protest.

"He used poor judgment," she said, "and for that he has earned your censure. But as to the other . . . matter—"

"The matter!" Sandro burst out, his forearms bulging with muscles as he planted his hands on his hips. "It would have been rape. A brutal mass attack. You could have died. Whatever his reasons, my noble son is responsible."

She stared at the floor.

"Laura, you must bring charges against every one of them," Sandro commanded. "My son included."

Marcantonio stiffened, and resentment gleamed in his eyes.

"It's too much to hope for a sentence of death against noblemen, but you could demand banishment." He glowered at his son. "Regardless of the

verdict, you will leave at once for Swabia to manage
our dairy concerns there."

"Swabia!" Marcantonio jumped back as if his
father had unsheathed a knife. "Jesus! That's beyond
the pale of the civilized world."

"Precisely," Sandro snapped. "You belong there."

Marcantonio aimed a malicious sidelong glance at
his father. "And if I refuse?"

Sandro's face changed. It was as if some inferno
sprang to life inside him. His eyes flared; he seemed
to grow and swell. "Try me, Marcantonio," he said in
a low, deadly voice. "Just try me. I'll bind and gag
you, and put you on the ship myself."

Marcantonio deflated before his father's fiery regard.
The young lord was still beautiful, Laura observed, but it
was a wilted, corrupt beauty, all the more evident in the
face of Sandro's sudden passionate vitality.

"You're to leave on the evening tide," Sandro
informed him. "Go to your rooms at once and start
packing."

Marcantonio drew himself up with an effort. He
seemed about to reply, but the terrible incandescence
on Sandro's face stopped him. Turning on his heel, he
marched from the room.

His whispered invective to Laura as he passed by
chilled her to the bone, but she held her face impassive,
not reacting to his insult or to his stench of sweat, wine,
and sea air that brought memories of her ordeal flooding
back. If she allowed even the slightest crack in her
façade, she would crumble like an ancient fresco.

She stared across the room at Sandro. Unbidden
came earlier memories: discovering he had laid down
a fortune to purchase her innocence. Her initial terror
of his savage embrace. His brusque attempt to scare

her. And then his fierce tenderness, the sudden burning glory of his caresses, the sweet wine of his kisses. With skilled, subtle hands he had changed from demanding seducer to tender lover. Had they not been interrupted, she would have given herself to him fully. The possibility snatched her breath.

"—the necessary papers to secure the arrests," he was saying.

Startled out of an explicit fantasy involving hard-muscled limbs and soft, sweet kisses, Laura blushed. "I'm sorry, my lord. I wasn't listening."

"I said, we need to draw up papers so I can arrest your abductors."

Her hands flew to her face. "No!"

"What?"

Reliving the event in her mind renewed her terror. "I won't bring charges against those men."

"They're knaves, villains. They tried to hurt you, Laura."

She thought of the young nobles chained to the galley oars. In her mind's eye, thirty-one patrician faces glared at her. She envisioned herself trying to bring the sons of Venice to justice.

"It won't work, and you of all people should know it," she said bleakly. "The high courts would scorn a known courtesan. My future as a painter would be ruined. I'd never win commissions if I offended the nobility. I'd be giving up a lifetime of dreams for the doubtful possibility of winning revenge, my lord."

"You're a fool, then. Will you buy your success with your body and your silence?"

His words turned the air in the room cold. "We'll speak of it no more, my lord. Instead, I want to tell you something Adolfo said last night."

Sandro's hands pressed on the desk until his knuckles shone white. "Yes?"

"He had those broadsides printed by Aldus. After what he tried to do to me, I don't think it beneath him to have committed other . . ." She shuddered. "Other crimes."

Sandro stood very still, but she could see the thoughts flickering like clockwork behind his eyes.

"We should investigate the possibility," she said.

"I shall. You needn't worry about that, for you're still shaken. The events of last night—"

"Yes," she said angrily. "Let us talk about last night. Why did you leave me?" The question burst out; she had not meant to sound so accusing.

He flinched, and his guilt was tangible—the set of his shoulders, the grim and agonized lines of his face. "Laura." He came around the desk and held out both hands.

Suddenly she saw other hands reaching for her, grasping. She backed away. His eyes rounded in amazement and consternation. Then he pressed his arms to his sides. "They should pay for the fear I see in your eyes."

"My lord, I mean no insult," she said, twisting her fingers into the folds of the gold robe. "It's just that . . . I welcome no one's touch at the moment."

"Forgive me. Laura, you must believe that if I'd known what was going to happen, nothing could have dragged me from your, er"—incredibly, he blushed—"from your side."

"Then why did you go?" She remembered the concern in Jamal's eyes, the urgency of the *zaffo*'s whisper. "What's happened?"

"The *bravo* who attacked you has died." His face pulled taut; the lines of strain about his eyes and mouth deepened. A day's growth of whiskers gave him a dark, shadowy look.

Shock and grief rushed over Laura. She pressed her hands to her throat and shook her head in denial, even as the truth screamed through her. "My God," she whispered, "I killed him."

"No," Sandro said hurriedly, leaning forward as if he wanted to hold her. "He was recovering. In fact, he regained consciousness, was beginning to speak." Sandro's eyes darkened. "He was killed—stabbed—in the hospital."

She felt the color drain from her face. "But who? Why?"

"I know only that it must be the same animal who performed the other killings. The *bravo* knew something about this plot and had to be silenced before he could tell me."

Laura sank to a nearby chair. Sandro's grief, his sense of futility, weighted her down as well.

"I arrived just as he was breathing his last," Sandro finished grimly.

Laura winced at the self-hatred in his face. She knew what he was thinking. While he was dallying with her, a man was being savagely murdered by a villain who had eluded him for several frustrating weeks.

"Did he say anything to you?" she asked, consumed with the need to know.

"Yes, but I can't make sense of it. Something about—" Sandro broke off, and his head snapped up. "This is police business, and I've no call to discuss it with a civilian."

Laura shot to her feet, her terror over the ordeal the previous night suddenly forgotten. "A civilian?" she demanded. "Is that all I am to you, my lord?"

His posture took on that tight, controlled, defensive stance she was beginning to recognize and resent. "Yes," he said.

"Oh, I see." Rage gave life to her legs; she paced the room like a soldier on parade. "Simply a civilian." She brought herself face to face with him and stood on tiptoe to glare into his eyes. "Not the person who gave you your first lead about Moro. Not the person so close to the truth that two attempts have been made on my life. Not the person who was responsible for your seizing the *bravo* in the first place, and—"

"Laura." He took a step back, looking surprised and, oddly, not displeased by her burst of temper. His dark eyes aglow, his sculpted mouth quirked, he said, "All that is quite true, but—"

"I'm not finished." She dipped into her far-too-small reserve of courage and delved to the heart of the matter. "The true reason I deserve to know all the facts of this case is that, last night, we nearly became lovers."

For the second time this morning, and probably for the second time in his life, Sandro Cavalli blushed. "No." His denial was swift and certain. "Nothing could be further from the truth."

"Oh?" She was possessed by the impulse to hear him admit that his iron control had slipped last night. Five minutes more and he would have let her take up permanent residence in his heart. "And did I imagine the way you touched me, the way your kisses felt on my mouth and throat and breasts?" Ah, she was making inroads into his taut control, for his shoulders seemed to tremble slightly. "Did I imagine," she pressed on, "the way you groaned when I touched you, or the lovers' phrases you whispered in my ear?"

"I whispered nothing in your ear!"

She nearly smiled at his self-righteous outrage. "But you did, my lord. You said that I tear you to pieces, that you wanted to fly away with me, that you never truly wanted anything in your life until you met me."

Horror burst inside Sandro's head. The words would be forever etched, like a scar of shame, upon his soul. Didn't she know that *he* had been the one pretending? A woman like Laura could never want him. He'd surely only imagined her response, her cries of ecstasy, for how could she desire an old man like Sandro Cavalli?

No, he thought. He had to deny that last night was anything more than a lesson she needed to learn. To deny that his need for her had consumed him like a forest fire. He had to stop the unthinkable from happening. He had to stop himself from falling in love. Hopelessly in love with a woman who wanted only momentary passion. If he didn't pull back now, the madness would grow, devour him; he'd lose all sense of himself and his place in the world.

She had pushed him too far. Pride forced him to lash back.

"Don't be ridiculous," he snapped. He stared at the dying embers in the grate, because he could not face her when he lied to her, when he buried the knife in her heart. "You've managed to deceive yourself about my motives last night. My dear innocent, I merely wanted to show you the true lot of a courtesan. You see, I had the same purpose as Marcantonio. By my callous behavior I hoped to turn you from the brothel."

"You weren't callous," she said, her voice low and aching, as if she were trying to dispute his words. "You were gentle and loving and—"

"Damn it, Laura." Though he still did not look at her, he sensed her hurt. "You fell victim to manipulation. I was toying with your emotions to show you that, as a courtesan, you'll be at the mercy of whatever man happens to claim you for a night. Some will be brutal, others will be tender, but either way, you'll have no power over them—none at all. If they choose to exploit your passions, you'll have no choice but to submit."

"I don't believe you," she said in a low, horrified voice. "It was more than that. You desired me."

"I don't want you, Laura," he forced out. "I never did. Last night was all an act."

Laura sat silent for a long time, gazing into the embers of the grate. In the street below, a lamplighter called out the time. She felt like an injured victim awakening after a bad accident. At first the jagged pain hovered at the edges of her consciousness; then the agony moved in, coming on like a rogue tide, flooding her with all-engulfing agony.

"I see." Her voice was amazingly calm. With a self-possession that surprised her, she went before him and dipped into a curtsy. Damn him! Why didn't he look at her? "Forgive me, my lord," she said. "In my utter stupidity and gullibility, I did not recognize your noble purpose."

He seemed to find some fascination in a red-and-gold tapestry on the wall. "No apologies necessary, madonna."

"But you must accept mine."

"I'd rather hear you say you won't go back to the *ridotto.*"

"I won't go back to the *ridotto.*"

Ah, at last he looked at her, and his face was filled with surprise and gratification. "Good," he said briskly, and deep in his eyes she saw the light of high triumph. "Under the circumstances, it's the only decision you could have made." He hesitated, and for a rare moment he looked uncertain. "It was the Trentuno, then, that changed your mind?"

Laura, too, hesitated. Even before the abduction, she had decided to abandon her career as a courtesan. She would find some other means to finance her art. But oh, how smug Sandro would be if she admitted he was responsible for her transformation. Unable to bear more of his self-satisfaction, she merely said, "As a civilian, I assume my reasons are my own."

The eager light left his eyes, and she was glad. "You'll stay here, then," he declared. "I'll assign you a maid and a duenna. You'll have the entire fourth floor for—"

"No," Laura said quietly.

He stared at her. "No?"

"That's what I said, my lord." She walked to the door and turned back. "As soon as Yasmin wakes, we'll go to the convent together. It's safe for civilians there."

"Very well." His face was bleak and haggard.

"It's better this way, my lord," she hastened to say. "You live such a—a well-ordered life here. Everything is so precise. I would be a terrible disruption. I'm most untidy, I keep no regular schedule, and I work obsessively. You'd never be able to abide my presence."

"Oh. Well, then. I'll see that you're taken there in my gondola. Naturally, I'll send a guard."

"No. I won't stand for it. The convent is a place of retreat and safety. Don't profane it with the presence of your nosy men."

He scowled. "I assume," he said, "you're joking.

My men will be there, make no mistake." He turned away.

An aching melancholy engulfed her, for she sensed that their association—surely she could not call it a friendship—was coming to an end. He was strait-laced and infuriating, dictatorial and overbearing, but she would miss him. She would miss his hidden tenderness, his argumentative nature, and, most of all, his moments of pure romance.

"Just make certain the guard is discreet and doesn't disturb the solemnity of the sisters." An unsettling thought occurred to her. "My lord, about Yasmin . . ."

"Yes?"

"Madonna della Rubia won't take kindly to losing her, even for a few days."

"She no longer belongs to Madonna della Rubia."

Laura gasped. "How do you know that?"

"She's been sold."

"No!" Awful possibilities coursed through Laura's mind. Yasmin might belong to a harsher master. "Who?" she forced herself to ask. "My God, not Thorvald the Swede."

For the first time in a long while, Sandro smiled. It was a wary smile, but it warmed her heart nonetheless. "Jamal," he said. "I paid Madonna della Rubia, then gave her to him."

Laura leaned against the doorway in surprise and relief. "He'll set her free, then."

"I believe that's up to Jamal."

"If he knows what's good for him, he'll manumit her. Now, if you'll excuse me, my lord, I'll just fetch Yas—" A loud noise interrupted her. She turned to see Sandro's steward rushing toward them. In his wake thundered six grim-faced ducal lifeguards.

"My lord, you have vis—"

"Out of the way, madonna," said one of the men, brushing past Laura. The crimson feather in his biretta marked him as their captain. Even as he entered the room, he was unfurling a long document.

"Is something amiss? What's the meaning of this?" Sandro demanded. His weariness vanished; he stood as erect and alert as a soldier under inspection. His gaze snapped from the official to the guards. The latter shuffled their feet and stared shamefacedly at the floor.

The captain cleared his throat and handed Sandro the documents. "A summons from the doge, my lord. You're to appear before him to answer for the crimes you committed last night."

Laura gasped, and Sandro spoke as if his mouth were filled with sand. "Crimes?"

"Adolfo of Urbino and twenty-nine other nobles have accused you of unlawful seizure and enslavement."

"Oh, please," Laura burst out. "This is too ridiculous. Those men abducted me, and Sandro was only performing his duty in protecting a citizen of the republic."

The captain regarded her as if she were a small rodent. "That, madonna, is for our courts to decide."

She wondered if the official recognized the white-hot fury in Sandro's eyes. She supposed he didn't, for he merely turned back toward the door, saying, "We're to escort you, my lord." He gestured. "If you please . . ."

Walking like a condemned man to the gallows, Sandro followed the official out. He paused by his steward. "Send word to Jamal. And see to the needs of our guests," he said, and then he was gone.

* * *

"Your lover will be fine—eventually," Yasmin said. In the plaster-walled dormitory of the convent, she looked exotic and out of place.

"He's not my lover," said Laura, staring idly at a fresco of Saint Agnes she had painted when she was twelve.

Yasmin's catlike gaze probed her. "He will be."

Laura loosed a bitter laugh. "He made it perfectly clear that he has no interest in being my lover. And I'm not so certain I want him, either."

"You will," Yasmin said. "You must live down the ordeal of last night. He might be the one to heal you."

Laura tore her eyes from the painting. Not a bad effort, yet too controlled, too primitive. "I don't want to be healed. I just want to paint."

"Then you don't care about the charges against him?"

She remembered the awful twisting that had wrung her insides when Sandro had been hauled off; she felt again her rage at the injustice. "Of course I care. Sandro saved me from a terrible ordeal."

"He is wise for a Christian, and knows the law."

"He offended the most noble houses of Venice." Laura hugged her knees to her chest and fought down her agitation and worry. "Perhaps I should bring charges against them after all."

"Do not be foolish," said Yasmin. "No one would believe you." She eyed the bars of fading sunlight on the flagstone floor. "It is time for my evening prayers," she said and left with her rolled rug tucked under her arm.

Laura slumped against the wall. Yasmin was right. Sandro Cavalli was a noble in his own right, but he was an individualist, too. While others devoted themselves to currying favor, Sandro kept the peace. For that, he might well pay with his life.

The sunlight on the floor faded from bronze to purple,

marking the endless minutes of Laura's worry. Then she heard footsteps, and the door of the dormitory burst open. In rushed Magdalena and Celestina, their habits fluttering like dark wings. With a cry of desperation, Laura embraced them both.

In shaking hands, Magdalena held a crumpled document. "Laura. Is this true?"

Laura winced at the broadsheet her abductors had printed: *On 16 February 1531, Laura Bandello satisfied everyone.*

"No," she said, a shiver coursing through her. "Sandro Cavalli stopped them before . . . before . . ." As the memories leapt out to assault her once again, she covered her face with her hands. "God! I was so scared. There were thirty-one of them, and—"

"The Trentuno, was it?" Celestina demanded.

Her furious tone jolted Laura out of her misery. "Y-yes. Sister Celestina, I never thought you would know about such a horrible thing."

"I know," she said, darkly and coldly. "It's an atrocity. She grasped Laura's hands, and her grip bit with barely suppressed violence. "Men are evil, Laura. God may favor them, but you must turn your back on them all. I thought you were strong enough to stand up to them, but I was wrong," she said fiercely, leaning forward so that Laura smelled the sulfurous scent of her laboratory. Celestina, always so cool and self-possessed, had never shown this wrathful side of her nature before.

Magdalena broke the tension of the moment. "Mother, please don't get yourself into a passion over this. It's done, and Laura is safe with us, God protect her."

And four *zaffi* stationed outside the convent, Laura recalled.

"It will be like old times now that you're home," Magdalena said. "It's best to come home after you've been hurt."

Laura didn't want to think about the future, not now. She seized the moment to change the subject. "I'm safe, but the Lord of the Night is not."

Celestina's eyes gleamed with interest. "What do you mean?"

"He saved me from the Thirty-one, but now he's being censured for his actions."

"Sandro Cavalli was always one to meddle in the affairs of others. No doubt he will get exactly what he deserves."

"Mother!" Magdalena looked shocked. "He saved Laura from terrible violence. Do you feel no gratitude toward him?"

Serenity settled over her like a well-worn cloak. "Of course. God's ways are a mystery to mere mortals."

Yasmin returned, her rolled rug tucked under her arm and her face serene as it always was after her devotions.

Laura scrambled to her feet and made hasty introductions. Magdalena gaped in open astonishment at the beautiful African woman. "I recognize you from Laura's sketches," she said.

Yasmin favored her with a regal nod, but her brows were drawn in confusion. "And I recognize the two of you. You seem taller in person."

"You're the slave who befriended Laura, then," said Celestina, not without compassion. "I do not believe in slavery, even of heathens. There is nothing more heinous than subjugating the human will. Here, we are slaves only to the Lord."

Yasmin took no offense, for she was accustomed

to the ignorance and suspicion of Christians. "It is my lot."

"Oh!" Laura slapped her forehead. "How could I have forgotten to tell you?"

"Tell me what?"

"You belong to Jamal now."

Yasmin's eyes glittered dangerously. "He bought me?"

"Sandro did, and he deeded the papers to Jamal." Laura studied her friend. Yasmin's features seemed carved in mahogany. "Aren't you pleased?"

"Pleased that I have changed hands like a camel between traders?"

Then Laura understood. It was pain, and not anger, that ate away at Yasmin. She hurt because Jamal would have her as a slave, but not an equal. "He'll free you," she said. "You'll see."

Magdalena asked, "Is it true that Marcantonio Cavalli was the man who invented this whole scheme?"

"How did you know that?" Yasmin asked sharply.

"Marcantonio!" Laura dove for her cloak. "Magdalena, you're a genius."

"Where are you going?" Celestina demanded.

"To find Marcantonio before he leaves Venice."

"But why?" Magdalena asked. "He tried to hurt you, Laura. He's a horrid man."

"He ended up hurting his father instead." Laura tugged on the hood of the cloak, one she had borrowed from the chest in Sandro's house. She snatched up the broadsheet. "And now Marcantonio is going to have the chance to make up for what he's done—if I can get to him in time."

11

"I do not understand your brand of justice, Your Eminence." His hands bound, Sandro stood before the doge in the Great Chamber, his head high, his pride in tatters. "Have I not served you well all these years?"

"Exceedingly well." Andrea Gritti looked both weary and nervous as he eyed the others in the chamber: members of the Council of Justice and the Council of Ten, clerks and magistrates, and—flanked by their powerful families—the men who had abducted Laura Bandello.

"Then why, my liege?" Sandro demanded. "Banishment for life is a fate reserved for murderers and traitors."

"And for a man," shouted the fiery duke of Urbino, "who abuses young nobles, chains them like galley slaves to oars. Your rash insult has brought you low, my lord."

Sandro ignored the gibe; Urbino's son and the others had deserved their punishment.

Gritti looked torn, his gaze darting to and fro, his

fingers twisting the tassels of his cushion, as he eyed Sandro and then the roomful of angry lords. Sandro realized that he had dug his own grave. In the years of his service, he had unveiled corruption in most of the noble houses of Venice. Individually, they had submitted to justice while their peers laughed behind their hands. But Sandro's mistake had been in censuring them collectively. United by their common hatred, they meant to see him fall.

"My lord, please approach the dais," Gritti said.

Sandro mounted the five steps to the huge chair. "Yes Your Honor?"

"You must understand my position," Gritti whispered so that none but Sandro could hear. "Were the matter solely my own, I would impose no punishment. I do not doubt that events occurred exactly as you described them. However, there is none here to corroborate your story."

A fresh wave of resentment rushed over Sandro as he remembered Laura's refusal to accuse her abductors. "You're correct," he said. "None will speak for me, save my years of loyal service."

The doge gripped the gilt arms of his chair. "The Trentuno is an abomination I have always deplored. Such acts were far more suited to my late and unlamented father."

"Then let me stay," Sandro said in a low pitched voice. "I ask this not for myself, but for you. There is still a killer at large. You're in danger, my liege."

"Nonsense. You've surrounded me with more guards than the Pope. I have not one, but three tasters who sample my food for poison. A footman takes apart my bed each night to examine it for asps and scorpions."

"The precautions do not ease my mind," said Sandro. "Have you thought anymore on those documents we found at the printer?"

Gritti tugged at his pointed beard. "I've thought until my head aches. I can find no reason for the extra names."

Sandro's assistants had investigated each man. Most were retired *condottieri,* living on the spoils of old battles. Sandro considered mentioning the document Adolfo of Urbino had commissioned from Aldus, but knew he would get no cooperation from the doge. "Look," he said, "if you let me stay until I apprehend the assassin, then I'll accept banishment with no further argument."

"No," said Gritti, "I can't help you. I'm not some prince whose word is law, but an elected official. These men can override me with a single vote. Perhaps if you retracted your accusations against the young lords—"

"Never," Sandro stated. "I stand by exactly what I said. Those little bastards mock the law. They would have torn Laura apart."

"Laura, is it?" Gritti lifted a thick eyebrow. "What is she to you?"

Everything, he thought bleakly. "She's a young artist of prodigious talent. But even if she were the lowliest streetwalker on the Ponte di Tetti, she would not deserve the abomination those knaves visited upon her."

"So you won't retract your accusations?"

"Not in this life."

Gritti shook his head. "How has someone so noble managed to live so long?" His hand trembled as he made a dismissive gesture. "Step down my lord.

Much as I regret it, I must read the terms of your banishment."

With his bound hands in front of him, Sandro turned and walked down the stairs. So this, then, was the fate of a man who lived by a strict code of honor and self discipline. He had spent his life serving his beloved city, first as warrior, then as *condottiere,* and finally as Lord of the Night. He had lavished devotion on la Serenissima as if she were a cherished mistress. Without Venice, he was nothing. A sentence of death would have been a kinder punishment than banishment for life.

Gathering the shreds of his pride, he went down on one knee and faced the doge.

Gritti raised his staff of office. Clerks poised their quills to record Sandro's shame.

The doge opened his mouth to speak.

"Wait!" Laura Bandello skidded into the Great Chamber. Her entrance had the effect of a whirlwind stirring a staid and venerable old forest. Men dropped their jaws, stared at her, and whispered amongst themselves.

With obvious effort, she slowed her pace. Her hood fell back and her hair tumbled down around her shoulders, framing a face that glowed like the sun.

Elation and dismay warred within Sandro as he rose to his feet. Even after he had done his best to hurt and belittle her, she had come to defend him. Foolish baggage. Her disruption would do nothing to improve his lot.

She turned to glare at the young men who had terrorized her only the night before. None would meet her eyes.

Her courage broke Sandro's heart, yet, strangely gave him strength to face what lay ahead.

Doge Gritti gaped at her. The Council of Ten gaped at her. Judges and clerks and nobles gaped at her. Sandro remembered that most of them were seeing her for the first time.

Recalling his own first encounter with her, he realized anew how extraordinary she was—not merely beautiful, but vibrant and colorful and strong, like a sunbeam intensified by a curved glass.

Drawing a deep breath, she summoned dignity despite her disarray and approached the dais. "I am Laura Bandello." With a flourish, she snapped open a large sheet of parchment. Sandro read the large letters, and it was all he could do to keep from throwing his head back and howling in rage.

"You see, Your Serenity," Laura said in a hard, clipped voice, "this is what the young lords intended for me."

Whispers hissed from the men gathered in the hall. The doge paled and recoiled in distaste.

"Lies, all lies!" someone shouted.

Laura aimed a disdainful look at the group of nobles. "I have brought with me the man responsible for the crime against me."

Into the hall strode Marcantonio, splendidly dressed, his head held high, his hat in his hand. "It's true, Your Serenity," he said, bowing down before the doge. "I take full responsibility."

Sandro's thoughts raced. So, Laura had sought out Marcantonio, had faced him despite what she had suffered at his hands. My God, he thought. With a mother like Laura, Marcantonio would have grown to greatness.

"It was my idea to abduct the young lady," Marcantonio confessed, his beautiful face a mask of solemn shame. "I thought it a mere carnival prank. It's my fault our revels got out of hand, and my fault that my friends suffered at the galley oars. If anyone is to be punished, then punish me."

Sandro's ears rang with shock. Never before had Marcantonio accounted for his own behavior.

"This open confession sheds new light on the matter," Gritti said, a sigh of relief puffing his cheeks. With a wave of his hand, he summoned his three chief advisers to the dais.

Sandro caught Marcantonio's eye. "Why?" he whispered.

"Because of Laura," Marcantonio whispered back. "Father, she has forgiven me. Can you?"

Sandro could not speak. His heart was full of respect for a brave young girl, and compassion for a troubled young man. Across the room stood Laura, gazing at him with shining eyes.

The majordomo came forward and whispered something to her, and Sandro could guess what it was: No woman, not even the dogaressa, had ever entered the hallowed Great Chamber when council was in session. It simply wasn't done.

For a moment Laura looked mutinous; then she flashed Sandro a smile and departed.

"What could be taking so long?" Laura said, pacing the convent dormitory. "It's past midnight, and there's been no word from the doge's palace yet."

"Impatience turns minutes to hours," Yasmin said from her bed. "Lie down, Laura. Your pacing could wake the dead."

"But it's all so simple." Laura walked more

briskly. "Marcantonio told the truth for once in his life." She pressed her hands to her eyes, which burned from lack of sleep. For a moment, she wished Magdalena were here with her; in the old days, they often sat up all night and talked of their hopes and dreams, their troubles. But they had grown apart; tonight Laura had only Yasmin, and Magdalena was in the chapel, spending the night on her knees in private prayer.

Reviewing the events of the day, Laura shuddered to think she had almost missed Marcantonio; he was already aboard the roundship. Persuading him to come to the doge's palace had been easier than she had anticipated. For hidden deep inside Marcantonio was a kernel of decency which no doubt Sandro had planted. When he heard his father faced a great shame, Marcantonio had seemed almost grateful for the chance to clear his conscience.

Laura's throat constricted as she envisioned Sandro in the Great Chamber, his hands bound like a common prisoner's and his head bowed as he submitted to the unwarranted wrath of his accusers. The sight had filled her eyes with tears. Even if Sandro had toyed with her affections, he was at heart a man of great integrity and did not deserve to suffer for an act of heroism.

"Yasmin, I can wait no more." Laura fetched her cloak. "I'm going to make Guido take me back to the palace."

"There is no need," said a cold voice from the doorway. "The Lord of the Night is here." Celestina shivered as she lifted the lamp she carried. "This is a place of retreat for women, but since your return, it's been crawling with men."

"I'm sorry, sister." Suppressing a surge of elation, Laura took the lamp. "Where is he?"

"Outside, at the almsgate."

Laura ran, heedless of her bare feet and the borrowed robe flying open to the night air. She passed the chapel where Magdalena prayed, and it seemed to be empty. Perhaps Magdalena had tired or had cast herself prostrate on the floor.

At the gate, she saw Sandro waiting, his tall form cross-hatched by the shadows of the iron bars.

"Sandro." She was too weary and elated to address him properly. "They've set you free, then."

"Not exactly." He cleared his throat. "At least not until after Lent. My sentence of banishment has been commuted from life to forty days."

"You should not be punished at all," Laura said stoutly. "Where will you go, my lord?"

"To the mainland." He propped his shoulder against the stone wall and gazed at the golden city lights. Longing and regret shone in his eyes. "I have a country house on the river Brenta."

She knew it haunted Sandro to have to leave his investigation in the hands of others. "What of the men who abducted me?" she asked.

"Marcantonio is on his way to Swabia. The others will soon be banished, too—to Dalmatia, Cypress, Circassia. Officially, they're off to take care of family business."

"Thank God," she said, pressing her hands to her chest. "Thank God they're all gone."

"Not quite all of them," he said. "Adolfo of Urbino is in the Gabbia."

A chill raced down her spine. "You think it was him all along, then?" Sandro said nothing, so she reasoned it out for herself. "It has to be. He had a glass dagger. He had business with the printer. He's known to consort with low-living *bravi.*"

Sandro lifted one eyebrow. "You make a neat case, madonna."

"For a civilian."

"We have enough evidence to hold Adolfo in custody, but not to convict him of plotting against the doge." Sandro balled his fist and slammed it against the wall, giving her a rare glimpse of the turmoil inside him. "Damn it! I have to leave the questioning of Adolfo to others."

She wanted desperately to cheer him, for he had the aspect of a defeated man. "It must be very beautiful at your estate."

"I'll let you judge for yourself," he said.

She cocked her head to one side. "What do you mean?"

"You and Yasmin are coming with me."

Surprise turned swiftly to resentment. "No."

He drew his hand slowly along his jaw. "Look, we're both too tired to argue. Just get your things and you can yell at me on the barge."

"Would you please stop trying to control my life?" she shouted, clutching the bars of the gate to glare at him through the gaps. "I'm heartily sick of it, my lord."

"That hardly matters to me," he said coldly. "You're still in danger, probably even more so now. Your abductors might well steal back to Venice to seek revenge. Since I can't be here to protect you, I'm taking you out of harm's way."

"I never asked you to protect me!" she cried.

"Oh, no?" His angry voice cut like a knife. "Would you have declined my help last night?"

Laura fell away from the gate. She felt the coldness

of damp grass about her ankles. Damn him, he was right. How could she go on with her painting if she was constantly looking over her shoulder, wondering if a *bravo* or some resentful young lord was stalking her?

"All right," she said sullenly, "but I'm taking my work with me."

"Damn it, Laura, there's no time. If I'm found in the city past dawn, I—" He broke off. "Just get your things."

"What will happen if you fail to leave by dawn?"

"I won't fail."

"Tell me, damn you."

"Damn me all you want, but hurry."

"I have to collect my supplies from Maestro Titian's studio." Without giving him time to object, she hastened back to the dormitory.

A frisson of excitement sneaked down her back. For better or worse, she was going on a voyage with the Lord of the Night.

Torches blazed in sconces along the waterline of Titian's house. Sandro frowned as he stepped from the gondola onto the steps and peered into the open door. It was the middle of the night, yet servants scurried through the halls as if it were midday.

Titian came running to meet him in the foyer. The artist looked haggard but agitated, his thin, pale legs sticking out below the hem of his nightgown. "That was quick. I only summoned you five minutes ago."

"I received no summons," said Sandro.

Fortunato, the little dog, raced into the room, his claws scrabbling on the marble floor. With a hideous growl, he made a lunge for Sandro, but Laura snatched him up before he could attack.

Titian ran his hand through his beard. "Then how did you know to come?"

"We didn't," said Laura. "I'm here to get my things."

Sandro swung around to scowl at her. "I thought I told you to wait in the gondola."

"Is that another of your rules for civilians?"

"Laura . . ."

"I couldn't bear it. Jamal and Yasmin refuse to even look at each other. Their silence was hurting my ears."

Titian grinned at the exchange. "What do you mean, you're getting your things?"

"I'm going to the mainland with Lord Sandro," she said, diplomatically omitting the reason for their departure. "There's no time to explain." She dipped her head. "I'm sorry, maestro. I know I have much to learn from you, but I shall have to finish my last paintings for the Academy without your guidance."

Vito, the apprentice, raced to Titian's side. His cheeks puffed with exertion. "We've found nothing in the garden, maestro. Where shall we search next?"

"Leave it, Vito," said Titian. "The authorities have arrived."

Vito took the snarling dog and walked off.

Sandro returned to the matter at hand. "What's amiss?"

Titian's eyes glittered with fury. "An intruder broke into the studio. I heard a noise, and when I saw what he'd stolen, I summoned you."

Sandro's fatigue fled. His senses buzzed with the excitement of the hunt. "What did he steal?"

Titian turned toward the stairs. "Come. I'll show you." To Laura he added, "You should come, too."

Moments later, they stood in the gallery where Titian had kept his paintings of Laura. The walls that had been graced by the mythical beauties were bare.

Laura gave a small moan and fell back against Sandro. His arms came up to hold her. He could feel her trembling and hear her short, quick breaths.

He, too, felt a sense of violation, of anger and fear. He remembered his first reaction to the paintings. Now, some nameless intruder had taken them all.

"Is anything else missing?"

"No." Driving his fingers into his long hair, Titian prowled the empty gallery. "And somehow, that makes things worse. The thief knew exactly what he was after."

"The paintings were so large," Laura said in a faint voice. "How could he have stolen all five at once?"

"They were unframed," Sandro said. "A strong man could have made off with them easily enough." The keen edge of fear cleared the last vestiges of weariness. This theft was linked with the murders. Or was it? Perhaps his feelings for Laura clouded his logic. Any man would want her. Her beauty could inspire obsession in a saint.

A commotion from below drew them to the head of the stairs. A team of *zaffi,* headed by Sandro's chief deputy, had arrived.

"Go and collect what you need," Titian said to Laura.

"We can't bring your canvases with us tonight," Sandro said quickly. "I'll send for them once we reach my country home."

She opened her mouth to begin a furious protest,

but he turned away before she could say a word. He went below and started issuing directives. The deputy glared at him resentfully; the policemen stared at the floor. Frustration tore Sandro apart. For the next forty days, he was no longer Lord of the Night. This was only the first of many investigations that would take place without him.

Very gently, Titian touched Laura's cheek. "Do you really think he'll let you paint? I have nothing but respect for Sandro Cavalli, but he doesn't understand an artist's soul."

Laura sighed and leaned her forehead on her teacher's shoulder. "You're right, maestro. But for now, I have to trust him."

"Country home," Laura said wryly as the barge moved up the Brenta River and docked at the villa. "So this, my lord, is your 'country home.'" She gaped at the stately manse. Arcaded wings, veneered in brick and decked with ornamental stone, spread grandly to each side of the soaring building.

Still gawking, she stepped from the barge. Orchards and vineyards covered the rolling hills that rose behind the palatial home. Walls of pollarded poplars and rows of neat box hedges encompassed the gardens.

It was evening, and a few workers walked down avenues bordered by pleached bays, heading toward a cluster of cottages in the distance. The scene held such serene, bucolic beauty that Laura felt an ache in her throat. Now with an accusing note in her voice, she turned again to Sandro. "You should have prepared me for this."

He looked both confused and tired, and for a

moment she fancied him an exhausted angel fallen to earth. While his guests had slept during the voyage across the lagoon and up the river, Sandro had stayed awake, no doubt eating himself alive about having to leave his beloved city.

"Prepared you for what?" His voice was gravelly.

"My God, you really don't understand, do you?" Laura stepped aside as an army of servants began carrying masses of goods from the barge to the house. "Don't you realize the treasure you have here?" She indicated the acreage with a broad sweep of her arm. "I thought such places existed only in Bellini's paintings."

"Laura. Every noble in Venice keeps a country retreat. By some standards, my home is modest." His nostrils flared as he stifled a yawn. "Didn't you know that?"

"I've never been away from Venice."

Surprise stole his fatigue for a moment. Then he gave a small smile. "Forgive me. I wasn't thinking."

When they entered the house, the last of Laura's regrets about coming here vanished. The grand houses of Venice, cramped into narrow spaces along the canals, were built on principles of verticality. Here, with all the space in the world, the house rambled and sprawled in a labyrinth of halls, solars, sitting rooms, ballrooms, and rooms that seemed to have no purpose other than to absorb the golden sunlight that streamed through bank after bank of clear glass windows.

Laura and Yasmin were conducted to adjoining guest chambers. Laura threw open the double doors that separated their rooms and spun around with a cry of delight. "Can you believe we will live here, Yasmin? Please, tell me I'm not dreaming."

"You are not dreaming. We are penned here like deer in a park."

"No, we're free," Laura insisted. "I shall finish my paintings for the Acad—"

"Do you truly believe he'll let you?" Yasmin's eyes glittered dangerously. "He is more just than most, but he is still a man. He will find excuses to leave your painting supplies in Venice, for I assure you, he does not take you seriously."

Laura tried to deny the observaton, but Yasmin was wise in the ways of men. Sandro considered her ambitions inappropriate, and might use the sojourn at the villa to try to change her mind about being a painter. "Well, it's just for forty days, and then we're truly free."

"You will do as you please." Yasmin crossed into Laura's room and stood at the tall windows, which framed a view of the greening hills in the distance. "While I will still belong to that—that deceiving African."

"Oh, Yasmin." Laura went and took her hands. "Is it so very bad, then? You won't have to endure the attentions of men as you did at the *ridotto.*"

"But at least there I enjoyed some time to myself. Now I am at his beck and call all hours of the day and night."

The petulant note in Yamin's voice struck Laura with a flash of understanding. "And *has* Jamal called you?" she asked slyly.

"No." Yasmin glided across the room like a cat on the prowl. "That does not mean he will not." Seeming eager to abandon the topic, she went to the door. "Lord Sandro has provided a chest of clothing. I will sort through the garments and see if there are any we can use."

Evening had drawn to a close, and purple-gray darkness spread over the estate. Laura sat at the window, pondering the issues she would discuss with

Sandro on the morrow. Something had to be done about Yasmin; Jamal had to be made to understand that he could not be her master.

The other matter troubled Laura even more. What if Yasmin had guessed the truth? What if Sandro truly did not intend to allow her to paint? She had given up her freedom at his command; now she was at the mercy of his dictates.

She walked decisively to the desk. An array of fine paper lay on top, and dry ink filled the carved horn. Fetching a few drops of water from the basin, she dipped a quill and penned a note to Sandro. Summoning a footman and ordering him to deliver the message to Lord Sandro seemed strange, but at the same time the role of lady of the manor felt deliciously decadent.

Laura let her worries slip away as she eased into the bed. The grand bed she had occupied her last night at the *ridotto* had been designed for show, and in truth the lumpiness of the mattress had been ill disguised by the fluffy white counterpane. This bed, in contrast, had been designed for one simple purpose: comfort. The mattress billowed as she sank into it, and the faint scent of dried lavender was released by her movement. The sheets were not harsh linen, but a fabric Laura recognized as pure silk, so fabulously expensive that she almost felt guilty wallowing in the softness. Almost, but not quite.

Resting her head on a huge pillow, which she imagined was stuffed with swans down, she fell into blissful sleep.

At eight o'clock the next morning, Sandro held her note in his hand. He had known, even before his gaze fell to the embellished L at the bottom of the page, that it was from her. Each penstroke showed the art of the manuscript miniaturist: The letters were finely drawn and even, and yet Laura gave them a unique flare, with whimsical scrolls and flourishes that were the hallmark of her irrepressible spirit.

A pity he had no intention of complying with her request.

A summons indeed. Even the doge couched his commands in more polite terms than Laura had.

He read her words one last time: *Meet me in your offices at nine of the clock. L.* No respectful salutation or humble closing, simply a bald command.

She should know better. The Lord of the Night, even while in exile, did not obey commands from eighteen-year-old female artists.

His fingers tensed to crumple the note, but something stopped him. Though the words offended, he had no doubt that this was a small work of art. It was also the first note she had ever sent him. Embarrassed by his own sentiment, he slipped the paper into his black fustian doublet. Shaking his head, he walked down the hallway to his suite of offices.

The carved double doors stood ajar. Sandro stepped soundlessly onto the thick Turkish rug, a rich prize seized from pirates years earlier. To his utter annoyance and unwelcome delight, Laura was there.

Just as at their first meeting, she was unaware of his presence as she gazed out the tall double windows. This time—thank God and all the saints and apostles—she was fully, even demurely, clothed. She wore an old day dress of Adriana's.

The thought brought a prickle to his skin. Adriana had worn the dress when she was just sixteen.

As always, Laura was in motion, swaying back and forth in a private dance step performed to music he wished he could hear.

What did she see outside to make her sway with rapture? His formal gardens of the *vigna* were in the foreground, and farther out lay his vineyards on the southern slope, and to the east were the orchards, the trees fluffy as clouds with pink-tinged white blossoms. With rakes and hoes slung over their shoulders, workers headed out toward the fields, and women in aprons and kerchiefs worked in the herb garden, which was ringed by gnarled olive trees.

To Sandro, the scene was pleasing, well ordered. The workings of a successful estate. It gave him satisfaction, not rapture.

Suddenly irritated, he asked, "What are you doing here?"

She turned, and the smile on her face was as warm as the sun. She looked fresh, well scrubbed, almost neat but for the wildness of her long black hair. Impossibly, maddeningly, young.

Rightfully, willingly, his.

"You're early, my lord," she said, ignoring his question.

"Early for what?"

"For our meeting."

"I had no intention of granting you an appointment."

"I know. I'm only a civilian. That's why I made certain to arrive before you." Taking a soft roll from her apron pocket, she held it out to him. "Have you had breakfast?"

Of course he'd had breakfast. Wherever he went, he always took, at precisely six o'clock, a Spartan meal of watered wine and hard cheese.

Breadcrumbs drifted to the pristine carpet. "Put that away," he said.

She shrugged and took a bite.

Stung by annoyance, he said, "I have work to do."

She laughed. "You'll not get rid of me, my lord."

He resigned himself too easily. "Very well. What is it you wish to see me about?"

"Could we walk outside and talk?" she asked. "The day is so bright, and I'm still new to this place."

He agreed because, he told himself, she was getting breadcrumbs on his carpet. Moments later they passed through the garden and meandered along the woven fence that bordered the pastureland. She walked far too slowly, falling behind each time he tried to increase the pace of his purposeful strides.

He tried not to notice that she wore no shoes, that her bare feet crept daintily through the budding clover. He tried not to notice the way the wind breezed through her hair, the way a few dark curls wafted caressingly down her back.

But he did notice. Damn the girl, he did.

Annoyed, he stopped and leaned his elbows on the fence. A small herd of cows and one rangy, grizzled bull grazed in the shade of a large tree.

"Can we get to the matter at hand?"

"Of course." A veritable fount of good cheer, she clambered up onto the fence and perched there, hooking her slim bare ankles into the slats and bracing herself with her hands. She threw back her head, letting the breeze fondle her graceful throat.

Sandro scowled at the cows. Three had calved recently and stood patiently by as their offspring drank their fill.

"Well?" he prompted.

"It's about Jamal and Yasmin." Laura had a frustrating way of hesitating until his patience was sapped, then delving straight to the heart of the matter.

"What's amiss?" he asked.

"Everything, as far as Yasmin's concerned."

"How can that be? We brought her away from the *ridotto.*"

"And into another sort of bondage."

"Jamal's a fair man. He'd never treat her ill."

"Owning her is not treating her ill?" Laura regarded him with disgust. "I want you to tell Jamal to set her free."

"He won't do it."

"Why not?"

"Because he loves her."

To Sandro's exasperation, her eyes filled with tears. "He loves her," she repeated. "Yet he holds her in bondage. The logic of that escapes me."

Sandro wondered what his cherished—his only— friend would think if he knew that Sandro was discussing his affairs with a meddlesome lady artist who was too young, too ripe, and too wise. "Jamal believes that owning Yasmin is the only way he can hold her."

"God!" She threw up her hands and nearly fell off the fence.

Sandro reached out to steady her, and found his hands cradling her firm, rounded buttocks. Thoroughly disconcerted, he dropped his hands.

She eyed him over her shoulder. "Was there ever a creature more foolish than a man?"

"Yes," Sandro said curtly, stepping back. "A woman."

She glared down her nose at him. "I'll disregard that."

"As you wish."

"Does Jamal truly think he can find happiness by keeping the woman he loves as a slave? A man should offer his lover her heart's desire. Doesn't he know that?"

"Jamal believes he lost any chance at happiness the day he was seized by the Turks and had his tongue cut out."

"He's wrong. He must know Yasmin wants his love, desperately. She'll never accept it so long as she's a slave."

"Then they're at an impasse. And it's none of your business."

"Oh, posh. Have you no imagination, my lord? No faith in the power of love?"

To his eternal shame, he did. Right now he could imagine her lying naked in the grass, her hair spread upon the carpet of clover, her lips bruised by his kisses, her eyes misty with ecstasy.

"I have no imagination," he stated, placing his foot on the bottom rung of the fence to hide his body's reaction to the brief but vivid fantasy.

Common wisdom decreed that a man's desires waned as he aged. Sandro was still waiting for the loss. Who the devil invented trunk hose, anyway? Even worn with a codpiece, the tight woven garment gave a man no privacy, no privacy at all.

"The solution is simple," Laura said, blithely unaware of his discomfort. "Yasmin will accept Jamal once she becomes his equal."

"Jamal believes he can only be her inferior because of his affliction."

"She adores his affliction. After spending most of her life in a brothel, don't you think she's sick of the prattle of men?"

"Fine, but how do we convince Jamal of that?"

"Just cloak it in imperatives as you are wont to do," she teased. "How neatly we have solved this."

"It is . . . neat." He'd give her that, nothing more.

She sobered, became wistful. "Why can there be no simple solutions for us, my lord?"

"I don't know what you mean."

"Oh, yes, you do." The smile returned. "You just won't admit it yet." Her attention strayed. "Doesn't that bull worry the cows?"

"No, he stopped breeding years ago. Doesn't even think about mating. I've always meant to have the knacker come for him."

"Don't you dare! He's wonderful."

Sandro scowled at the old stud. "He's useless."

She gazed enraptured at his battle-scarred hide, the one broken horn. "He has such character, my lord. Such appeal. Do you not see beauty in anything, my lord? Anything at all?"

I see beauty in you, his heart cried out while his stomach twisted in frustration. "Certainly not in an old bull too long past his prime. I ought to put him out of his misery."

"Oh, you." She elbowed him in the shoulder. Hard. His face must have betrayed him, for her eyes lit with sudden understanding. "You're not talking about the bull, are you?"

Reason told him to pull back, to turn away. Her beautiful eyes, aglow with sympathy, called words from him that he never should have spoken. In a raw, aching voice he said, "I was always at the center of my world. I always knew exactly who and what I was—Lord of the Night, and Venice was my home."

Suddenly she was at his side; he had not seen her

drop to the ground, but she was there, putting her arms around him, pressing herself against him, leaning up to kiss his lips.

Shocked by her brazen assault, he pulled back. "This is not what I need, Laura."

She stared at him, the hurt bright in her eyes. "Then what *do* you need, my lord?"

"My work. It's the one thing that brings me fulfillment."

"So do I," she said quietly, "but you won't give me that."

"What do you mean?"

She planted her hands on her hips. "You promised you would bring my supplies, and I see no sign of them, none at all."

Sandro almost smiled. He had assumed her natural penchant for prying would have led her to the observatory, which he and a small army of servants had spent most of the night turning into a studio for her.

She had angered him; he would not smile. "Come with me," he said, turning on his heel.

Laura was annoyed by his silence, but she respected it, too. She had obviously touched a raw nerve and did not wish to throw salt on the wound. As they passed again through the herb garden, she wondered what was in store for her. Although Sandro claimed to love order and predictability, he never failed to surprise her.

He led her up a flight of stairs and through an area of the house she had not seen yet. The marble halls and ornate doorways intrigued her. They came to the end of the long hall and stood before a pair of double doors.

Sandro grasped the latch and threw open the doors. Laura stepped inside. Her mouth opened, but she could not speak, for she had the incredible sensation that she was standing in the middle of a dream.

Not even the greatest masters of the age had a studio such as this. The room was octagonal, and five of its walls had tall, clear windows. Overhead was a glass dome through which the light streamed like rays of purest heaven.

Three easels had been set up, and each held one of her works in progress. Low tables were arranged nearby for her pigments and oils. Most astounding of all was the view out the window: the vine-draped rolling hills, the gardens, the lawns, the pasture where the old bull grazed.

Laura hugged herself, when in truth she wanted to hug him. "My lord," she breathed, "bless you. This is the most perfect, the most won—" She broke off, staring at him. He stood watching her, more wonderfully handsome than she had ever seen him. His eyes were bright, his mouth curved in a smile, and with a start she realized he was enjoying her pleasure.

The feelings that had been pressing at her heart for weeks suddenly burst forth. Before he could defend himself, she launched herself into his arms.

"Sandro, I love you." She covered his face with kisses and rushed on, giving him no chance to respond. "I know you don't want me to, but I do. And I know you'll try to resist me, but I mean to stay in your life, in your heart."

"Jesus! Stop this." He made a strangled sound of pure agony in his throat and set her aside. Sweat had broken out on his brow. "Don't be foolish, Laura."

"But—"

"I appreciate your gratitude," he said stiffly, and his withdrawal from her was a tangible and loathsome thing. "I always try to see to the needs of my guests. I'm glad the studio pleases you."

"Oh, it does, immensely." Now was not the time to argue with him. Her admission had frightened him into a state of denial. She moved to a table where fresh paper and sketching pencils lay waiting. "I shall make the most remarkable pictures here."

She spun around to see that the doorway was empty. She ran to the passageway, but saw no sign of him, only heard his footsteps on the stairs.

She sighed, leaning against the doorframe. What a strange, wonderful, infuriating man he was.

Frustrated, she slammed the doors shut. For good measure, she shot the iron bolt to lock herself in. Yanking a smock from a hook, she threw it over her head and tied it on with a savage tug.

Stalking to one of the easels, she faced the canvas. It was blank as yet, an amber field that she had prepared with an undercoat. This was to be a botanical still life; the Academy required at least one.

"Damn him." Laura went to a long worktable and set about mixing her colors, grinding a marble roller over the pigments, pulverizing them with satisfying pressure. She worked doggedly, relentlessly, with more energy than she had ever had before.

She found herself mixing colors she hated: brown-black, umber, flame, harsh vermilion. She jerked a selection of boar's bristle brushes from a holder and faced the canvas as if it were her sworn enemy. As if it were the Lord of the Night.

All her training dictated that she make a detailed sketch of her subject in charcoal. Logic told her she was wasting precious time and materials on work the Academy would never, ever accept.

Sandro Cavalli had pushed her beyond reason. In her present mood, Laura was beyond rules, beyond convention. She succumbed to the mad urge to flout accepted practice. She wanted all her feelings to pour directly from her soul onto the canvas.

She hesitated no longer, but launched herself at the canvas. She stopped thinking and only felt. She used her brushes like knives, eschewing the delicate strokes she had always excelled at, and slathered on the dark, hated colors. The utter disorder, the breaking of every rule, filled her with a hot, dangerous sense of power. The colors spread out to the edges of the canvas and then bled down and off, seeming to move of their own accord. Laura wielded the brushes like a sculptor with a chisel: She did not lay her images flat, but shaped them until they took on a life of their own.

She spent hours in her frenzied endeavor. At some point she heard a knock at the door and banished the caller with an angry roar that Maestro Titian would have applauded. She had no awareness of the passage of time, of the discomfort of standing and working her arm with savage speed and power. Only when the light waned to long red-gold rays through the skylights did she stop.

Yet she would not have stopped simply because of darkness. She could have painted stone blind, using only the certainty of her emotions to guide her.

She stopped because she was finished.

Feeling weak and drained, she set aside her brushes and stepped back to view the havoc she had wrought.

The image was powerful, imaginative, alive . . . and deeply disturbing.

"My God," she whispered, gaping at the work that had come from the secret depths of her soul. "What have I done?"

12

Sandro pretended that Laura's self-imposed exile did not bother him. She stayed in her bright, sunlit studio for days, not coming out to eat or sleep; God knew how she managed her privy needs. The servants reported that she accepted a small meal each day, opening the door only wide enough for the tray to pass through.

He tortured himself with the memory of the words she had uttered: *Sandro, I love you. I know you don't want me to, but I do. And I know you'll try to resist me, but I mean to stay in your life, in your heart.* The words that had made him want to run for his life.

One day when he could stand it no longer, he walked outside and stopped below the windows of her studio. A foolish move, for the room was high on the second story, having been used as an observatory in the past.

From the ground, he could see only vague flashes of movement within, but in his mind's eye he saw her clearly: disheveled, her hair wild, her eyes impenetrable, her soul consumed by her work, her heart closed to all save her art.

Feeling unsettled, he walked back into the house. Laura had warned him about her habits the first time he had insisted she live under his protection. Her words called across the weeks to him: *I would be a terrible disruption. I'm most untidy, I keep no regular schedule, and I work obsessively. You'd never be able to abide my presence.*

A fair warning. He just had not expected it to be so hard to bear her presence in his life.

Spying activity at the river landing, he hurried down, grateful for the distraction. It was Jamal, returning on the barge from Venice.

"What news?" Sandro asked, pulling Jamal away from the bustling servants.

Jamal shook his head. *Nothing.*

Sandro felt both relief and annoyance. His city was still at peace, but no progress had been made toward uncovering the plot against the doge, either.

"No murders," he said. "Any thefts?"

None reported, Jamal signed.

"Any leads on the theft of Titian's paintings?"

No.

Something was troubling Jamal, though. His obsidian eyes darted to and fro as if he were trying to hide his nervousness. "Come," Sandro insisted. He started back to the house and led the way to his favorite solar.

"Jamal," said Sandro, gesturing at a horsehair-stuffed ottoman, "sit down."

Jamal did so and watched Sandro through opaque black eyes.

"It was a mistake for me to give you Yasmin."

Jamal sat forward, his face a carved mask of fury.

Sandro waved his hand. "No, no. Of course I don't

want her for myself. What I'm saying is, no man should own her. She's miserable."

Pain flashed across the usually stoic face. Jamal spread his huge hands in query.

"I want you to grant her manumission."

No. No. I would die first, came the expected reply.

"Damn it, Jamal, she wants to love you, but she can't so long as she's your slave, don't you see that?"

Jamal sat very still for a long time. His hoop earring caught a glint of sunlight through the window. Then he scratched on his slate. *When did you become so wise?*

Sandro's throat itched. He coughed. "I've been thinking about . . . certain matters of the heart."

He waited as Jamal wrote again. *If I free her, she'll leave me.*

"If she leaves, she was never really yours in the first place," said Sandro.

A gagging noise escaped Jamal. He thrust himself out of the chair and left.

A soft knock sounded on Yasmin's door. "Laura?" She came up off the couch, set aside the dress she had been altering, and hurried to the door. She had seen nothing of her friend these past days, and was beginning to worry. Laura often got herself into a passion over her work, but never before had she immersed herself this long.

So involved was Yasmin in these thoughts that she did not realize her caller had not responded. She pulled open the door and stumbled back.

"Jamal!"

Her gaze took in his stern, carven face, his muscular

chest beneath the half-open brocaded vest, the uncertainty in his eyes.

He stepped into the room and handed her a document. She read Italian poorly; Latin not at all. But she recognized the names of Sandro Cavalli and Madonna della Rubia.

She eyed the document with distaste. "This is the deed to my person, is it not?" she asked coldly.

He nodded, taking the paper back from her. Her heart ached as she gazed at him. When they had first met, she had understood him completely. His lack of speech was no impairment to her, for his eyes spoke from the heart. A subtle precise signing of the hands, a shrug of the shoulders, could convey an idea more clearly than mere words.

But now he had set himself as her master. He had become a stranger to her.

He made a soft humming sound in his throat and walked to the grate. Crumpling the paper in his large hand, he tossed it onto the embers. The deed smoldered, then took fire. Jamal stood watching with his back turned to her while the paper burned to charred black leaves.

Yasmin waited, her heart in her throat, until he turned back to face her. "Does this mean," she asked, "what I think it means?"

Yes. Yes, you are free.

"Free," she whispered, and the word tasted like jasmine honey on her tongue.

Where will you go?

She blinked in startlement. "Go? I wish to go nowhere, Jamal, my beloved. I wish to stay with you." She watched as his face lit with the blessed miracle of a smile.

"That is," she said, stepping into his strong arms, "if you will have me."

"My lord." The footman toyed nervously with the braid on his jerkin.

Sandro felt a stab of annoyance. "Yes? What is it? Can't you see I'm busy?"

The footman dubiously eyed the surface of Sandro's perfectly ordered desk. The estate business had taken him no more than an hour. Now he had nothing to do. Nothing. He could not even pretend he had work to do.

"Er, it's about your guest, my lord. The lady artist."

"Laura?" Sandro shot to his feet. "What about her?"

The footman ran a finger around his collar. "Well, my lord, she's stopped answering our knocks. The door's locked tight. She hasn't taken a meal since early yes—"

Sandro did not wait to hear the rest. He raced from his study and pounded down the hall to the staircase to the studio. Visons of Laura, collapsed from starvation, exhaustion, fatigue, tortured his mind. What a fool he had been to respect her privacy. What a stupid, heartsick fool. He had thought her isolation would bring her to realize that he wanted nothing from her but to further her career as an artist. Instead it might have killed her.

He did not bother trying the door; he knew she had bolted it from within. Standing back two paces, he shot out one foot and slammed it with all his might at the door.

Pain exploded up his leg. With a howl, he landed on his backside. Cursing, he scrambled up and glanced behind to make sure no one had seen.

He set his jaw and positioned himself again. He was too old for this, for kicking down doors to get to recalcitrant females. The thought renewed his strength. He kicked once more, probably shattering his ankle. The stout bolt held.

Grimly Sandro shed his doublet, then yanked off the batiste sleeves laced to the shoulders of his chemise. He stepped back. This time, solid stone could not keep him out.

He squeezed his eyes shut. His foot burst outward. At the same instant, the doors swung inward, opening wide. Momentum sent him careening inside.

His feet came out from under him and he slammed down flat on his back. The air left him in a whoosh. Stars cavorted before his eyes. Wheezing, he blinked to clear his vision.

And found himself staring at Laura's bemused face.

"You might have knocked," she said, a faint but infuriating note of accusation in her voice.

She was lucky he lay winded and unable to speak, for the words screaming through his mind were not the words of a Christian man.

"Here," she said, sticking out her paint-stained hand. "Let me help you up."

While his every bone and muscle took fire with each movement, he ignored her hand and forced himself to his feet. He staggered, then propped his elbow on the doorframe and affected a nonchalant pose. "Actually, I would have knocked, but I was told you'd locked yourself in and stopped answering."

She cocked her head to one side. "I suppose I was too involved in my work."

Sandro looked at her for the first time in a week. To be charitable, she appeared no worse than the beggar children at their posts outside the Church of San Rocco. She appeared no better, either.

Her skin was ghost pale, translucent; he could see the tracery of lavender veins at her temples. Patches of feverish brightness colored her cheeks. Her hair was even wilder than usual; she had attempted to tie it back with a bit of rag, but the curls spilled free, adorning the nape of her neck, her shoulders, her breasts.

Her borrowed dress, one Adriana had worn a lifetime ago, hung limp and soiled with paint and oil. Its shapeless state accentuated the angularity of her prominent collarbones and hipbones.

"My God," Sandro said, resisting the urge to scoop her up and cradle her like an infant to his chest, "you look like a starveling." What kind of host was he that he would let a guest starve herself to death?

She touched her stomach as if her body were a stranger. "Do I? But I've never been more . . . I don't know . . . full to brimming." She yawned, stretching her arms luxuriously over her head. Her breasts, Sandro observed wryly, had not suffered from the fasting; they thrust out as full and enticing as ever.

She smiled, and he saw a deep inner serenity in her eyes as if all her troubles had been purged from her. "And now, my lord," she said, "I think I shall avail myself of your *bagnio.*"

As she started down the stairs, he gaped after her with his mouth hanging open. A bath? he thought dully. She had nearly ripped the heart out of him, had caused him to bruise every working part of his body, and she wanted a bath?

Rubbing his aching head, he hobbled into the studio. The smell of fresh paint hung harsh in the air. Perhaps if he saw what she had been up to all these days, he would understand.

The paintings stood propped against the walls; three of them rested on easels. He knew little about artists, but realized that she had been extraordinarily prolific, for most paintings took weeks or months to complete.

Sandro stared in disbelief and dread at the work Laura had done. The pictures were, he realized, a chronicle of her experiences and emotions over the past several weeks.

There were the two *bravi*, arrayed like popinjays, leering out at the viewer, weapons drawn. This was no ordinary portrait, but a living, breathing impression. The picture revealed rather than represented a certain moment in Laura's life. Sandro felt her terror, her helplessness.

The next scene depicted Gaspari, the young printer whose body Laura had discovered. She had depicted his face with one hand curled beneath it, the eyes wearing an expression of eternal startlement. Again, the painting defied convention; there was motion in the picture, and isolation, and soul-deep grief.

The frenzied pace of her work showed itself vividly in the scene aboard his galley, when Marcantonio and his friends had abducted her. She had placed herself in the picture, only none but Sandro would ever recognize her in the cowering pile of white robes and black hair on the deck of the galley. The play of torchlight over the faces of her attackers gave frightening life to the scene. The picture personified malicious domination. The evocative work sparked Sandro's anger as powerfully as the reality had the moment he had come upon them.

For a long time, he stared at the horrible scene of violence on the verge of erupting. Then it hit him: He realized that, more than any testimony sworn before prelates and judges, this painting told the truth. No man with a shred of compassion could see this as fiction, for only one who had experienced the terror could paint it so realistically.

One canvas was turned to the wall. The back of it was dated the same as the day he had shown her the studio, the day she had disappeared.

Gingerly, half afraid of what he would see, Sandro turned the painting around and stood back to view it.

The first painting Laura had created was of the bull in the meadow. She had set the scene at night, the sky done in thick purple layered over black, paling around a shrouded moon. She had spared the old bull no vanity, had depicted every scar, every bony line, every imperfection, right down to the broken horn.

And yet the picture did not evoke pity or disgust. Laura had given the beast a strange sort of beauty, a tired nobility, a sense of pride and dignity that commanded respect.

It was, even to Sandro's inexpert eye, a masterpiece. The art world would never be the same once the masters had seen this. What could have inspired her to take a common, even lowly beast, and exalt it in a great work of art?

He noticed words etched in the thick paint at the bottom of the picture. Bending low, he read: *A Vision of Sandro.*

*   *   *

Laura blessed the Romans for instituting the invention of the *bagnio.* She applauded Sandro Cavalli for reviving the tradition. His bathhouse made the one at the brothel look like a mud puddle. The round, domed building had colonnaded arches that opened to the outdoors. The tub itself was a deep pool of marble inlaid around the edges with mosaic tile. An opening in the roof let in the bright midday sun; a hypocaust beneath kept the water at a perfect warmth.

Sighing, Laura lathered herself with perfumed soap, then dropped her head back and dipped her hair to rinse it.

"Enjoying yourself?"

The sardonic question brought her jolting upright. The warm, soap-clouded water barely covered the tops of her breasts. She smiled. "Yes, thank you, my lord."

He seemed discomfited standing there, pacing back and forth, a tic throbbing in his temple. He had removed his sleeves, and the laces trailed down his powerful arms. Her fingers itched to sketch him like this—shirt open at the throat, his bare arms shining with sweat, his face stamped with wisdom, weariness, and immovable integrity. Drawing the living, breathing Sandro Cavalli would be far more instructive than lessons with a male model.

Sandro leaned against a fluted stone column. "I don't suppose you'd care to explain yourself."

"I'm bathing. Surely my actions speak for themselves."

"You know what I mean, Laura. Don't evade me. I've borne many insults in my life, but never have I been likened to a bull ready for the knacker's yard."

"Oh, Sandro. I'm not sure I even understand myself. Here, I'll get out and I'll try to explain." Remorseful, she vowed she would make it up to him. She placed one foot on the bottom step leading out of the pool.

Sandro's eyes widened, then narrowed as he apprehended her purpose. Did he know how handsome, how wonderful he looked to her, in his rumpled, sleeveless shirt and his windblown hair?

"Later," he said, turning on his booted heel. "I'll find you later, when you're decent. And then, by God, you've a few things to answer for."

13

"*She's not in* the solar either, my lord," said the footman. "Cook said she ate half a loaf of bread in the kitchen and drank some soup. After that . . ." The servant spread his arms.

Sandro scowled in annoyance. He always kept a schedule; civilized people did not simply wander about aimlessly at any hour of the day, especially a woman who had come close to death more times than a Borgia heiress. "Check her room again, and that studio. And then—"

"My lord, she would not be inside on such a day," Yasmin interjected, calmly and smoothly. "You must learn to look at things through Laura's eyes."

Impossible. Sandro took pride in the fact that he never could, never would, think like Laura. For to discard his long-held principles, to think like his whimsical guest, would be to become young again, to believe in dreams.

"I shall decide what I must and must not do," he stated.

"As you wish, my lord. You might consider that

she has been confined for days in the studio," Yasmin went on. As she stepped into the estate offices, the African woman looked more beautiful than ever. She had not changed from the goddesslike icon she had always been, yet now the softness of serenity hovered about her. Gone was the feral, predatory look; in its place was a catlike contentment.

Amazing, thought Sandro. Laura had been right.

Why can there be no simple solutions for us?

Angry, he snapped, "Just tell me where she is."

Yasmin's nostrils flared. "Outside taking the air, my lord. I know not where precisely."

Sandro searched the gardens, empty now in the bright glow of early evening. The row of workers' houses crouched in the slanting rays of the sunset. In the lane, bare-legged children chased each other with sticks; their sweet, abandoned laughter reminded him poignantly of Laura.

He walked between the rows of grapevines. Tiny green grapes were pushing out of delicate clusters, and Sandro was startled by the beauty, the newness of the growth.

From the slope, he could see the pink-and-gold sunlight spreading over the orchard, imbuing the fluffy white blossoms with precious color. It was the only place he had not looked.

Stepping between the rows of blooming apple and pear trees, he felt as if he was entering a cave of gilt and white. The breeze stirred the myriad petals, and they rained down, drifting, exuding a perfume of such delicacy that he closed his eyes and inhaled.

A change, a shifting, started inside him, a sense of impending discovery, as when the wind stilled before a storm. After a moment he started walking again, and the air had the quality of syrup, a fog of rich color and scent that filled his senses.

He felt no surprise when he found her. She lay in the soft grass at the base of an apple tree, sound asleep, her cheek pillowed on her hand.

She looked like a child, clad in a clean blue skirt and white peasant's blouse, her freshly washed hair a shining black river curling across the grass. The flurry of white petals, flickering in the golden sunlight, added a sense of unreality to the scene. She was a study in color and light—the rich abundance of her hair, the subtle lavender of her black-fringed eyelids, the vivid red of her bowed lips.

Do you not see beauty in anything, my lord?

Ah, he did now; his throat ached with the beauty he saw and felt in the depths of his soul. He was not especially grateful for the transformation. To open his heart to beauty was to admit that he was alive, on fire with yearning, and impossibly drawn to Laura Bandello. She might find joy in beauty, but for Sandro it meant only pain—pain for the futility of his own desires.

She stirred and gave a little sigh. He could see her waking slowly, her eyes shifting behind the closed lids. My God, he thought. Where was Titian when one needed an image maker?

All at once Sandro remembered his anger, his humiliation.

"Laura."

Her eyes blinked open. A vague, dreamy smile spread across her lips.

"Hello, my lord." She sat up, placing her palms flat on the grass and looking at the light filtering down through the petals. "*Ecco*, I've slept the day away."

He waited for her to stand, and when she didn't, felt a stab of impatience. "Please don't get up."

"I wouldn't think of it."

"True, you never do." Reluctantly he lowered himself to the ground. He felt ridiculous, like some vain patrician posing in an overly flattering bucolic scene. She was making him into a puddle of overaged sentimentality; he had best get to the matter at hand before she noticed his weakness.

"You exhausted yourself painting," he commented.

"I did, didn't I?" She shook back her hair, exposing the slim curve of her neck. Then she picked up the jar that lay beside her, uncorked it, and drank deeply.

Fascinated, Sandro watched her pale throat move with each languorous swallow.

She drank her fill, and like a peasant wiped her mouth on her sleeve. "Cider," she explained. "From the barrels in the cellar. Would you like some?"

Sandro drank, burningly aware that his lips were touching where hers had. The cool, sweet cider, with its crisp bite, soothed the dryness from his mouth and throat.

He set down the jar and faced her.

"What do you think of my paintings?" she asked.

He cleared his throat. "I'm no judge of fine art."

"That's not what I asked. I want to know what you thought, what you felt, when you looked at them."

"Most of them were . . . disturbing."

A frown puckered her brow. "I thought so, too."

"Then why did you paint them?"

"Art isn't always a matter of healthy nymphs and bowls of pomegranates, my lord."

"Your pictures lack the detail I'm accustomed to seeing."

"I know." She pushed her finger at her lower lip. "I realized that as I was working on them. I didn't want to paint detail. I wanted to paint . . . I don't know . . . impressions. Feelings."

"Then you succeeded."

"Did I?" She cocked her head to one side. "What feeling came to your mind?"

Sandro had an urge to loosen the fastening at the neck of his shirt. "Lust. Youth. Violence."

She tucked a strand of hair behind her ear. "The pictures will probably cost me my chance to join the Accademia."

"Either that, or they'll elect you Master Painter."

Delight lit her eyes. "Do you mean it?"

"It's possible."

"Then you liked them?"

"I've told you before," he said a bit stuffily, "I never lie."

"Good." She dropped her head and peeked at him shyly. "I'm sorry you're angry about the bull."

Her comment brought his sense of humiliation rushing back. "Are you?"

Gazing up at him, Laura looped her arms loosely around her knees. "Yes."

She hated the bleakness in his eyes, hated that her painting was the cause of his displeasure. "I'm sorry you're upset, not sorry I did the picture. There's a difference, my lord."

His hand twitched. For a moment he looked as if he'd like to slap her. Laura did not think for a moment that he would. Sandro Cavalli might break her heart, but he would never, ever, raise a hand to strike her.

"Would you let me explain?" She wanted to run

from his silence and the censure in his eyes. "Please."

"I can't think what there is to explain," he grumbled. "The picture speaks for itself."

She ruffled her fingers over the soft grass. The beauty of his estate captivated her. How could he live in such a place and be so cold of heart? "The picture speaks, but you miss the meaning. I didn't intend to mock you."

"Oh? Then enlighten me, please. I'm burning to know why."

Laura studied his fierce, craggy face, his shuttered eyes. "I did it to express my feelings about you."

"Ah, you succeeded, then. You managed to show me as a stringy, useless old beast."

"Is that really what you saw in the painting?" He did not reply, and she took heart from his hesitation. "Did you not see the strength, the nobility, the dignity?"

He coughed. "All right, you meant well, then. I overreacted. It's not every day I see myself portrayed as an animal."

She leapt on the opening he had inadvertently given her. "I'd like to paint your true portrait." Eagerly she came to her knees and leaned forward. "Would you let me?"

"No." His answer came swiftly, with implacable certainty.

"Oh." She sat back on her heels. "I didn't think you would." Again her gaze moved over him, taking in the stiff set of his shoulders, the firm unsmiling line of his mouth. "You protect your feelings well, Sandro," she whispered.

A familiar guarded look crept into his eyes. "What do you mean?"

"There's passion in you, and fire and wildness. But

you keep these things so deeply hidden that very few even know they're there."

"Oh." His mouth pulled into a humorless smile. "And you, in your infinite wisdom and advanced age, are one who knows."

"Yes. So do Aretino and Titian. And Jamal, of course."

"I had no idea so many people were privy to my inner soul."

"Only because we want to be," Laura said, moving close, preparing to take the risk of her life.

She could stand the watching, the wondering, no longer. He swore his lovemaking the night at the brothel was merely a lesson. But sometimes she caught him looking at her or heard a certain inflection in his voice, and she wondered if he hid true desire behind his sense of duty.

Reaching out, she stroked his cheek. His skin was rough with tomorrow's beard, his bones strong and prominent beneath her fingers.

He held himself very still, though his eyes reflected a look of alarm. "What are you doing?" he asked.

She brought her other hand to his cheek and leaned close, entranced by the way his eyes caught the spears of light from the setting sun.

"You don't understand the words I say, my lord. You don't understand my paintings. Perhaps you'll understand this."

Without giving him a chance to reply, she pressed herself against him and kissed his lips. He made a hissing sound as if she had burned him, but he did not push her away.

Instead, his voice erupted in a groan of pure passion and he held her tightly, his arms a welcome vise.

And then the kiss was no longer hers, but something of his own invention. His mouth claimed hers, possessed hers, at once both giving and taking. She tasted the sweetness of the cider they had drunk; she discovered the warm inner wetness of his mouth. He held her closer still, pressed his mouth harder, so that her head bent back and her face was raised to his like a flower to the sun.

His tongue plunged and then receded, and her response was a deep tugging, as if a thread of sensation linked her mouth with her feminine core. Wetness flooded her and she gasped, startled.

He pulled back immediately, and she could see his struggle to turn away from her.

"Sandro," she said, aching at the war that twisted his features. "Don't stop. Please."

"My God," he said. "Do you think I'm made of iron?" His hand trembled as he loosed the string that laced up the back of her blouse. "I have gone insane, and at the moment I don't care."

"I don't, either," said Laura.

"I couldn't stop now if I tried."

"I don't want you to."

"I could devour you whole and never suffer a moment's regret."

"Please do, Sandro."

Laughing in nervous delight, she fell against him. Her hands caressed his shoulders and back, and she felt his tension flow out beneath her touch. That she could give him ease filled her with contentment.

Taking her hands, Sandro brought her to her feet. He lifted her hands to his lips and kissed them. "You're a child," he said, in one final effort to stop himself.

"If you believe that, my lord, then you don't know me at all." Yes, in his arms she was woman, all woman, eager and powerful and wanting.

"I can't marry you, you know," he said solemnly, with complete honesty.

Laura was amazed that he would think she expected marriage. Patricians did not marry base-born commoners. Not unless they wanted to end up like Guido Lombardo, and Sandro had far too much pride for a life of obscure poverty. Marriage to the Lord of the Night was one dream she never dared to contemplate.

She laughed. "I don't want you to marry me, my lord. I just want you to make love to me."

He expelled his breath on a sigh of relief. A nightingale whistled in the trees. Petals floated down, sprinkling his shoulders, lodging in the folds of his biretta.

He cleared his throat. "This is hardly the place to . . . er, such things should be done in the privacy of a bedchamber."

Her eyes followed the path of a petal tumbling down his broad chest. "Who says?"

He brushed the petal away in annoyance. "*I* say."

"Ah, the Lord of the Night has spoken."

He offered her his arm. "Shall we go?"

She ignored his courtly gesture. She didn't want to leave the orchard, to give him time for misgivings, to lose the magic of the tense moment. Once, just once, she'd like to see him lose control. "No," she said.

His eyebrows rose. "No?"

"We'll stay right here." Enraptured by the anticipation swishing in her ears, she gazed down at the carpet of grass flecked with pink-and-white blossoms.

"Here?" He looked panicky, nervous. "It simply isn't done. What of your modesty?"

"I have none where you're concerned." She stepped forward, placing her palms on his chest, over the fine linen of his chemise. She slid her hands upward over his pounding heart, his heated flesh. "Sandro, I want our loving to be . . . different for you. Special. Memorable."

He looked dubious, and she went on, "You're surely a man of experience and, despite my training, I'm new to this. I want at least something to be new to you, too."

"You are," he said, his hands grasping her hips and coasting up over the inward curve of her waist. "Everything about you is new, Laura." He gazed into her eyes and a familiar pain flickered over his face. "God. You're so . . . clean. So untouched. I think—"

She stopped him with a finger to his lips. "Don't you dare start thinking. You become insufferable when you think. Damn you, I *want* this. So don't stand there and ponder logic or excuses."

"Stop me, then," he said urgently. "Stop me from thinking."

She wound her arms around his neck and lifted herself on tiptoe. They kissed hard, and a deep, inner pulsing overcame her. He pulled her blouse from the waistband of her skirt. His rough palms abraded her nipples. She whimpered, wanting, craving more. He removed his hands to skim the blouse down her shoulders, and then discarded the skirt and smallclothes. She stepped out of the pool of clothing, feeling curiously shy. Although it was evening, the sun was still strong, the light hard and golden. True, she had bared herself for Titian; his friends and apprentices had scurried in and out during the sittings, but this moment was different. Etiquette among artists and models was one of professional detachment.

With Sandro, she felt no detachment at all, only hot, urgent desire and a soul-deep need to know she pleased him. Her cheeks tingled with a blush.

He was staring at her as if he had seen a celestial vision. She smiled—hesitantly, tremulously. "Your turn, my lord," she whispered.

"Patience, *carissima*," he said, hauling her against him. His hands were like warm water flowing over her, molding every curve and plane, around, across, and into her with a tenderness that stole her breath away.

Laura had a vague memory of Portia's diatribe on the most picaresque means to get a gentleman out of his clothing, but the knowledge fled on a storm of desperate need. Her fingers found the closures of his doublet and unfastened them. The stiff garment resisted, but he helped her rid him of it. His shirt with its laced-on sleeves went next, followed by trunk hose and smallclothes that caught on his boots before, with an oath, he kicked them off.

The Lord of the Night stood naked before her. He cast a wistful glance at the untidy heap of clothing. "No," Laura said, guessing his thoughts. She could not wait while he carefully folded each garment.

Taking his hands in hers, she stepped back to look at him.

He flushed. "Damn it, I told you I was too old for—"

"Shut up, Sandro." She gazed at him steadily. Sandro's body bore the marks of hard living, of battles and sea voyages and hours in the sun. He was rough, raw, and brown. He was perfect, and she told him so.

He accused her of idle flattery, and she proved him wrong with a kiss that sent them tumbling onto the grass.

He stretched out full-length beside her, propped on one elbow so that his free hand had full access to her supine form. She arched upward, and his hand found her breasts, cupping each one and then holding the second while his tongue traced a ring around the peak. Round and round it went, flicking out to sear her with sensation until she cried out in wanton need. He fastened his mouth on her and drew the nipple past his teeth. Laura felt the same wonderful sensations she had the last time, only now she feared no interruption and had no question about his motives.

While he suckled her, his hand skimmed down to her knees and then traveled slowly upward. When he encountered her slick readiness, he moaned softly and slipped one, then two fingers inside while his thumb made a circling motion that launched her on an updraft of sensation and made her mad to hold him, to touch him.

Her hand closed around him, her fingers moving over the warm ridges of his manhood. His body convulsed, and he lifted his head to curse softly, in surprise, as if he had not expected to respond with such swift intensity.

He nibbled a path up her throat and caught her earlobe between his teeth. "Laura," he whispered. "What you do to me . . . Jesus, I'm on fire . . . I don't want to hurt you. . . ."

"You won't." She kissed his jaw. *Not that way.*

He primed her tenderly, compellingly, and when she could stand the waiting no longer she opened her legs. He slid over her, bracing his hands on either side

of her head while he kissed her deeply. Then, discon-
certingly, he stared into her face as he entered her by
inches.

She felt the resistance of her own body and tilted
her hips to ease his journey. Next came a dull pressure but no pain, for his expert caresses and her own
yearning had made her ready.

Still he looked at her, searching her face.

"What do you see?" she whispered.

"Heaven."

I love you. She mouthed the words, then cupped
his neck with her hands, lifting her head to kiss him.
Her invitation compelled him to move. The rhythm
started slowly and evoked pulsations that originated
deep inside and radiated outward, bathing her in rip-
ples of warmth. She had never expected to know full
womanly pleasure, and her surprise added a sharp
edge to the exquisite sensations.

She had never expected to adore her first lover,
either.

Small, breathy sounds escaped her as if she were
running up a hill, higher and higher, intent on reaching the top. The rhythm quickened, and she rose
higher still, hovered for a long, breath-held moment,
then burst into an explosion of color and light.

Sandro stopped moving. His body snapped like a
bow; then she felt the intense spasms as he poured
into her. The movement renewed her ecstasy and she
soared with him, airborne, swirling like petals on the
wind, then drifting slowly, settling, relaxing. . . .

Stunned to immobility, Sandro lay atop her, their
bodies still joined, his face buried in her mass of hair.
He could not think, could not move. Coupling had
never been like this for him. Never. Were he a youth

of eighteen, he could not have had a more profound response. All other women faded to shadows before the brilliant intensity of Laura, a girl with the heart of a woman and the body of a goddess.

She had said she wanted this time to be different. Special. Memorable. If she only knew how well she had succeeded.

He had thought to take her swiftly, unthinkingly, to slake his lust and then be done with her.

Now he knew how foolish the idea had been, how easily he had deceived himself. He was far from done with her.

Horrified at the implication, he lifted his head and kissed her soft, moist lips. Incredibly, the taste of her roused him again. Obeying the rare impulse, he began to move once more, his knees grinding into the grass, his gaze fixed on her face. The drowsy, replete haze in her eyes lifted and she looked fierce, greedy, wanting him again, grasping his pumping buttocks and urging him on.

In a far-off corner of Sandro's mind, he acknowledged the unlikelihood of an encore performance. Not in twenty years had he felt pleasure like this. Not in all his life.

Her passion crested, and she gasped, her velvet sheath wringing a response from his body and wresting a cry from his lips. He knew he was saying her name, knew he was speaking words better left unsaid, but he had lost control of himself. For the first time in his life he became a creature of sensation and emotion; feelings overcame logic, smothered reason, buried common sense. To stop the flood of words, he kissed her and did not pull away for what seemed an eternity. A wave of pleasure convulsed him, and then at last he relaxed, slipped away from her to lie at her side, with his body curved around hers.

She breathed deeply. Her hand crept across his bare chest, fingers twining into the curly hair. He wished fiercely, futilely, that he could be young again, a fiery gallant who would do battle to win her heart and kill to keep it for himself.

"Sandro," she said, then hesitated. "Is it all right . . . to talk?"

"Why wouldn't it be?" Her drawn-up knee beckoned, and he sculpted its shape in his big rough hand.

"Part of me is afraid to say anything. Afraid I might, I don't know, change what's happening between us, break something."

Something is already changing, Laura. The convictions of a lifetime.

He tore his mind from the thought. Seized by impulse, he scooped up a handful of fallen petals. Lifting his hand above her, he let the petals drift downward, sprinkling her breasts and stomach and thighs.

"I'm listening," he prompted.

"I never knew," she said, watching his hand, "never expected it to feel like this."

He smiled wryly, then bent his head. Blowing lightly, he scattered a few petals from her stomach. Goosebumps sprang out on her skin. "You lived in a brothel for six months, and you weren't told about the nature of physical pleasure?"

"Of course I was."

He scattered more petals over her, fascinated by the pattern they made on her body.

"My God, Sandro, what are you doing to me?"

She moved against him, and her breast brushed his chest.

"Since the brothel was remiss, I'm showing you the nature of physical pleasure. What did you expect, Laura?"

"I expected some . . . agreeable sensations, but I never knew a fire would consume me, that your touch would reach so deeply inside me. There was a moment when I didn't feel human at all, but a spiritual being floating toward the heavens. Is that blasphemy?"

"Probably." And thank God for her gift of words.

"I don't care. Sandro, am I crazy, or did you feel it too?"

He hesitated. Never, ever, had a woman spoken this way to him. To make love was one thing; modest people averted their eyes afterward and dressed decorously, pretending the coupling had never happened. Laura, it seemed, intended to pick it apart like a critic studying a painting. If he admitted how he felt at this moment he would be lost, a prisoner of desire, his carefully guarded privacy no more than dust under his feet.

He dragged his gaze from her. "The young," he said, sitting up to draw on his hose and boots, "always feel more intensely."

"That's ridiculous." She watched him lace up his codpiece, and, with a devilish grin, poked her finger at it.

"Quit that." He jerked away.

"I've always wondered about these. What does a man keep inside it?"

"That," he said, lowering her blouse over her head, "depends on the man."

She pushed her arms into the sleeves. "What do you keep in yours? Bonbons? Silver coins?" She scooped up a handful of petals and tossed them at him, and for a moment she looked unreal, a faerie imp in a kingdom of flowers. "Padding?"

He shoved his feet into his tall cuffed boots. "Nothing," he said with a sigh, "but trouble."

He said no more as they finished dressing. He did his best to ignore her, to disregard the feelings that bubbled up like a fountain inside him. He felt confused, disoriented, like a convict just released from the Gabbia. In the deep lavender light, Laura looked ghostly, a creature borne on air and laughter to a place he could not follow, did not belong.

She tugged at the drawstring of her skirt. "Sandro, I want to stay with you tonight."

"No."

"Why not?"

"Because I'll hurt you, Laura. We'll both be hurt."

"How can you know that?" she demanded.

"I cannot give of myself the way you can, Laura." Bleak regret for a lifetime of missed opportunities settled over him. "When my first wife discovered my inability, it drove her to another man's arms."

"She was a fool to tolerate your remoteness," Laura insisted. "I will not." She threw her arms around him with an exuberance that nearly knocked him off his feet. "Don't you see? It's all clear to me now. I was born to be with you."

"I thought you were born to paint."

"Then I was born for two purposes. Oh, Sandro, I shall do the most wonderful paintings, and you—"

"We don't suit, Laura. Get used to it."

"Oh, don't we? I wonder then, about the things you said when you were so deep inside me that our souls touched."

Sandro wondered too, for he had no memory of the words. "A man is not responsible for words uttered in the heat of passion."

"You told me you never lie."

"I don't."

"Good, because you said you loved me."

"Laura." His heart sinking, his soul in torment, he took her by the shoulders and gazed into her eyes. "At the moment, I'm sure I meant it. You're beautiful, incredibly responsive. You made me feel young again, as if I could conquer the world. Can you blame me for speaking out of gratitude?"

She stiffened. "Men don't ordinarily profess love by way of saying thanks."

"Those were hardly ordinary circumstances. Laura, we must forget what we did. Our differences in age, in station—our very opposite natures make a future together impossible."

She took his hands and stared solemnly into his eyes. "Then let's not think of the future, my lord. I make you happy right now. Isn't that enough?"

Urgent need overcame his misgivings. He groaned in frustration as he swept her into his arms. Even as he took her to his own chamber, even as he undressed her and made love to her again, he knew they were making a grave mistake. They were allowing their involvement to deepen when they should be pushing each other away. He would hurt her; it was just a matter of time before the pain would start.

But as Laura's cries of joy rose to the silken canopy of his bed, he didn't care.

* * *

Their passion held the world at bay. For Sandro and Laura, there was only each other—long nights of lovemaking, longer days of anticipating it. They shared secret looks across the supper table, intimate laughter as they fumbled in the wine cellar, thirsty after hours of athletic sex.

Sandro moved through the days in a state of sweet exhaustion. It was not the fatigue of old age, but a pleasant numbness that kept him insulated from the reality that he was a man in exile, banned from doing his job of protecting the citizens of Venice.

Laura had done it all, he thought one day as he lounged on his bed, naked atop a tangle of sheets. She took him out of himself, gave him a purpose beyond his role as Lord of the Night.

He picked up a Jaffa orange and dug his thumb into the stem. A spritz of orange zest moistened his hand, and he peeled the golden fruit slowly. It was Laura, Laura who made him aware of the simple, sensual pleasure of peeling an orange without a knife. Greedily he tore off a section and bit into it, savoring the burst of juice in his mouth.

"Stop it," she said, looking up from her sketch-book. "You're making me hungry."

He sent her a lazy smile. "That's the idea. Come here."

She clutched the sketchbook to her chest and pointed a charcoal-smudged finger at him. "It's taken me a week to convince you to sit for me. I won't waste the opportunity."

He glanced down the length of his reclining body. "Sitting? This is sitting?"

"It's just a figure of speech." Frowning in concentration, she rubbed the paper with her finger to blend the charcoal. "Oh, Sandro," she said, her attention still riveted to the drawing, "this is the finest study I've ever done. I'm going to paint a magnificent portrait of you."

"I don't doubt that you will. Pity no one will see it."

She made a few long strokes with her stub of charcoal, then highlighted with a bit of chalk. "What's that supposed to mean?"

He sucked thoughtfully on a section of orange. "You don't really think I'd allow a picture of myself in the altogether to be made public."

"Art is meant to be shared."

"Not this time, Laura."

She shrugged, unconcerned, and they spoke no more as she drew. Sandro had never spent a day in his life abed, and he found himself reveling in the decadence. Seeing Laura's deep absorption, the way her eyes studied him and her clever hand flew confidently over the page, he smiled. He would never understand what she found so fascinating about his naked, battle-scarred body. He had always regarded it as a utilitarian device with all its parts in satisfactory working order. He saw nothing extraordinary in his broad chest with its mat of silvering hair, his long lean legs knotted with sinew, his big shoulders, one scarred by a saber cut, the other bearing a shiny burn mark from a gun that had misfired.

Yet despite his flaws, Laura seemed to find endless fascination in him—even when she wasn't drawing him.

He enjoyed the rest of his orange, then settled in to watch her work. He had long since reconciled himself to her genius and was no longer frightened by the power of her work. She was a study in complete concentration, her eyes drinking him in, then misting over as she transferred the image in her mind to the page before her. She drew pictures the way she did everything else—with restless energy, boundless exuberance, and a *joie de vivre* that was infectious.

The thought raised memories of her lovemaking. He had never known a woman to be so giving. She was generous with her kisses and her caresses. She was bold and adventurous, never failing to surprise and delight him. She adored the bliss, indulged in it, made no moralistic excuses for her behavior. She was a sensual creature, uninhibited by convention or training, and that aspect of her enchanted Sandro. She was as creative in sex as in art, and her inventiveness was infectious. He had lived his life by rules and conventions and the expectations of others. He had never, until the first time he had made love to her, acted solely for the sake of pleasure.

As she continued working, he watched her with unabashed delight. She wore one of his long robes. The crimson satin, many sizes too large, gaped open in front to display her shadowy cleavage. Her loose hair tumbled over her shoulders and down her back. Her bare feet were hooked around the legs of her chair, and the unladylike pose gave him a particularly fine view of her thighs.

"Sandro." She sent him a censorious look.

"What? I'm being still."

Laughter glinted in her eyes. "Part of you is restless."

It felt good to laugh at himself as he followed her gaze to the erection his lusty thoughts had caused. *"Carissima,* I can think of only one way to correct this situation."

Her eyes went smoky and liquid, but she held her

sketchbook like a shield. "I ought to draw you just like that to show you for the lecher you are."

"I was a perfect gentleman until you came along."

"It's a good thing I did, then. Perfect gentlemen are bores."

He feigned a yawn. "I'm getting bored at the moment. Modeling should be limited to fruit in bowls or spaniels and dead pheasants."

"Please, Sandro. Just a little longer."

He held out his arms. "Come here."

"I want to draw."

"You can draw later."

"No."

"No?" Moving slowly, he coiled like a snake and then stood beside the bed. "I think so, Laura."

"You're being unprofessional."

"At modeling? True." In two swift strides he reached her, forgetting his curiosity about the sketch as he set aside the charcoal and pad.

"No," she said again, jumping up and darting out of reach. "I won't—" She broke off and shrieked as he cornered her.

Laughing, he picked her up, slung her over his shoulder, and stalked toward the bed. She beat her fists on his back. "You . . . barbarian! Hun! Troglodyte! *Bestiaccio!*"

As he flung her down on the bed and pinioned her wrists over her head, the epithets dissolved into helpless giggles, which stopped only when he devoured them with a kiss. He had never known it was possible to laugh while making love.

Then the mirth left them both. Standing over her, still keeping her wrists pinned, he parted the robe and sank into her, not bothering to see if she was ready, not surprised to find that she was. Bending slowly, filling her with himself, he pressed on her a kiss that tasted of the orange he had eaten.

With a muffled cry, she brought her legs up and locked them around him, rocking back her hips to offer him even deeper entry.

His free hand found her nipples, bringing each erect, readying her for his mouth. He suckled deeply and was so moved by her pleasure that he almost attained his own.

No, he thought, he was not some green youth. As swiftly as he had come to her, he pulled back, ignoring her cry of startlement and dismay. "Hold still," he whispered in her ear, then slid down the pale, satiny length of her, his hands lingering on her breasts while his mouth went lower, drawn to the dark, rich scent of her. His tongue laved her salty folds of flesh until she gasped three times in quick succession, then held her breath and finally, gloriously, rewarded him with a rush of sweetness.

Surprise and delight glowed in her eyes as he entered her again, her channel slippery now and still convulsing with her climax. The sensations brought him to the limit of his control, and with a hoarse cry he vaulted over, thundering into her, imagining, strangely, that his seed was absorbed by her body, that this act was making him part of her, bonding them irrevocably.

She drew him down and kissed him, and her eyes flew open in wonderment.

He laughed softly. "It's the taste of love, *carissima.*" When they parted, she looked amazed, replete, and so happy that he wanted the moment to last forever.

For a long while he simply held her and wished he could believe that their passion was more than an idyll, a fantasy. They were removed in time and place from the life that shackled him with the demands of duty, and consumed her with the lure of ambition.

After a time, a knock sounded at the door. Grumbling, Sandro tugged the robe back over Laura and slung the sheet negligently about his waist. He tried not to grin at the shocked face of the footman. None of his servants save his valet had ever seen him less than fully attired, yet here he stood in a makeshift toga, his hair tousled and his mouth moist with the essence of Laura.

"Yes?" he asked. "What is it?"

"A message for you, my lord." The footman handed him a folded, heavy piece of paper and then left, scratching his head in bewilderment.

Sandro turned back to Laura, breaking a familiar seal, and frowned at the spidery writing.

"What is it?" she asked.

For a moment, her disheveled, well-loved state drained his mind of thought.

"Sandro?"

"Oh." He cleared his throat. "It's an invitation. From the marquis and marchioness of Mantua. They're having a soiree at their country villa tomorrow night." He paused, then said, "I suspect they wish to atone for their son's misbehavior."

She swallowed audibly. He guessed that, like him, she had forgotten that the rest of the world existed. "Will . . . will you go?"

"We'll both go," he said, acting on an impulse he hoped he would not regret.

Her eyes widened. "Sandro, I couldn't. I'm hardly fit for polite society."

"Nonsense. You're charming, Laura."

"To you, perhaps, but you have strange tastes."

He laughed.

"I don't want to see them, Sandro. How could I, after what their son did to me?"

A painful tightness squeezed his chest. "My son was involved, too, and you've forgiven me. The men who tormented you that night have been exiled as well." He dropped the note, returned to the bed, and took her in his arms. "Never hide because of what happened, Laura. None of it was your fault."

"But people will think otherwise. I was sold in a brothel, for God's sake. They'll say I deserved everything I got."

"Only if you hide and let them think the worst."

"Are . . . are you sure?"

"*Carissima,*" he said, brushing aside her robe, stroking her intimately, and steering her back toward the bed, "trust me." He held her close and whispered into her hair. "You'll conquer them heart and soul, Laura. You have a talent for that."

"Have I?" She turned her head and kissed his cheek.

"Yes," he murmured, his desire taking wing. "God, yes."

14

The ballroom of the marquis of Mantua filled Laura with awe—and a sense of impending doom. Standing next to Sandro at the grand entrance to the *salone,* she gaped at the soaring, vaulted ceiling with its Bellini frescoes, the marble arches, the gilt plaster trimmings, and the daunting whirl of glittering nobility. In contrast to the classic simplicity of Sandro's villa, this place was gaudy and overly bright.

They were greeted first by the famous triumverate of Venice: Titian, Aretino, and the architect Sansovino.

"Divinissimo!" Aretino boomed, bouncing up the steps of the *salone* to meet them. "How good that you have come." The writer swept his arm to encompass the crowded room. "You see, since you are not in Venice, she has come to you."

Indeed, Laura saw a large portion of the city's patrician population in the huge hall. Amid a fog of expensive perfumes, a cacophony of voices mingled with the sound of banging utensils, clinking glasses, and sweet music.

Aretino scooped her into a bear hug. "How is my

bellissima? Is the Lord of the Night treating you well?"

A blush stole to her cheeks. Aretino looked from Sandro to Laura, and then at his two friends. "*Ecco!* I don't believe it!" he brayed. "They're lovers!"

Laura held her head high, for she felt no shame in her passion for Sandro.

"Christ, Pietro," Sandro said, "you've got a big mouth."

Those nearby were already sending speculative glances in her direction. Fans went up and whispers hissed behind them.

The duke of Urbino sidled near and aimed a contemptuous glance at Laura. "So now we know why she barged in on the council session," he said. "She lied to protect her lover."

Sandro moved so swiftly that Laura almost didn't see him. One moment he was standing next to her; the next he had one fist clutching the duke's shirt-front and was drawing the startled man close. "Say one more word, Francesco, and you'll find yourself floating face down in the Brenta."

"Here, now," Urbino blustered as his face paled. "My son is in prison because of her."

"No," said a woman, hurrying forward. "Our son is in the Gabbia because of his own behavior."

Laura stared in amazement as the duchess of Urbino inclined her head. "The passions of youth can be dangerous. It's time Adolfo learns to keep himself in check." She handled her husband as a mother would a recalcitrant child, leading him away and plying him with a cup of marsala.

"A most sensible woman," said Sansovino. He linked his arm with Sandro's. "The sooner we stop the talk, the better. Let's start a rumor about Pietro."

Titian placed his hand at the small of Laura's back and drew her away from the others. "I assume it's true."

"Yes, maestro. I just wish Messere Pietro hadn't alerted half the people in this room."

"And you're happy, Laura? This is what you want?"

"Yes." The problem was, she wanted Sandro for her own. For always. But he couldn't give her that.

"I've heard Sandro's generous with his mistresses."

Laura stood still. Titian handed her a glass from the tray of a passing servant. The stem of the goblet felt like ice in her hand. "Mistresses?"

Titian blinked in surprise. "Surely you know all men have a mistress or two. Or four," he added under his breath.

Laura took a drink of wine, but its coolness failed to soothe her burning throat. She tossed her head, feigning nonchalance. "I suspect he has many."

"He's been widowed for a long time, Laura. You don't think a man like Sandro Cavalli has lived like a monk."

She thought of Sandro's lovemaking, the fierceness of it, the frequency of it. Titian was right.

Jealousy seared her heart, but she refused to give in to the pain. Sandro had made her no promises. He had offered her nothing but the passion she craved. She was a fool to want more.

"Have you learned anything new about the stolen paintings?" she asked, eager to change the subject.

"No. Sandro's subordinates have found no clues."

Laura shuddered; the idea of a stranger, a thief, possessing such intimate pictures of her was unsettling. "I've been working, maestro." She found herself anxious to tell her teacher of the breakthrough in her art. "I have a wonderful studio."

"Lord Sandro allows this?"

"Of course. You were wrong about him, maestro. He understands my ambition. I've produced five paintings."

His eyes widened. "Five? I rarely produce five in a year."

"I know. These are . . . they're different. They speak for me. It's the best work I've ever done."

He nodded, and she knew he understood that she spoke without conceit. "If you think the work is good, then it must be," he said. "You'll need the new paintings."

A shadow of apprehension darkened her heart. "What do you mean? Have you heard from the masters at the Academy?"

"Yes." Titian took her hand and pulled her through a set of tall glass-paned doors to the loggia. The cool evening air enveloped them, but failed to relieve her sense of dread.

"They didn't accept me, did they?" she said, girding herself to let go of a lifetime of dreams.

"No," said Titian. "They did not, despite all my exhortations."

"Is it because my art is poor?" she asked, burning to know. "Or because I'm a woman?"

"Not one man dared to dispute the quality of your work," Titian said.

"Damn." Laura slammed her open palm down on the stone railing. She glowered out across the lawn at the glistening black ribbon of the river. "If it were my art, I could change that—try harder, do better. But I can do nothing about my sex. How dare they reject me because I'm female?"

"I didn't say they rejected you." A smile peeked from the middle of his full beard. "I said they haven't accepted you . . . yet."

Whooping for joy, she took his hands and spun him around. "Tell me! Tell me what to do next."

"We need more examples of your work."

"I have them." She hugged herself. Never had she felt so confident, so hopeful. Even the thought of Sandro's mistresses could not dim her giddy anticipation. Once the Academy accepted her, she could compete for commissions; she would be free and independent.

She would not need Sandro Cavalli anymore.

The notion overwhelmed her with a sense of bleakness.

"I'll take your new paintings back to Venice with me tomorrow." Titian could not hide his uncertainty; he glanced at a burbling Neptune fountain and shuffled his feet.

"What's wrong?" Laura demanded.

"Is there an anatomical painting among your new works?"

Laura swallowed hard. She could not progress to journeyman until she demonstrated her expertise with the human form. She thought of the reams of studies she had done of Sandro. She had sketched him from every possible angle: lounging in bed, standing at a window with his back to her, lifting a glass of wine in salute. Two days earlier she had begun her painting. She had rendered her favorite sketch onto the prepared canvas, and the image that had taken shape was powerful, growing out of the canvas like a sculpture emerging from stone. The work, she knew, would prove beyond doubt that she not only could depict the human form, but that she could give it life and pathos and potency.

"Yes," she said, finally answering Titian's query. "I'm working on one now." Sandro had already made his feelings clear on the topic of exhibiting the picture. He did not want his private image to be displayed. She respected his view, for who was more private than Sandro? But what of respect for her and her ambitions?

Titian started back to the *salone*. "Send it when it's finished." He paused at the entrance and turned back. "You'll succeed, Laura. I vow you will."

"Will what?" Sandro stepped out to the loggia as Titian returned to his friends.

"It's so exciting." Laura threw herself into his arms. "The Academy has evaluated some of my paintings. The maestro thinks that once I submit the new ones, I'll be accepted."

"I don't doubt that you will." His voice was taut, modulated.

She wanted him to be happy for her, but realized that he knew, as she did, that her success would take her away from him. "I'll have my own studio in Venice," she said. "I'll—I'll be on my own." She pressed her cheek to his chest. "Sandro, will you miss me?"

He tipped up her chin and asked, "What do you think?"

Without waiting for an answer, he kissed her hard, devouring her, causing her back to arch and her hands to clutch at his shoulders. He held her, shoving forward with his hips while his hands gripped her buttocks. Her feet left the ground. She put one leg around him, held on, and tried to forget about tomorrow.

"*I* taught him that," said a feminine voice.

Startled, Laura dropped to the ground. She backed away from Sandro to find four beautiful women staring at them. The speaker was a petite, curvaceous redhead.

The sable-haired woman next to her slapped a silk fan rhythmically on her open palm. "Perhaps you did, Gioia, but only after *I* told you he liked it."

"Oh, hush, Barbara, don't be so smug," said the tall one, perusing Laura with sharp hazel eyes. "Can't you see Sandro's new plaything is a complete original?"

"You're right, Arnetta," said the last woman. "Fresh from the manger."

"Funny," said Sandro, rubbing his jaw. "I remembered you as ladies of refined manners. Your behavior proves that memory can play tricks on a person." He spoke with casual aloofness, but Laura felt his rage. Suppressed violence emanated like body heat from him.

"Madonna Laura," he said, all courtly formality now, "I'd like you to meet Madonnas Barbara, Gioia, Arnetta, and Alicia. Former . . . acquaintances of mine."

His mistresses. Laura's heart turned to stone. One day, he would probably refer to her, too, as a former acquaintance.

"*Such* a pleasure," Arnetta effused, taking Laura by the hand and practically dragging her from his side.

"We all have *so* much in common," said Gioia. "Come, we really must lift a cup in salute."

Sandro stepped forward, but Laura shook her head. She was more than equal to these she-buzzards circling for the kill. She was morbidly curious about the women who had held Sandro's affections. "Do stay here, my lord," she said, mimicking the precious, affected speech of the ladies. "I'm most eager to get to know your former acquaintances."

The minute they were out of Sandro's sight, Gioia demanded, "Who the devil do you think you are?"

Laura blinked in surprise. "We've just been introduced." She gazed at them with feigned pity. "I'm told women of a certain age tend to be forgetful."

"One thing we'll never forget," snapped Alicia, "is your impertinence."

A horrible thought struck Laura. Perhaps these ladies had known about her from the start. Perhaps they had hired the *bravi* to do her in. Unthinkingly, she took a step back.

"You think you're on top of the world now, but he'll bring you low," Gioia warned.

"See that man over there?" Arnetta pointed to an elderly, tartan-clad Scots nobleman who sat in a velvet corner chair, staring fixedly into an empty goblet. His other arm rested on a golf club, which he used as a cane. "He's the duke of Dinn. Fabulously wealthy."

"I'm impressed," said Laura. "Is he yours?"

"He happens to be my betrothed." The ladies shuddered in synchrony. "Sandro arranged the match. He's in the process of finding suitors for the others."

"Oh." Laura toyed with the seed pearls on her jeweled bodice. "Pity you can't attract husbands on your own." She savored their gasps of outrage.

"Listen, you little slut," Gioia hissed, "we know what you are and where you came from."

"And where you're going," Arnetta added.

"The Lord of the Night has sunk low," Alicia said, "pilfering counterfeit virgins from cat houses."

Arnetta gestured angrily at the elderly duke. "That's what you have to look forward to if you stay with him."

Given Sandro's prejudices and Laura's own ambitions, staying with him was a doubtful prospect. But never would she admit that to these harpies.

"Unlike you good ladies," she said, dipping into a curtsy, "I have a career. I shall not need a man to take care of me."

"Oh? But you like men. I hear you satisfied *everyone.*"

Laura hoped the golden candlelight would hide her sudden pallor. Although conquered, her fear still lingered. Insolently she looked them up and down. "And I hear *you* ladies *can't* satisfy anyone."

"Here, now." Clapping his hands, Pietro Aretino breezed into the group. "So you've met at last. I've been looking forward to this."

"Bestiaccio," grumbled Alicia.

"Ah, Laura, I know Sandro introduced the good ladies to you, but I doubt he did justice to their virtues—which are considerable for women in their dotage."

The furious ladies sailed away in a rustle of watered silk and high dudgeon. Laura closed her eyes, leaned back against Aretino's chest, and let out a long-held breath. "Thank you, Messere Pietro."

"You didn't need rescuing," said a woman's voice. "You were magnificent."

Laura opened her eyes and stared at the lady who had spoken. The newcomer was beautiful—chestnut-haired, tall, and elegant, with well-defined features and soft, dark eyes. Her face was so strikingly familiar that Laura forgot her manners and said, "Adriana?"

Sandro's daughter held out a pale, slim hand. "Most people do know me by my father."

"I'm sorry." Laura squeezed the cool hand. "I didn't mean—"

"It's nothing." With a refined nod to Aretino, Adriana led Laura to a table laden with food. Humor sparkled in her eyes. "Even if you weren't wearing my dress, I'd have known instantly that you were Laura."

Laura blushed and looked down at the dress. It was high-waisted and made of sapphire silk velvet. Garnets edged the oversleeves, and tissue of the sheerest white silk showed through the slashings of the sleeves. She had never worn a gown of such staggering luxury. "Madonna, I didn't mean to presume—"

"Don't be silly," Adriana said with a laugh. "The blue looks better on you, anyway. The good Lord gave me only one body, and not enough time on this earth to wear my costumes. Between Franco and Papa, I own enough to clothe all the beggars of Venice. It's disgraceful."

Laura quickly understood the affection in Sandro's voice on the few occasions he had spoken of his daughter. Adriana was everything Marcantonio should have been: straightforward, charming, intelligent, generous.

"Thank you, madonna. I'm glad you don't mind."

"Laura." Adriana took her hand. "I don't mind a thing that you do." She twined their arms together and started a progress around the ballroom, nodding at lords and prelates as she passed, pausing here and there to introduce Laura in terms that would have flattered a saint. Only Laura felt Adriana shaking with laughter at their drop-jawed expressions.

Adriana's connections to both Sandro and the son of the Capo of the Council of Ten had endowed her with a formidable status among the nobles of Venice. By showing open regard for Laura, Adriana was bringing her among the ranks of the respectable.

"I appreciate what you're trying to do," she murmured around her fixed smile. "But it won't work. I'm baseborn; I lived in a brothel, and I was abducted by the sons of these people. I don't even want to be accepted by them."

"I'm just trying to make things easier for you."

They reached a private corner away from the crowd. Laura disengaged her arm from Adriana's. "Why?" she asked.

"Because of what you've done for me. See, I've shown myself for the selfish baggage that I am, but I won't lie to you."

Laura heard echoes of Sandro in the statement. "What have I ever done for you?"

Adriana laughed. "You've given me the father I've always dreamed of having."

"I don't understand."

"You've changed him. All my life, he was stern and demanding. I almost never saw him smile, and certainly never heard him laugh. And now look at him." She gestured.

Across the room, Sandro stood with one arm draped around Aretino and the other around Titian. They were singing at the tops of their lungs. Sandro's face was flushed, his eyes sparkling, and his posture completely relaxed.

"I always considered him an old man, even when he was young. You've given him youth." Tears sprang to her eyes. "A while ago, when you were out on the loggia, he danced with me for the first time ever. And he—he told me he loved me."

"Of course he loves you. He always has."

"He never told me. Not once. Until tonight."

"Perhaps being away from Venice has been good for him."

"Do stop making excuses," Adriana insisted. "It's you. When he fell in love with you, he changed."

"He's not in love with me," Laura said swiftly, frantically. "He denied it, and it's well he did. An affair of the heart would make everything . . ." She cast about for the right word. "Impossible."

"Well, it's too late now. He loves you. Everyone can see that."

"Then his feelings will change very soon."

"True love never changes, only grows and deepens."

"It will this time." Solemnly, feeling torn to pieces, Laura explained about the painting. "I must submit the nude of Sandro to the Academy if I'm to win acceptance."

"It's that important to you?" Adriana asked. "You'd risk my father's love to win your journeyman's status?"

"I'm only his mistress." Laura turned away. "Aren't I entitled to my own dreams and ambitions?"

Adriana pulled her back. "I do understand. I think it's wonderful. Send the painting, Laura. It will be good for my father to put love before pride."

Laura shook her head. "Your father," she said sadly, "would never choose love over pride."

Her heart tripping, Laura held her hands over Sandro's eyes as she guided him into the studio. "Just another few steps," she said.

The studio looked curiously empty after Titian had taken the five paintings to the Academy. He had pronounced them astonishingly original. She was glad the pictures were gone. By painting them, she had purged herself of nightmares; now they belonged in the past where they could not touch her.

She did miss the bull. Or rather, she had until she had completed the portrait of Sandro.

"Any time now," he prompted with good-humored impatience.

She stood behind him and positioned him in front of the easel. "Promise me something," she whispered, pressing her cheek to his back and finding comfort in the rhythmic thud of his heart. "Promise me you'll look at the painting—really look at it—before you decide whether or not you like what I've done."

"It's that bad?"

"No." With complete certainty she said, "It's that good. But you might take a few minutes to appreciate the work."

Trying to keep her hands steady, she took them away from his eyes, then stepped forward to watch his reaction. She prayed he would understand.

Sandro blinked, and the picture leapt out at him, grabbed him on some awful visceral level, and held him spellbound.

Even as his mind screamed in outrage, part of him knew with terrible conviction that he was viewing the best painting she had ever done.

And God, he hated it.

She had shown him standing at a window, his shoulder propped on the embrasure and one knee drawn up, the foot braced on the ledge. She had set the scene at night. The only source of illumination came from the milky mist of moonlight flowing through the open window, streaming over him like water from an evening cascade.

The details in the room were muted by shadow so that the eye was riveted to the man alone. He stood naked in more ways than one.

She had done the unthinkable—had violated accepted practice and depicted him exactly as he was, not as he wished he were. She had highlighted his long, tousled hair with streaks of silver. She had allowed light and shadow to carve his true age in his features. With a merciless, unblinking eye she had shown every scar and seasoned sinew on his body.

His face was turned in profile. The hard line of his jaw feathered away to softness, giving him a strangely contradictory look of both ferocity and dreaminess. It made the viewer wonder what events had brought him to this tense, pensive moment. Had he just left his lover's bed, or was he a warrior on the eve of battle? Were his thoughts carnal or spiritual? Was he man or god?

Sandro's throat seemed to close. She had stolen his soul, laid his private self bare for all the world to see. And then, in case there might be any doubt, at the bottom she had titled it *Il signore di notte.* The Lord of the Night.

"Well?" she asked in a rush, as if she had been holding her breath.

"It's . . ." He cleared his throat. "It's like the bull."

"You hated the bull."

"Yes," he said, feeling suddenly weary and defeated. "I hated the bull."

"I'm not surprised." She spoke briskly, nervously. "Few people actually like pictures of themselves. Truth be told, I'm rather relieved that Titian's paintings of me are gone. They were masterpieces, but I never liked them."

He gave a start of surprise. "How could you not like them? Those pictures are radiant. They show the true character of the subject."

"As this one," she said, "shows yours."

He knew better than to succumb to flattery, but in

spite of his misgivings, he felt a sense of awe at the stark honesty of the portrait.

"Remember what you promised," she said. "Don't decide about the picture yet."

"When can I decide?"

She idly picked up a clean paintbrush. "Oh, after I've had a chance to gain your sympathy."

"Really? And how do you propose to do that?"

"The same way," she said, unclasping the row of fasteners at the front of his doublet, "that I did the painting." She slipped her hand inside the neck of his shirt.

His skin tightened under her touch. Doublet and shirt fell away. "And . . . how did you accomplish that?"

"You have the most uncompromising features I've ever seen, my lord. To show that, I used a brush of boar's bristle and sculpted your face as much as I painted it." Her deft fingers loosed his trunk hose. He stepped out of his boots and clothing as if in a dream.

"And yet," she whispered, her breath a warm mist on his chest, "there is a tenderness in you, which I could only show by blending with this." The brush in her hand drew a feathery circle around his naval and then traveled slowly, erotically, downward. "It's made," she explained, "of the finest sable."

"Jesus," he said, gritting his teeth as she used the brush to paint an invisible picture upon his flesh. The fine wisps of precious sable swirled around his groin, took the measure of his hardness, traced a path around his hips to travel the curves of his back and buttocks. "Laura . . ." he said, then forgot what he was going to say.

Surely no woman had ever enticed a man in this manner. His code of behavior was extensive and detailed, but he could think of no rule to govern the conduct of a man being roused by a woman armed with a sable brush.

"You're thinking again," she chided. "I can tell. You always get this crease right here"—she touched the brush to the spot—"between your eyebrows. Don't wonder what to do next. Just let your heart guide you for once in your life."

He gave an involuntary shudder. "Much more of this and my heart will lose out to my . . ." His voice trailed off and he caught her against him. It was amazingly easy to succumb to her unusual seduction, particularly for a man who had, until recently, never acted solely out of desire.

In moments he had her undressed and took the brush from her, torturing her in turn with light, teasing caresses until they tumbled into the nest made by their discarded clothing. He loved her with a wild, savage hunger that suffered no fits of conscience, no misgivings of honor. Her joyfully wanton response urged him on, sweeping them both into a whirlwind of hard, brilliant color and then leaving them sated, almost bloated with fulfillment, sweaty arms and legs entwined.

"So," she said at last, propping her chin on his chest. "Now what do you think of the painting?"

He gazed at the easel, at the naked, troubled, dreaming man standing in darkness. The picture revealed too much. She knew him too well, and that frightened him, for it illustrated the power she had over him.

"I suppose you've given me a certain . . . puissance," he admitted.

A smile flashed across her face. "I have, haven't I? Sandro, it's the best picture I've ever done. The others were a breakthrough for me, but this one . . . this one proves I have it."

"Have what?"

"The gift. The magic."

"You do, Laura."

"Then it's enough."

"Enough for what?"

"For the Academy to accept me."

An icy snake of fear coiled low in his belly. He pushed her aside and got up, hurriedly donning his clothes with jerky movements. She followed suit, eyeing him warily. "What's wrong, Sandro?"

"So that's what this seduction was all about," he bit out. "You thought to lull me into compliance."

Her features fell in dismay. "No! But I must submit this painting to the Academy. They won't accept me without it."

"Paint a different picture."

"It has to be this one."

"Then give the subject a different face."

"I can't change the face. There's only one face for this body. Yours. Anything less would be a lie, and I only paint the truth." She gazed at the portrait, and the love shining in her eyes made him wince . . . and wonder. Did she love him, or a fantasy she had created on canvas?

"I won't allow it." He gestured angrily at the picture. "How do you think I would feel, Laura, to have all of Venice looking at me?"

"It's a noble portrait. An honest one. Everyone would look at you with respect."

"Ah, respect." Anger roiled like storm-heavy clouds inside him. She had seduced him just to get her way; he wanted to punish her for that, for making him believe she loved him. "That's what I need now,

isn't it, Laura? For I've lost it all. Banished from
Venice, living in exile with a whore—"

The horrified look on her face stopped him. Immediately he knew he had gone too far, had cut her too
deep. Like a cornered animal, he had lashed out, his
unthinking aim to hurt, to tear her tender heart to
pieces.

"Laura," he said hoarsely, "I didn't mean that."

She had gone completely pale, and her wide eyes
were great pools of agony in her chalk white face.
She stumbled back a few steps and fumbled at a worktable. When she turned to him, she clutched a palette
knife in her hand.

My God, he thought. She meant to kill him in
order to stifle his objections.

He took a step forward, hands ready to deflect the
first blow. She seemed not to see him. With a cry of
pain she lunged toward the painting. The knife
moved toward the center of the canvas.

"No!" The shout broke from him as he leapt
forward, clutching her hand and stopping it in
midarc. "Laura, what the devil are you doing?"

"I never should have painted this," she said, her
breath coming in panting sobs.

He drew her to him and felt her pain then, felt it
rush like a tremor through her body. Her hand convulsed around the handle of the palette knife.

"Leave it, Laura," he said. "We're both . . . over-
wrought."

The knife dropped and skittered across the floor.
"All right," she said, her shoulders slumping in
defeat. "Good night, Sandro. Sleep well."

He let her go, his heart aching at the smallness,
the slowness of her as she retreated from the studio

and crept down the stairs. Part of him wanted to go after her, but another part knew that it was too late to take back the things he had said to her.

He glanced at the painting, and a low curse escaped him. It *was* a masterpiece. It *would* win her election to the Academy.

If he let her submit it.

If he humbled himself, laid himself bare for all of Venice. Why was it so damned important to her? They were happy here, alone together, passing the time making love or sharing companionable meals with Yasmin and Jamal. Wasn't life at the estate enough for her?

No, he conceded bleakly. She wanted more. So did he. Her happiness was false, the contentment of a bird in a cage, and his resistance kept her there because he knew no other way to hold her.

The truth struck him with the force of a blow. His fear, his obsession, he finally admitted, lay at the heart of the dilemma. Letting her send the painting would take her away from him, lift her into the exclusive, rarefied realm of celebrated artists. Commissions would pour in; she would be too busy for him.

While still an apprentice, she had no means of support. She was dependent on him; she belonged to him.

The words he had spoken to Jamal came back to haunt him: *If you free her and she leaves you, then she was never yours to begin with.*

How wise he had thought himself; how smug he had been. Now he understood Jamal's panic at the thought of giving freedom to the woman he loved.

Sandro gazed at the private, revealing portrait, and the dilemma pounded at him. Set Laura free . . . and lose her. Or deny her, and keep her.

* * *

Laura came awake in the middle of the night.
After leaving Sandro, she had stared at the ceiling
and despaired until she fell asleep. Upon waking, she
felt no sense of relief. His bitter, hateful words still
squeezed like a weight upon her chest. *I've lost it all.*
Banished from Venice, living in exile with a whore—

The room looked alien to her, for she had not slept
here in days. Sandro had taken her to his bed. She had
fooled herself into thinking he had let her into his life.

Gathering a yellow silk robe around her, she
walked barefoot to the studio. Moonlight and shadows danced on a breeze through the large room.

She went to the easel to look at her painting, to try
to find some reason for his hatred. She had spilled
her heart and soul upon the canvas, and the result
had offended him.

The painting was gone. Horror and denial climbed
up in her throat. Gone!

How could he? she asked herself. The portrait represented the very best of her skill and talent. He had
taken her future. Stolen her chance at independence.

But why? To destroy or hide it?

Racing through the house, she searched every
room and closet, but within minutes, the terrible
truth struck her.

Both Sandro and the painting were gone.

I know where he went.

Laura read the message on Jamal's slate and raised
her eyes to his grave face.

She turned in disbelief to Yasmin, who held her

tight. Laura had roused them from comfortable, love-sated sleep to tell them what had happened.

"He says he knows where Sandro went," she told Yasmin.

"Then he probably does." Yasmin used a corner of her robe to wipe Laura's face. "The two of them are as brothers."

Laura shot up and clutched the front of Jamal's caftan. "Where? Where did he go to destroy my painting?"

Not to destroy.

"How do you know that?"

"Because he knows Sandro," Yasmin stated.

Jamal showed her the slate again. *Gone to Venice. Lovesick fool.*

Fatigue and sorrow and confusion hummed in Laura's ears. "Why?"

To give your painting to the Accademia.

Laura fell back against the bedpost. "He wouldn't."

Jamal's nod assured her that he had. Panic swept through her. "He can't! He's not allowed in Venice."

Grimly Jamal presented the slate to her again. *Allah preserve him if he is caught.*

Sandro prayed he would not get caught. Displaying the portrait at the Academy was humiliating enough. He did not need the added trouble of being apprehended violating the terms of his banishment.

He pulled up the collar of his cloak and decided there was little danger of being recognized. Mist shrouded the quiet early morning. Like a thief, he had entered through the cellar of the Academy. In half darkness, he had located the gallery where Laura's other paintings hung. Even in the dimness, the power of her work struck him. Taken as a group, they represented a rare and unique genius. With shaking hands, he had hung out his soul for all to see. In a short while, the masters would gather in front of the picture.

Sandro crossed the Pescaria where the fishermen were just starting their day, and headed for his waiting barge. His tightlipped bargemen had instructions to stay put.

A group of local militiamen came staggering through the plaza, drunk after a night of revelry. Sandro tugged up the collar of his mist-damp cloak and swept past. One soldier eyed him curiously.

As he passed by the Church of San Rocco, the bell tolled. Black-garbed widows hurried to morning mass. One of them brushed close to him, and for a moment he thought she spoke to him, but dismissed the possibility as soon as she passed by.

On the water side of the piazza, he saw his barge, its bulky decks rising out of the mist. A flock of doves lifted, the muted clapping of wings adding rhythm to the morning bells. Taking the painting to Venice had violated every code of behavior he had ever known. He had broken the terms of his banishment. He had displayed himself naked for all to see.

He had committed an act of supreme foolishness. An act of love, the first such sacrifice he had ever made. He prayed this folly would be the last.

When the team of ducal guards seized him just as he was about to board, he concluded that it would be, and thanked God for small mercies.

15

"*Jamal thinks we* should start searching here, at the Piazza San Marco," Yasmin explained.

Laura stood impatiently as the craft docked at the quay in front of the grand Byzantine plaza. The soaring campanile and the winged lions of Saint Mark rose in splendor above a surging, shouting crowd. A procession of some sort was in progress; she could see the tasseled red umbrella that always shadowed the doge when he went out in public.

"Why here?" she asked, jumping out of the boat and earning a glare from the lighterman, who had not yet made the mooring lines fast.

Moments later, she discovered the horrible, outrageous answer on her own.

Pushing through the crowd, she made her way toward the bobbing red umbrella of the doge. Two long lines of ducal guards flanked the head of the republic. State inquisitors surrounded the doge's litter. Nine members of the Council of Ten followed. The tenth member walked at the rear with his hands tied in front of him.

"Sandro!" Laura whispered. Love and pity choked her as she took in his haggard face, his blank, dead eyes, the bloody stripes that soaked through the shirt on his back.

"My God," she said half to herself. "What's happened to him?"

A stout man in a butcher's apron frowned. "Just got here, did you?"

"Yes." She tried to break through the ranks of militiamen holding the crowd at bay. A burly soldier pushed her back.

"You're too late," the butcher said, his face dark with indignation. "The interesting part's over."

"Interesting part?" Laura shivered with dread.

"The flogging." The butcher rubbed his hands on his apron. "The Lord of the Night made nary a sound. Just stood there like a statue, staring off at God knows what." The butcher shook his head. "The city is appalled, for he's been good to us. Sometimes he was the only one to stand between the common man and the nobles."

"If everyone is appalled, why not act? Defend him, speak out—"

"Against them?" The butcher gestured at the fierce guards with their pikes and swords. "I think not."

Her heart in pieces, Laura lurched toward the parade again, but the butcher held her back. "No need to endanger yourself. All that's left now is to clap him in the Gabbia."

"In prison?" Nausea washed over her in a wave. She recalled her short stay in the damp darkness. Now Sandro would reside there.

"No!" The yell burst from her, and desperate strength propelled her through the ranks of guards.

She knew she couldn't help Sandro, but neither could she stand by and see him humiliated before the city he loved.

Moving swiftly to elude the guards, she planted herself directly in front of the doge. "Stop this!" she yelled.

Andrea Gritti stared at her in outrage. Sandro swore. Two men came forward and started to haul her away.

"Let go," she said furiously, jerking free of the guards. "Don't you remember me?"

His face pinched in concentration, the doge looked to his councillors as if seeking help.

"I came forward the last time you committed an injustice against Sandro Cavalli," Laura said. "He's dedicated his life to the security of Venice. How can you force him to endure this treatment?"

"The woman's right," someone shouted, and Laura recognized the voice of the butcher. A few others took up the cry, and the crowd surged like a forest disturbed by a restless wind.

Sandro's blank eyes stared at Laura. In that moment she forgot the hateful things he had said to her the night he had left. If it would ease his agony, she would endure a lifetime of his temper.

"Laura," he said hoarsely, "stay out of this."

"Young lady, your insolence will cost you," said the doge. "Lord Sandro broke the law."

"Your Worship!" Pietro Aretino's voice boomed from the back of the crowd. Flanked by Titian and Sansovino, and trailed by the master of the Academy, he fought his way forward.

Behind them came a red-draped litter, the conveyance of the wife of Andrea Gritti, the dogaressa. At her side walked Adriana, who took one look at her father and started to weep.

"Good prince," Titian said, invoking the humility that so pleased his patrons, "surely you'd not incarcerate the newest member of the Academy."

Laura's knees went weak. "You mean . . . I . . . "

Titian smiled triumphantly. "Yes, maestra. It was that last painting that convinced all the skeptics. Your portrait of the Lord of the Night."

Confusion spun through her head. "No one has seen that painting."

"Half of Venice has seen it," Jacopo Sansovino assured her. "The other half is clamoring for a view."

"It's brilliant," said the dogaressa, emerging from her litter. Benedetta Vendramin Gritti fixed a regal gaze on Laura, although she addressed her husband. "You won't lift a hand against this woman, Andrea. I mean to offer her a commission immediately."

Laura's head reeled. Jamal had been right after all. Sandro had risked his pride and his freedom to bring about her election to the Academy.

His selfless gesture was a knife to her heart.

"With your permission, my prince," Aretino said.

Gritti nodded to allow him to approach. The writer bent to whisper something in the doge's ear.

The color drained from the doge's face. He opened his mouth to speak. At first no sound came out; then he said, "Release Lord Sandro at once."

As he stood at the door of the neat, modest house in the Merceria, Sandro felt as gawky as a lovesick suitor. Eight days had passed since the scene in the Piazza San Marco. Eight eventful, torturous days.

The doge had taken him to the palace, showered

him with praise and gifts, and begged him to return to his post as Lord of the Night.

Why? Sandro had asked, knowing it was neither friendship nor compassion that had motivated Andrea Gritti.

Fear, not loyalty, had compelled him to lift the banishment.

The doge had looked frightened, for during Sandro's absence Gritti had managed to convince himself of Adolfo's guilt.

He had been wrong. Another murder had occurred the night before. The victim was a ship's chandler at the Arsenal.

It took a murder, Sandro reflected bitterly, to make the doge lift his banishment.

Not once during the week had Sandro gone to see Laura. She had flooded his office with letters, had come in person to see him, but he had instructed his servants to send her away. He did not want her gratitude.

The madness was over; she had reached her goal of joining the Academy, and he had settled back into a role that was as familiar to him as a pair of old boots.

With one significant difference.

He was not the same person who had run his ministry, his business, and his life like well-oiled clockwork. Now he was a man who felt pain and passion, mirth and grief and joy. Laura had awakened him to a rich world of emotion, and he could not forget that despite his return to the orderly, arid existence he had known before.

For eight days he had fooled himself into thinking that he could live without her. Then, early this morning, he had watched from the window as a flock of birds had risen from the lagoon, their wings gilded by the sun. He had looked at his Spartan breakfast of dry bread, hard cheese, and watered wine, and had remembered that he and Laura used to lie naked in bed, eating Smyrna dates and honey for breakfast.

In that instant, the solution had come to him. He did not have to live without her.

To bolster his confidence, he thought of all her letters and visits.

The bouquet of posies felt sticky in his hand. He could not believe he was taking her flowers. He had not been himself since he had first set eyes on Laura.

He rapped smartly on the door, then held his breath. After a few seconds, the door opened and a servant bade him enter.

A servant, for Christ's sake. Laura had wasted no time in establishing her new household.

"The maestra is in her studio," the woman said. "She does not wish to receive any vis—"

"She'll see me," Sandro said, brushing past. At the end of a hallway, he saw a light-filled solar.

She stood behind an easel in the center of a room filled with sunlight and cluttered with the tools of her trade. On a worktable lay a series of studies of Dogaressa Benedetta Vendramin. All he could see of Laura was a pair of bare feet moving to and fro, the paint-stained hem of her smock swaying with the motion as she hummed tunelessly.

A flood of tenderness washed over him, but in its wake came terror. She seemed perfectly content without him, while for the past eight days he had been insane with wanting her.

He cleared his throat. At the same moment, the small black-and-brown dog came racing in through the garden door. Yapping in outrage, it launched itself at Sandro and clamped down on a familiar target. His boot.

"Fortunato!" Laura pulled off the dog and tucked it under her arm. "My lord, you really shouldn't provoke him so."

Sandro aimed a glare at the growling, trembling beast under Laura's arm. "I came to tell you that I am in receipt of your letters," he said, instantly hating the stiff formality in his voice.

She turned the dog back out into the garden and shut the door, ignoring a howl of outrage. Then she rushed to Sandro like a bright-eyed, eager child. Her hair was caught negligently with a piece of twine, and her face and hands were smudged with paint. Never had she looked more beautiful, or more shockingly youthful, to him. He had never felt more haggard, his back on fire from the flogging.

She flung her arms around him, clinging, kissing his throat and chin and cheeks, anywhere her lips could reach. A few weeks earlier he would have fussed about getting paint stains on his clothing; now he merely gave it a passing thought. He had clothes to spare, but there was only one Laura.

Gently, trying to deny the unutterable joy of seeing her again, he disengaged himself from her and held out the bouquet. "These are for you. I'm afraid we've crushed a few of the carnations, but—"

"You're jesting, are you not?" She took the flowers, buried her face in them, and inhaled.

"Jesting?" he asked. "Jesting is beneath me."

She laughed and lifted her face. "Maybe so, but bringing me flowers is not. What a wonderfully sweet gesture."

God help me, he thought.

"Congratulations are in order," he said. "Are they not?"

"I've been congratulating myself for a week." She

spun around, her arms outflung. "Look at this place, Sandro! The dogaressa rented it for me, with three servants and enough money to buy all the supplies I need. She wants me to have every convenience while I work on her portrait."

"It's very nice."

"I owe it all to you. After we quarreled and I dis-covered the painting was gone, I thought the worst. I thought you had destroyed it. I never dreamed you would make such a sacrifice."

I would do anything for you.

He tried to smile nonchalantly. "Hanging naked on a gallery wall is not half so bad as I feared. I've endured a few jokes, but they don't bother me." He decided not to mention the flood of invitations that had come from dozens of Venetian ladies. He looked around the well-appointed room. "You've gotten what you wanted."

"Yes." Her agreement lacked emphasis. "Why did you wait until now to come?"

Because I was afraid.

"I was busy."

She braced her hands on the table and regarded him steadily. "There's been another murder, hasn't there?"

His blood chilled. He had meant to protect her from the knowledge. "Yes," he said. "How did you know?"

"Since I can't even sneeze without Guido observ-ing me, I assumed you reopened the case." She rubbed her hands up and down her arms. "It was like the others, wasn't it?"

The gory image flashed in his mind, and he nodded. To the amazement of his staff, he himself had gone to inform the victim's family. He himself had heard the cries of the young widow, the wails of the two now-destitute children. Before Laura, he had lacked the strength to expose himself to the grief of a family.

"Who was the victim this time?" Laura asked.

If he didn't tell her, she would ask strangers until she found out. "His name was Solonni. He was a chandler at the Arsenal. At the time he was murdered, he was preparing torches to light the state barge for next week's ceremony."

He knew with complete certainty that the scene of the crime was more than coincidence. Each victim had some connection with the doge. This very moment, Sandro's team of investigators was searching the giant galley from stem to stern.

"So Adolfo is not the killer," Laura concluded.

"No. He was in the Gabbia when this last murder took place."

"So you still have no idea who the assassin is?"

"No." But he was getting close. He could feel it, like the brush of a cobweb in the dark. He was starting to understand the assassin, to sense the cold satisfaction of the kill.

"Is there anything I can do to help?"

"No, damn it. Stay out of it, Laura. I'm not asking you or ordering you to. I'm begging you."

"From commanding to begging," she said. "I like that."

He took a deep breath. "I want to offer you more than protection."

She looked at him in surprise.

"Laura," he said quickly before his courage left him. "I have a proposal to make to you. An offer."

"A p-proposal?"

"Yes." He took her hand and brushed his lips over her knuckles. "I want you to be my mistress."

"Your m-mistress?"

"I'll buy you a house—any house you choose, with a studio and an army of servants."

"No." Her voice was low and rough with horror. "I don't need you to provide a house or jewels or servants for me." She snatched her hand back. "I need more."

"I don't understand."

"I need all of you, Sandro, and if you can't give me that, then I want no part of you at all."

Sandro's heart sank to his knees. Had she tired of him already, found a young lover, foresworn men altogether?

"You can't refuse me," he said. "Damn it, Laura, you were happy with me at the villa. You liked making love, sharing meals, spending time together."

"That's true," she admitted desolately. "But I had no idea our parting would be so . . . shattering."

He gripped her shoulders. "We needn't be apart, Laura."

"No. I cannot accept your terms."

"Why not? My proposed arrangement provides the perfect solution."

She pulled away. "For you, perhaps. I'm very busy. When people heard about the commission of the dog-aressa, they all wanted to hire me, too. If I choose, I can have commissions to last many years."

"You cannot spend every waking moment on your art."

"Oh, and so I should squander my free time servicing you?" Her voice lashed at him like a whip, and her hair swirled like black fire around her beautiful, angry face. "And when you're tired of me, will you marry me off to some rich old lord as you did your other mistresses? Everything's so neat and simple to you, Sandro. But not to me."

"Why are you so offended? You were going to be a courtesan, Laura."

"Yes," she said hotly. "But no man has ever made me feel as cheap and insignificant as you just have." She turned away, looking suddenly very small and forlorn. "I wish you would leave now, my lord. I have work to do."

"Such a wise decision," Magdalena said. "You were right to refuse him. I'm proud of you."

Laura sighed and moved restlessly around Magdalena's room. The familiar surroundings failed to ease her anxiety. "So am I," she said, pressing her back against the tall armoire. "I still hurt when I remember the way he treated me."

"I know." Magdalena rose from the desk and took Laura's hand; she kissed her cheek, lingering for a moment. "It does hurt to lose one you love. When you went away, I was miserable. But I knew you'd come back to me."

"It's good to be back, to be painting. My work keeps me sane these days."

"I heard you were accepted at the Academy." Magdalena's face lit with delight. "What are you working on?"

"A very important commission. That's why I came here today. I need a special pigment from your mother. You won't believe this, Magdalena, but my first job is a portrait of the dogaressa."

Magdalena gasped. "The consort of Andrea Gritti!"

"Yes. Isn't it incredible?"

"No! Stay away from the doge and all his family. It's too dangerous for you."

Laura frowned. "I don't understand. How can

painting for an influential lady be dangerous?"

"I know about the murders," Magdalena said. She paced in agitation, her gait uneven and her hands toying with her rosary. "Every victim was someone close to the doge. At least wait, Laura. Wait until the danger is over."

"What's all this talk?" Celestina glided into the room, bringing with her the familiar smells of her alchemy.

"Mother," Magdalena said urgently, "Laura is doing a portrait of the dogaressa."

Celestina's mouth tightened. She glared at her daughter with fire in her eye. Laura ached for Magdalena, for Celestina had a way of giving a simple look the knife edge of cruelty. "And what business is that of yours?" she demanded.

Magdalena seemed to shrink inside her habit. "I just don't think . . . it's a good idea."

"Laura is getting the acclaim she wanted. Can you not be happy for her?"

"No," Magdalena snapped, suddenly exhibiting a rare rebellious streak. "I don't want any harm to come to Laura. I would *die* if anything happened to her."

Celestina's hand shot out and cracked against Magdalena's cheek. "Enough," she shouted. "Your duty is to love the Lord, not interfere in Laura's life."

In stunned disbelief, Laura rushed forward and put her arms around Magdalena. She shot a censorious look at the nun. "Magdalena didn't deserve your anger. She's wrong about there being any danger in my commission. Still, I won't have you abusing her."

Celestina took a deep breath and her face smoothed over, serene once again. "You're right, of course." She cupped Magdalena's chin in her hand and kissed her cheek. "Forgive me, child. I acted out of turn. It's not like me to bring pain to an innocent."

She left, and so did Laura. She could do without the special pigment.

On the eve of Ascension Day, Laura walked on a cloud out of the ducal palace. The ever-present Guido Lombardo followed at a respectful distance. She knew he burned to find out the result of the private audience, but she did not speak to him. In her mind she relived the scene in the residence quarters again and again.

The doge and his consort had received her as an honored guest. Her three servants had set the shrouded portrait before them. Laura had felt light-headed with anxiety as she waited to unveil the portrait, the fruit of days of working and reworking until she was satisfied that her painting of Madonna Benedetta was perfect and true.

With a shaking hand she had removed the shroud.

Andrea Gritti and his wife had simply stared at it.

Laura died a thousand deaths awaiting their reaction. Had she been too bold, too radical? Conventional painters depicted every hair, every thread of clothing. Drawing inspiration from Titian's style, Laura had painted what she saw as the essence of the dogaressa. During the sittings for the preliminary sketches, she had come to know Madonna Benedetta as a handsome, energetic woman. In the portrait, Laura had wasted no art on the sumptuous, pearl-encrusted *dogalina* or the lavish jewels. She had gone straight to the heart of her subject, and the result was a vigorous, unusual picture.

But in those first few moments, her confidence had slipped.

Until Madonna Benedetta spoke: "It's brilliant."

Her husband had agreed heartily. On impulse, Benedetta had suggested that the official unveiling take place in a suitably dramatic setting: on the state galley *Bucentaur,* during the ceremonial marriage to the sea.

"Tomorrow," Laura said aloud, quickening her steps as her thoughts returned to the present. She was full to bursting. She had to tell someone her news. Guido would not do; he had never pretended to understand her passion for painting. By all rights she should go to Titian. For the longest time, he alone had believed in her, had let her immerse herself in his world of color and light.

Yet she knew his reaction would be purely professional. Right now she needed emotion—joy, amazement—to validate her triumph. There was only one person in the world who could give her that.

But when she arrived at Sandro's house and stood unannounced outside his offices, she began to have doubts. They had quarreled at their last meeting, had hurt each other. Two weeks had passed since then.

Today was different, she told herself. Sandro wanted her to succeed regardless of the damage they had done to the tender bud of their new love.

Bolstered by the thought, she knocked at the door and pushed it open. Her heart ached at the sight that greeted her.

Sandro sat at his desk. His hair and clothes were as meticulously neat as they had been on the first day she had met him. His face had that same hard, angry look, as if the world displeased him.

She had almost forgotten this Sandro Cavalli, this arid soul encased in ice. Apparently he had forgotten the freedom, the laughter, and the intimacy they had shared.

He glanced up. A look of unbearable hope lit his eyes.

In that moment, Laura realized her mistake. "My lord," she said, hurrying forward, "I didn't come because I reconsidered your offer."

A chill seemed to pervade the air. "Oh? Then what do you want from me, Laura?"

She had wanted to blurt out her tidings, have him pick her up and swing her around in joy. Now she realized, with bleak disappointment, that an awkward distance lay between them.

"I have . . . news, my lord. I showed my painting to the doge and his lady, and they . . . they approved." She frowned. Her recounting made it sound as dull as a rainy day.

"Excellent," he said crisply, straightening a pile of perfectly straight papers. "I'm not at all surprised. I never disputed your talent, Laura."

"No, you disputed my right to use it," she shot back, infuriated by his impassive attitude. He acted as if the idyllic weeks at his villa had never happened, as though he had never been swept away by passion.

"You're wrong," he said flatly. "My offer doesn't mean you would have to give up your art."

"I suppose," she said, "I should be grateful. Most women of my station would be honored." *But I want more, Sandro. I want to be part of your life, not just the woman you visit when you feel the need.* Pride held the words in.

He twirled a quill pen between his fingers. She remembered his wonderful hands on her, working a dark, sweet magic that touched her soul.

"Where are Jamal and Yasmin?" she asked suddenly,

a safe question that drove out the warm liquid sensations she had begun to feel.

A small smile lifted his mouth. "I see little of them these days. They're fitting out one of my cogs, and live aboard."

"Why?"

"They're planning a voyage. To Algiers, then back to Jamal's people in Africa."

"I thought Jamal had vowed never to go back."

"Yasmin changed his mind. You see, Laura, it's amazing what the right woman can do for a man."

Had she changed him? No, Sandro's life was back in the same rigid order it had been before she had come along. With one difference. Because of her, he had been beaten, humiliated. He had lost his son.

"I'll miss Yasmin," she said. "I have few friends to spare."

"You'll have more friends than you can count once people see your portrait."

She pushed a finger at her lower lip. "No, it's not the same. After today, I'll never know if people like me for who I am, or for what I can create on canvas."

"Laura, a long time ago I asked you if you could stand the loneliness, the struggle, the heartbreak of being an artist."

"My answer hasn't changed." She set her hands on her hips and glared at him. "I've not found heartbreak in art, but in being your lover."

Abruptly he got up from the desk and crossed the room. Just the sight of his lean, athletic body filled her with need, and when he grabbed her and pulled her to him, she lost all power to resist.

"God, Laura, don't say that," he implored in a rough whisper. As he spoke, he backed her against the tapesty-covered wall. "I never meant to hurt you."

She had forgotten how sweet he tasted, how sensitive she was to his touch. Within moments her skirts were up, her legs locked around him, and her senses in flames. Their joining was swift and savage, her pleasure shattering, and the aftermath unexpectedly peaceful.

"I'm sorry," he whispered into her ear.

"Don't be." She put her forehead against his, kissed him, then shook out her skirts. "I wanted you."

"Then damn it, why won't you accept my offer?"

"Because it's not enough, Sandro."

"Come here," he said, lacing on his hose. "I want to show you something."

Curious, she followed him out to the long open gallery with its arcaded windows. What a wondrous place his house was, with its marble halls, light-filled rooms, private gardens, the *altana* on the roof abloom with potted plants.

She could never be a part of his home. A man's mistress was required to keep herself separate, confined to the shadows of his life.

He stopped at a small, jewel-like painting on the wall between two pillars. "This is new," he said. "It just arrived from Verona."

It was exquisitely done in soft light and muted colors. The subject was a family—six children at play on a green lawn, their gestures and poses utterly authentic. In the background stood a man and a woman, their features indistinct, yet the overall theme of family love united them all.

"It's marvelous," she said. "So sensitive. I've never known an artist to so capture the essence of children. Raphael's cherubs look stiff and formal compared to these."

"So you like it?"

"Immensely."

"So do I. Aretino told me about the artist and I bought this painting on a whim, just on the strength of his opinion." He seemed incredulous that he would do such a thing.

"Who is the artist?"

"Maestra Catalina Bolla."

"Titian has mentioned her, but I know very little about her."

"She mainly does decorative works. Stays away from large canvases."

"I wonder why. She's so talented."

"All those children in the picture are hers."

"She has six children?"

"Yes. And it hasn't drained her talent, Laura. No other artist I've ever seen depicts children like this."

"My lord, what are you saying?"

"That she didn't let her career eat up her life."

"You're forgetting one fact," Laura retorted, already leaving, too hurt to tell him about her part in the ceremony tomorrow. "She has the love of a husband."

As Laura ran from Sandro's house, she heard him calling after her, but ignored him, for to be with him, to look into his eyes and know he would never be hers alone, was torture.

Guido came along awkwardly, obviously embarrassed by her display. Laura didn't care. She needed a friend now.

She rushed to the convent and ran to Magdalena's room. Dismay enveloped her as she realized her friend was gone.

Shaken, she lowered herself to the bed and buried her face in her hands. Damn him. How dare he flaunt the painting in her face? What was he trying to say?

Small, decorative pieces were fine for Bolla. She found fulfillment with her family. Laura had nothing but her art. And—if Sandro got his way—a lover on occasion. She wanted more. She needed more.

Wiping her face with the hem of her fancy court dress, she went to Magdalena's desk to leave her a message. She found a broken pencil, but no paper.

She went to the armoire to search for something to write on. The doors swung open with a whoosh, lifting her hair. For a moment, she thought she saw a flash of color. Shaking her head, she took a piece of ragged-edged paper from the top shelf, sat at the desk, and wrote a note informing Magdalena that she would be aboard *Bucentaur* for the Sposalizio tomorrow. What pleasure it would give Magdalena to see how far Laura had come.

As she went to shut the closet, she glimpsed something colorful again. Curious, she peered into the closet. She brushed aside the extra novice's habit. What hung beneath brought a frown to her face. It was a set of boy's clothing—a fustian jerkin, trousers, hose. What would Magdalena be doing with these garments? She had probably collected them for charity, Laura decided, moving them aside.

Behind the hanging clothes, she spied the corner of a painting.

A soft gasp left her lips. Only one artist worked with those brush strokes. These were Titian's stolen paintings.

Apprehension clutched at Laura as she pulled out one canvas. A cry of horror broke from her.

It was the painting of her, as Danae. The face,

breasts, and groin had been savagely gouged and slashed with a knife.

With shaking hands, Laura pulled out the other stolen paintings. Each had been destroyed, stabbed and shredded with a violence that chilled her.

For a moment she could do nothing but stand and hold her throat, fighting to stall the sickness before it erupted. Magdalena had done this. Magdalena had stolen the masterpieces from Titian's house. Magdalena had mutilated them.

Why?

These paintings celebrated, revered, and exalted feminine beauty. A quality Magdalena had never, would never, possess. Perhaps jealousy—the frustration and futility of a woman imprisoned by a deformity—had driven her to this mad, rash act. Or perhaps she truly did resent the life Laura had chosen instead of taking the veil.

The proper and lawful thing to do would be to call Guido, who waited outside. Magdalena would be arrested—perhaps by Sandro himself—and charged. The Council of Justice might show mercy and allow Magdalena to serve her penance in the convent.

Or Magdalena—Laura's brilliant, troubled friend—might go to prison.

A deadly calm settled over Laura. Very carefully, she replaced the paintings and closed the armoire. Putting a glass paperweight over her note, she left calmly, quietly. She would never betray her friend.

16

On the day of the Sposalizio, the most auspicious water pageant of Venice, Sandro sat alone in the Great Chamber of the doge's palace. He glared at the maw of the lion's mouth on the wall; he'd found few messages there, and none relating to the plot against the doge. He paged through the reports an assistant had just brought him—a gunpowder theft, probably for fireworks; a domestic quarrel in the Merceria; a Murano glassblower selling trade secrets to the Germans.

Sandro pinched the bridge of his nose and fought the fatigue that dragged at him. He could find no way to the bottom of this plot. His men had searched the state galley; the dignitaries who would be aboard had been questioned and questioned again. None, not even the friends of the doge's late father, merited further investigation.

Night Lords were stationed as thick as an army regiment in the ceremonial flotilla. Soon, Sandro himself would join them, for the events of the day made him uneasy. The trail of gruesome murders had been leading up to this day.

During the bright spectacle of the Sposalizio del

Mare, boatloads of noblemen, wealthy merchants, and religious houses would escort the state galley out into the lagoon. Amidst music, song, fireworks, and gun salvoes, Venice would renew her vows to the sea that gave her life and prosperity.

Although he knew he must go soon, Sandro wanted no part of the festivities. Even a symbolic marriage twisted the dagger of pain in his heart.

He had lost her.

Unless.

Out of the depths of his yearning, an idea took shape in his mind. It grew and blossomed and burst to vivid life. It was the only solution left to him.

He must marry Laura.

He shuddered beneath the weight of his momentous decision. Marrying Laura would force him to give up the honor that had kept him alive all these years.

Marrying Laura would give him a new kind of honor—that of living and loving sincerely, not out of a sense of duty. He wanted her with a passion that destroyed his former convictions.

If she would have him.

Doubts marched through his mind. *I don't want you to marry me*, Laura had said at the villa. *I just want you to make love to me.*

Had she meant it? Early on, she had told him she didn't want babies. She was young and healthy; he wasn't exactly on the shelf yet. Judging by the frequency and ardor of their couplings, pregnancy was a distinct possibility.

Perhaps, too, there was another reason for her refusal. She had her whole charmed life ahead of her. And she was smart enough to know that, although she had enjoyed her dalliance with Sandro, she might one day find another man. A younger man.

The thought boiled like molten lead in Sandro's gut. Nothing, not even an army of Turks, had ever frightened him more.

She loved him. She had to. But would she open her future to him?

Sandro wanted to find out for certain. He would swallow his pride, humble himself, beg her if he had to.

A strange sense of peace drifted over him. All his life he had been dictated to—by his family, by the generals he had fought under, and by his duty to the republic. He'd never done anything simply because he wanted to. All his choices had been made for him: whom he had married, the business he carried on, his career as Lord of the Night.

Not once had anyone asked him what he wanted.

Not once had he even bothered to ask himself.

He did now, and the answer blazed in his mind. He wanted to marry Laura, even if it meant giving up his noble status. The loftiness of his rank, the wealth, the bowing and scraping of underlings meant nothing if he didn't have Laura.

He decided to go see her after the ceremony. Thank God, he thought, she was safe at home.

He stood to go, touching the dagger that rode in a sheath at his hip. A whisper of sound, barely audible, stopped him. His senses came alert, and he looked around the room.

Empty.

The back of his neck prickled as he walked to the mouth of the lion. Reaching inside, he felt a folded piece of paper.

When he read the message, his hands began to

shake. *Laura will be aboard* Bucentaur *for the Sposalizio. Stop her, or she will die with the rest.*

Panic rushed like ice water over Sandro. He raced out a side door and down a narrow flight of stairs toward the street. Just as he reached the opening, something heavy and sharp, dense as iron, came down on his head. Stars flashed behind his eyes. He roared in pain and fury; he groped for his knife, but the blow came again. And again, throwing him back on the stairs.

"No!" he said, feeling darkness fall over him. "No, not now. . . ."

Laura gazed at the receding shoreline of Venice. The city looked magnificent today, with flowers blooming on the balconies, bright silk banners fluttering from poles, garlands draping every rail, and the archway at the Lido decked in bunting. From her vantage point on the grand state barge, the lacy palaces looked like dollhouses of spun sugar.

All around the barge bobbed a flotilla of barcas, galleys, cogs, gondolas, and innumerable skiffs. Sunlight, lowering fast toward evening, flashed off the water. It was a perfect day.

Almost.

Laura leaned her elbows on the gilt rail. Inside, she felt empty, missing Sandro so much that she ached.

"Courage, little one," said a smooth, melodic voice behind her.

She turned around and, despite her troubles, smiled at Florio. He was resplendent in robes of blue velvet and gold braid, a mourning brooch pinned at his shoulder. Beneath a biretta decked with peacock feathers, his hair floated on the breeze.

"What's wrong, Laura?" he asked. "A moment ago you looked as if you wanted to fling yourself into the lagoon."

She laughed. "There's no danger of that, my friend. I've managed to collect enough patrons to keep me painting into my dotage." She leaned against a torch fitting, and the smell of pitch and paraffin wafted to her.

"Then why the long face?"

Florio was a friend, and wise. She could tell him her troubles. "I've fallen in love with Sandro Cavalli."

Florio gave a low whistle. "The Lord of the Night?"

"Yes."

He shook his blond mane in wonderment. "That dry stick of a man? He's too conservative for you."

She laughed without humor, for she alone knew how sensitive and seductive Sandro Cavalli could be. "He's perfect for me," she said. "He just won't admit it."

"Then make him."

"I don't know how."

Florio chuckled. "You spent six months in a brothel, and you don't know how?"

She thought of the blazing passion she had learned at the hands of Sandro. A warm spasm came with the memories of their intimacy, yet a chill emptiness followed. "It's not just a matter of making love. In that, we're compatible. But we're from different stations."

Florio lurched toward the rail as a pair of liveried men shouldered past. *"Gesu,"* he muttered. "This barge is crawling with Night Lords." He touched Laura's hand. "I suppose Sandro Cavalli protects what's his."

"I'm not his—"

A blare of cornets burst from the raised prow of

the galley. Flame bearers lit the hundreds of torches that marched along the gunwales of the huge craft. Excitement flooded Florio's eyes. "I have to go. I'll be performing next, and your picture's about to be unveiled." He bent and kissed her cheek. "Perhaps I'll have you paint me one day."

She smiled after him, but her amusement faded as she made her way past nobles, clerics, Night Lords, and nuns toward the stern. Andrea Gritti and his wife sat upon thronelike chairs beneath the red ceremonial umbrella. Candles as thick as a man's arm burned in the gilt urns flanking them. An easel with the shrouded picture stood a few feet away.

Laura felt hot and self-conscious as the nobles gathered to hear the doge expound on the skills of Venice's newest artistic talent. The moment should be one of triumph for her. Instead, sadness dragged at her. After today, she would start down her path alone, leaving Sandro behind for good. She had tried her best to love him, to become part of his life. Tried, and failed.

A ducal aide stood ready to unveil the portrait. From the bow of the huge ship, Florio's voice rose in crescendo. Laura held her breath.

With a flourish, the aide removed the shroud.

Gasps hissed from the crowd.

Laura stared in horror at the picture. While outraged voices shouted in protest, she clutched at her stomach and stepped back until she touched the rail.

It was the same as the others. The portrait of the dogaressa had been savagely stabbed and slashed to ribbons.

The dogaressa hastily motioned Laura to her side. "Do you know anything about this?" she asked.

"No." Laura's lips, her tongue, her whole body felt numb. "I swear to you, I don't."

"Andrea's men will get to the bottom of this, I promise," said Benedetta Vendramin. Already, a ducal aide was taking the ruined canvas below. "I'm sorry, Laura. Henceforth all your portraits shall be kept under constant guard."

Laura thanked her, curtsied low, and withdrew. The vandalism was soon forgotten by all save Laura as the revelry got under way.

She shivered despite the balmy warmth of the April evening. Magdalena had destroyed the portrait just as she had the others. But why? What prompted the secret hate Magdalena harbored?

They had been friends since childhood. But lately their paths had diverged. Still, in deference to the friendship they had once shared, Laura intended to confront Magdalena in private and find out what had driven her to this wanton destruction. Perhaps Magdalena was envious of Laura's advancement to the Academy. Perhaps she was hostile to the idea that Laura had taken a lover. Whatever the reason, Laura would try to make Magdalena understand.

She lifted her face to the cooling breeze. Her court dress of figured velvet felt heavy and confining. She yearned for the days at the villa, when she had dressed as a peasant and run, with the river breeze rushing through her hair, into Sandro's waiting arms.

She shook her head, wanting to flee. But there was no escaping a pain beyond bearing, no escaping the deep, terrible love that Sandro had rejected.

In the prow, Florio began another barcarole. Murmurs of appreciation swept through the passengers, for his voice brought to mind a chorus of angels.

"Were there enough room on these crowded decks," said a man as he walked toward her, "I would ask you to dance, madonna."

Laura tried to summon a polite smile, but managed only a stiff nod. The man was crudely handsome with yellowed teeth and small, sharp eyes. His velvet cloak was threadbare at the hem.

Sweeping off his hat, he bowed. "Please, dear lady, don't let that unconscionable prank spoil your evening."

"I wasn't even thinking of the painting," she said softly.

"Good. I mean to enjoy myself. I was in the service of Andrea's father some twenty years ago. What a surprise to receive his summons, and to see so many of my comrades from years long past."

Laura stopped pretending to listen and looked out to sea. Youngsters in skiffs surrounded the galley and begged for coins and tokens from the noble passengers. Florio's tenor voice reached a spine-tingling high note. The scent of burning torches eddied on the breeze; soon the fireworks and gun salvoes would begin, for night was on its way. Sandro's time.

Laura ached for him. She longed to hear him promise to love and cherish her. But Venice espousing the sea would be the only vow spoken this night.

He prayed he would reach her in time. His head throbbed where he had been struck, and his shoulders screamed with the fire of exertion. Upon waking in the dark stairwell, he had spared no time to think or plan; he had leapt into a boat and started rowing.

Bucentaur rose like a jewel on the horizon, glittering gold and red, populated with dignitaries.

None of them realized it was a death ship.

Sandro cursed himself for not deducing the truth sooner.

Blisters formed and burst on his hands. He ignored the sting and kept rowing. The setting sun of the April evening beat down upon his neck. He disregarded the heat and pressed on.

The ship lay a hundred yards distant now. Smoke from the torches along the rails puffed into the air.

Sandro's boat lurched as it collided with a gondola. He said nothing to the cursing gondolier as he went on, a machine powered by muscle, sweat, fear, and determination.

Why? he asked himself, the question like a flail slicing his back. Why hadn't he realized?

With each stroke of the oars, he ticked off another bit of evidence. The altered program from the printer, containing the names of men the doge could not recall inviting. They must be marked for death. The last words of the assassin in the hospital. He had been trying to warn Sandro of the plot to blow up the barge. And finally, the evidence that had reached him only hours ago: the theft of the gunpowder.

With the warning he'd found in the lion's mouth, all had clicked into place.

He should have guessed the plot sooner. But his mind had been so muddled with agonized love for Laura that he had not been able to think clearly. Perhaps the blow to the head had unclouded his brain at last.

Fifty yards lay between him and the galley. One thought pounded in his mind: Someone was going to blow up *Bucentaur* and all her passengers.

Later he would wonder who had crafted such an ingenius and cold-blooded plan, and who had attacked him in the stairwell. For now, he could only pray he reached the galley in time.

Fireworks and artillery salvoes popped off here and there. With each small explosion, Sandro squeezed his eyes shut and cringed. A beautiful tenor voice was singing a barcarole.

At last, his small boat came alongside the galley. He grabbed onto a huge oar, ignoring the curse of the oarsman within. Clinging fast, he started to climb toward the oar port. The oar behind him swept up and knocked him into the lagoon.

Chill saltwater flooded his eyes and burned the wound on his head. Sandro surfaced, gasping for air. Much to the amusement of people in gondolas and crafts all around him, he grabbed the oar again. Hand over hand, he moved toward the hull. Wedging his booted foot into a gilt-framed oar port, he grasped the rail and swung himself over, onto the deck.

Looks of outrage greeted him. He made no apologies for his sodden state, but yelled, "Abandon ship! She's going to blow!"

No one moved. The doge and his lady exchanged a glance. "Have you completely lost your mind, my lord?" Doge Gritti demanded.

Sandro looked around frantically for Laura. Twilight was creeping over the lagoon. A crowd of hundreds thronged the decks. He could not find her.

"This ship has been planted with explosives," he said. "Get off now, before they blow."

"Explosives, my lord?" the doge said. "Where are they?"

Sandro ground his teeth and paced the deck, his boots squishing over the planks. "I'm not sure, I—"

He broke off, for he was wasting time arguing. These well-dressed nobles were not about to throw themselves into the water on the strength of a rumor. His only chance was to find the explosives and dump them overboard.

Smoke from a torch soaked in paraffin seared his nose. He recalled the death of the ship's chandler in charge of illuminating the galley. Now he knew the reason: so the culprits could put their own man to the task.

"The torches," he shouted, racing to the nearest one. He flung the burning top into the water. In the space where the torch had been, a twist of rope smoldered slowly. The base of the torch fitting looked to be of solid wood, but it was plaster; the rim broke between his fingers.

Stepping back, he kicked it hard. The base crumbled. A rain of black powder showered the deck.

Murmurs of horror came from the passengers.

"Well done, my lord," said the doge. "Now that it's over—"

"It's not over," said Sandro, rushing to the next torch, flinging it into the water and shattering the powder-filled base. He aimed a furious look over his shoulder. "Damn it, help me."

Nobles and Night Lords cast off their robes. They swarmed along the gilded deck rail, dismantling the bombs. Sandro ordered a group to go below and search there.

Spying Laura at the prow, he raced toward her. In seconds, he took in her sumptuous crimson gown, her cap of gold chenille, the dark veil of her hair flowing down her back. In seconds, he fell in love all over again.

"I want you off this ship," he stated.

"No." She pulled the fuse from the torch holder, blackening her hands with deadly powder. Nearby, Florio wrestled with the next torch.

Sandro clenched his jaw. "Do it, Laura. Here, I'll help you—"

"I'm not leaving, Sandro, and you can't make me."

Pandemonium broke out on the galley. Jamal boarded the galley from a ship's boat to help extinguish the torches. There were hundreds of them. Hundreds of passengers, too, their lives all in Sandro's hands.

At last the torches were all extinguished, and the barge was thrown into purple shadow. Sandro allowed a small measure of relief to seep like warm wine into his bones.

Until Laura clutched at his arm and pointed. "Sandro, the doge!"

At the stern, the doge and his consort sat beneath the red state umbrella. The standing candles in their huge gold-painted urns had burned to stubs.

"Jesus!" Dread churned in Sandro's gut as he fought his way down the crowded decks toward the stern. He shoved past patricians and clerics and dignitaries. A contessa who did not move quickly enough found herself sprawled on her velvet-clad backside.

No one heeded Sandro's shouts of warning as he closed in on the last and biggest of the bombs. Whipping a glance behind, he saw Jamal and Florio following him.

The low candle flames spat tiny sparks that danced on the tops of the holders. Sandro grabbed a cup of wine from someone and flung the contents upon one of them. The fuse hissed as if in protest, then continued to burn steadily.

Cursing, Sandro hugged the barrel-sized container.

In his mind he saw the bomb detonate, saw himself blown to pieces, a feast for fish and seabirds.

The urn dragged at Sandro's arms. The fuse shot sparks at his eyes. He heard Jamal and Florio grunting as they staggered toward the rail with the other.

Hurry, Sandro told himself. Aloud he bellowed, "For the love of God, help me!"

The doge seemed stunned to immobility. Choking from a noseful of sulfurous smoke, Sandro picked up the urn and lurched to the rail. The stench of burning powder seared his eyes. Any moment now—

The urn teetered on the rail, then toppled over. It detonated, with a thunderous report, as it fell.

The explosion erupted in a fount of water that rose like a mushroom and showered the deck. Cold seawater slapped Sandro to his knees. The barge shook as if it had been rammed by the hand of God, then rocked in the aftershock.

The shouts and screams subsided to stunned silence. A single gull cried out—a plaintive, unknowing cry to heaven.

His muscles aching, his hands stinging, and his legs weak with relief, Sandro braced himself on the deck rail and stood. He turned, and there was Laura, racing toward him, stumbling without apology over the still-grumbling contessa, leaping over benches and coils of rope to get to him.

Still no one spoke. Laura, her face as beautiful as the springtime, launched herself at Sandro. Her golden cap trailed down her back, and her hair flew free, a cascade of midnight waves.

With a cry of desperation, he pulled her into his arms. He buried his hands in her hair and turned her face up to his.

"Laura. God, I nearly lost you."

"Me? Oh, beloved, you could have been . . . I could have lost *you.*"

"Would that distress you?" he asked.

She placed her hands on his cheeks. "You know the answer to that."

"I came to ask you something."

She looked around at the crowd, all of whom were watching them curiously. "Here? Now?"

"Let them gawk." He winnowed his fingers deeper into her warm, silky hair. "Will you marry me, Laura?" The words came in a rush and he plunged on, heedless of the hundreds of astonished listeners.

His naked image hung at the Academy; why should he not bare his soul now as well? "Be my wife. I know I'm an old soldier, a man past my prime, but I vow I'd respect your career, let you paint—"

"Oh, do shut up." She looked like a petulant child. His heart sank. Then she spoke again. "You're saying everything except what needs to be said."

"My God, Laura, if you refuse me, I'll—"

"You love me, don't you?" She laughed at his flabbergasted expression. "I should have guessed! When did you know, Sandro? And why didn't you tell me immediately?"

He stopped the questions with a long, heartfelt kiss that tasted of the seawater that had drenched him and the desperation that had driven him. Sighs wafted from a dozen nearby ladies. When he lifted his mouth from Laura's, he smiled down into her face. "Perhaps I didn't tell you, *carissima,* because you haven't given me a chance."

He stepped back and sank down on one knee

before her. More feminine sighs soughed from the crowd, but Sandro saw only Laura: her dress damp and glittering in the low light, the dark nimbus of her hair framing the face of the woman for whom he would lay down his life.

Solemnly he took her hand and carried her fingers to his lips. "Laura, it's true. I love you."

Murmurs of approval greeted his declaration. The only reaction he noticed was Laura's. Joy lit her face; then she burst into tears.

He came to his feet and gently folded his arms around her, whispering into her hair, "Is that such a disaster, then?"

"No. I mean, yes. Oh, Sandro, I don't know." She placed her palms on his cheeks and gazed steadily into his eyes. "I tried so hard not to want too much from you. But I couldn't help myself. I wanted all of you. I wanted you to hold nothing back, to give me everything."

He kissed a tear from her soft cheek. "And I will. Believe it." She looked so enchantingly disbelieving that he smiled. "I'll give you children if God wills it. I'll give you lazy days spent in the shade of an olive tree, and long winter nights holding you as we sit before a fire. If you but wish it, I'll braid daisies into your hair, or dance in a vat of grapes for you."

She laughed unsteadily. "You'll forfeit everything you hold dear, Sandro. Your nobility, your status in the Council—"

He pressed a finger to her lips. "To have you, I would give up the surety of my soul."

He felt mad, crazy; he wanted to howl at the moon and commit all the sins he had been too stiff-necked and prideful to contemplate before.

"What matters," she said, "is whether or not you can live with such a future."

"Darling," he replied, lowering his head to kiss her, "I'd best marry you before the moon rises." As his lips touched hers, love rose like a fountain in him, and he knew he had made the right choice. She clung to him, and her lips were sweet, warm, and giving, full of promises that made nothing else matter.

Distantly he heard the sound of music and a wonderful tenor voice. It was Florio, paying tribute to a love so strong that Sandro had proclaimed it before a boatload of people. Finally, Laura pulled back and regarded him almost shyly. "Ah, Sandro. I wish I could take this moment and lock it away in a chest somewhere so nothing can ever spoil it."

He smiled—a silly, joyous grin that made him feel years younger. People started talking again, laughing and singing and moving about. "This was one feast day no one will ever forget."

Laura's heart filled to bursting as she laughed with him—the giddy laughter of relief and wonder. From the corner of her eye, she saw the doge beckoning to them. When Sandro approached the thronelike seat, Andrea Gritti and his wife both stood, a rare honor.

"My lord," said the doge, "I have no words to tell you the depth of my gratitude."

"The emergency is over," Sandro said, unperturbed, "but we still must find the culprit."

"And you will," said Benedetta Vendramin. "We have every confidence in our Lord of the Night."

The doge summoned Jamal and Florio. To Jamal he gave a balas ruby of incalculable value, taking the pearl-encrusted ornament from the chain around his own neck. Jamal accepted the token with a deep salaam. To Florio, the dogaressa offered a sapphire brooch. She pinned it to his velvet robes and kissed his cheek. "Daniele would have been proud of you today."

Florio swallowed hard. "I only wish I could have saved 'him, too."

Gritti stroked his beard as he looked at Sandro. "Your reward—"

"Your Serenity, I need none for the disposition of my duty." Sandro bent and kissed Laura's cheek, then went below to the oar deck to make certain there were no more hidden hazards.

Laura stood awkwardly before the doge and his consort. Then she curtsied and was excused. The cacophony of music and fireworks pounded in her ears. When she turned, she found herself looking at Magdalena.

She opened her mouth to greet her friend, but no words came out when she saw what Magdalena held.

Two glass stilettos, one in each hand.

Magdalena crouched low in a fighter's stance, the mound of her back exaggerated by the posture. Her eyes glittered more brightly than the weapons. She seemed not to see Laura; her fiery regard was fixed on the doge.

"Magdalena!" Laura cried, but the word was no more than a shocked whisper.

In the exuberant celebration, no one heard. No one noticed the strange, black-clad person launch herself at Doge Andrea Gritti.

With no time to think, Laura threw herself at Magdalena. Glass flashed, and a hot sting grazed the back of Laura's wrist. A shattering sound drew the attention of Jamal, who planted himself protectively in front of Laura and the doge.

"Guards!" someone shouted.

Feet pounded on the deck as militiamen came to seize the murderess. Laura stared in horrified grief at Magdalena—her lifelong friend. The guards were coming closer, moving cautiously, for Magdalena still held one dagger. Her pale face was as hard as stone. Her hands were steady as she lifted the remaining stiletto and aimed the point at her breast.

"No!" Laura screamed, breaking away from Jamal and leaping toward Magdalena.

She was too late. The deadly point penetrated Magdalena's robes and pierced her body. Her eyes rolled up, and she sank to the deck.

Laura was on her knees in an instant, cradling Magdalena's head in her lap. Blood pulsed from the wound and darkened the black fabric. The wimple and coif fell back, and Magdalena's thin, oily hair spilled out.

"My God, Magdalena," Laura whispered through her tears, "what have you done?"

"It's . . . finished." Magdalena's tongue seemed thick. "Never meant to hurt you . . . I always loved you . . . you. . . ."

"Then why, Magdalena?" Laura could feel her friend growing heavy and limp, slipping away. "Please, I must know."

"I had to kill . . . him."

"Doge Gritti?"

Magdalena blinked slowly. "My . . . father."

Laura barely heard the disbelieving gasps and shocked whispers. She felt Sandro's presence behind her, but her attention stayed fixed on her friend. A strange clicking sound came from Magdalena, and she breathed her last.

Laura clung to the numbness of shock, for it was all that kept her from dissolving into a fit of mad weeping. Slowly she raised her horrified gaze to Andrea Gritti.

"Is this true? You fathered Sister Celestina's child?"

"Celestina?" Tears of despair ran down his face and slid into his beard. "It must be so."

Benedetta buried her face in her hands.

"We were . . . *inamorati* many years ago, before Celestina took the veil. I swear to God, I never knew I fathered a child."

Sandro gently laid the body supine on the planks and drew Laura to her feet, pressing her cheek to his chest. "How could you not know, Andrea?"

Gritti stared with bleak regret and pity at the deformed body of his child. "It was in my days as a *condottiere*. You remember, Sandro, for you fought by my side. I spent months away from Venice, fighting in Cyprus, Corfu, Ravenna. But why would she attack me now, after all these years?"

"I intend to find out," Sandro said.

A cleric bent over the body and closed the eyes.

"It's over," Florio whispered, clearly torn by grief at what he had witnessed and rage at what Magdalena had done to Daniele.

"Yes," Laura echoed, turning her tear-bright gaze up to Sandro. "It's over." She shuddered and added in an aching whisper, "But for one matter. Someone must tell Celestina."

17

Late that night, they married in a subdued ceremony in a chapel in the Church of San Rocco. Sandro had laid waste to laws governing the reading of the banns and the procurement of special licenses, and no one dared gainsay the Lord of the Night.

He felt a quiet joy as they spoke their vows, and he slipped an heirloom Cavalli ring, glittering with cool sapphires, on her finger. When she softly kissed his lips, love and contentment radiated from his new, beautiful, indecently young wife.

Titian, Aretino, Jamal, and Yasmin attended them. Their smiles and felicitations lent warmth to an event so shadowed by tragedy.

On the church steps, Aretino slapped his rock-hard girth. "I've not seen such high entertainment since the sack of Rome."

"And you'll likely not see it again, thank God," said Titian.

Pietro Aretino eyed the married couple speculatively. "Are you sure you won't let me write it down? Such drama! The mighty Lord of the Night baring his soul on the deck of a ship before all the princes of Venice—"

"No." Sandro tried to keep the smile from his voice.

Yasmin embraced Laura. "We sail for Algiers with the dawn tide," she said.

Laura blinked back tears. "I knew you were leaving. I only prayed it wouldn't be so soon."

"It is time to rejoin our people." Yasmin stepped back beside Jamal. "Is it not?"

He gave a regal nod. Despite the uncertainty in his eyes, he stood strong and proud, no longer a prisoner of his affliction.

Sandro clasped hands with his old friend. "I've been thinking of putting Guido Lombardo in your post."

Jamal's grip tightened. Then they were in each other's arms for a moment before parting.

As their four witnesses dispersed, Laura stood with her back to Sandro, his arms circling her from behind. There would be no wedding feast, no week-long revels to celebrate their union. They needed no salutes or speeches or endless wedding toasts to affirm their love. The contentment of a quiet embrace satisfied them both.

"What a day of sorrow and joy this has been," Sandro murmured into her hair.

"It has." She turned to face him, resting her palms on his chest. "There's something I must do before we go home."

"Celestina?" he asked gently.

"Yes. Despite all the horrible things Magdalena did, her mother will still grieve."

"I'll go with you."

"No. She'd want to see me alone. She's never been easy with men, and now we know why."

"All right. I have some things to take care of at the ministry."

She shuddered, knowing he had to go over the coroner's report, to record the cold details of a young woman's death.

"Very well," she said. "I'll be waiting at the convent."

He started toward the ducal palace across the piazza. After a few steps, he turned, smiling.

"What pleases you so, my lord?" she asked.

"I was thinking . . . we'll share a bed for the rest of our lives. I can't remember ever being so pleased by a notion."

Celestina's room lay in darkness. Chemical smells hung thick and noxious in the air. Laura paused in the doorway, having argued her way past the nuns who insisted Celestina wanted no visitors.

A trembling shape sat in front of the single square window.

"Sister Celestina?" Walking gingerly to avoid upsetting the littered worktables, Laura went and knelt beside her friend's mother.

"Laura." Celestina grasped her hand, holding so tight that it hurt. "I thought you would come to me."

"How could I not? Magdalena was my friend."

"And my child."

"She is with God now."

"I know. My child was not a bad person."

"No." Laura bit her lip. "Was it madness, sister?"

"My child was not insane." Celestina spoke with clipped certainty. "Only . . . impatient."

"I don't understand, sister."

"Magdalena burned to see justice served. When

the plan failed, she took matters into her own hands."

"Plan?" Laura's mind whirled in confusion. "Sister, did you know of this plan?"

Celestina got up, drew Laura to her feet, and pressed her shoulders so that she was sitting on the hard wooden chair. "I heard you were wounded," she said.

"It's nothing. The glass didn't break, so the poison didn't touch me."

"Let me bind it for you."

Laura said nothing as Celestina fumbled with flint and steel to light a small glass lamp. If it comforted Celestina to minister even to so minor an injury, then so be it.

The wick flared and a tallow smell added to the chemical odors. As Celestina lifted the lighted lamp, Laura found herself staring at a leather folio lying under a table. On the flap was the doge's seal of office. It was the satchel Daniele Moro had been carrying on the night he was killed.

A chill skittered down Laura's spine.

"Now, about that cut . . ." Celestina turned. In her hands she held a razor-sharp knife.

Alone in the justice ministry, Sandro worked by the light of a candle. He didn't feel his usual sense of accomplishment upon solving a crime, for this one was no neat parcel to be filed away. Three men were dead and a disturbed young woman had killed herself. The doge of Venice had been almost blown to pieces, then shamed before his most important nobles.

Only the prospect of a blissful wedding night kept Sandro from despair.

He combed through the facts of the case, trying to make sense of things. Magdalena had killed and mutilated three men in order to plant explosives on the state galley.

Why? he asked himself. Why murder a boatload of people in order to take revenge on the father she hated? Why not simply kill the doge alone?

He knew now that Magdalena must have been responsible for the warnings he had received through the lion's mouth. Both messages had been about Laura.

But why would Magdalena set *bravi* after Laura if she did not want her harmed? Why would she tell Sandro about *Bucentaur,* then bash him over the head and foil her own plan?

It was all part of the mystery, the madness of a deranged mind. Magdalena had taken her secrets with her to another world.

The sound of footsteps drew Sandro from his reverie. He looked up to see a robed figure coming toward him.

"Dr. Marino." Sandro stood to greet the coroner.

Carlo Marino bowed. He seemed agitated, yet curiously hesitant. "My lord . . . about the body."

"Of the woman, Magdalena?"

"There's something I think you should know about the deceased. She . . . wasn't a woman."

Sandro's eyes narrowed. "My dear Dr. Marino, I think you should explain yourself."

"Magdalena was born male. From the look of the corpse, I'd say castration took place at birth."

An icy finger of horror touched Sandro's spine. "You're saying . . ."

"Magdalena seems to have been raised a girl. The, er, alteration, accounts for the smooth skin, the softness of the muscles."

"It was done at birth, you say?"

"Or shortly after."

Sandro's blood ran cold. Magdalena had not acted alone, but in concert with her—his mother.

Celestina, who at that very moment was with Laura.

The lock of the door clicked like a death rattle. Celestina pocketed the key, then calmly turned to face Laura.

"For privacy," she explained. "I know you have a lot of questions."

Fear held Laura mute as she stared at the knife in Celestina's hand. "You were behind the plot. Why hold the doge responsible if you never even told him about Magdalena?"

"His neglect could be forgiven. But there's something else."

"He seemed sad when he spoke of your *amor.*" Perhaps Celestina would let down her guard. Perhaps, if Laura stalled for time, Sandro would weary of waiting for her and come searching.

"By the time I realized I was carrying Andrea's child," Celestina said, "he had gone off to battle. Some skirmish involving the Pope's saltworks, as I recall. So I approached his father. I knew he was a powerful man, but I didn't realize how ruthless he could be."

"Ruthless? In what way? Didn't he offer to help you?"

Celestina grimaced. "He told me he would meet me on his barge in the river Brenta and, all trusting, I went. He wasn't there, but his lackeys were. Thirty-one of them."

Laura's hands flew to her throat. "Oh, God. No."

"Yes. The Trentuno. My punishment for loving his son. They were all there, you know, the men who violated me that night."

"Where?" asked Laura. "Where were they?"

"On *Bucentaur.* I arranged it."

Laura began to understand. Celestina had altered the printed list of dignitaries, the invitations. She had made certain each of her tormentors received a summons.

"I would have killed them one by one, but it was too risky. I might have been caught before I finished."

"I see. But it was you who killed the others."

"Yes."

"And . . . m-mutilated them."

"As all men should be. Even Gaspari, that young printer. He was not among my tormentors, but he suffered my fury nonetheless. Think of it, Laura. Thirty-one of them, and I an expectant mother. No doubt my child's deformity was caused by my suffering that night."

Laura pitied Celestina, for she knew firsthand the feelings of terror, powerlessness, humiliation, and rage.

"Celestina, why did you send the *bravi* after me? I had nothing to do with any of this."

"You wouldn't use the potions and cosmetics I gave you."

Sickness rose in Laura's throat. "They were poisoned."

"Yes."

"Why? Celestina, you were like a mother to me!"

"You wouldn't leave events alone, Laura. I planned this for years, and couldn't allow you to stand in the way. You kept asking questions and carrying tales to Lord Cavalli. And then . . ." Celestina sighed, and her eyes clouded. "There was Magdalena."

"What about her?"

"Magdalena was falling in love with you."

"It was the love of two friends, Celestina—" Laura

broke off as she realized the woman was not listening.

"Such a beautiful baby," she said, running her thumb down the blade of the knife. "At birth, there was no sign of the deformed back. Ah, he was an angel come to ease my suffering."

"He?"

Celestina nodded dreamily. "My son. Only I didn't want a son, but a daughter. And so I arranged it."

Laura stared at the knife, thought of Celestina's other victims, and knew the truth. She felt horrified, and deeply, desperately sad as she pondered the shambles of Magdalena's ruined life.

"Yes, he loved you," the nun mused. "I took away his maleness, but I could not excise his feelings for you."

Laura remembered the slashed paintings. It was not the act of a jealous girl, then, but of a frustrated lover.

"Celestina," she said softly, "I must go."

The dreamy haze left the nun's eyes. "My goal has not been accomplished. I'm sorry. I can't let you stop me now."

Brandishing the blade, she started toward Laura.

Sandro ran with demons of terror snapping at his heels. His frantic footfalls rang through the streets and alleyways of Venice. All his life he had loved this city in all its glittering splendor. Now, tonight, la Serenissima was a sinister place. A place that had spawned a madwoman. The woman who would kill his beloved.

God. Laura might already be dead.

As the notion assaulted him, Sandro increased his speed. *Not yet,* he prayed as he ran. *Please not yet.*

At the convent, he ripped open the gate and exploded into the courtyard, startling a few nuns who were on their way to midnight prayers. A few female voices lifted in protest. He ignored them and took the steps two at a time.

He sped through the shadowy cloisters to the door of Celestina's room. He jerked the handle, knowing even as he did so that his way would be barred.

The sound of breaking glass and the ominous thumps of a struggle reached him. "Laura!" he roared.

"I'm here," came her frantic cry. "Help me!"

Sandro hurled himself against the stout timbers. He bruised and battered himself, but the door would not yield.

Cursing, he pounded back down the stairs and climbed the side of the building, bloodying his fingers on the rough stone. On the sloping roof atop the room, he bent to see the window several feet below.

He could not reach it.

Closing his eyes, he gripped the lintel over the window, tucked his chin to his chest, and threw his feet over his head.

He landed with a bone-crunching thud on the floor. Splinters of broken glass ground into his shoulders. He came to his feet to find Celestina with Laura pinned against the wall. A sharp blade stabbed at Laura's chest.

"No!" he yelled, leaping across a littered table. A lamp fell. Flame rushed across the stone floor and licked at the leg of a chair. His hand clamped around Celestina's wrist. The knife dropped. Sparks flew as a sulfurous compound caught fire.

Celestina jerked her hand away. She reeled back while Sandro pulled Laura into his arms. "I'm all right," she said, then: "Celestina, no!"

He turned to see the nun put an amber flagon to

her lips. The firelight rose around her, already devouring the hem of her habit. She lifted the flagon in a silent salute, then swallowed the contents.

"You can leave me now," she said, calm despite the smoke and flames that consumed her. She dropped the flagon. It rolled to Sandro's feet. "I've taken care of everything."

Chilled, Sandro picked up the flagon. It reeked of aconite. She had swallowed enough poison to kill a bullock.

A week later, Laura smiled nervously at her husband and mouthed the words, *I love you.*

Sandro squeezed her hand, but kept his gaze trained on the dais. The entire Council was in session, and the great hall teemed with dignitaries, ambassadors, and friends.

Laura walked forward, holding her husband's arm and thinking about their wedding night. Was it only yesterday that he had taken her as his wife? Only last night that he had held her, and wept with her, and then made love to her so tenderly that she had wept again?

It seemed they had been together forever.

Yet despite Sandro's strength, despite his heartfelt pledges and the adoration that shone from his eyes, she feared their audience with the doge.

The summons had held an ominous tone. Laura had no doubt that today, Sandro would lose everything. Even her love, fierce as it was, could not shield him from the censure of Andrea Gritti. For the civil offense of marrying a commoner, Sandro would be stripped of his nobility, his offices.

All he would have left was his wife.

His daughter, Adriana, caught Laura's eye and smiled encouragingly. Laura wished she had a measure of Adriana's optimism. She could not help thinking that one day Sandro would resent her for causing his fall from grace.

The walk to the dais seemed endless. They passed the courtesans of Madonna della Rubia. Portia and Fiammetta dabbed tears of happiness from their eyes. Florio gave her a wink. Guido Lombardo and the *zaffi* held their hats over their hearts. Ambassadors and princes watched with frank interest. When Laura and Sandro reached the dais, they made their obeisance.

"I've read your report, my lord," said Doge Gritti.

Sandro nodded. "An extraordinary and tragic tale."

"I swear to you, I knew nothing of what my father had done to that poor woman." Gritti's voice quavered with grief. "When I returned from the war, I was told she had taken the veil and would not see me. I sent a generous monthly allowance to the convent, but was never allowed to see Celestina."

He cleared his throat, and his voice gathered strength. "I want all to know that for their crimes against an innocent young woman, the thirty-one have been banished. In addition, I have seized their assets and created a fund to protect the courtesans of Venice. I know it's not enough, and that it comes twenty years too late. But it's all I can do."

"I understand, Serenissimo." Sandro bowed stiffly, and Laura felt the tension in the muscles of his arm.

"Now, as to you, my lord," the doge went on, "and this unusual love match you have made. Yes, we know it's true love, for you said so before all of us."

Chuckles came from the assembly, and Sandro flushed. "I have apparently forsaken privacy and dignity on all counts. But to my great surprise, I would say it a hundred times and more," he stated, and Laura squeezed his hand. "I love my wife."

"By law, you are to be stripped of your nobility. My lord, marrying a commoner simply isn't done."

Laura braced herself. What was he feeling, knowing he must relinquish all he had been, all his life? *Don't hate me, Sandro. Please, don't hate me.*

He seemed to sense her thoughts, for he said, "In the battle between love and honor, I am the victor."

"Indeed, you are. And more, my lord. Laura is no commonor. Her courage and deeds have ennobled her. I hearby proclaim her a True and Special Daughter of the Republic."

Gasps of surprise, then cheers came from all quarters: From artists and courtesans and *zaffi* and patricians alike.

His face bright with amazement, Sandro bent to kiss her as the noise crescendoed.

Aretino elbowed his way through the throng. "All right, *superbossio,* this is your last chance. One epic poem, entitled 'Lord of the Night.'"

Sandro laughed. "Don't bother, old friend. They'd never believe it." He smiled down at Laura and drew her away from the crowd. The noise and movement and clamor seemed to fade around them as they drifted into their own soft, separate world of contentment. "How easy it is to laugh at life when you're around, *carissima,*" he said.

Laura's heart was full, her throat aching, and for the first time in her life she fell victim to speechlessness. But no matter; they had years to share, long golden summers on the Brenta and endless revels in Venice. She and Sandro had journeyed together into the dark realms of danger, but now the dawn beckoned, for she was safe in the arms of her Lord of the Night.

History of Passion . . .

Dearest Reader,

Don't be deceived. Behind her demure smile and guarded gaze even the most proper lady has a secret. But what happens when the sting of betrayal, ache of sacrifice, or ghosts of lovers past return, threatening to shake that Mona Lisa smile?

This summer, Avon Books presents four delicious romances about four women who are more than what they seem, and the dangerously handsome heroes who are captivated by them. From bestselling authors Elizabeth Boyle, Loretta Chase, Jeaniene Frost, and a beautifully repackaged edition by Susan Wiggs.

Coming May 2009

Memoirs of a Scandalous Red Dress

by *New York Times* bestselling author

Elizabeth Boyle

Twenty years ago, Pippin betrayed her heart and married another in order to save Captain Thomas Dashwell's life. Now their paths cross again and Pippin is determined not to let a second chance at love slip away. Dash's world stops when he sees her standing aboard his ship but promises himself he'll never again fall for the breathtaking beauty.

$\mathcal{D}$ashwell's nostrils were filled with the scent of newly minted guineas. Enough Yellow Georges to make even the dour Mr. Hardy happy. Nodding in satisfaction, he whistled low and soft like a seabird to the men in the longboat.

They pulled up one man, then another, and cut the bindings that had their arms tied around their backs and tossed the two over the side and into the surf.

That ought to cool their heels a bit, Dashwell mused, as he watched the Englishmen splash their way to shore. His passengers had been none too pleased with him last night when he'd abandoned their delivery in favor of saving his neck and the lives of his crew.

Untying the mule, he led the beast down the shore toward the longboat. It came along well enough until it got down to the waterline, where the waves were coming in and the longboat tossed and crunched against the rocks. Then the animal showed its true nature and began to balk.

The miss who'd caught his eye earlier came over and took hold of the reins, her other hand stroking the beast's muzzle and talking softly to it until it settled down.

"You have a way about you," he said over his shoulder, as he walked back and forth, working alongside his men, who were as anxious as he was to gain their gold and be gone from this precarious rendezvous.

"Do you have a name?" he asked, when he returned for the last sack. This close he could see all too well the modest cut of her gown, her shy glances, and the way she bit her lip as if she didn't know whether to speak to him.

Suddenly it occurred to him who, or rather what she was, and he had only one thought.

What the devil was Josephine doing bringing a lady, one barely out of the schoolroom, into this shady business?

"What? No name?" he pressed, coming closer still, for he'd never met a proper lady—he certainly didn't count Josephine as one, not by the way she swore and gambled and schemed.

As he took another step closer he caught the veriest hint of roses on her. Soft and subtle, but to a man like him it sent a shock of desire through him as he'd never known.

Careful there, Dashwell, he cautioned himself. If the militia didn't shoot him, he had to imagine Josephine would. "Come sweetling, what is your name?"

There was no harm in just asking, now was there?

The wee bit of muslin pursed her lips shut, then glanced over at her companions, as if seeking their help. And when she looked back at him, he smiled at her. The grin that usually got him into trouble.

"Pippin," she whispered, again glancing back over toward where Josephine was haranguing Temple and Clifton for news from the Continent.

"Pippin, eh?" he replied softly, not wanting to frighten her, even as he found himself mesmerized by the soft, uncertain light in her eyes. "I would call you something else. Something befitting such a pretty lady." He tapped his fingers to his lips. "Circe. Yes, that's it. From now on I'll call you my Circe. For you're truly a siren to lure me ashore."

Even in the dark he could see her cheeks brighten with a blush, hear the nervous rattle to her words. "I don't think that is proper."

Proper? He'd fallen into truly deep waters now, for something devilish inside him wanted to make sure this miss never worried about such a ridiculous notion again.

But something else, something entirely foreign to him, urged him to see that she never knew anything else but a safe and proper existence.

A thought he extinguished as quickly as he could. For it was rank with strings and chains and noble notions that had no place in his world.

"Not proper?" He laughed, more to himself than

at her. "Not proper is the fact that this bag feels a bit lighter than the rest." He hoisted it up and jangled it as he turned toward the rest of the party on the beach. "My lady, don't tell me you've cheated me yet again."

For indeed, the bag did feel light.

Lady Josephine winced, but then had the nerve to deny her transgression. "Dash, I'll not pay another guinea into your dishonest hands."

No wonder she'd brought her pair of lovely doves down to the beach. A bit of distraction so he'd not realize he wasn't getting his full price.

"Then I shall take my payment otherwise," he said, and before anyone could imagine what he was about, he caught hold of this tempting little Pippin and pulled her into his arms.

She gasped as he caught hold of her, and for a moment he felt a twinge of conscience.

Thankfully he wasn't a man to stand on such notions for long.

"I've always wanted to kiss a lady," he told her, just before his lips met hers.

At first he'd been about to kiss her as he would any other girl, but there was a moment, just as he looked down at her, with only one thought—to plunder those lips—that he found himself lost.

Her eyes were blue, as azure as the sea off the West Indies, and they caught him with their wide innocence, their trust.

Trust? In him?

Foolish girl, he thought as he drew closer and then kissed her, letting his lips brush over hers. Yet instead of his usual blustering ways, he found himself reining back his desire. This was the girl's first kiss, he knew that with the same surety that he knew how many casks of brandy were in his hold, and ever-so-gently, he ventured past her lips, slowly letting his tongue sweep over hers.

She gasped again, but this time from the very intimacy of it, and Dash suddenly found himself inside a maelstrom.

He tried to stop himself from falling, for that would mean setting her aside. But he couldn't let her go.

This Pippin, this innocent lass, this very proper lady, brought him alive as no other woman ever had.

Mine, he thought, with possessiveness, with passion, with the knowledge that she was his, and always would be.

He wanted to know everything about her, her real name, her secrets, her desires . . . His hands traced her lines, the slight curve of her hips, the soft swell of her breasts.

She shivered beneath his touch, but she didn't stop him, didn't try to shy away. Instead, she kissed him back, innocently, tentatively at first, then eagerly.

Good God, he was holding an angel!

And as if the heavens themselves rang out in protest over his violation of one of their own, a rocket screeched across the sky, and when it exploded, wrenching the night into day with a shower of sparks, Dashwell pulled back from her and looked up.

As another rocket shot upward, he realized two things.

Yes, by God, her eyes were as blue as the sea.

And secondly, the militia wasn't at the local pub bragging about their recent exploits.

Laura seated herself, and Sandro took the opposite chair. The fire crackled cheerily in the marble framed grate. "Have you run afoul of the law, madonna?"

"Of course not." She folded her hands demurely in her lap. "My lord, I have information about Daniele Moro."

Her words pounded in Sandro's head. Disbelief made him fierce. "How do you know of Moro?"

"Well." She ran her tongue over her lips. Sandro knew women who spent fortunes to achieve that beautiful shade of crimson, but he saw no trace of rouge on Laura. "I have a confession to make, my lord."

A denial leapt in his throat. No. She could not be involved in the butchery of Moro. Not her. Anyone but her. "Go on," he said thickly.

"I heard you speaking of Moro to Maestro Titian." She leaned forward and hurried on. "Please forgive me, but I was so curious, I couldn't help myself. Besides, this might be for the best. I can help you solve this case, my lord."

He didn't want her help. He didn't want to think of this innocent lamb sneaking in the dark, listening at doorways, hearing of the atrocity that left even him feeling sick and soiled.

Without thinking, he jumped up, grasped her by the shoulders, and drew her to her feet. Although he sensed the silent censure of Jamal, he ignored it and sank his fingers into the soft flesh of her upper arms. He smelled her scent of sea air and jasmine, saw the firelight sparkling in her beautiful, opalescent eyes.

"Damn you for your meddlesome ways," he hissed through his teeth. "You have no business poking your nose into the affairs of the *signori di notte.*"

She seemed unperturbed by his temper, unscathed by his rough embrace. She lifted her chin. "I'm well aware of that, my lord, but remember, I did warn you of my inquisitive nature."

"Then I should have warned you that I have no use for women—inquisitive or otherwise."

She lifted her hands to his chest and pressed gently. "Your fingers are bruising me, my lord."

He released her as abruptly as he had snatched her up. "My apologies."

"I wouldn't worry about it, but Maestro Titian will

question me about any bruises when I model for him."

Sandro despised the image of Laura laid out like a feast upon the artist's red couch, lissome and sensual as a goddess, while Titian rendered her beauty on canvas.

"Do you truly have no use for women, my lord?" she asked. "That's unusual, especially in so handsome a man as you."

Sandro ignored her insincere compliment and paused to consider his four mistresses. Barbara, Arnetta, Gioia, and Alicia were as different and yet as alike as the four seasons. For years they had fulfilled his needs with the discretion and decorum he required. In exchange, he housed each in her own luxurious residence.

"It's my choice," he said stuffily, settling back in his chair. He did not need to look at Jamal to know that he was grinning with glee.

"Well, I believe my information could be useful to you." She sent him a sidelong glance. Not even the demure brown dress could conceal her lush curves. "That is, if you're interested, my lord."

As she sank gracefully back into the chair, he stared at the shape of her breasts, ripe beneath their soft cloak of linen. "I'm interested."

She smiled, the open, charming expression that was fast becoming familiar to him. "I happened to mention the murder of Daniele Moro to my friend Yasmin—"

"By God," he snapped, "don't you understand? This is a sensitive matter." He gripped the chair arms to keep himself anchored to his seat. "You can't go airing police business all over the city."

"I didn't." She seemed truly bewildered. "I told only one person."

"You could endanger yourself, madonna. The killer is still at large."

"Oh. I'm not used to having someone worry about my welfare."

"It is my vocation to worry about the welfare of every citizen of the republic."

She shifted impatiently. "Never mind all that. I found someone who saw Daniele Moro on the night he was killed."

Once again, Sandro came out of his chair. *"What?"*

"I'll take you to meet this person, my lord."

"Do that, and I'll think about forgiving you."

Don't Tempt Me

by _New York Times_ bestselling author
Loretta Chase

Imprisoned in a harem for twelve years, Zoe Lexham knows things no well-bred lady should . . . ruining her for society. Can the wickedly handsome Duke Lucien de Grey use his influence to save her from idle tongues? A simple enough task, if only he can stifle desire long enough to see his seductive charge safely into respectability . . .

Zoe went cold, then hot. She felt dizzy. But it was a wonderful dizziness, the joy of release.

Now at last she stood in the open.

Here I am, she thought. _Home at last, at last. Yes, look at me. Look your fill. I'm not invisible anymore._

She felt his big, warm hand clasp hers. The warmth rushed into her heart and made it hurry. She was aware of her pulse jumping against her throat and against her wrist, so close to his. The heat spread into her belly and down, to melt her knees.

I'm going to faint, she thought. But she couldn't let

herself swoon merely because a man had touched her. Not now, at any rate. Not here. She made herself look up at him.

Lucien wore the faintest smile—of mockery or amusement she couldn't tell. Behind his shuttered eyes she sensed rather than saw a shadow. She remembered the brief glimpse of pain he'd had when she'd mentioned his brother. It vanished in an instant, but she'd seen it in his first, surprised reaction: the darkness there, bleak and empty and unforgettable.

She gazed longer than she should have into his eyes, those sleepy green eyes that watched her so intently yet shut her out. And at last he let out a short laugh and raised her hand to his mouth, brushing her knuckles against his lips.

Had they been in the harem, she would have sunk onto the pillows and thrown her head back, inviting him. But they were not and he'd declined to make her his wife.

And she was not a man, to let her lust rule her brain. This man was not a good candidate for a spouse. There had been a bond between them once. Not a friendship, really. In childhood, the few years between them was a chasm, as was the difference in their genders. Still, he'd been fond of her once, she thought, in his own fashion. But that was before.

Now he was everything every woman could want, and he knew it.

She desired him the way every other woman desired him. Still, at least she finally felt desire, she told herself. If she could feel it with him, she'd feel it with someone else, someone who wanted her, who'd give his heart to her. For now, she was grateful to be free. She was grateful to stand on this balcony and look out upon the hundreds of people below.

She squeezed his hand in thanks and let her mouth form a slow, genuine smile of gratitude and happiness, though she couldn't help glancing up at him once from under her lashes to seek his reaction.

She glimpsed the heat flickering in the guarded green gaze.

Ah, yes. He felt it, too: the powerful physical awareness crackling between them.

He released her hand. "We've entertained the mob for long enough," he said. "Go inside."

She turned away. The crowd began to stir and people were talking again but more quietly. They'd become a murmuring sea rather than a roaring one.

"You've seen her," he said, and his deep voice easily carried over the sea. "You shall see her again from time to time. Now go away."

After a moment, they began to turn away, and by degrees they drifted out of the square.

Coming August 2009

Destined for an Early Grave

by *New York Times* bestselling author

Jeaniene Frost

Just when Cat is ready for a little rest and relaxation with her sexy vampire boyfriend Bones, she's haunted by dreams from her past—a past she doesn't remember. To unlock these secrets, Cat may have to venture all the way into the grave. But the truth could rock what she knows about herself—and her relationship with Bones.

If he catches me, I'm dead.

I ran as fast as I could, darting around trees, tangled roots, and rocks in the forest. The monster snarled as it chased me, the sound closer than before. I wasn't able to outrun it. The monster was picking up speed while I was getting tired.

The forest thinned ahead of me to reveal a blond vampire on a hill in the distance. I recognized him at once and hope surged through me. If I could reach him, I'd be okay. He loved me; he'd protect me from the monster. Yet I was still so far away.

Fog crept up the hill to surround the vampire, making him appear almost ghost-like. I screamed his name as the monster's footsteps got even closer. Panicked, I lunged forward, narrowly avoiding the grasp of bony hands that would pull me down to the grave. With renewed effort, I sprinted toward the vampire. He urged me on, snarling warnings at the monster that wouldn't stop chasing me.

"Leave me alone," I screamed as a merciless grip seized me from behind. "No!"

"Kitten!"

The shout didn't come from the vampire ahead of me; it came from the monster wrestling me to the ground. I jerked my head toward the vampire in the distance, but his features blurred into nothingness and the fog covered him. Right before he disappeared, I heard his voice.

"He is not your husband, Catherine."

A hard shake evaporated the last of the dream and I woke to find Bones, my vampire lover, hovered over me.

"What is it? Are you hurt?"

An odd question, you would think, since it had only been a nightmare. But with the right power and magic, sometimes nightmares could be turned into weapons. A while back, I'd almost been killed by one. This was different, however. No matter how vivid it felt, it had just been a dream.

"I'll be fine if you quit shaking me."

Bones dropped his hands and let out a noise of relief. "You didn't wake up and you were thrashing on the bed. Brought back rotten memories."

"I'm okay. It was a . . . weird dream."

There was something about the vampire in it that nagged me. Like I should know who he was. That made no sense, however, since he was just a figment of my imagination.

"Odd that I couldn't catch any of your dream," Bones went on. "Normally your dreams are like background music to me."

Bones was a Master vampire, more powerful than most vampires I'd ever met. One of his gifts was the ability to read human minds. Even though I was half-human, half-vampire, there was enough humanity in me that Bones could hear my thoughts, unless I worked to block him. Still, this was news to me.

"You can hear my *dreams*? God, you must never get any quiet. I'd be shooting myself in the head if I were you."

Which wouldn't do much to him, actually. Only silver through the heart or decapitation was lethal to a vampire. Getting shot in the head might take care of *my* ills the permanent way, but it would just give Bones a nasty headache.

He settled himself back onto the pillows. "Don't fret, luv. I said it's like background music, so it's rather soothing. As for quiet, out here on this water, it's as quiet as I've experienced without being half-shriveled in the process."

I lay back down, a shiver going through me at the mention of his near-miss with death. Bones's hair had turned white from how close he'd come to dying, but now it was back to its usual rich brown color.

"Is that why we're drifting on a boat out in the Atlantic? So you could have some peace and quiet?"

"I wanted some time alone with you, Kitten. We've had so little of that lately."

An understatement. Even though I'd quit my job leading the secret branch of Homeland Security that hunted rogue vampires and ghouls, life hadn't been dull. First we'd had to deal with our losses from the war with another Master vampire last year. Several of Bones's friends—and my best friend Denise's husband, Randy—had been murdered. Then there had been months of hunting down the remaining perpetrators of that war so they couldn't live to plot against us another day. Then training my replacement so that my uncle Don had someone else to play bait when his operatives went after the misbehaving members of undead society. Most vampires and ghouls didn't kill when they fed, but there were those who killed for fun. Or stupidity. My uncle made sure those vampires and ghouls were taken care of—and that ordinary citizens weren't aware they existed.

So when Bones told me we were taking a boat trip, I'd assumed there must be some search-and-destroy reason behind it. Going somewhere just for relaxation hadn't happened, well, *ever*, in our relationship.

"This is a weekend getaway?" I couldn't keep the disbelief out of my voice.

He traced his finger on my lower lip. "This is our vacation, Kitten. We can go anywhere in the world and take our time getting there. So tell me, where shall we go?"

"Paris."

I surprised myself saying it. I'd never had a burning desire to visit there before, but for some reason, I did now. Maybe it was because Paris was supposed to be the city of lovers, although just looking at Bones was usually enough to get me in a romantic mood.

He must have caught my thought, because he smiled, making his face more breathtaking, in my opinion. Lying against the navy sheets, his skin almost glowed with a silky alabaster paleness that was too perfect to be human. The sheets were tangled past his stomach, giving me an uninterrupted view of his lean, taut abdomen and hard, muscled chest. Dark brown eyes began to tinge with emerald and fangs peeked under the curve of his mouth, letting me know I wasn't the only one feeling warmer all of a sudden.

"Paris it is, then," he whispered, and flung the sheets off.

At Avon Books, we know your passion for romance—once you finish one of our novels, you find yourself wanting more.

May we tempt you with . . .

- **Excerpts** from our upcoming releases.

- Entertaining **extras**, including authors' personal photo albums and book lists.

- Behind-the-scenes **scoop** on your favorite characters and series.

- **Sweepstakes** for the chance to win free books, romantic getaways, and other fun prizes.

- Writing **tips** from our authors and editors.

- **Blog** with our authors and find out why they love to write romance.

- **Exclusive content** that's not contained within the pages of our novels.

Join us at
www.avonbooks.com

A V O N   *An Imprint of* HarperCollins*Publishers*
www.avonromance.com

Available wherever books are sold or please call 1-800-331-3761 to order.

FTH 0708